THE COW

For the men in this special 2-in-1 collection nothing is more important than the family that surrounds them and the women they love.

From cowboy hats to baby booties, and horseback rides on the range to candlelit dinners for two, these romances are sure to lasso your heart.

We dare you not to fall for these rugged men who know the value of a hard day's work, hold family loyalty in the highest regard and would do anything for the love of a good woman!

TINA LEONARD

is a *USA TODAY* bestselling and award-winning author of more than fifty projects, including several popular miniseries for the Harlequin American Romance line. Known for bad-boy heroes and smart, adventurous heroines, her books have made the *USA TODAY,* Waldenbooks, Ingram and Nielsen BookScan bestseller lists. Born on a military base, Tina lived in many states before eventually marrying the boy who did her crayon printing for her in the first grade. You can visit her at www.tinaleonard.com, and follow her on Facebook and Twitter.

TINA LEONARD

More Than Expected

H HARLEQUIN® COWBOYS AND BABIES

Recycling programs
for this product may
not exist in your area.

ISBN-13: 978-0-373-60612-2

MORE THAN EXPECTED
Copyright © 2014 by Harlequin Books S.A.

The publisher acknowledges the copyright holders
of the individual works as follows:

THE COWBOY'S TRIPLETS
Copyright © 2011 by Tina Leonard

THE COWBOY'S BONUS BABY
Copyright © 2011 by Tina Leonard

Printed in U.S.A.

CONTENTS

THE COWBOY'S
TRIPLETS

Many thanks go to Kathleen Scheibling,
for believing in this series and always having faith
in me, and editing my work with a sure hand.

There are many people at Harlequin
who make my books ready for publication, most
of whom I will never have the chance to thank in
person, and they have my heartfelt gratitude.

Also many thanks to my children and my husband,
who are enthusiastic and supportive,
and most of all, the generous readers
who are the reason for my success.

Chapter One

"A dark night for Peter D. Callahan is being alone in his room."

—Jeremiah Callahan,
who knew his toddler son all too well.

"The Diablos are running." Pete Callahan turned from the frost-speckled window, letting his words sink into the sudden silence. His five brothers and Aunt Fiona looked at him.

A shiver touched Pete. The shadowy, misty mustangs running like the wind across the far reaches of the ranch meant magic was in the cold night air. According to legend, the Diablos only ran as a portent of something mystical to come. The Diablos were real—and magical in themselves—but Pete didn't believe in mystical magic, the oogie-boogie kind of magic. Nor did he believe in pushy old beloved aunts trying to rule from the grave, as his aunt Fiona was hinting she would.

Jonas Callahan ignored his brother's inopportune comment and resumed gently badgering their dear aunt. "You've suggested your time is running out," Jonas said to Fiona, who shrugged, dismissing the light sarcasm in his tone. Fiona was holding court in the massive library at Rancho Diablo in New Mexico. His brothers lounged around the room in various states of stubbled beards and dirty jeans, fresh from working the ranch. They were trying to assuage her worries, let her know that they were there for her in all matters—though if anybody did not need help, it was their cagey aunt.

"I am seventy-nine," Fiona said. "Please speak to me with respect. You make me sound as reliable as a vintage bedside clock."

"You've just told us that you're leaving Rancho Diablo to one of us based on a dream you had," Pete said. "We're more interested in your health than in your will, Aunt Fiona."

"Oh, poppycock." She sniffed, clearly put out with her six nephews. No doubt she thought they were trying to mollify her, coddle her to get into her good graces. It annoyed Pete.

"You all want Rancho Diablo because it was your parents'," Fiona said. "Let's be honest about our motivations."

If that wasn't calling the kettle black.

"Aunt Fiona, I speak for all of us—" Pete gestured toward his sprawling brothers who were only too content to allow him to beard their celestial-minded, determined aunt "—when I say that we don't believe in dreamscapes, incantations, voodoo or rubbing the venerated bellies of mystical bunnies dating from the time of Lewis Carroll. So our motivation is simple. We love you. Most of us live here at Rancho Diablo because we love you, as much as you seem inclined to look for an ulterior motive. The ranch is our livelihood, but it isn't everything."

Murmurs of assent rose from his brothers. His aunt

gave him a disapproving, sour look. She was a tiny woman, a petite bundle of dynamite in a prim navy-blue wool dress. Her only concession to the bitter cold was what she called her bird boots—knee-high, lugged soles, fur-lined. White hair was pulled severely back from her face in an elegant updo she called a bird's nest. It did have the same sort of peculiar order of a mourning dove's nest, but it was attractive. There wasn't a spare ounce of flesh on the diminutive woman, which made people at first meeting assume she was fragile.

She was not.

"Nevertheless," Fiona said, her eyes bright behind her glasses, "I am following my dream."

"You do that." Pete crouched to stoke the fire. He wondered if it would be easier on their beloved aunt if he had gas-lit logs installed in the seven fireplaces throughout the huge ranch house, and decided she'd resent the implication that she couldn't take care of her home herself. The smell of cookies hung in the air, lingering with the fragrances of Christmas and home, which was, Pete thought, how their wily aunt managed to lure her nephews to the house so often, although they would have surreptitiously checked on her and Burke anyway. Home-baked cookies and other to-die-for gastronomic delights—they simply had it too good, courtesy of Fiona.

"Since Pete doesn't care about his stake in Rancho Diablo, that leaves it to the rest of you to see which of you will take over the ranch. When I'm gone, naturally. Which might be any day now." She held a tissue to her nose. "This is the third cold I've had this month. My immune system is so weak."

Jonas straightened. "You said nothing about feeling weak."

"Not that you would care, Doctor." She rubbed her glasses clean and replaced them on her pert nose. "Burke, please bring the brandy. We are all in need of a bit of fortification. Except Pete, who is always above the fray."

Her faithful butler went to do her bidding. Pete sighed and sat down on the leather sofa, where he had a premier seat to stare out the window at the frozen landscape. Guilt was a familiar parenting tool, and she'd been employing it with greater frequency of late. The problem was, he knew all about Fiona's Secret Plan, so he had plenty of guilt heaping on him from all sides. It sucked being the responsible one. "I'll take the damn brandy," he said as Burke offered him a snifter. Right now, he could use a stiff one.

"The terms of the deal—which have also been written into my revised will—are thus. The first of you who gets married to a suitable woman, has a family and settles down, will inherit Rancho Diablo. You may not sell the land or house, of course, without all six of you being in agreement. That is what was revealed to me in my dream."

Pete sighed. Their stubborn aunt was hatching more mayhem for their lives. He knew she was serious about this plan, and the mischievous side of him thought she was cute and downright smart to try to pull this on his brothers, who richly deserved the trap Fiona was springing on them. They'd fall for it, too, in his opinion, though they should know better. Nobody left ranches worth millions of dollars in land value alone to relatives based on a dream, not to mention expecting them to compete for it, especially not using the tool of marriage. None of them even had a serious girlfriend. Pete scowled at his brothers.

The problem was that the plan was sound—but the material Fiona had to work with was sadly lacking.

There was Jonas, the eldest, a successful surgeon who surely had his pick of hot doctors and nurses. He kept himself busy amassing a reputation as a hard-working, best-in-class cardiac guy. Jonas was a typical girl-magnet: tall, dark as the ace of spades, square-jawed. All good stuff, but clueless with women, basically a bonehead with every subject except science and research. A typical nerd, and useless to Fiona's Secret Plan, in Pete's opinion.

Pete continued the roll call. There was Creed, who wouldn't send women screaming from his appearance, but was too wild for most men, let alone women. Creed was a typical badass, the kind of man ladies loved like grandmas loved tea. Creed, unfortunately, would never love anything but rodeo and the ranch. No marriage material there.

Creed's twin, Rafe, was a strange blend of nerd and reckless cowboy. Sometimes he wore his long jet-black hair in a braid down his back. Other times he shaved his head. The best way Pete could describe his free-spirited brother was "out there"—egregiously, studiously out there on the edge. One day a woman might reel him back in to planet Earth, but Pete wouldn't put down a twenty on it.

Judah was a champion bullrider. He had ladies in every town. He was popular with everyone, and blessed with good fortune and athleticism. Judah's face was cut by the hand of Michelangelo: strong, precise and manly.

Women left undies in his gear with phone numbers. One enterprising young lady had herself carried into his hotel room in a maid's cart. Judah hadn't been able to resist the French maid's costume, nor the heiress who'd wanted a cowboy fling and had flown him to Paris for a weekend of French cuisine and French-kissing and everything else that entailed. Judah was a kind, damaged soul and ladies adored all that haunted mystique. But Judah had never chosen just one woman to be his girl. Pete thought Judah overworked the Eeyore routine, but he had to admit it worked brilliantly for his brother.

Finally, there was Sam. No one needed to worry about Sam's zeal for the altar. Stockier and more muscular than the rest of them (which meant he could kick just about anybody's ass who messed with him), Sam carried a chip on his shoulder that had everything to do with confidence, swagger and being the youngest. He knew there was something different about him, which didn't help. He'd come "later" as Jonas always put it, and Pete thought Sam had grown up not exactly understanding his place in the world or the family. Nobody worked harder than Sam, but then sometimes Sam would disappear for days.

Pete shook his head. Fiona was barking up all kinds of wrong trees with this latest plan. He'd consider his brothers candidates for group therapy rather than matrimonial bliss. *But that's just me,* he thought, *and I tend to be a doubter.*

He supposed he'd be the closest to suiting Fiona's ridiculous offer. He at least had a Saturday-night thing going on. Still, being Mr. Saturday Night wasn't likely to be upped to two nights a week, much less a full lifetime.

Pete sighed. He admired their Irish aunt who loved

to dabble in drama. He had to hand it to her—there was never a moment when she wasn't trying to fix their lives. Fiona certainly had her work cut out for her this time, but he knew she would stick to it until she considered her job done and done well.

"When was this dream?" Jonas asked, shifting his long legs as he reached for another Christmas cookie from the silver platter on the side table. Pete thought a heart surgeon should be watching his cholesterol, or at least the toxic-waste levels in his body, but no one could eat just one of Fiona's cookies. Jonas could be counted on to talk some sense into the redoubtable aunt, and Pete relaxed a little. Surely the rest of the brothers could see that there were as many holes in this plan as in Swiss cheese—and his guilt would go away once he knew they'd safely figured Fiona out. After all, what would stop any of them—all of them—from running out, hiring a woman to fake a marriage and perhaps a pregnancy, and then cashing in? Pete swallowed, not wanting to think about his little aunt pushing up daisies.

"It wasn't so much a dream, it was more a *premonition*," Fiona said. "It occurred when I talked to a nice lady at the traveling carnival."

Creed sat up. "Traveling carnival?"

"That's right. She was standing outside her tent. There was a sign on it that read Madame Vivant's Fortune-Telling. Several of the ladies from the Books 'n' Bingo Society decided it sounded like fun. So we went in."

Pete heard Rafe groan. He agreed with the sentiment. Was their adorable, feisty aunt beginning to show the start of some affliction that would affect her mental capacity? His blood ran cold at the thought.

"As a matter of fact, I've invited her here tonight. Burke, please show Madame Vivant into the library."

Pete watched as his lunkheaded brothers seemed to transmogrify in the face of a beautiful woman. Jonas looked like a petrified tree felled by an ax, and the rest of his brothers were practically drooling like babies. He was embarrassed for them. Pete smelled enticing perfume, heard the jingle of tiny charms she wore on silver bracelets. No more than five foot two, Madame Vivant was a delightful babe of about twenty-five. He'd bet the whole "dream" was a ruse for her to get hitched to one of them. Madame Fortune-teller his ass—more like Madame Shakedown Artist.

This was bad news. No woman of good intent should jingle when she walked. It was as *look-at-me!* as a lady could get.

Pete decided Fiona's scheme was getting out of hand. She wasn't supposed to bring the catnip to the mice, was she? It was dirty pool, and he had to draw the line somewhere.

A guy could only enjoy watching his brothers get worked over by Fiona for so long.

"You have to leave," Pete said, towering over the tiny redhead. He refused to notice the trim waist, the delightful peachy bosom, the sweetly curved hips under the undulating black skirt that had his easily-led-astray brothers reeling. Once again, Pete realized, it was up to him to save them from themselves. "Take your bells and your parlor tricks out of here. And don't bother taking Burke's pocket watch," he said, neatly removing it from the velvet pouch she carried. He'd seen it poking out and recognized it instantly. It was one of the butler's prized possessions.

Burke cleared his throat. "I gave her that, sir. I asked her to help me with a personal matter."

Pete looked at the butler he'd known ever since Burke and Fiona had come to the ranch to care for the boys. He softened his words for Burke—he'd protect him, too. "No doubt she has played with your mind as well. Never mind. Once you're off the property, Madame Vivant—if that is your real name—all will be right again."

Cool green eyes considered him. "Tough guy, huh?"

"That's right. Off you go, little gypsy." Pete congratulated himself on his excellent handling of the situation—until Jonas spoke up.

"Not so fast, bro," Jonas said. "It's cold outside. I'm sure we could offer our guest a cup of cocoa, couldn't we, Burke?"

The butler nodded and went off to do Jonas's bidding. Jonas continued staring at the gypsy as if his brain was locked in gear. Pete scowled. Surely Jonas—steady-handed Jonas the surgeon—wouldn't get the hots for a *gypsy*.

He should have put a stop to this in the beginning; he was practically an accomplice. But he hadn't counted on his brothers being super boneheads—just greedy. He opened his mouth to throw water on the scheme, confess everything, too, but Fiona shot him down.

"Pete!" His aunt's voice cracked like a whip. "You're being rude to an invited guest, and one thing we aren't at Rancho Diablo is *rude*."

He shrugged and went to lean against a wall. "If you think I'm going to be part of a séance or machination on her part to confuse you, I'm afraid we're not going to fall for the plan, Aunt." There, that was a piece of delicious Broadway acting, if he did say so himself—

although he was still worried about Jonas. Sam was young and hotheaded, so he might have expected Sam to latch on to their visitor, or wild-at-heart Creed might have been an easy target. Any of them but Jonas, who was still stonelike and staring—rapt, mesmerized.

Creed, Rafe, Judah and Sam all crossed their arms, gazing with interest at the fortune-teller. They seemed very interested in the tale she was about to spin. Pete would have to keep a close eye on Fiona since no one else seemed inclined to play protector to their giddy aunt.

The next thing Pete knew, Jonas was lying on the floor staring up at the wood-beamed ceiling. Madame Vivant stood over him, staring down at his brother. Jonas said, "My lucky, lucky eyes," and Pete wondered if Jonas had hit his head on the way down. Pete was getting really nervous. He glanced at Fiona to see if she was worried about the effects of her Secret Plan, but she seemed more interested in the warm drink Burke was handing her.

"What happened?" Jonas asked as Madame Vivant moved to help him up.

"You fainted," she told him.

Jonas raised a disbelieving brow that made Pete proud. For a moment he'd feared his older brother was going to drown in a pool of misplaced desire.

"I'm a doctor, and a damn good one. I think I'd know if I'd fainted."

"You fainted, bro," Rafe said. "Went down like a sack of hammers."

"Made a real funky sound when you fell, too," Aunt Fiona said. "When you were just a little thing, I used to ask you if you'd stepped on a frog when you made that noise, Jonas. Brings back memories—"

"That's enough." Jonas stared at the petite redhead. "You did something to me."

"You don't believe in spells," she replied. "A doctor wouldn't believe in such things, would you?" She took his hand in her much smaller one and helped him to his feet with a surprisingly strong yank.

"I felt fine before you walked in," Jonas replied, his voice crabby, and Pete relaxed. Jonas had obviously recovered his good sense when he fell out of his chair, or whatever the hell he'd just done. *We're all working too hard. Or we've had too much Christmas vacation with the holiday-loving aunt.*

"Can we get on with this?" Aunt Fiona asked, her tone impatient. "Madame Vivant can't stay long. The carnival's train moves on tonight."

"After she's stolen the family heirlooms," Pete muttered.

"We don't have any of those," Sam said. "Bro, sit over here so I can keep an eye on you. You're making an ass of yourself."

This was tough coming from the baby. He'd changed that boy's diapers! Pete felt tired suddenly, and not soothed by the brandy Burke pressed on him.

"Your aunt asked me here to interpret—explain—the dream she had while in my tent," Madame Vivant said. "Your family home is in jeopardy."

Pete rolled his eyes. He couldn't help it. He knew he was being churlish, and a thirty-one-year-old man shouldn't be. Of course the family home was in danger. The culprit was sitting next to his aunt on her velvet footstool. Why couldn't anyone but him see this?

His brothers were mesmerized. They leaned forward like schoolboys, hanging on every word that dropped from Madame Vivant's sweet ruby lips. Even Jonas went back to being spellbound, looking as if he might jump into her lap any second. Pete just glared at her. "In danger from what?" he demanded. "Or whom?"

As if he didn't know.

"That has not been revealed to me," the fortune-teller replied, her voice soft.

He shook his head. "And so we're all supposed to get married, and have a child—"

"That's your aunt's solution," the gypsy said.

"Look," Pete said, tired of the conversation. He and his brothers had work to do on the ranch. He didn't want to leave this woman here to prey on his innocent aunt's fears. She loved Rancho Diablo with all her heart. She'd kept it running after their mother and father had died, had raised all of them to manhood. He was always up for a joke on his hammerheaded brothers, but Aunt Fiona's scheme was getting out of hand.

Suddenly, Jonas spoke. "I'm not going to allow you to continue this charade until you tell me your real name. This Madame Vivant crap is for beginners, and I am no easy mark. I want your name in case I have to have the law hunt you down."

Her eyes widened.

"Jonas!" Fiona leaned forward. "I'm going to ask you to leave if you insist upon being a pest."

Jonas refused to release the gypsy's gaze. Something was definitely happening to his normally uptight brother.

"My name," she finally said, "is Sabrina McKinley."

"Your real name? Or one of many aliases? I've got

a good mind to call the cops right now," Jonas stated, and Pete was pretty certain his brother meant it. Jonas seemed to be fluctuating between protecting their aunt and rampant sexual desire, and if he wasn't so worried, Pete might have enjoyed the drama.

"It's my real name." She stared back at Jonas, unafraid of his growing ire. "I might remind you that I don't know any of you. I came alone, knowing there would be six men and only a frail elderly woman here—"

Pete expected his aunt to utter a loud "ha!" but she only sighed and pulled an afghan around her shoulders.

"You've convinced her she's ill," Jonas said, outraged. "She was fine last I saw her. You've toyed with her mind, made her think she's dying—"

Madame Vivant—Sabrina—shook her head. "I have no dark powers."

"Hypnotism isn't a dark art?"

She gasped. "How dare you?"

"Let her finish, Jonas," Rafe said, interrupting the two verbal combatants. "She's not going to hurt anybody by saying whatever she wants to say."

"I'm going to do this," Fiona said, "in fact, I've already changed my will. Regardless of what misguided thoughts you have about my mental state, the time has come for me to make a decision about Rancho Diablo." She looked around at all of her nephews. "Which of you truly feels a special connection to Rancho Diablo? Would want it to be yours? You, Jonas, are the eldest," Fiona said, "and marriage might suit you."

"And you have a bid on a ranch sixty miles to the east," Sabrina said. "You've been thinking about having your *own* working ranch."

Pete supposed she expected them to be amazed that

she knew this bit of information, as if they were in the presence of a mystical mind-reader. Pete *was* surprised his brother was thinking about owning a ranch in New Mexico, since he had a successful surgical practice in Dallas, Texas. Fiona must have told Sabrina.

"Sorry, I don't feel like cooperating," Jonas said, sounding more in control of his faculties, to Pete's relief. "I'm not getting married, having a baby or playing hoodwink-the-gentle-aunt."

"Nevertheless, you will be considered, Jonas," Fiona said, her tone firm. "Should you marry and produce multiple heirs, you will be considered for Rancho Diablo."

"Multiple heirs?" Creed asked.

"Naturally," Fiona said. "Whichever of you has the *largest* family should inherit the property, which makes sense on several levels. That's what Madame Vivant suggested, and I think it's an excellent plan to ensure that none of you try to hire a woman with a child to fool me or my executor." She shot Jonas a stern look. "It's not like my own kin doesn't know a little something about hoodwinking the gentle aunt."

Pete silently conceded Fiona's point. Over the years they had done their best to pull the wool over the bright aunty eyes, with varying degrees of success. She'd grown up on a farm in Ireland with eleven brothers, so she knew a lot about what boys—men—could get into. It had been like living with a kindly old jailer.

Still, they'd done their best—and had occasionally succeeded.

"Now, I don't expect any of this to happen overnight," Aunt Fiona continued. "In fact, given the nature of your extreme bachelorhoods, it could be *years* before any of you settle down. Therefore, I have set forth these plans with an executor in an airtight will and testament. *Airtight*."

Pete rose to his feet. "Jonas, you get the job of trying to talk sense into our beloved aunt."

Jonas smiled a lazy come-and-get-it smile at the gypsy. "I'm not so certain Aunt Fiona's plan doesn't have some merit. I'm not totally opposed to settling down."

Pete had expected all five of his brothers to follow him out the door in a cavalcade of loyalty and righteous indignation. But to a man, they wouldn't look at him.

He was outnumbered, voted down. Aunt Fiona's Secret Plan was surely succeeding beyond her wildest dreams.

"Fine. I'm going to check on the horses. Then I'm bedding down. None of you, and that includes you, Jonas," he said, sweeping a hand toward his brothers, "come crying to me when you find yourselves ensnared by Mata Hari here."

By that moniker he meant their aunt as well—she was such a bad storyteller—but Sabrina looked at Jonas with big, sexy, fake-concerned eyes. *Oh, boy,* Pete thought. *That's danger dressed in a sweet tight top all right. Jonas is a marked man.*

He decided it would be fun to watch Jonas fall like a granite boulder for a woman. Pete grinned, suddenly feeling no guilt at all.

Jonas stood, catching Pete by surprise. "Well, I'm out like a trout," Jonas said. "It was a pleasure meeting you," he told Madame Vivant.

"You can't leave," Pete said, "The fun's just beginning."

"I've got patients," Jonas reminded him. "Got to catch a plane back to Dallas. Pete, I leave tonight's discussion and everything that follows in your more-than-capable hands."

"Oh, hell, no," Pete said. "Don't you leave me holding the bag, Jonas."

"Sorry. Duty calls."

"Duty?" Pete realized Jonas was really leaving. This was bad for Fiona's trap. Pete didn't want her trap slamming shut on *him*. "Jonas, we have a problem here."

"No worries," Jonas said, kissing their aunt goodbye. "You'll take care of everything, Pete." He departed as though he hadn't spent the past half hour ogling the gypsy like a tomcat eyeing a nice, juicy mouse.

Pete glanced at his aunt, wondering if Jonas's exit blew up her plan, but she was staring at him as though she expected him to do something, and Pete sighed.

It was hell being Mr. Responsibility.

Chapter Two

Pete hadn't exactly meant to tell Jonas to blow it out his ass, but when his older brother pulled a fast escape, leaving him in charge of a room full of lunatics, Pete wondered if he'd yanked Jonas's chain a bit hard. He hadn't seen his brother's gaze light on a woman like it had lit on Madame Vivant in…well, since Nancy had left him at the altar five years ago.

Madame Vivant—Sabrina McKinley—wasn't a woman who had accosted their tender aunt with a wild story to prey on her feebleness. Pete had taken Fiona and her blue-rinsed friends to the fair. He'd happened to be standing outside the tent when Fiona and her three co-conspirators had hatched the plan with Sabrina. Hatched and hired, while he'd listened through the walls of the tent. He'd tried hard not to laugh. It wasn't such a bad plan. And he would never give away Fiona's Secret. His brothers had this one coming to them. If there had ever been a group of guys who needed to be thinking about their futures a bit more, it was probably the Callahan brothers.

Himself excluded, of course. He could just sit back and watch the fun as his brothers scrambled to win the ranch.

He eyed the door through which Jonas had departed. Their more surly, tightly controlled brother wouldn't be able to stand the suspense. He'd be back, unable to keep himself from interfering. Jonas loved Fiona. The doctor in him wouldn't be able to stand the thought that he hadn't given her a decent evaluation. He'd think *strong pulse, lungs clear, heart rate excellent,* but all the while Jonas would be worrying like crazy. That was part of Fiona's MO, tugging on just the right heartstrings.

Pete leaned back, winked at Madame Vivant, and grinned. This would be great entertainment during January, a traditionally long, cold month on the ranch.

"Get your popcorn," he told Sabrina.

"I beg your pardon?" She glanced back at the door through which Jonas had exited.

Pete smiled. "He's a bit of a hothead."

She raised her chin and turned to Fiona. "I must be going, Miss Callahan."

Four brothers jumped up to walk her to the door. "Stay," Sabrina said. "I don't need to be walked to my car."

"Goodbye!" Fiona got up and made her way to the door, gently pushing her nephews out of her way. "Thank you so much for coming out. Good luck at your next stops! *Adh mór ort!*"

Sabrina went out with a jingle of bells and reluctant sighs from his brothers.

"You shouldn't listen to people like that, Aunt Fiona," Creed said. "Cute as she is, that fortune-teller doesn't know any more than the weatherman about what lies in the weeks ahead."

"That's right," Judah said. "We're going to take good care of you."

"Always," Rafe said.

And Sam said, "You better believe it."

Fiona blinked. "I don't want you boys looking after me. I want you looking for wives!"

Pete chuckled, deciding to give Fiona's plan a boost. "Wouldn't hurt to have some pretty ladies around this place."

Creed glared at him with indignation. "Women cause nothing but trouble."

"That's true," Judah said. "Did you ever see a more miserable man than Jonas when Nancy ran off?"

Rafe shook his head. "It would take more than a woman to get me to the altar. I love this ranch, Aunt Fiona, but damn, I'm not putting my neck in a noose to get it."

Sam shrugged. "I'm afraid I agree with them, Aunt. A woman just isn't worth all the heartache."

Fiona's jaw dropped. Pete almost felt sorry for her.

"Do you mean you intend *never* to marry? None of you?" she demanded.

Four brothers shook their heads.

"I've got plenty to do around here," Creed said. "No woman wants to be abandoned for the life of a cowboy."

"They all want to play *Desperate Housewives* these days," Rafe said. "High maintenance is not for me."

"But surely there are women out there, women from this very town, who are of stock that can appreciate this way of life?" Fiona said.

"Aunt," Judah said, his voice gentle, "we live two hundred miles from the nearest city. We live on five thousand acres of dirt. There are no malls, no restaurants—"

"There's Banger's Bait and Tackle," Fiona said.

"They serve a mean catfish. Not to mention Mr. Sooner has been grilling burgers in his backyard for the last twenty-five years, and they're the best I've ever put in my mouth. You can't get a finer burger!"

Sam rearranged the wool afghan around his aunt's shoulders. "Don't worry," he said, kissing her cheek. "You and Burke can live here as long as you want. We'll work the ranch, the way we always have. We just don't want you getting so upset."

Fiona blinked, then looked at Pete. "You're awfully quiet, nephew."

He didn't know what to say. Truth was, he'd had his eye on a gal for quite some time, in fact, for the past fifteen or so years. But Jackie Samuels was less inclined to settle down than he was. She'd said a hundred times that what was between them—*their big secret*—was all she wanted. He couldn't figure that out. Wasn't a girl supposed to want to drag a man to the altar? Wasn't that part of the fun? She did the chasing, and he did the complaining, while she enticed him to the state of wedded bliss?

When Pete had asked her that, Jackie had shot back, "Why should I buy the steer when I can get the steak for free?" It was a question he hadn't considered before.

Pete went to stare out the window. Darkness had fallen so that all was visible was a wide range of inky nothing. They needed to put spotlights up in the trees around the ranch, and maybe some lamps on the fences. That reminded him—Jackie had a window or two at her tiny cottage he'd noticed needed repairing as well.

"I'm going out for a while," Pete announced. He felt sorry for Fiona because her Secret Plan had blown up on her, after she'd gone to the trouble of hiring an actress to help spin her diabolical and amusing web. Pete felt more sorry for himself, though, because he didn't stand a chance with the woman he loved.

JACKIE SAMUELS HAD NURSED enough grumpy patients in her life to develop a fairly thick skin, but Mr. Dearborn was about to make a dent in her good temper.

"I don't want to take any medicine," Mr. Dearborn said.

Jackie said, "Doctor's orders, Mr. Dearborn. You need to take this antibiotic, and then I'm going to give you a pneumonia shot. It's important to keep you well this winter so you don't have to come back." She handed him a glass of water.

Recognizing the take-no-prisoners tone of her voice, Mr. Dearborn took the medicine, then bared an arm for the injection.

"All done. Didn't hurt a bit, did it?"

"No," Mr. Dearborn said, "but I'd rather you quit bothering me."

"And you'd rather not be in this hospital." She covered him with a warm blanket and gave him a smile. "Try to get some rest before I bring you a small treat."

His face lit up. "Chocolate?"

"Yes." She placed a hand on his wrist, taking a pulse while he was thinking about his treat. "But you have to stop complaining every time I bring you your medicine. Please."

He wrinkled his nose, his white brows beetling. "You realize that when I complain, you bring me chocolate."

She sighed and took her clipboard from the table. "Yes, I do, Mr. Dearborn. I'll be back later."

She left his room and returned to the nurses' station. "Why do men have to play games?" she asked Darla Cameron.

"It's in their DNA," Darla answered. She looked at Jackie, her bright-blue gaze excited. "You're never going to believe it, but Candy Diamond has decided to sell her wedding-gown business."

Jackie blinked. "Isn't that bad? Diamond's Bridal is the only place to shop for gowns and nice dresses for two hundred miles."

"It might be bad," Darla said, "except you and I are going to buy the business."

Jackie shook her head. "I want no part of wedding gowns and nervous brides. I get enough complaining around here as it is."

Darla flopped some papers down in front of her. "And yet, check out the income from Candy's business."

Jackie stared at Darla for a moment, realizing her friend was serious. Her gaze moved to the column of figures and the paperwork Darla was tapping with a graceful finger. "Why is she selling if her business is so lucrative?"

"Needs to retire. And so do we," Darla told her. "Think of it, Jackie. No more bossy doctors. No more grumpy patients. We'd be our own bosses."

Jackie thought about Mr. Dearborn, one of her favorite patients. She liked caring for people. Sometimes the hours were long, but she was single. There was no one to inconvenience in her life. No family counting on her.

No husband, either. Pete Callahan, the secret love of her life, didn't care when she worked. Pete was the only man she'd ever made love with. He would marry her in a flash, he always told her—not that she believed him. He was an inveterate footloose cowboy, an enigmatic

Prince Charming who claimed he was in it for the real kiss, only to drift off at the last second.

This bridal shop might be the closest she ever got to being a bride. "I don't know," Jackie said. "What do we know about running a business?"

"My mom runs the Books 'n' Bingo," Darla said. "I've learned a bit about managing a mom-and-pop shop."

"But brides," Jackie said, thinking about all the drama involved with weddings, "there's a reason they're called bridezillas."

Darla shrugged. "It'd be nice to do something new for a change. I wouldn't mind smelling gardenias and lilies instead of antiseptic and other things. Not that I don't love most of my patients," Darla said, "but I'm ready for a new challenge."

"I guess you're right." Jackie looked at the line of figures again, her heart beginning to race with some excitement and a little trepidation. "Let me think about it tonight, okay? I need to come up with all the reasons I can why this is a very bad idea."

"I'd let your name be first on the door," Darla said.

Jackie blinked. "Samuels and Cameron's Bridal Shop? I think we'd be better off with something else."

Darla smiled. "Or Callahan," she suggested. "Callahan and Cameron."

"No." Jackie grabbed a wrapped piece of chocolate from her purse to take to Mr. Dearborn. "Even if I go into the wedding-gown business with you, Darla, I guarantee none of those gowns will ever be on my body." She only loved Pete, and the fact was, Pete only loved Rancho Diablo. He teased her about marriage, but both of them knew that he wasn't serious. Underneath it all,

Pete was happy with their noncommitted-committed relationship. They kept quiet about it, they met in absolute secrecy, keeping the town busybodies from planning their wedding and naming their future children—and after all these years, she couldn't change the game. She had nothing to offer him in the way of family, if he wanted that, and surely he did.

They'd never talked about it. But even Pete had to notice, with his penchant for making love "bareback" as he put it, that a pregnancy had never arisen. There'd never even been a false alarm. It wasn't that she was taking unnecessary chances; she was over thirty. She would have been thrilled to become pregnant. Even just making love on Saturday nights should have produced a bingo at some point.

She was infertile.

"Maybe once Pete sees you around all those beautiful white gowns, he'll pop the question," Darla said.

"I don't think I can get pregnant," Jackie said, "and I'm pretty sure he would want a big family like his own."

Darla stared at her. "Aren't you on the pill?" she asked in a whisper.

Jackie shook her head. "I rarely have a cycle. In all my life, I've probably had ten."

Darla thought about that for a minute. "Maybe Pete's been fixed. Or maybe he has a problem."

Jackie laughed. "He has problems, but I don't think fathering a baby would be one."

"Some men have low sperm counts."

"Maybe." Pete was pretty virile, though. Jackie wouldn't bank on him having a problem.

"Well, anyway. Think about the bridal shop. We'll

worry about getting Pete Callahan to the altar later. I'm sure we can spring a proper trap if we put our heads together." Darla went off, whistling, to check her patients.

"That's not what I meant!" Jackie called after her. Darla waved a backward hand at her and kept going. But it was true. Jackie wasn't ever going to marry Pete. She knew it just as certainly as she knew the stars were going to shine in the dark New Mexico skies tonight. If she could get pregnant—maybe. But a family man would want a family, and so far, she wasn't a baby-mama kind of girl.

I'd love Pete's babies.

Short of magic, it wasn't likely.

"DON'T WORRY SO MUCH," Pete said as he climbed back through the bedroom window of Jackie's small house. "If you're going to jump around like that, I'm going to nail my finger. Then you'll have to nurse me."

Since there was nothing sexier than Jackie in her nurse's uniform, he really wouldn't mind her taking very good care of him. But she didn't laugh, the way she usually did. She watched him fit the frame a second more, then she left the room. He made sure it slid shut without a whisper, then followed her into the kitchen.

"Coffee?" she asked, avoiding his hands when he reached to grab her.

"Just you," he said, "as usual."

"Pete," Jackie said, "I think I'll go to bed early."

He looked at her, admiring her dark hair, darker eyes. She had springy little buns and an energy he loved, and he couldn't wait to get her in the sack. Why else did a man fix a woman's windows when they warped from drifting snow? He couldn't wait to run his hands over that perky butt. She had a back that curved just right into his body, and a—

"Pete, I don't know how to tell you this," Jackie said, and he tried to snap his focus back to where it needed to be. His little turtledove was awfully jumpy. Tonight was clearly going to be conversation-first night, and he was okay with that. As long as he got to hold her, Jackie could talk all she liked.

"Go ahead. I'm listening."

"All right." Jackie turned delicious dark eyes the color of pure dark cocoa on him. He watched her lips as she hesitated. God, he loved her mouth. If she wanted to talk for an hour, he'd just sit and watch with pleasure. As long as she let him kiss that mouth, he was a happy man.

"I think it's time for us to…"

He grinned. "To what, sugar?" He had a feeling he knew where this was going, and it couldn't be more timely.

"I'm so sorry, Pete," Jackie said, taking a deep breath. "But I don't want to see you anymore."

Chapter Three

The jackass—he actually *laughed*. Jackie stared at Pete, all the tears she'd been trying not to cry drying up to nothing.

"Come here," he said, reaching for her, "you're tired. You've had a bad day. Come tell big ol' Pete all about it."

She squirmed out of his arms, though she never had before. "No. It's nothing like that. It's just time, Pete."

He watched her, his dark-blue eyes wide with unspoken questions. Pete wasn't the kind of man who talked a lot. He wouldn't bug her to death about what she was thinking. In a minute, he'd shrug, decide the pastures were greener elsewhere, and off he'd go.

She just had to wait out this awkward moment.

Yet, as his gaze refused to release hers, she knew she'd not only caught him by complete surprise, somehow she'd also wounded him. She was shocked by that more than anything.

"Jackie, you mean a bunch to me," Pete said.

"And you mean a lot to me." Jackie reexamined her feelings for the hundredth time, and came to the same conclusion as before: It was time to end what was a non-serious relationship between them. Maybe these new feelings had started when Mr. Dearborn protested his medicine—for the hundredth time. Perhaps it had been knowing that nothing was going to change about her life, not tomorrow or the next day, if she didn't stop going along with the currents that flowed in their predictable patterns in Diablo.

But when Darla had mentioned changing their entire livelihoods, Jackie had known she was being handed the only chance she might ever have to change her whole life.

Maybe it shouldn't have meant ending her relationship with Pete, too, but what she had with him was just as much of a road to nowhere as anything else. By the hurt expression on his face, she wondered if she was being selfish. But the bottom line was that she was in love with Pete Callahan, and he was not in love with her, and after fifteen years of loving the man and five years of sleeping with him, she knew their pattern was just as predictable as any other in her week. She would find him in her bed, he would ravish her, adore her body from toe to nose and then he'd depart before dawn to feed cattle and horses.

And she'd see him again—the next Saturday.

"I'm sorry," she said to the pain she saw in his eyes.

And he said, "I am, too, sugar." He stroked one work-roughened hand down her chin-length hair, then her cheek, put his hat on and left.

This should feel different, Jackie thought. *My heart should be shattering.*

But her heart had shattered long ago, when she'd realized there was no future for her and the hottest cowboy to ever walk Diablo, New Mexico. Oh, she knew the ladies were gaga about the five other Callahan men, but in her opinion, only Peter Dade Callahan made her heart jump for joy every time she heard his name, saw his face, felt his hands on her.

Eventually, a girl had to move on with her life.

She grabbed her cell phone, dialed Darla. "I may run by and take a look at those papers again."

"I was hoping you'd be tempted," Darla told her.

"I just might be," Jackie said, listening as Pete's truck pulled from her drive. "I'll be there in a few minutes."

PETE THOUGHT HE WAS pretty good at reading women. In fact, there were times he'd thought he could write a book on the vagaries of the female mind.

Jackie had caught him so off guard he wondered how he could have missed the signs. Had he not just loved her within an inch of her life last Saturday night? She'd cried his name over and over so sweetly he'd been positive he had satisfied her every desire.

Now he was left to scratch at his five-o'-clock stubble with some puzzlement. Last Saturday night had been the last time he'd seen Jackie. He'd hidden his truck around back, as he always did. She liked to keep their relationship private, a plan he agreed with, thanks to the Diablo busybodies. Nobody wanted the Books 'n' Bingo ladies fastening their curiosity on them—it was a recipe for more well-meaning intrusion than a man could stand.

Jackie had cooked him dinner, and then, because she'd worked all day, he'd rented a movie, a chick flick. As the movie rolled, and guy got girl, Pete had massaged Jackie, starting with her shell-shaped toes, the delicate arches of her darling feet, then had even bent over to plant tender kisses on her ankles. The flower-patterned sofa in front of her TV was soft and puffy, a veritable haven of girlieness, and he loved sitting there on Saturday nights like an old-fashioned date.

Then he always carried Jackie into her white-lace bedroom, his angel ensconced in gentle frills and woman's adornments, and he made love to her with a passion that he felt from the bottom of his heart.

In his mind, there was nothing better than Saturday nights with Jackie. It was so much a part of his routine—their routine—that he wasn't sure how he could live without it.

Apparently, she thought she could.

His heart felt as if it had been kicked.

He parked his truck and went inside the house. Aunt Fiona looked at him, her Cupid's-bow mouth making an O. "You're home quite early, Pete."

"Change of plans," he said, not about to share any details. Anyway, there was nothing to share. No one knew about him and Jackie, so there was nobody he could tell about the breakup, even if he wanted some sympathy, which he damn well didn't.

He wanted a handle of whiskey and a quiet room in which to nurse his pain.

"Did something happen?" Fiona asked.

"Like what?" he asked, rummaging through the liquor cabinet. Damn if he knew where Burke kept the goods.

"I don't know," Fiona said. "I just don't think I've ever seen you home at this hour on a Saturday night. Probably not in five years—ohhh."

He stopped moving bottles, pulled his head from the cabinet again. "What 'ohhh'?"

"Nothing. Nothing at all." Fiona went back to crocheting something that looked like a tiny white Christmas stocking.

He stared at her creative project, perplexed. "Are you making a *baby bootie?*"

She shoved the white thing into a basket at her feet. "Pete, if you're going to come home early on a Saturday night, that's your choice. But that doesn't mean you have the right to poke your nose into my business."

His jaw went slack. Nosiness wasn't something he'd been accused of before. He was known for being close-mouthed, secretive, even aloof. If Fiona was making baby booties, it was none of his business.

Yet, perhaps it was. Baby booties meant that Fiona had a taker for her plan. And that was a problem for him, because he wanted Rancho Diablo, and the woman he'd figured was a surefire deal had just given him the brush-off.

"Who are you making it for, Aunt Fiona?"

She cleared her throat. Got to her feet, sending him a cool, none-of-your-business stare worthy of a general. She took her basket and disappeared down the hall.

Pete lost his desire to drink. He shut the cabinet, then after a moment, left the house.

He felt lost in a way that he never had in his entire life. His woman had just left him; what would he do if he lost his home as well?

There was only one thing to do: He had to drive to Monterrey and watch the rodeo. Gamble a little, sing some karaoke, maybe let a sweet cowgirl calm his broken heart for the night. Chat with some buddies, go to cowboy church tomorrow morning—and then maybe this terrible problem would have gone away.

Maybe.

"COME TO BED, my Irish knight," Fiona said two hours later when Burke came into the bedroom they shared clandestinely.

"My wild Irish rose," Burke said, taking off his long coat and cold-weather cap. "I've been thinking."

"Think quietly, husband," Fiona said. "Pete came home tonight. We don't know where he might be lurking."

Burke glanced up as he stripped off the corduroy trousers he wore to oversee the locking-up of the old English-style house. A manor, her brother Jeremiah had wanted, just like the ones he'd seen in England before he'd had money. So that was what he'd built.

Jeremiah hadn't lived here long.

"Why is Peter here?" Burke asked.

"My uncomfortable suspicion is that he and Jackie may have had a wee falling-out."

Burke put on a robe made of Scottish wool and sank into his comfy leather armchair in front of the fireplace and directly across from the bed where his wife looked darling in her frilly white nightcap and flannel nightgown. "He said nothing?"

"No. But Pete's been the soul of discretion about his Saturday nights for so many years." Fiona sighed. "He wouldn't be here if something unfortunate hadn't occurred between them." Fiona hoped her pronouncement about the ranch hadn't stirred some sort of disagreement between them. Privately, she'd had her money on either Pete or Jonas to be the first to the altar. Stubborn Jonas had shocked her by walking away from the deal stone-cold. Now Pete might not be in quite the position she'd hoped he was in for a small nudge toward marriage. That left Creed and Rafe, Judah and Sam—none of whom she'd put a long bet on.

"Then I may have other bad news," Burke said, taking out his pipe carved from burled Irish wood. "All the other boys are in the bunkhouse."

"All the boys?" Fiona sat up straighter. "They're never home on Saturday nights! This is our night!"

"Be that as it may," Burke said, "they're engaged in a game of poker in the main bunkhouse." He drew with satisfaction on the pipe, then leaned over to stoke the fire.

"Burke! How can you be so calm! They're supposed to be competing against each other for Rancho Diablo!"

Burke smiled. "You've done an admirable job with the boys, Fiona. Now it's our turn. As I said, I've been thinking."

"Thinking about what?" Fiona didn't want to take her mind off her charges—although they weren't really her charges anymore, she supposed. They were full-grown men, responsible for their own happiness.

Still, the only way a man was happy—truly happy—was with a woman. Look at Burke, after all. He was the happiest man she'd ever met. Fiona smiled with satisfaction. Of course, he'd always said he preferred his creature comforts of home and hearth.

Her nephews didn't seem to share that opinion. They were more the type to fly the coop. Where had she gone wrong with them? Had she not been the best mother figure she knew how to be? And Burke...well, Burke had done as she'd asked. He'd remained a butler, not a stand-in father figure, which she thought the boys might have resented. They'd kept their marriage secret in order that the boys would always know that they were first priority for her, first in her heart. That she had done for her younger brother, Jeremiah, and his wife, Molly, a promise kept she'd never regretted.

"Let's renew our vows," Burke said. "I ask you, my love, to marry me in front of the whole town. Your Books 'n' Bingo ladies can be your bridesmaids."

Fiona stared. If Burke had suggested that the answer to their dilemma was for her to sprout wings and fly, she couldn't have been more shocked. She'd be more likely to sprout angel's wings because the man was about to give her heart failure.

Burke looked so earnest, with his bright-blue eyes and ruddy cheeks framed by very un-butlerish longish white hair, that she didn't dare stamp on his romantic tendencies, however much she felt that he wasn't thinking about her problem very seriously.

"Burke, we can't do that. You know I promised Jeremiah and Molly that I would see their boys to adulthood."

"And you've done that admirably." Burke smiled at her. "Sometimes I just sit and chuckle about how skillfully you've played your hand with those ruffians, Fiona."

"But they aren't married. They have no children. And have you forgotten, most importantly, that Rancho Diablo is going to be sold?"

This was the part that frightened her the most; the nightmare that kept her awake at night. She had failed Jeremiah. The castle of his dreams, the home where he and Molly had imagined raising their sons, wasn't really hers to raffle off to the brothers as she'd claimed. "Burke, they simply have to focus on their lives."

"Fiona," he said, getting up to lie on the bed with

her, cradling her head to his chest, "they *are* concentrating on their lives."

"They'll hate me for losing the ranch."

"No."

"In a year, when it's all over, and the Callahan name is nothing but synonymous with a joke and pity—"

"Fiona, you sell these boys short. Anyway, they're not even boys anymore. They're full-grown men. Why not just tell them the truth, instead of forcing them to find brides they may not want?"

"And the secret at the bottom of the stairs?" She looked up at her husband. "What do we do about that? And about their parents? Do you suggest I tell them that Jeremiah and Molly are still alive as well?"

Burke laid his pipe on the nightstand tray next to him and stroked his wife's head. "You worry too much, Fiona. It will all work out."

He'd always said that. She wasn't convinced this time. Rancho Diablo was in trouble. She could tell the brothers, see if they could raise enough money to somehow buy it back. Once they found out she'd put it up as a guarantee for a deal that had gone south, they might be able to do something. She probably owed it to them to tell them what had happened.

She couldn't. They couldn't help, she knew. And Jonas already had his eye on another property due east of here. He said he wanted his own place. Sympathy was her last card—community sympathy against that evil Bode Jenkins, their neighbor, and the scurvy bounder who'd convinced his daughter, the Honorable Judge Julie Jenkins, to cast their ranch as payment for the deal she'd greatly underestimated. Plus she owed a fearsome amount of taxes on a property that wouldn't be theirs in another year.

No one knew yet—but it would hit the grapevine soon enough. Fiona wasn't certain how much longer she could keep the dam from breaking. Her friends would always be her friends, but the boys—the boys she'd pledged to raise—stood to lose everything.

"Damn Bode Jenkins," Fiona said. "He outfoxed me good this time. I wish he'd...I wish he'd fall into a river."

"Fiona," Burke murmured, patting his wife's head as she started to cry against his chest, "the boys are always going to love you."

She wished she could be certain of that.

Chapter Four

The bunkhouse door blew open. All five brothers glanced up. Snow and frigid wind blasted in with Jonas, who stamped his feet on the outside mat before closing the door.

"Look what the bad weather brought in," Pete said. "Couldn't make it to the airport?"

"Had no intention of leaving."

Pete took Jonas's coat and hung it on the hook in the entryway. His brother looked tired. "So where the hell have you been?"

"Following Miss Cavuti or whatever the hell her name was."

"You mean Madame Vivant. Sabrina McKinley." Pete chuckled. "I figured you had an eye for her."

"I do. And you should, too. Two eyes, in fact." Jonas glared at Pete, then around at the other brothers who sat on the dark-brown leather sectional, watching them. "Am I the only one who thought her story sounded odd?"

Sam shrugged. "Aunt Fiona can take care of herself. And Burke wouldn't let her come to any harm."

Pete applauded their youngest brother's common sense. Pete hadn't foreseen Jonas being so suspicious that he might follow the fortune-teller—if that's what she really was. Truthfully, Jonas was right to be suspicious, but he'd be better off putting all the suspicion on their dear Aunt Fiona.

Pete slapped Jonas on the back. "Well, join us for poker, bro. I'll grab you a beer, if you want."

Jonas shook his head. "No. All I want is some hot, black-as-night, stand-a-spoon-in-it coffee. It was colder and the snow was higher where those gypsies are now. I about froze my tail off."

"Where's their next stop?" Rafe asked.

"North of here. Buzzard's Peak or something like that. Think they're on their way to Montana." Jonas drank from the steaming mug Pete handed him.

"What makes you think they're headed to Montana?" Creed asked.

"They stopped at a truck stop to fill up." Jonas sank into the leather sofa with a sigh of appreciation to be home. "I got out to refuel, and spoke to one of the drivers."

"Sabrina didn't see you?" Rafe asked.

Jonas shook his head. "No. I'm sure she was bundled inside somewhere, counting whatever money she got from Fiona."

Pete smirked and reached for the cards. "Fiona wouldn't part with much hard-earned cash, Jonas."

His brother eyed him. The other men sat silently, waiting. It was not unusual for Jonas and Pete to have a difference of opinion. They were fifty-fifty on the outcome, Pete thought with satisfaction. And this time, he was holding all the cards.

"All I know," Jonas said, "is that Fiona's up to something. That bit about us getting married and having a bunch of kids is a smokescreen for something bigger."

Judah took the cards from Pete and began to deal. "Like what?"

"That's what I aim to find out." Jonas set his mug down and rubbed his hands. "I'm starting to thaw."

"Listen," Pete said, "Fiona has always looked out for our best interests. Why be so suspicious, Jonas?"

Jonas glared at him. "Why wouldn't she just divide the ranch between us, if it's simply a matter of her needing to write a will? All of us are financially capable. It's not like she's having to protect the ranch from us doing something stupid with it. I'm not saying that I want Rancho Diablo, particularly, but it is home. And I have to wonder why Fiona just didn't offer it to us and let us decide, instead of making us play marriage roulette for it. It bothers the hell of out me."

The brothers sat lost in their own thoughts, the only noise the popping of the roaring log fire. Pete wondered whether Jonas was so sore because he was the only one of them who'd once been within a foot of a wedding altar, then decided it was typical of Jonas to look out for the rest of them.

Pete studied his brother. "Jonas, we can decide whether to do this Fiona's way or not. You don't have to big-brother us anymore."

"Yeah?" Jonas glanced up, spearing his brother with a frosty gaze. "So how's finding a bride going to fit into your Saturday-night routine with Jackie Samuels, Pete?"

The brothers snickered. Pete thought about socking Jonas a good one, right in the nose, but it wouldn't solve anything, because Jonas was right.

He sighed. "Not too damn good."

"Jackie said no?" Sam asked.

"Look," Pete said, "no one's even supposed to know about Jackie and me, okay? So I don't really feel like discussing it."

"Dang," Creed said, "we all figured you'd be first to the altar. Then the rest of us would be off the hook."

Pete's brows went up in disbelief. "How would that work?"

"You'd get married, and we'd keep working the ranch, just like we do. Of course, we'd have to beat the hell out of you until you went to a lawyer and divided the ranch up between all of us." Rafe grinned. "That was the plan, anyway."

"Let me get this straight," Pete said, his tone as sour as his gut had suddenly become, "you wanted me to be the fall guy in this deal. As soon as the ranch was out of Fiona's control, you were going to highjack me into splitting it up between all of us."

"That's right," Sam said, "and it was a helluva good plan. We didn't count on you muffing the proposal to Jackie, though."

"Probably should have," Creed said. "If I'd bet a fiver on that, I'd be money-up right now."

Pete sank back into the sofa. "Here I thought I was doing a deal on you, and you were plotting against me and my new bride and family. You're a bunch of jackasses."

"What's that?" Judah said. "Did you say *we're* a bunch of jackasses?" He smirked at his brothers. "Who wants to hold Pete's head in a bucket of snow until he confesses?"

The brothers rose like a well-muscled, united wave. Pete put up a hand of surrender. "Calm down. All I was keeping from you—and it's just a small thing, nothing like what you were up to—"

"We'll decide that by family vote," Jonas said, "don't leave out any of the details."

Pete was torn. He hated to blow up Aunt Fiona's excellent plan. On the other hand, Jonas had a great point. Maybe the fortune-teller *had* done something to Fiona's mind. He had no idea, after all, exactly how much coin had changed hands. There'd been no sign outside the tent at the fair indicating a fee for services.

"Pete," Sam said, his voice deep with warning. "Don't sit there and concoct a story, or we will hold you in censure."

That was bad. Last time one of them had been censured by the other brothers, Rafe—the unlucky bastard—had had his face tattooed in his sleep by a nice, usually calm lady—Judge Julie Jenkins next door. Rafe had been done in by his own twin, as Creed had opened the door for Julie. She'd brought an indelible red-ink pen, and the brothers had merely guffawed as she approached Rafe, who had crashed on the sofa. Rafe had been on a bender, so he hadn't noticed until he'd gotten up the next morning to go to Mass and had found himself looking like something out of a girlie revenge flick. His entire face had been covered with tiny hearts, probably fifty of them.

Julie was no pushover, and she thought Rafe was an ass. He hadn't tried to get smart with that little lady twice. Pete winced when he thought about Rafe scrubbing his face for days after Julie's sneak attack. Fiona had given Rafe some rubbing alcohol, but in the end, only time had worn away the tiny hearts on his face. His brothers had ribbed him for days, and Rafe had been unable to leave the ranch for the sake of machismo. If Rafe hadn't been in a state of censure with his brothers, they would never have let a miffed female in to pen her revenge on his face. They would have at least stopped her at five, maybe ten, hearts. They'd never asked Rafe what had gotten him crosswise with Julie, and he'd never offered any information. Pete wasn't eager to suffer a similar fate. "Fiona hired Sabrina to tell us the ranch was in trouble."

"Hired her?" Judah repeated. "Madame Vivant didn't work a nefarious plan on her?"

Pete shook his head. "Nope. I'm sure Fiona's as right in her mind as any of us. No one would ever take advantage of her. Not easily, anyway." He looked at his brothers' incredulous faces. "I feel bad ratting out her plan."

The poker game was abandoned. They were in a bigger game now, Pete thought. "At the time, I thought it was funny. She was trying to maneuver us into settling down. I had a girlfriend already, so it wasn't—"

"You were going to cheat us," Creed said. "You were getting a head start."

"No—" Pete began, then he slumped in the sofa. "Yeah."

They considered him with disapproving expressions.

"It's no different from you thinking you had me set up to fall first, thereby letting you off the hook," Pete said in defense of himself. "And I didn't feel that it was any of my business to spoil Fiona's plan."

"This is true," Sam said, "but we've always known we had to look out for each other."

Pete sighed. "Oh, shut the hell up. None of you wants to get married anyway. So don't act like you could have caught up with me if Jackie had said yes."

"Assuming you're not shooting blanks," Jonas said darkly. "Five years of dating is an awful lot of raincoats. I've never seen you make a run to the drugstore."

Pete felt a flush run up his neck. "There's nothing wrong with my gun, thanks. Jackie's probably on the pill or something."

Sam's mouth fell open. "You never asked her?"

"Hell, no. She's a nurse. What could I tell a nurse about birth control?" Now that his brothers were ribbing him about it, though, Pete wondered. He'd never seen anything in Jackie's house that looked like birth control pills. In fact, he'd never known her even to take cold medicine. She was a big believer in homeopathy, when appropriate, and eating healthy like a granola-starved hippie. Fresh food was the key to life, she'd say, setting a snack in front of him, and he'd smile and eat and mostly stare at her, not caring if she fed him dirt so long as he got into the sack with her.

"Damn, you're not much of a stud," Judah said, "if you don't even know whether you should be wrapping up."

Pete jumped to his feet. "There is nothing wrong with my—with me! I could have children if I wanted them, if Jackie wanted them." He didn't know if she did, but he wasn't going to admit that. Now that he thought about it, he and Jackie hadn't done a whole lot of talking about big life issues.

"Sit down. We're just trying to figure out what to do here." Jonas shoved him back down into the sofa, with a determined thrust that collapsed Pete. He felt as though his world was spinning, anyway. Did Jackie want children? He assumed that particular desire was baked into the DNA of all women. "Anyway, I never got around to asking her to marry me. She—" He took a painful swallow of beer. "She ran me off."

They took that in for a minute with an assortment of grunts and empathetic groans.

"Sorry about Jackie," Sam said. "Sucks, dude."

Pete glanced up at the first vote of sympathy he'd heard from his brothers, realizing how much he appreciated the sentiment. His other brothers reached over and either clouted him on the back or punched him in the arm. He felt better, as much as he possibly could, under the circumstances. "Guess you'll need a different plan."

"It just doesn't make sense." Jonas glanced around at his brothers. "There has to be something pushing Fiona to be this drastic. I had my doubts about that little con artist she brought in, figured she'd at least hang around to try to worm something out of Fiona or the ranch, but she seems to have been happy to take her fee and go." He squinted at Pete. "Why the hell were you going to let us all get caught in a noose, bro, if you knew it was a set-up?"

Pete shrugged. "Wouldn't kill any of us to settle down."

"Might kill me," Sam said. "I live a monklike existence."

This earned hoots from his brothers. Pete rolled his eyes. "Anyway, I thought it was kind of cute to hear Fiona and her bingo buddies trying to put one over on us. I figured I was pulling one over on her by hearing her plans."

"But still," Rafe said, "you planned to have the jump on us since you already had a woman picked out. I don't know if I feel good about that."

"I had a girl picked out," Pete said, trying not to wince, "but who knows if she would have wanted children immediately? These things take two people, and all the decision wasn't mine. So I was only ahead in the fact that I had a woman I thought I had a relationship with."

"Oh, I don't care about any of that," Judah said, pulling out his wallet. "I think I've got some hot-date phone numbers in here from the last rodeo. I can probably catch up pretty quick, if you guys want to let Fiona think her plan is succeeding. What does it hurt to give her a little pleasure?"

Creed shook his head. "I say we go to Fiona and tell her we're all joining the priesthood. That'll frost her."

Pete laughed, then straightened. "No! We can't give her any reason to suspect that we know anything."

Jonas looked at him. "We can't decide our futures based on emergency trips to the marriage license office."

"Do you currently base your future on more sound decisions than what Fiona has suggested?" Pete looked around the room at his siblings. "I don't think any of you realize this, but Fiona wasn't just our guardian. She wasn't just a parent. She keeps a lot of secrets in her drive to be our number-one protector and cheerleader."

Sam laughed. "You make it sound like she and her little friends sit around and plot all day."

Pete nodded. "Don't kid yourself. That's exactly what she does."

They went silent again. The wind howled outside,

picking up a violent sound. Pete wondered if he should drag one of his brothers out with him to check on the cattle and the horses. The wind whipped so hard over their bunkhouse that it reminded him of crying ghosts, something he'd always wondered about when he was a child. He'd always felt that ghosts lived just as freely at Rancho Diablo as the Callahans did.

Maybe the ghosts hung around because they liked it here. Pete was determined to feel positive about anything he could concerning Rancho Diablo.

"Let's make a pact," Sam said suddenly. "One of us—whoever can do it first—will get married. Try to have kids. The rest of us will be hellaciously good uncles."

Everyone stared at Sam.

"Since you're only twenty-six," Jonas said, his tone wry, "that almost makes your suggestion a bit callous."

Sam shook his head. "I might have my eye on a gal. You don't know."

Pete sighed. "He may have a point. Only one is needed for sacrificial-lamb status, as long as everyone agrees that once Fiona has given the ranch over to us, we formally split ownership in a lawyer's office."

"It's a bad idea between brothers," Judah said. "Not that I don't trust all of you, but Fiona is trying to play us off against each other. No telling what rabbit she might pull out of her hat next." He looked at Pete. "Besides, you seem to know more about her than the rest of us. These secrets she's keeping that you're hinting at—are they as much of a hairball as her marriage-and-kids plot? 'Cause while I trust everyone in this room, I'm not sure if you deserve trust, Pete, considering."

"He's right," Jonas said. "You seem to have information that could affect the rest of us."

"No," Pete said, "I mean, I just know her too well. Fiona works constantly on our behalf. All I meant was that she…she keeps things to herself." He was uncomfortable under his brothers' laser scrutiny. There wasn't a whole lot of trust being beamed at him.

"Can you give us an example?" Creed asked. "I'm getting mighty pissed about all the secrecy surrounding what should be my life."

"I don't know what all she keeps under her hat," Pete said, becoming defensive and somewhat hostile himself. "The only thing I know for sure is that she and Burke are married. And that's not such a big secret, is it?" Pete looked at all his brothers for confirmation that the bombshell he'd just dropped was, in fact, just a tiny one.

Five faces glared at him.

"Fiona is married to the butler, and you didn't tell us?" Jonas demanded. "Are you insane? When did this happen? You don't think this affects our futures?"

"Not really," Pete said, feeling his hackles rise. "They did it about a hundred years ago, for crying out loud. I found the marriage certificate when I was digging around in the cabinets in the basement."

"Holy crow," Sam said, "you should've been a spy."

"You sorry sack of crap," Creed said, "why'd you keep that under your hat?"

Rafe looked shocked. Judah looked as though he might take a swing at something, chiefly Pete.

"Look," he said to Jonas, feeling that his eldest brother was the only one in the room who might defend him, "it was none of our business if she didn't want us to know."

"I don't know," Creed muttered, "seems like you've appointed yourself the keeper of the family secrets."

"Not so much," Pete said, "considering we've never known that much about our family anyway."

Chapter Five

After a few moments of stunned silence, Jonas said, "We've done enough talking, at least in my opinion. We're just getting mad, and we need to be focused on what to do about Fiona."

Obviously, any discussion of their family history was off the table. Pete was okay with that. He hadn't wanted to talk about Fiona anyway. Or their troubled family tree. "Suits me, if anybody has a game plan."

"No," Sam said, his voice quiet. "We can't do anything until we talk to Fiona."

"No," Pete said. "We can't let her know that we're on to her. She works so hard to wrangle us in the direction she thinks is right for us. And you know, a lot of times, that little aunt of ours has been right."

They digested that. Jonas poked at the fire again. Sparks erupted with a pop and a log crashed to the bottom of the grate. Judah squatted in front of the fireplace to toss in a couple of logs. Overhead a fan swirled in a lazy motion, keeping the air stirred. Family photos lined the mantel, mostly black-and-white memories of the brothers. Fiona loved to take pictures of them. She was good with a camera and had captured their growing-up years with skill. Under the sofa, a hand-worked rug by a Native American artisan warmed the stone floor. Other decor they'd picked up on jaunts into Santa Fe graced the large, beam-ceilinged room, mementoes of what Fiona called family getaways. She'd bought a van, the biggest one she could find, and all the boys and Burke would pile in while Fiona drove them all over the Southwest once a year. She'd been a great parent. Pete swallowed. He didn't want her feelings hurt. "Look, let's just forget about it, okay? None of us want to get married, not really. So it doesn't matter."

"Yeah, so what happens to the ranch if something happens to Fiona?" Rafe asked. "She said she hasn't been feeling well."

Jonas sat up. "I'll check on her tomorrow."

"Rafe's right." Creed brought the coffeepot and a plate of cookies Fiona had left in the kitchen over to the table. "Anything could happen. We're going to have to ask her."

"You ask her, Jonas," Pete said.

His older brother shook his head. "No. We'll have a family meeting at the appropriate time."

"In the spring," Pete said. "It doesn't matter right now, does it? Christmas vacation doesn't seem like the time to bring up family issues."

"It's the third of January. Technically, vacation is over. And she started the discussion," Sam reminded him. "She brought in the fortune-teller."

That was true. There was no defense Pete could offer. "I wish I hadn't said anything."

"You know what I wonder," Sam said, ignoring Pete's doubts, "is where our parents really are."

All six brothers sat like stone statues, cookies left on the tray, seconds ticking loudly on the mantel clock.

Pete felt hair stand up on the back of his neck as regret washed over him. He'd opened up a box of trouble with his tale of Fiona's plot to make them family men. "Our parents are buried somewhere in a graveyard, Sam."

Jonas looked at Sam. Sam stared back at Jonas.

"Go ahead. Say it," Sam said. "I know what you're thinking."

Jonas jumped to his feet, paced the room. Turned away from the brothers. Scrubbed at his chin, took a deep breath. Pete wondered what the hell was going on. He felt deep waters eddying around them and hoped they weren't all going to drown. Something was going terribly wrong in the family—and it had to do with Rancho Diablo.

"I'm not so sure our parents are buried anywhere," Jonas said, as he turned back around. "We've never seen their graves."

Judah blinked. "Did we ever ask?"

Pete shook his head. "I didn't. Why would Fiona tell us they'd died if they hadn't? Why did she and Burke come from Ireland to raise us if they weren't gone?" A bad feeling wrapped itself around Pete, a question that had always been at the back of his mind but which he'd ignored. Wanted to ignore still.

"What Jonas isn't saying," Sam said, "is that I came later. And he remembers it."

They all looked from Jonas to Sam. Pete felt a snake of worry start in the pit of his stomach, pulling tight.

"So that's why he thinks our parents might not be deceased," Sam said. "And that's why he's suspicious about Fiona cooking up a plan to have us compete for the ranch." Sam looked at Jonas. "Right? That's why you really followed Madame Vivant?"

Pete crossed to the window, staring into the darkness, feeling the cold pane against his forehead. Nothing good was going to come of this night, and he wished he'd kept his big mouth shut. He and his brothers had always been close but reserved, keeping to themselves a lot.

He felt further apart from his brothers than ever.

There was a cauldron of family secrets stewing away—they all kept them. It protected them somehow from the underlying sense of not-quite-normal that surrounded the ranch. He glanced up at the moon—a fat, round harbinger of time. No one had yet mentioned the old Navajo who arrived like clockwork every year on the night before Christmas. He and Fiona went to the basement and stayed for an hour, and they had no idea why. Burke always sat with the brothers in the library, keeping them busy with conversation and cookies when they were young, and later with whiskey and a list of items he said needed to be conquered at the ranch. They'd always thought of this as their yearly Burke business meeting, their chance to help out Fiona and Burke with the running of the ranch. Now Pete realized Burke had merely been keeping them busy, away from the real business which was being conducted underneath the house.

Something was going on, something that had to do with Fiona's sudden desire that they settle down. Pete thought about Jackie, wondered what she was doing, debated whether she'd mind a late Saturday-night visitor, even though she'd just sent him away.

He felt certain she hadn't changed her mind in the few hours since he'd left her place. Probably she hadn't, but as the snow swirled outside and his brothers mused about Callahan family problems, Pete made a break for freedom.

"I'm going out," he said, jamming his hat on his head and buckling up a long oilskin coat.

"Bad night for it," Sam warned. "Could be snow drifts as high as your ass."

"It's okay," Pete said, "I'm already in up to my ass. Can't get any worse."

He hurried to the barn, checked the horses and saddled Bleu, a huge black stallion suited to riding over snow and ice. Didn't panic easily. Kind of like Pete, who hated dark emotion and stress—he wanted nothing more at this moment than to get away from a rising sense of panic he couldn't explain.

HE TAPPED ON JACKIE'S front door after noting that her car was parked alongside the house. Dangerous, thanks to the snow. He'd advise her to put it away, or do it for her if she wanted.

She came to the door, her expression curious and not necessarily pleased. "Pete! What are you doing here?"

He wished he'd ignored his urge to see her at all costs—he felt unwelcome, worse than he had back at the bunkhouse with his brothers.

"Come in," she said. "Tie Bleu under the eaves."

Usually she said, *Put Bleu in the barn,* so there wasn't a chance he was being asked to resume their comfortable Saturday-night routine. Bleu had been tied under the eaves before and he'd be fine, but it was going to be a quick visit, in this cold weather. "I won't be long," he muttered to Bleu, "so don't give me that face."

The horse blew out his disdain for being treated like

a common yard ornament. "Sorry," Pete told him, "this is important."

He went inside, staying at the front door on the pretty floral rug. "You're all dressed up," he said, surprised that she wasn't in her nightgown at this hour. *Old routine,* he reminded himself. *Back when we were us.* The black dress and boots she wore made him realize how much he was going to miss her in his life.

Well, it didn't take a dress and boots for Jackie to be hot, but he realized how many times he'd taken her out on a date. *Zero.*

"What can I do for you, Pete?"

He gazed into her dark-chocolate eyes, feeling as if he were drowning. *Say you didn't mean to send me out of your life. That it was all a mistake.*

"I'm not sure. I just wanted to see you." That sounded so lame he frowned. "Wanted to check on you."

That didn't sound any better. Jackie shook her head. "I'm fine, as you can see."

Great. Here he stood, a giant useless doofus, taking up her time when she clearly had some place to go. "Jackie—"

"I'm sorry, Pete." She did look regretful, which helped somewhat. "I have an appointment. You caught me just as I was leaving."

An appointment at eight o'clock at night? That was a polite way of saying she had a date. There was nothing else Jackie could be doing looking as hot as she did.

Pete had no idea how their steady relationship had jumped the tracks as it had.

"Okay. Thanks." He drank in her heart-shaped face, the slight confusion that lifted her dark brows. She really didn't understand why he'd come. Didn't feel the same things he did. "Good night, Jackie."

"Good night, Pete."

She watched him go out the door and untie Bleu. He swung up into the saddle, glancing back at her. She stood under the porch light, her arms wrapped around herself, the way his arms wanted to be. Needed to be.

He felt too helpless to do more than wave a hand at her to say goodbye. The gesture felt more like surrender. She waved back, and he rode away, which also felt like surrender.

JACKIE WATCHED PETE disappear into the night, Bleu anxious to be off again as Pete gave him free rein. She closed the door, her heart heavy. Maybe she wasn't making the right decision. Pete had been her guy for so long it was hard to think about him never holding her in his arms again.

"Change is necessary," she reminded herself. "We weren't going anywhere."

A knock on the front door filled her heart with a sense of hope that shouldn't be there—but it was. "Pete?" she said, opening the door.

A woman stood on her porch. She looked cold, her reddish hair shining under the porch light, her nose pink from the harsh conditions.

"Can I help you?" Jackie asked, now wishing she hadn't answered the knock.

"I'm sorry to bother you this late," her visitor said. Her green eyes expressed true remorse at the intrusion. Jackie held her breath as a strange chill passed over her. "This is awkward," her guest continued, "but Fiona Callahan sent me."

Jackie blinked. "Why?"

"She said you might want to talk to me." The woman shrugged delicate shoulders that were covered by a black wool poncho. "My name is Sabrina McKinley. I'm a fortune-teller with the circus that just came through town."

"You don't really tell fortunes?"

"I tell people what they want to hear."

Why would Fiona send a charlatan to her? "I don't need to hear anything. But thank you for stopping by."

She started to close the door, hesitating when Sabrina spoke.

"Children are a blessing," Sabrina said. "You have been blessed three times."

I don't want to hear this. This woman knows nothing about my life. "I'm sorry," Jackie said. "I don't mean to be rude, but I have an appointment, and—"

"It's all right," Sabrina said. "Can you tell me how to get to Bode Jenkins's house?"

"Bode Jenkins?" Jackie took a more thorough look at her visitor. "Why do you want to go there, if you don't mind me asking?"

"Fiona thinks he might need to talk." Sabrina shrugged, the poncho moving gracefully as she did.

Bode didn't talk to anyone, not much anyway. He'd eat this tiny woman alive for showing up on his porch. Yet, it wasn't her place to interfere. "Can I ask you a question?"

Sabrina smiled. "People usually do."

"Oh. Right. No, I meant…did you tell something to Fiona?"

"Client confidentiality," Sabrina said. "I'm sure you understand."

"Absolutely." Jackie didn't. On the other hand, she wouldn't want this woman talking about whatever she knew about her.

Oh, baloney. This lady knows nothing about me. It's all hogwash.

Sabrina stepped away from the door. "It was nice meeting you."

Jackie stared after her as she went down the porch steps and crunched off in the snow, leaving tracks with her small boots. Why was Fiona mixed up with a gypsy?

"I—" Jackie told herself not to get involved. Yet a visitor could get lost around here when she didn't know her way, especially with snow obscuring everything. She was going to be totally late to Darla's, but did it matter? Talking about the wedding business could wait thirty more minutes. "If you follow me, I'll take you by the entrance to the Jenkinses ranch."

"Thanks." Sabrina smiled. "The new business is a great idea, by the way. You should always follow your heart."

Once again, chills ran over Jackie that weren't weather-related. She decided to ignore Sabrina's words—maybe Darla had mentioned it to Fiona, who'd told Sabrina—but at the same time, she couldn't help but feel that the wind was blowing just a bit colder. She hurried to the car. "I'll drive slowly, so you don't lose sight of my taillights."

Nodding, Sabrina got into her truck. It was an old one, a white Ford that had seen better days. Jackie shook her head and started her own car—and felt the strangest jump in her stomach. A flutter, like a butterfly moving across her abdomen.

She glanced out at the horizon, and her breath caught.

Black horses ran across the horizon, tails and manes flying. It was beautiful and mystical, and Jackie suddenly thought about the black Diablos. But it couldn't be them. She was a good twenty miles away from Pete's ranch. And though Pete swore they were real, everyone else thought they were a myth dreamed up by the crazy Callahans. Fey Fiona and her Irish tales.

The wild hoofbeats she was hearing were nothing more than her own blood pounding in her ears.

Chapter Six

"She kind of wigged me out." Jackie glanced at Darla thirty minutes later as she sat in her friend's living room sipping hot tea. Their business papers were spread out on the table in front of her, but Jackie couldn't stop thinking about Sabrina McKinley. "I've never talked to a fortune-teller before. I don't know why it spooked me."

"I wonder at Fiona for sending her to your house," Darla said. "No matter. You got her to Bode's, and I feel bad enough for her having to pay a call on that troll."

Jackie looked down into her cup. She did, too. "So, where do we start?"

"Here are some ideas on financing. Here is the new spring inventory that has already been bought for next year." Darla pointed to different papers. "Best of all, here are the orders that are outstanding already for next June. Who would have thought we had so many antsy brides around Diablo?"

It was almost like reading a gossip sheet. Jackie gasped as she looked down the list of names Darla gave her. "I didn't know all these people were engaged!"

"And lucky for us they are." Darla grinned. "Love is definitely in the air."

Jackie felt a shard of pain go through her. Love was in the air, but not for her. Pete did not love her. He was going through some break-up pangs, probably, but they would pass. She knew her guy. Pete lived in the moment. He didn't think about the future, or life beyond the next Saturday night.

She was the worrier, the seeker. "This is great. This is just what I need."

"Really?" Darla beamed. "I was hoping you'd say that! Let's break out some champagne, partner!"

Jackie smiled, then remembered the strange flutter in her stomach. "Maybe just a soda for me. I've got a bit of a nervous stomach tonight for some reason."

Darla peered at her. "Do you think you might have a bug? There's been a lot of flu going around the hospital."

"I don't think it's a bug." Jackie felt a bit peaked. "Is it warm in here to you?"

"I'm fine," Darla said. "Let's go in the kitchen and get you a cold drink."

Darla got up and Jackie followed, although not with any enthusiasm. She wasn't certain ice would be enough to make her feel better. "So, if we decide to buy the wedding boutique, when do you plan to turn in your resignation?"

"I already did." Darla plunked three cubes into a glass, filled it with ginger ale and handed it to Jackie. "I gave my two weeks' notice, and I'm happy to be free."

Jackie nodded. "I will be, too." She thought about Mr. Dearborn, who loved to stir her up. "I'll miss it, but I do need a break."

Darla smiled. "Are you and Pete having some kind of little romance problems?"

Jackie blinked. "Why?"

"Just checking. You seem a little out of sorts."

The warmth was definitely back, despite the ginger ale, but this time it was embarrassment. "We broke up tonight."

"What happened?" Darla looked concerned. "This is a small town. You know better than to think you can keep something like that quiet around here. Tell me everything before I hear it through the grapevine."

Jackie shook her head. "How long has everyone known?"

"Since your mother told Fiona, and she told all her buddies at the Books 'n' Bingo Society. Which includes my mom." Darla grinned at her. "We've all known forever that you were sweet on each other."

"Why didn't you say anything?"

Darla shrugged. "I just thought you'd mention it to folks if you wanted to. Besides, it isn't like I don't know something about having a crush on a Callahan man."

"Really?" Jackie tried to picture Darla with any of the brothers and couldn't come up with one who could elude her gutsy, determined friend. "Who?"

"I'm going to wait five years to tell you, just like you did. Let's see if I can keep a secret that long," Darla teased.

"Tell me now."

Darla shook her head. "Unlike you, my secret crush has no idea I think he's a total stud. And we're going to keep it that way, unless I can figure out a spell to get him to notice me."

"I guess you could always ask Sabrina. She seems to know everything."

Darla glanced at her. "She really got to you, didn't she?"

Jackie perched on a bar stool at the counter. "She said I was going to be blessed with three children."

"Wow," Darla said, "that's better than a home pregnancy test." She giggled.

Jackie felt better just mentioning it. "Silly, huh?"

"Completely weird. Don't let it bother you."

"I'm not sure it altogether bothered me." Jackie looked at Darla, then smiled. "I felt sorry for her."

"She tells you you're going to have three kids, and you feel sorry for her? I'd be feeling sorry for myself."

"You don't want children?"

"If they were Judah's children, I'd have all he wanted." Darla grinned. "I could be a happy, barefoot and pregnant bride if the man involved was Judah Callahan."

"Judah! I should have known you'd fall for a hard case."

"I like a challenge, what can I say?" Darla smiled. "But unless it's with him, I won't be having children. I'm a career woman. I want to make enough money to buy my own tiny ranch." Darla looked around her house. "I love it here, but I want a place where I can have horses."

Jackie nodded. She understood. A Callahan man, a ranch, horses, children—wouldn't that just be heaven?

"So why'd you and Pete break up?" Darla asked. "You look so sad."

"I don't really want to talk about it." Jackie sipped at the ginger ale, feeling another squirm in her stomach. It was strange. She was never sick, never had aches and pains.

"You may not have a choice," Darla told her. "You looked sad when you came inside, and now you look like you've lost your dog. People will figure it out."

Jackie sighed. "We broke up because it wasn't going anywhere."

"Where did you want it to go?"

"Someplace different than Saturday-night sex."

"Oh. I suppose just asking for additional Monday-night sex was out of the question?"

Jackie smiled. "I don't know. We'd been in a routine for so long it had become a rut."

Darla looked at her. "How did Pete take the news?"

She remembered him standing on her porch, staring at her with hungry eyes. "He didn't say a whole lot."

"Typical Callahan."

Jackie felt another butterfly float across her stomach. "Listen, I think I'm going to head out. What papers do you want me to sign before I go?"

Darla grinned. "Several papers. And we'll need to go to the bank on Monday. But," she said with a teasing smile, "if the fortune-teller's right and you turn up pregnant, you have to model one of our gowns at your wedding."

"Oh, sure," Jackie said, "fat chance."

But deep inside her heart, Jackie knew she would have loved to have had a child with Pete. "Hey, let's take a drive."

"A drive where?" Darla asked.

"Over to the Jenkinses."

Darla hesitated before getting up to put her long blond hair into a ponytail. She pulled on a knitted cap and a wool jacket. "I'm ready to ride."

"You don't mind?"

"I totally understand. You'd feel better if you knew that Mr. Jenkins hadn't yelled three years off the life of your new friend. Or shot her." Darla shrugged and turned the lamps down. "The thought crossed my mind, too. She must have some strong magic or Fiona wouldn't have sent her to the bear's den."

Jackie got up to follow Darla to the door. "I don't think she has any mystical powers at all. I think she's just one of Fiona's friends."

"That's not saying much. I'm one of Fiona's friends, or at least my mother is, and I don't have any powers. Shall we stop at the drug store on the way and pick up a test for you?"

"No, thanks."

"Wouldn't it be funny if the fortune-teller was right?"

"No," Jackie said, "it would not."

Ten minutes later, Jackie and Darla stood on Mr. Jenkins's porch, stamping their feet to get the snow off. They could see Sabrina's old truck in the gravel drive.

"I can see them through the window," Jackie said.

"Not that we should be spying, but scoot over so I can see." Darla stepped up to peer inside. "They look like they're having a friendly chat."

"Yeah." Jackie was surprised Bode Jenkins had let Sabrina into his house. He was known for being rude to visitors and stingy with his hospitality. "Are they drinking tea?"

"And eating brownies, I think. Those are Julie's brownies," Darla said. "I recognize the frosting on top and the tiny white chocolate chips. She gives them out every year for Christmas."

A flash of indigestion hit Jackie, surprising her. She,

too, looked forward to the judge's brownies, so why had her stomach suddenly pitched?

Fear. "We should go," she murmured. "We don't want Mr. Jenkins to think we were—"

"Being nosey, which we are. Maybe we should ring the bell and see if we can get ourselves invited in for tea and one of those brownies, though."

"Hi, Jackie! Darla!"

Jackie swallowed a gasp, whirling. "Julie! Hi!"

Darla had jumped a foot beside her, but now all she said was, "Hi, Julie. We were just about to ring the bell."

Julie's brown eyes twinkled. "Come on in. Dad's got a visitor, but he won't mind a few more."

"We wouldn't want to bother anyone," Jackie said, and Darla said, "Sure, we could come inside for a minute."

"Let me help you with that firewood," Jackie murmured, taking a few sticks of it from Julie though the judge clearly had it handled.

Darla pulled the door open for Julie. "Was there anything special you were stopping by about?" Julie asked.

Darla's eyes met Jackie's. "We were going to get your thoughts on a business matter," Jackie said. "We should have called first."

"We always have visitors, and you're always especially welcome," Julie said, including both of them in her gracious words.

It was true. Julie did get lots of callers, mostly men who weren't afraid of Bode waving a shotgun at them. Cakes and pies were known to make their way with some frequency to the Jenkinses household, particularly if a grievance had been settled in someone's favor.

"Jackie, Darla, this is Sabrina McKinley," Julie said.

"She's a home-care provider who's come to visit Dad. Please come in and sit down, and have some tea with us."

"Hello, Sabrina," Jackie said. Darla murmured a greeting as well. Sabrina smiled at them, and the indigestion Jackie was suffering turned up a notch. "Good evening, Mr. Jenkins."

"You're interrupting," Bode said. "Do you know what time it is? Past time for a social call!"

Jackie and Darla backtracked to the door. "You're absolutely right, Mr. Jenkins. We're so sorry. Julie, we'll call you tomorrow."

"You don't have to go—" Julie began, but Jackie already had the door open.

"Good night, all. It was good to see everyone," Jackie said.

"At least take some brownies with you," Julie said, holding out a napkin with two on it.

Darla snatched the brownies. "Thanks, Julie. We'll take you to lunch one day this week. Good night, everyone!"

They hurried to the truck. Jackie was out of breath after scrambling through the slushy snow. "Gosh! That's what we get for trying to busybody as successfully as Fiona!" Jackie cranked the ignition and gunned the truck down the snow-covered gravel drive.

"I thought you said Sabrina was just a garden-variety fortune-teller." Darla chewed her brownie happily. "These brownies are great. Are you going to want yours?"

"No." Nausea swept Jackie at the mention of food. "Maybe I am coming down with a bug."

"Perhaps we should carry a line of christening

gowns, maybe even matching mom-and-me bride and baby gowns."

"I'm not pregnant," Jackie said, still thinking about Sabrina. Very tough to put anything over on Judge Julie. The home-health-care provider story was an angle Jackie hadn't envisioned.

"We'll see," Darla said. "Everybody's stories seem to be changing pretty fast. Good thing you're in the mood for change, huh?"

"Yeah," Jackie said, "I'm a real big fan of change."

ON SUNDAY MORNING, Pete noticed Fiona looked shocked—and none too pleased—when all of them piled into the van. This was nothing different from their usual routine. Whoever was available on Sunday mornings jumped in the van to go to Mass with Fiona and Burke.

"Good morning, Aunt Fiona, Burke," Pete said, as they all grabbed their usual seats.

She turned to glare at them. "What are you doing?"

"Keeping you company, just like we always do," Pete said, to a chorus of accompanying grunts from his brothers.

"You should be out looking for wives," she said, her doughy little face sweet—determined, yet sweet.

"Don't you worry about a thing, dear aunt." Pete patted her on the shoulder. "We've come up with a solution to the problem."

She brightened. "You have?" She cast a slightly optimistic glance over the carload of big men. "I'm so happy to hear it. Did you hear that, Burke? They have a solution!"

Burke started the engine. "Windshield wipers are stuck. Just a minute." He got out of the van.

"So tell me," Fiona said. "Don't make me wait."

"Sam's going to get married," Pete said.

Fiona's eyes went wide. "Sam?"

Sam nodded. "If it makes you happy, Aunt Fiona, it's no skin off my nose."

She glanced around the van. "Anybody else?"

"Nope," Pete said. "Sam's getting married, so Sam will get Rancho Diablo."

"You're all nutty as fruitcakes if you think I'm going to fall for this," Fiona said. "What a bunch of sissies!"

Pete blinked. "None of us, with the exception of Sam, are ready to settle down. So we forfeit."

Fiona turned back around. Pete could see her staring out the window, watching Burke as he picked ice off the wipers. "Well, then," she said, her tone deceptively enthusiastic, "whom are you going to marry, Sam?"

Pete glanced at Sam, as did all the other brothers. Fiona turned to pin her youngest nephew with a watchful look that was all Fiona. They'd seen that look too many times over the years not to heed the warning to tread carefully.

"Well, I—" Sam glanced around to his brothers for help. They hadn't planned that far into their scheme. Pete looked at Sam. Jonas sighed, rolling his eyes, which for some reason, seemed to force his youngest brother to a decision.

"I'm going to marry—" Sam gulped. "I thought I might ask Madame Vivant, er, Sabrina. It was love at first sight," he finished with a flourish.

The van went as silent as a coffin.

"Really?" Fiona asked. "Have you even talked to her, Sam? I thought she'd left town."

"No." He shook his head. "She was at Bode Jenkins's last night."

Now everyone stared at Sam.

"And you know this how?" Jonas asked. "I was up quite a bit north of here following their train, so I'm not sure how she could have been at Bode's."

"Oh, she was." Sam nodded enthusiastically. "I saw her go in, and when she left, I went out and talked to her."

Pete noticed Jonas getting real red around his fancy church-shirt collar. "I thought you were in the bunkhouse with us."

"I went out to check on the horses. Thought I heard something, got worried about wolves." Sam grinned. "And there she was, like Little Bo Peep who'd lost her way."

"Sheep, she's supposed to lose sheep," Pete said, not sure if his brother was embellishing the tale or not. All Sam was supposed to do was convince Fiona he intended to marry for the ranch. He was supposed to soothe Fiona.

What Sam was doing was making Jonas madder by the minute. Pete watched with great interest as Jonas's brows slid lower, practically pinching together.

"That woman is off limits," Jonas stated.

"Why?" Sam asked.

Burke got back into the van, letting in frigid air, but it couldn't have been any colder with the eldest and the youngest Callahans staring each other down.

"Because there's no such thing as love at first sight." Jonas stared out the window.

"Huh." Fiona turned around, clearly unimpressed.

"Sounds like a fish tale to me. I'm not buying it, Samuel Callahan."

Sam glanced around at his brothers for help. Pete shrugged. "Don't look at me. I've got no girl to marry."

"Pitiful," Fiona said. "Just pitiful. Burke, hurry and get us to church. I'm no saint, and my patience is wearing thinner than it's ever been."

Sam and Jonas were still glaring at each other. Creed and Rafe stared out opposite windows, and Judah looked as though he couldn't care less about the whole scheme.

Pete shrugged again, about to suggest that they go into town for pancakes after church—just to change the subject to a topic less likely to inflame the entire family—when he saw a familiar truck pull into their driveway.

"Oh, look," Fiona said, her tone a lot more happy. "It's Jackie! Jackie!" Fiona called, waving out the window. "Do you want to ride with us?"

"There're no more seats," Jonas observed.

"She can sit on Pete's lap," Fiona said over her shoulder.

A vision of his aunt forcing Jackie to ride in his lap to church fired Pete's limbs to motion. He flung the door open and jumped from the van. "We're on our way to church, Jackie," Pete said, noticing how beautiful she looked in a long red skirt and white fluffy sweater. "Did you need something?"

"Yes," Jackie said, her voice soft. Even at twenty paces he could tell she wasn't herself. "Can we talk, Pete?"

Chapter Seven

"Of course we can talk," Pete told Jackie. To his family Pete said, "You go on. I'll catch up." He closed the van door and crunched across the snow to stand in front of Jackie. "Are you all right?"

"Yes." She swallowed, her eyes sparkling in the sunlight that cast cold brightness over the morning. "No. Maybe I'm not totally all right."

"Come inside." Taking her by the arm, he led her indoors. She wore white mittens, a white scarf and a cream-colored coat, which set off her dark hair. But it was the look in her eyes that caught Pete's attention. Her eyes were sparkling, but it wasn't a happy sparkle. "Have you been crying?"

She didn't reply. Instead, she took several deep breaths.

She was scaring the hell out of him. Pete's heart skipped into faster beats. "Come sit down," he said, taking her by the arm and leading her into the family room of the main house. "Can I get you something? Water?"

"No. Thank you."

He waited, his breath caught in his chest. Whatever she wanted to talk about, she seemed to be hesitating. Maybe she regretted giving him the boot. Was there a chance she wanted him back? His heart soared at the thought.

If he could only be so fortunate.

"Jackie," he said, "tell me what's on your mind."

"I think I'm pregnant," she said, so softly he nearly missed what she said.

He couldn't help the grin that spread over his face. "What did you say?"

"I think I'm pregnant." And then she burst into tears.

"Oh, wow." He laughed, delighted. "This is great! Why are you crying?" Suddenly, he was bewildered. Why was she crying? Wasn't a baby a great thing? A miracle?

"Because I'm pregnant!"

"Oh, no, no, don't cry, Jackie," he said. "I'll take care of you. And the baby."

She jumped to her feet. "I don't need to be taken care of."

"Well—" He stopped, considered the mulish set to her face. "You don't want me to take care of you?"

"No."

He frowned. "But that's what men do. They take care of their women."

"I am not your woman."

"If you're having my child, Jackie, you're my woman."

"You sound like a caveman." She blew her nose into a tissue, which he thought was darling. She was so upset—and just like a woman, insisted she didn't need help when she so obviously did.

"If you don't need anything from me, why did you come here?" Pete asked, trying to reason with Jackie. Make her understand that clearly she did need him.

"Because everyone in Diablo will talk. So I just thought you should be the first to know."

Pride puffed Pete up. "We'll get married, Jackie, and no one will be the wiser nine months from now."

That brought a fresh burst of waterworks.

"We never talked about marriage before. Not really. Not seriously."

"True," he said, pulling her toward him. She allowed him to rub her back as she buried her face in his chest for a moment. She felt so good to him. He'd been dreaming of a reason to touch her again, see her again and now he'd been handed this golden opportunity. He was going to be a *father*. "Aunt Fiona will be so happy."

"What?" Jackie raised her head to look at him.

"Oh, Aunt Fiona wants us all married." Smiling, he touched his palm to her cheek. "We need to be married and have children if we want her to will us the ranch."

She blinked, her dark-brown eyes wet with tears. "What are you talking about?"

"Rancho Diablo. Aunt Fiona seems to be trying to make us believe she's on her deathbed. She's not, of course. Jonas says she's strong as a horse and will probably outlive us all. But," he said, brushing his lips against hers in a fast kiss, "now she claims she's changed her will. Whichever of us gets married and has the most children will inherit the ranch."

"So Rancho Diablo would be yours, now that we're having a baby?"

Pete shook his head. "Not all mine. My brothers and I agree that we're going to split the ranch anyway. Only one of us needs to get married to get the ranch under Fiona's rules, right? So it was going to be Sam, because he…I don't know." Pete stole another kiss. "I think Sam figured it would be easier on him to get married. He's less set in his ways."

Jackie pulled from his arms. "But now it could be you. You could make this sacrifice for your brothers."

"It's not a sacrifice, Jackie." Pete reached for her hand, drawing it to his lips. "You know how I feel about you."

She nodded. "I do. Every Saturday night, I've known exactly how you felt about me."

He shook his head. "It wasn't how I feel *just* on Saturday nights. But with your schedule at the hospital, when else could we be together?"

"I'm buying a business," she murmured. "A bridal shop."

He grinned. "That's timely. Order up a dress, sweetie. We can fly to Las Vegas this weekend."

She backed up a couple of steps. "Pete, I didn't come here to get you to marry me. I simply felt it was important that you be the first to know that we're having a baby."

"And that's great. I'm thrilled. Boy, am I thrilled." He was. He wanted to whirl Jackie around the room in his arms, laughing. He couldn't understand why she didn't seem off-the-floor happy.

"I've got to go," she told him. "Thanks for listening."

He grabbed her hand as she turned to leave. "Where are you going?"

"Home." She looked at him, her delicate dark brows high above her beautiful eyes. His heart sank as he decided she looked annoyed with him.

"And you need to catch up to your family," she said.

He was pretty certain she was giving him the royal wave-off. "I can go to a later service. Right now, we have a million things to talk about. And, Jackie," he said, deciding to try to get a fast point in while he could, "I'd like you to start thinking of home as wherever you and I decide to live."

She shook her head, an imperceptible motion that he realized didn't bode well for him. "No, Pete. When I broke up with you, I didn't see a future for us. This doesn't change anything."

He stared at her. He couldn't swallow past the lump in his throat. Something told him to go easy, not to explode, not to lose his mind over what she was telling him. Now was not the time to push Jackie for decisions. Everything was too fresh, too raw. "All right," he said. "I guess I'll have to respect that."

She nodded. "Thank you."

When she pulled her hand from his, he didn't stop her. This time, he let her go. He listened as the front door closed, heard her boots crunching the snow as she walked to her truck.

He moved to a window to watch her. She got into her truck and he thought he saw her glance toward the house. Then she drove away.

He let out the breath he'd been holding. "Miss Jackie Samuels, you and I have a lot more talking to do," he murmured.

That little woman could run all she liked, but in the end, the only place she was going was right back into his bed—where she belonged.

Whether she believed that or not.

He was hit by a sudden urge to drive right down into Diablo and buy the tiniest pair of western boots he could find, dark-brown and masculine as heck and just right for a baby boy who would one day grow up to be a rodeo badass like all the other Callahan cowboys. "Yeehaw!" he yelled in triumph, punching the air with his fist. "I'm going to be a dad!"

JACKIE WAS DONE with tears. Done. Never crying another tear over Pete Callahan. The man was a dunce. "You do realize," she said to Darla when she met her at Diamond's Bridal so they could look over the stock, "that men are insane? They have some kind of chromosome that is unique to them that causes them not to think like rational humans?"

"Well," Darla said, "men say we're the ones who are wacky."

"Maybe." Jackie stepped inside after Darla unlocked the door. "All I know is that Pete Callahan takes the cake for crazy."

"Come look at this wedding gown." Darla held up a hanger sheathed in a white covering. "You won't believe your eyes. This one's vintage."

"Do we sell vintage in our shop?" Momentarily, Pete and his antics flew right out of Jackie's mind.

"Some ladies really like vintage, so I think we should. If you like the idea, that is. What do you think about this classic?" Darla unzipped the bag and carefully pulled out the fairy-tale creation.

"Oh," Jackie murmured, touching the tiny crystals and luminous sequins, "it's like something out of Cinderella."

"Exactly what I thought. So when Sabrina brought this dress to me—"

"Sabrina McKinley?"

"Fiona's friend." Darla nodded. "The one who's going to work for Mr. Jenkins."

Jackie blinked. "But isn't she a fortune-teller?"

"And we're nurses selling wedding and maid-of-honor gowns. Changing jobs isn't all that unusual. Some people like change. Like us."

Jackie looked at Darla. "Is she not going to do fortunes anymore?"

"I didn't ask." Darla hung the gown on a hook. Late-morning sun streamed through the window, dancing on the crystals. It seemed the wedding dress came alive with passion and wishes and dreaming.

"That's the most beautiful gown I've ever seen." Jackie's breath hung for just a second as she thought about wearing something that wonderfully lovely for Pete.

Darla zipped the gown back into its bag. "I bought it because it's totally stunning, and somebody will buy it, probably the first day our shop is open. We're in this to be profitable, and this gown is a sure sale." Darla headed to the back of the store. "And Sabrina said she was low on funds, so it seemed the right thing to do. I hope you don't mind that I bought it without consulting you. I promise never to make business decisions without you, but I couldn't resist the gown. I swear I could hear it talking to me."

"What did it say, exactly?" Jackie followed Darla after a cautious glance at the covered gown. Darla was right about the dress: it would make a woman feel like a princess on her special day. Jackie almost thought she heard a chorale of softly tinkling bells luring her back to it.

She turned off her imagination.

"It said, 'I'm perfect for your friend, Jackie,'" Darla said, stopping outside the storeroom.

"You'll wear it before I will," Jackie said, "I'm expecting a baby."

Darla turned to stare at her, then her stomach. "Sabrina was right!"

"Oh, pooh." Jackie dismissed that notion without a qualm. "You're a nurse. You know how these things work, Darla. A little nausea, some tiredness, more nausea, that's all the fortune-telling a woman needs to know she probably needs to take an in-home pregnancy test."

"Okay," Darla said, "last night you were swearing you weren't."

"I got suspicious, so I decided to take a test." Jackie sat on a stool. "I've been moody lately—"

"Just a little."

Jackie shook her head. "And so there it was. The reason for the moodiness, the desire for pickles and chocolate cake, all foretold by a little blue line on a stick."

Darla threw her arms around Jackie. "It's wonderful news!"

Jackie smiled. "I keep thinking I'll wake up and it'll be a dream, and then my toes curl and I pray it's not a dream." Jackie laughed. "I never thought I'd be a single mom, but for some reason, going into debt with this business makes me feel very optimistic about the future."

"Really? No regrets?" Darla asked. "You might prefer the steadier income of nursing."

"But not the late hours and long shifts." Jackie smiled. "Everything is happening at the right time."

"What did Pete say?"

The smile left Jackie's face. "That he's happy. He wants to get married."

Darla squealed. "You can still fit into the magic gown!"

"Now wedding gowns are magic?" Jackie laughed.

"Well, you never know." Darla flung her arms around Jackie again. "I'm going to be a godmother!"

"How did you guess?"

"Because I'd kneecap anybody else who tried to take my place." Darla squealed again. "So if Pete wants to get married—"

"No," Jackie said, the smile sliding away again, "we're not getting married."

"But if Pete wants to—"

"He really doesn't."

Darla snorted.

"He never asked me before. He was happy with our relationship just the way it was. I'm not going to drag him to the altar after I'd just broken up with him, Darla." Jackie peered into the stockroom, intrigued by all the boxes. "Let's get down to business and forget about weddings right now, okay?"

"Won't be very easy, considering where we work. But all right." Darla followed Jackie into the storeroom. "Pete's going to be a hard guy to say no to."

"Not really. If he gets married, he gets Rancho Diablo. Call me crazy, but I don't know if this marriage enthusiasm is about me or the ranch."

"He gets Rancho Diablo?" Darla asked. "All of it?"

"There's some complicated rubric of how the brothers would split it. They just need a sacrificial lamb to get married, and Fiona wants to turn over the ranch. Any of them can be the stooge, but Pete thought about me. I can't decide how I feel about being included in his caper."

"Is that what Pete said when he proposed? That this was great timing or something?"

"I can't really remember. It all sort of ran together. But that was pretty much the gist of it. I got the feeling it was a two-birds-with-one-stone moment for him."

"That's not good," Darla said. "That sounds like a business proposition."

"That's right," Jackie said. "Just like buying this shop."

"Oh, hell. That means Judah will have to find a bride!" Darla pulled out some veils that looked like they'd seen better days. "These are some of last season's leftovers that could neither be sold nor returned. We're not going to do a whole lot of this kind of vendor business. Besides, these are not magical." She put the veils back away. "What am I going to do?"

Jackie agreed; the veils were not "magical." "We'll make better selections, although it may take us some time to develop our own vendor relationships."

"I meant about Judah."

Jackie's gaze flew to Darla's. "You're serious, aren't you? You really are crazy about him." She looked into her friend's eyes, seeing the worry there. "You're in love with him!"

Darla nodded. "Always have been."

Jackie thought for a minute. "Well, if one of them has to get married," she said thoughtfully, "it could be Judah."

"Newsflash—he's never knocked on my door."

Jackie couldn't bear the look on her friend's face, a cross between resigned and hopeless. "Why don't you ask him out?"

"No. Didn't you just say that Callahan men have a

strange gene that makes them…strange? Who knows how he might take a woman making the first move?"

"It's not a first move. Judah could use a wife. Technically, it could be considered a date with his destiny."

Darla shook her head. "We focus on making you realize that you can't turn down a hot cowboy like Pete. Not when you're having his baby. You have to think of that, Jackie."

And then it hit her. Hard, like a snowball in the face: From now on, she was thinking for two.

JACKIE AND DARLA FINISHED going through the store's stock, examining every cabinet and drawer, checking out anything that needed to be repaired before they signed the final paperwork to take over the building and the business. "Everything feels very organized," Jackie said.

Darla nodded. "I agree."

The shop bell rang. Pete walked in, despite the Closed sign on the door, and Jackie's heart fell into her boots.

"Hello, Pete Callahan!" Darla said, cheery as all get out. "What's that you're carrying? A little friend?"

Pete set the black-and-white puppy on the counter. "Mr. Dearborn's wife, Jane, called about a litter of puppies. This is Fanny, a border collie. She's looking for a wedding shop to live in. That's what she told me, anyway."

Jackie picked up the puppy, cuddling her. "Hello, Fanny."

"I'm going to run grab a cup of coffee. Either of you want anything?" Darla asked, slipping on her down jacket.

"No, thanks," Pete said, and Jackie shook her head.

"Be back in a jiffy," Darla said.

"Pete," Jackie said when the door closed behind Darla, "what are you doing here?" She held Fanny just under her chin for support and comfort, the fat wiggly puppy body comforting. Jackie's eyes drank in the tall cowboy, even though she'd just seen him this morning.

Pete was too big, too manly, to be in a bridal shop surrounded by white gowns. The shop seemed smaller with him in it, as though the walls had shrunk. Jackie wanted to put the puppy down and reach for Pete instead, but she couldn't. She'd broken up with him. Hugging him, holding him now, wasn't fair to either of them.

"I stopped by to see your folks. They told me you were here." Dark-blue eyes stared at her, leaving so much unsaid.

Jackie hesitated, before handing the puppy back to Pete. He put the small creature inside his suede jacket, and Fanny seemed delighted to be up against his broad chest. Jackie forced her gaze back up to Pete's face. "You went to my parents' house?"

He shrugged. "I went by your house first. When you weren't there, I decided to check with your folks."

In the five years that they'd been seeing each other on Saturday nights, Jackie had never taken Pete over to her parents'. "They don't know about the baby yet."

"I figured as much. I didn't bring it up." He studied her for a moment. "Consider Fanny a bribe."

"A bribe?" Jackie looked at the brown-eyed puppy peering out over the jacket zipper. "For what?"

"Just think about making a family with me." Pete took her hand. "We need to be together."

She blinked. "Saturday-night fun doesn't translate into wedded bliss."

"I'm good with the sneak peek I got."

He grinned at her, slow and sexy and teasing, and Jackie's heart jumped. From the other side of the store, she could practically hear the magic wedding gown singing a siren's song of temptation.

But then what? What happened after the magical gown and the fairy-tale wedding? They'd never even mentioned *feelings* to each other. Never.

Jackie swallowed, telling herself to ignore the gown—and Pete.

"I brought you something else," Pete said.

He set a pair of the tiniest western boots Jackie had ever seen on the counter. Picking one up, she studied the hand-sewn leather.

"You're crazy, Pete Callahan. You don't even know if we're having a boy or a girl."

"They're unisex as far as I'm concerned."

Jackie couldn't help laughing. "I don't want these. I'll keep Fanny, though not as a bribe. Just because she's a sweetheart. I've always wanted a dog." She ran a finger along the puppy's nose, and Fanny rewarded her for the affection by trying to nibble on her finger. "I'll have to ask Darla if you can be our store pooch, Fanny."

Pete's mouth twisted in a wry grin. "Go out on a date with me, Jackie."

"No. No dating. We didn't for five years. No reason to start now."

He put a finger on her chin, pulling her close over the puppy's head, and gave her a long kiss. "There's several reasons. I'm going to marry you, Jackie Samuels. You might as well accept that."

She pulled away, wishing he'd kept kissing her instead of talking. "Pete, getting married at this time runs counter to everything I've ever believed a marriage should be about."

He took her hand, giving it a quick brush against his lips. Jackie couldn't take her eyes off his lips as they moved across her skin. "I promise to make love to you more than just on Saturday nights, Jackie, if that's what's worrying you. I promise to fit in an occasional Tuesday as well."

She turned away, not wanting to laugh. "Pete, it's not funny."

"Okay." He turned her back around. "I'm leaving now. I'm taking Fanny with me, because you're too busy for this wild girl at the moment. What time are you going to be home tonight?"

"We'll finish up around four. I should be home at five. Why?" Jackie didn't trust the gleam in Pete's eyes.

"Expect me to be waiting for you at your house. I'm going to have dinner ready for you, a fire in the fireplace and probably some romance on the side. If you're lucky."

"I'm not sleeping with you, Pete." She put a hard tone in her voice, so he would know that part of their lives was over.

"Oh, don't worry, Jackie. Like you always said, why should you buy the steer if you get the steak for free?" Pete gave her a devilish grin. "I'm all about the purchase now, so you're just going to have to do without, my sweet."

Jackie put her hands on her hips. "That's fine." *I'll try to sit on the sofa primly and act like I'm not lust-*

ing after your big gorgeous body, you ape. "Just so we have the rules straight."

He leaned over, giving her a quick kiss before she could protest. "The rules are straight. I expect you to stick to them."

"Pete Callahan, don't try to act like I was only after your body."

"Weren't you? I could have sworn you were always more than happy to get me naked, Jackie Samuels."

She gasped, outraged at his cockiness, although he was right. He just didn't have to rub it in, the louse. Pete laughed, turning to walk from the store. Jackie considered throwing something at him, but the only thing close enough was a veil, which wouldn't have quite the effect she wanted.

He stopped in front of the magic wedding dress, considering it through its clear plastic casing. "This would look beautiful on you," he said. "You should think about it before my son starts making you plump." He winked, knowing her blood was now on full boil, and waved Fanny's paw at her before leaving.

Jackie let out her breath, wishing she had thrown something, anything—and realizing she wished it was tonight already, when she'd be seeing Pete again.

Bad. Oh, that was a very bad sign. He was taking over her life, and she was letting him, as though they were already halfway to the altar, full speed ahead and never mind the reasons she knew better than to say yes to him.

Then her gaze lit on the tiny brown boots Pete had left on the counter. How long had she waited for Pete to show her that he cared? How many years had she hoped their relationship would turn into something?

Now it was—and it felt all wrong.

Baby boots—not booties. Boots. Already planning for a rodeo rider, a cowboy, a Callahan.

Jackie shook her head. *Forget about it, bud. I'm not raising a heartbreaker like you.*

Chapter Eight

The solution was simple. Jackie knew it as soon as she saw Judah striding across the town square. If Jackie could get Judah to ask Darla out, and things happened between them—what couldn't happen with a sexy male like Judah, and a smart woman like Darla?—then Pete would be relieved of the pressure to get married.

She'd be off the hook. All this rush-rush-hurry-hurry Pete would go away. They could relax, think about how they wanted to be parents apart from each other.

"Judah!" Jackie waved at the handsome cowboy, getting his attention before any of the females who'd suddenly appeared in the square could.

"Hi, Jackie." Judah grinned at her, walked toward her with that loose-hipped Callahan saunter. Pete walked just like that, and it never failed to make her knees weak.

"Listen, Judah." Jackie hesitated, trying to formulate a quick plan now that the object of her manipulation was in front of her. What would Fiona do? "Darla had a date tonight with a guy from out of town. She bought a new dress and everything. The loser stood her up."

Judah's gaze flashed with sympathy. "His loss."

Jackie smiled at him. "I hate for her to sit at home tonight when she was planning on going into Santa Fe."

"Does she like this guy?"

"Oh, no," Jackie said, her gaze honest and wide. "But I think he's crazy about her, and you know Darla. Never wants to hurt anyone's feelings."

"That's true," Judah murmured. "I wish I could help, but she wouldn't want to go out with me."

Jackie blinked. "Why do you think that?"

He shrugged, his grin sheepish. "Every man in this town has asked her out. She always says no. I wouldn't be any different."

Jackie didn't dare say *oh, but you would!* She wrinkled her nose, wishing she could do better at the art of chicanery, but she was no Fiona. No one was. She wasn't artful and sly, giving people that little push they needed to do whatever they really wanted to do in the first place. "That's too bad," Jackie murmured. "I was hoping you had some free time."

"Oh, I've got time. There's nothing to do around our place. We're just waiting out Sam's wedding."

Jackie stared up at Judah. "Sam's…wedding?"

"Sure." He grinned. "He's hot into planning the biggest shindig Diablo has ever seen. He'll probably be bringing a bride to you to fit for a gown." Judah winked at her. "Make it a doozy, okay?"

"A doozy?"

"Expensive. Eye-popping. One that will be talked about for days."

Suspicion flared inside her. "Judah Callahan, are you setting up your little brother?"

Judah laughed. "I'd never do that."

Only one of them had to get married. If Sam was

going to do it, then Judah might stay free long enough for her to figure out how to convince him that the only reason Darla was turning down male companionship was because she was waiting for him.

Honestly. Men were blind.

"And Pete doesn't have to get married," she murmured, not realizing she'd spoken.

"Pete? Nah. He'll never marry. Unless it's you," Judah said, giving her chin a little cuff. "And a little birdie told me you weren't in the mood for marriage."

"The birdie was smart." She frowned. Why was Pete telling her he was going to marry her if Sam was going to be the fall guy for the family? "Will Sam move away after he gets married?"

"No. He'll live at Rancho Diablo, just like always."

"What about the rest of you?" Her curiosity was killing her.

"We'll look for wives."

That didn't sound good. And Judah didn't look all that unhappy about the prospect. "Why the sudden matrimonial urge infecting you men?"

Judah laughed. "Whichever one of us has the biggest family gets the ranch. The race is on for all of us."

Jackie stiffened. Pete had left out that little detail. Pete was competing with his brothers, as if he was in a rodeo, and Pete had a head start on Sam because she was already pregnant.

"That rat," she said. "That lowdown, no good rat!"

Judah grinned. "You must be talking about Pete."

"I—" She hesitated, before realization hit her. "If you're telling me this, you're not exactly keeping it a secret."

He shrugged. "No reason to. It's best to toot your own horn if you're selling something, right?"

Every female within a hundred miles was going to set her cap for a Callahan cowboy, including Pete.

It shouldn't matter. Nothing had changed between her and Pete—no matter what that stubborn cowboy thought.

"Judah," Jackie said, inspiration hitting her in breathtaking fashion. "How would you like to come to dinner tonight?"

He raised a brow. "What's cooking?"

"Not what. Whom. Your brother," she said sweetly. "And Darla will be there." She hoped Darla didn't already have dinner plans. But having extra people around would foil Pete's plan to press her about marriage. She wanted no part of the Callahan marriage derby.

"Sure," he said, "I'd love to watch my brother slave over a stove."

"Great. See you around five."

He grinned. "Thanks."

"Not at all. It'll be fun."

Maybe it wouldn't be fun for Pete, but it was going to be fun to watch him stew. "I'm turning into Fiona," she told her friend when Darla sailed back into the bridal shop with her coffee.

"Is that a good thing?" Darla asked.

Jackie looked at the magic wedding gown, still hanging on its hook, and thought how wonderful it would look on her friend. Clearly the wrong signals were being sent between Darla and Judah, a problem easily fixed by a casual dinner among friends. "We'll find out," Jackie said. "Darla, I think I'll have a small dinner gathering tonight to celebrate our new business venture. Do you have plans?"

"I'm free," Darla said. "I'll bring dessert."

Jackie smiled. "Just bring yourself."

PETE HAD PLANS—big plans. He'd cooked up a storm, a romantic meal that would impress even the most reluctant of women. And he hadn't stopped there. Jackie's sofa, the scene of so many of their wonderful nights watching television, was sprinkled with red rose petals. There were candles glowing on the table. And the pièce de résistance—him. He'd found a tux and had himself suited up like a waiter. He planned to serve her like a princess, shower her with attention and spoiling and everything her heart could possibly desire.

He had on his lucky boxers, too.

"Lucky, lucky." He took Fanny out of the crate he'd put in Jackie's living room, not far from the television, and carried the puppy outside for a fast piddle. Absolutely nothing was going to destroy his quiet evening with Jackie. She needed to focus solely on him—the new him.

So he wasn't particularly pleased when Judah's truck came to a halt at the top of the driveway. Fanny gave a tiny yap, and gamboled toward the newcomer.

"Wow," Judah said, slamming his truck door, "you look like a dude."

Pete bristled. "I do not look like a dude. Why are you carrying flowers?" He glared at the pink roses Judah was waving around like he was some kind of prince. "Why are you here?"

"Jackie invited me to dinner." Judah grinned. "A gentleman always brings flowers. Hope you did, bro."

Pete thought about the petals he'd strewn around the living room. After the dude comment about his tux, Judah was really going to give him the business about petals. He was slightly relieved when Darla pulled up in her truck. Maybe he could get the two of them to shove off before Jackie got home from work. He planned on cooking for her—grilled steaks, mashed potatoes and toasted French bread slathered in butter—then massaging her feet. Her toes were especially sensitive, foolproof for relaxing her. Relaxation was key for getting into her bed, a place he intended them to be for the rest of their lives—no more selected evenings. Bed was the place he could help her see things his way. Pete was pretty sure he did his best communicating in bed. "Hi, Darla," Pete said, before realizing she carried some kind of pie.

Pie was good, but not today, because it might mean Darla was coming to dinner. He glanced at Judah, who was gazing at Darla, apparently too thunderstruck to speak.

Dork. Pete looked back at Darla, who was, he had to admit, a tall, hot, golden blonde who would have fitted right in someplace warmer than Diablo, someplace she could live full-time in a bikini. "Why are you bringing Jackie a pie?" he asked, hoping he'd missed some really good reason Darla would be showing up here.

"For dessert, silly," she said, handing it to him. "Jackie mentioned you Callahans love blackberry pie, and I might just tell you that these blackberries come from Jane Dearborn's specially frozen stock."

He didn't give a hoot at the moment about Jane Dearborn's coveted blackberries that she painstakingly froze every May. He was about to ask *why the hell are you handing it to me?* when three more vehicles pulled up in Jackie's drive. All his brothers hopped out, along with Judge Julie Jenkins, Fiona and Burke, and all were bearing covered casseroles or some kind of food item. If his eyes weren't deceiving him, Sabrina McKinley had also managed to snag an invite.

Everyone was here but Jackie.

"That little minx," he muttered under his breath. She'd outfoxed him. She was intent upon keeping every wall between them she could construct.

"Hey, Pete," people said as they filed past him carrying crockery and pot holders and other contraptions used for potluck meals. "Nice monkey suit. You the waiter tonight?" was asked by more than one person. With one last glance toward the road, he went inside to find Darla.

"Where's Jackie?"

"Closing up the shop. She said she'd be here soon." Darla glanced at the rose petals strewn everywhere. "How nice of you to have a celebration for our new store, Pete."

"Celebr—" He forced a smile. "Happy to do it."

"The rose petals are a great touch."

He glanced to see if she was ribbing him. She appeared to be paying him the first sincere compliment he'd gotten beyond the monkey suit and dude comments. "Thanks." He couldn't be rude now that he was apparently hosting a reception. "I'd probably better go check the kitchen and make sure my apelike brothers aren't ransacking it."

Darla smiled, waving a wineglass at him. "Bye."

He headed into the kitchen where it looked like Aunt Fiona and Burke were managing KP, plugging in cas-

seroles and sorting paper plates someone had thoughtfully brought. Sabrina was chatting with Julie, and his
brothers looked like stuffed scarecrows incapable of
conversation.

"At least *talk* to the humans with the female equipment," he muttered to the clump of men that were his
brothers, although right now was an inopportune time
for them to be needy. "If you're going to bag a female,
you have to somehow sneak up on them."

Sam grinned. "Is that what you've done with Jackie?"

"Hell, no. I haven't had a chance to do anything
yet." He took a deep breath, reminding himself that it
wasn't his brothers' fault they'd wrecked his carefully
laid plans for the evening. No, all the blame could be
placed at Jackie's door. "Go at least send out a mating
call," he advised them as he spied Jackie making her
way up the sidewalk.

Before any one else could go greet her, he met her at
the door. "Oh, no, you don't," he said, taking her by the
arm and dragging her over to a secluded spot behind
a massive trellis covered in winter-dead leaves. "You
pulled a fast one on me."

"Did I?"

She looked up at him, her dark eyes innocent. He
could tell she was having an inner giggle at his expense.
He vowed to kiss her later until she was very sorry for
trying to be such a smartypants. "Yes, you did. And I
want you to know that I've got your number now, little
lady. I won't be fooled so easily next time."

"Pete," Jackie said, and he raised a brow.

"Apology accepted," he said, "now shut up and kiss
me."

"That's not—"

He stopped whatever she was going to say by claiming her lips. Pulling her up close, he kissed her until she was breathless, his heart hammering like a thousand anvils being beaten inside his chest.

Then he pushed her away. She stared at him, her fingertips pressed against her lips.

"Now, you go inside and make a plate for me," Pete said, "and remember, I've got my eye on you."

"Maybe that's not what I want." She raised her chin at him, and he laughed, giving her a gentle pat on the bottom.

"Jackie, one thing I know about you is that you like me. You liked me well enough to have me on your sofa every Saturday night for the past five years. Nothing changed except you got pregnant, and now you have to somehow figure out how to get me to the altar."

He kissed her lips when they parted in outrage.

"It's okay," he said, "it might not be as hard as you think to get me there."

Then he kissed her once more for good measure, a sweeping kiss, possessing her mouth with his tongue, just to remind her how much she liked it when he carried her into her bedroom on Saturday nights.

THE NIGHT DID NOT go as Jackie had planned, and she had no one to blame but herself. She felt like a heel for destroying Pete's dinner plans, especially after she saw all the rose petals on the floor and sofa. She'd sent a guilt-ridden glance his way, then told herself to get a spine. He'd forced her to have this dinner, and she'd warned him she didn't want to rely on her pregnancy as a reason to reel him in.

Pete was still full of typical Callahan bravado, acting

as though the tux was part of the night's entertainment. Then when Fiona, fun-meister extraordinaire, pulled out Twister for "all the young folks to play," Pete had thrown himself into the game despite the tux.

But Jackie couldn't help noticing that Pete wasn't the only one bluffing a bit. Darla and Judah acted like polar opposites on a magnet; even Twister couldn't pull them near each other. They played, but it was like watching two mannequins stiffly maneuvering into positions. Sabrina and Julie and the other Callahan brothers all twisted like pretzels, quite willing to try to get into the spirit of the game, but Jackie was worn out from trying to smile.

She couldn't stop thinking about Pete's kisses, and how her body just wanted to rock into his every time he touched her. It was all she could do to slow her brain down, remind herself that there was no going back.

And then, when Fiona and Burke toasted her and Darla's new business venture, Jackie felt dishonest. These were her friends, most of them people she'd known all her life. She felt as though she was cheating them of the truth.

She felt as though she'd cheated Pete.

He followed her into the kitchen when she went to pull out some Christmas fudge to send home with everyone.

"I'm going to go," he said, and she nodded.

"Okay." But then she couldn't help being honest, at least just for the moment. "Pete?"

He turned to look at her, his dark hair falling over his blue eyes. Rarely did a man have the combination of sexy and handsome and sweet all wrapped up in one package. "I'm sorry about tonight. I meant to protect myself, and I ended up spoiling something you were trying to do for me. It was mean. And I'm sorry."

He touched her chin. "One thing you've never been is mean, Jackie Samuels. Scared, unsure and occasionally grouchy—"

She raised her brows, drawing a laugh from him.

"But you're not mean. I just rushed you. You've got a lot going on in your life right now." He dropped one hand casually to caress her still-flat stomach. "I'm the one who should apologize. But I guess I won't." He grinned at her. "It's better if I keep you just a wee bit annoyed with me. Eventually, you'll run out of reasons to say no."

"Maybe I won't."

"Yeah. You will." He kissed her eyelids, then her lips so softly she wanted to stay near him, touch him, all night. "We'll go slow. We can start over. I don't mind convincing you that the first five years were just good friends getting together on Saturday nights. And now the fun stuff can begin."

"You're scaring me," she said, leaning her head against his chest. "I want to believe that we'd be right together forever because we always were. I just don't think we are, Pete." It was hard to say that, but it was how she felt. People who loved each other didn't get together only on Saturday nights. They shared things, their lives, their hopes and dreams.

"Just don't forget that if I marry you, I have a head start on my brothers." He gave a sly wink. "There's so many dividends to getting one of your wedding gowns on you, it's all upside for me."

She crossed her arms. "Now *you're* being mean."

He laughed, and dropped a kiss on her nose. "I'm just

reading your mind, my angel cake. I leave you to your sweet dreams of what might have been tonight, and the exquisite joy I would have given you."

Jackie stared at Pete. "You think highly of yourself."

He grinned and left. She picked up a sponge, wishing she'd been holding it just a moment ago. It would have felt great to bean him with it.

Darla came into the kitchen to toss paper cups into the trash. "How did it go?"

"Insufferable," Jackie said. "The man is an ass."

Darla laughed. "And you love him madly."

Jackie didn't say anything, but in her heart, she didn't argue the point. She wished Pete would magically appear in her bed tonight, which was exactly what Pete claimed she really wanted. "I'm fighting admitting that. I may be losing."

"He seems to know you pretty well," Darla said, wrapping up the pies that had been brought. "He's got you completely flustered. Eventually, he's going to wear you down. And you'll be so happy you'll forget to say no."

Jackie thought about Fanny. Fanny could sleep with her tonight. "There's no way a baby should make two adults, who didn't have a real relationship before, have a relationship."

"I don't know. Maybe a baby is like a bandage. Patches up all the rough spots."

Jackie stared at Darla. "That doesn't sound right somehow," she said, wishing it were true.

Chapter Nine

Two weeks later, Jackie and Darla had the grand opening of their new shop. They'd decided to name it The Magic Wedding Dress, after the gown that Sabrina had asked Darla to sell for her.

"Not that we have any magic, personally," Darla had said.

"We're going to need magic to make this business venture work," Jackie replied. "Think magical. Think hard."

Owning a half store seemed magical enough to Jackie. It looked like a wedding cake, with white shutters and pink letters scrolled on the windows. She and Darla had selected cabbage-rose-flowered settees for the ladies to lounge on while brides tried on dresses. The whole effect was comfortable and bright and romantic, and Jackie loved it to bits.

Fiona brought some of her friends to the opening. Mavis Night, Corinne Abernathy and Nadine Waters surveyed the store with delight.

"Think of the things we can cook up now that we know someone in the biz," Fiona said.

"It's almost too good to be true." Corinne smiled at the young store owners. "There are a wealth of beau-

tiful gowns in here, Jackie. You must be so tempted!"
Corinne giggled, her blue eyes dancing behind her
polka-dotted-rimmed glasses.

"Not really," Jackie said, which wasn't entirely true.
Secretly, she'd held the "magic" wedding gown up to
herself once, surveying herself in the mirror. It *was*
magical. There was no label on the gown to tell where
it had come from, but it had never been worn. She wondered about Sabrina—and how much she'd talked Darla
into paying for the gown. She'd meant to check the business register and had forgotten in the excitement of getting everything ready for the opening. *I'll do it tonight.*

Nadine patted her arm. "I predict you'll be wearing one of these lovely creations by spring, my dear."

Jackie backed away, keeping the smile on her face.
"You ladies go pick on Darla. I'm going to check the
punch."

"Whew. So that's why you never wanted anyone
to know you and Pete were dating," Darla said with a
laugh when Jackie retreated into the stockroom. "Smart
move."

"It's just going to get worse once everyone knows I'm
expecting Pete's baby." Jackie sighed. "Maybe I'll ask
Sabrina which way her circus went and go join them."

Darla grinned and handed her a cookie tray. "Be
brave. They mean well."

Jackie carried the tray out and set it on the white-
linen-covered table. About twenty ladies milled around,
admiring the dresses and wedding gowns. It was all
going well. Even Fanny was on her best behavior, sitting in her basket with a pink ribbon around her neck.

Then Pete walked in, and all the ladies turned to send
delighted glances Jackie's way. Broad-shouldered, tall,

handsome, vital—he was every woman's dream prince. *Mine, too.* But then she shook the thought aside.

"I've come to lend my support to this shindig," Pete said, making his way politely through the crowd of ladies greeting him. "I've told my brothers that they have to put in an appearance, too."

"Why?" Jackie stared up at him, her heart practically in her throat. He was so handsome. When he looked down at her, his eyes sparkling like that, it was all she could do not to throw herself into his arms. *I should. Give the crowd of busybodies what they came for.*

He tapped her on the nose. "If you want to make this place a success, you have to have bachelors to be caught."

"You're setting up your brothers." Jackie looked at Pete in surprise. "Isn't that a little devious?"

"To dangle the lure in front of the eager fish in here?" He grinned at her, leaning forward on the counter so their conversation was private. "No way. It's high time they were caught."

She shook her head. "If they ever figure out what you're up to, they'll be annoyed."

"Well, it's all for a good cause." He looked around the store. "It's weird seeing you in here instead of at the hospital. I had fantasies about your nurse's uniform, you know."

Jackie warmed all over, in spite of herself. *Don't think about fantasies,* she told herself. *Fantasies are the past.*

"But the innocent-bride fantasy works just as well." He winked at her and took the cup Darla was offering him. "Don't you think, Darla?"

"What do I think?" Darla asked.

"That nurse or bride, white is a great color for Jackie."

Darla glanced her way. Jackie could feel the blush rise in her cheeks.

"Oh," Darla said, "Jackie's playing hard to get. You'll have to romance her with something other than the fashion color wheel if you're going to drag her out of her ivory tower." She went off to greet Fiona and company with a teasing smile on her face.

"Ivory tower, huh?" Pete asked.

Jackie glared at him. "Don't you have fences to fix? Horses to train? Chores?"

He took her hand, gently brushing his lips against it. Jackie's gaze followed him, as did twenty other pairs of eyes in the store. She flushed, the heat in Pete's gaze trapping her. "I'm heading out for a week or so with Judah," he said. "When I get back, I'm coming through the window of your ivory tower. Expect it."

Jackie couldn't think of a swift reply. Pete winked at her, turned and left, sauntering through the throng of admiring females. More than one woman shot a wistful gaze after Pete's very sexy behind.

Silence descended on the store as Pete departed. Jackie tried to catch her breath, but then the five other Callahan brothers suddenly pushed through the door, to the delight of the women inside. That meant that more ladies crowded into the store from the street, all eager to be wherever good-looking bachelors were. Out of the corner of her eye, Jackie could see Darla taking orders and ringing up sales; the ladies wanted new spring things to catch a Callahan with, no doubt.

The fire marshal's going to cite us, Jackie thought. *I'm pretty sure we have too many people in here. Too many single ladies wanting a man.*

She watched the Callahan brothers seat themselves on the cabbage-rose sofas and accept tea and cookies from helpful females. They seemed to be enjoying the attention. That was the problem, Jackie thought. Callahan men loved female attention. They ate it up like peach ice cream in summer, which put her in a totally sour humor, because she knew Pete was just the same, no matter how much he tried to act as if he wasn't.

Jackie bit back a little jealousy, telling herself that it was none of her concern what any of the Callahan men did with their bachelorhoods. Then she went to help Darla, and tried not to think about Pete leaving town for a week.

She already missed him.

AFTER THE RUSH was over and most of their guests had gone—and after the rascal Callahans had finished holding court—Darla turned to Jackie. "So, partner, this may work out."

Jackie nodded. "Did you ever have any doubts?"

Darla smiled. "I did. I just didn't share them. Kind of like you not sharing how you and Pete really felt about each other. That man is crazy about you! How did you manage to keep that under your hat for so long?"

Jackie shook her head. "Pete is not crazy about me."

"Trust me, he's crazy about you."

Pete *had* seemed different. Jackie frowned. "It's the baby. He was never this way before."

Darla laughed and pulled her blond hair up into a high ponytail. "I don't think it's the baby, Jackie. Maybe he was always crazy about you, but didn't express it the way you expected him to."

"All I know," Jackie said, "is that one day I decided

to change my life. I had to move on, from everything. Then you showed up with a new business, and I broke up with Pete and everything changed. I even have a dog." She picked up Fanny to take her outside. After being made the belle of the ball, Fanny was almost too excited to be excited about going out. "Of course, I love the dog. Come on, angel, you need to get out of the store for a minute."

She didn't make it to the back door before Darla called after her. "Jackie? Did you move the magic wedding dress?"

"Hang on," she told Fanny, "I promise your bathroom break is next." She went back inside the showroom. "It was on its hanger right there. Several ladies were ooh-ing and aahing over it." Jackie frowned. "Maybe someone moved it near the big mirrors to see how it would look on them."

Half an hour—and a Fanny excursion later—Jackie shook her head at Darla. "Are you sure you didn't ring it up for someone?"

"Trust me, I would have remembered it. I wanted it for myself." Darla looked stricken. "And I'd bought it from Sabrina. So I would have been extra certain to note the sale."

No one would have stolen anything from them. At least Jackie didn't think they would. But they'd searched the store over twice. They'd checked the register tapes and the receipts—nothing. "I can't imagine," Jackie said.

Darla sat down on a cabbage-rose sofa. "It's gone. Vanished."

Jackie held Fanny in her arms, stroking her fur absentmindedly. "It'll turn up, I'm sure."

"No one in town would dare wear it. We'd recognize it at once."

"And there wasn't anyone here who wasn't from Diablo." They'd had a steady stream of well-wishers and shoppers that day, all people known to them all their lives. "Let's close the shop up and go to my place for hot cocoa. I don't want to sit home alone wondering how a magic wedding dress disappears."

"Great idea. We just need a little Kahlua for the cocoa, and I'll feel a lot better." Darla put on her blue wool winter coat and locked the front door.

Jackie opened the drawer underneath the register to get her keys and saw a plain white envelope. *Jackie* was written on it in blue ink. "What's this?" she said to Darla.

Darla looked over her shoulder. "Open it."

Inside was cash, in hundred-dollar bills and a few ones. Jackie counted it. "Exactly the price of the magic wedding dress, plus tax."

Darla took the envelope from her. "I don't recognize the writing. It's so generic it could be male or female."

Jackie shrugged. "Someone who didn't want anyone to know they'd bought it."

"And they carried it out of here while we were busy with guests."

"We can't report it as stolen," Jackie said, "but I suppose we could get the sheriff to dust the envelope for prints."

"Except you and I have both handled it." This was true.

Pete had walked out empty-handed. She remembered because she'd been staring at his backside as he walked—and watching him jealously as other women tried to catch his eye. And she didn't think it was Fiona or any of her friends. Fiona would do a lot of things, but if she was buying a wedding gown for someone, she wouldn't be quiet about it. She'd want everyone to know. Shaking her head, she added the cash to the total of the night deposit they would make on their way home.

"Well, if it was magic, we'll never know." Sabrina followed Darla out the back. "Not that I really believe in magic anyway." She set the alarm and locked the door.

Darla shook her head. "I do. And I believed that gown was one day going to magically be mine. You could use a little magic in your life, too, you know."

It hadn't escaped Jackie that Judah had never come over to speak to Darla beyond a casual hello. Her matchmaking dinner the other night hadn't worked. "I'm no Fiona," Jackie said, picking up Fanny to carry her to the truck.

"No one is." Darla laughed as they walked together in the cool night air. Neither of them saw the shadows moving behind ivy trellises that framed the store, watching as they got into their trucks and drove away.

Chapter Ten

The next day, Pete decided the first thing he was going to do when he got back to Rancho Diablo was punch his brother Sam in the nose. He'd do it right now, he thought, fuming, except that Jonas was on the way and would probably take exception. Jonas and Sam might be seven years apart, but Jonas looked out for the youngest Callahan. "Just buy the damn horse and let's go," Pete groused.

"I don't know." Sam ran one hand over the ebony stallion's back. "We may not need another champion breeder."

"Why?" Pete glanced around the well-lit barn at Monterrey Five ranch, located just outside of Las Cruces. Workers milled around blanketing horses and filling water buckets. Outside, in a lighted ring, a woman was giving a teenager jumping lessons. They'd done business with Monterrey Five before, knew they were getting an honest deal. Pete didn't know what was holding up his brother, but it wasn't the horse. And if Sam wasn't going to buy the beast, Pete wanted to get on to the next stop on their list. The sooner they finished their errands, the faster he'd be back to Jackie. A week was a long time to be away from her.

"Oh, boy," Pete muttered.

Sam looked up. "What?"

"I just realized something." Realized that he'd always spent a week away from Jackie at a time, and never had he missed her this much. "I'm changing."

Sam stared at him. "Yeah, Dad. Growing up is probably normal for an expectant father."

"Not that kind of change." Pete revisited the notion of poking Sam in the nose. "Why are you being such an ass tonight?"

"I don't know. Full moon or something." Sam shook his head. "I'm not going to buy this pony."

"Pony?" Pete snorted. "He's got hooves the size of dinner plates."

Sam sighed. "I think Fiona's in trouble, Pete. And maybe the ranch."

"What ranch?" Pete glanced around him. Monterrey Five looked great to him. Well-run, busy, clean, well-stocked—the way he liked a ranch to run.

"Our ranch."

Pete looked closely at his brother. "What are you talking about?"

"Come on." Sam jerked his head, and Pete followed him from the barn. "Thanks, Pio, we'll let you know about the horse. He sure is fine."

Pio waved at them. "Thanks for swinging through. Come by on your way back if you can."

They got in Sam's truck, and Sam turned down the gravel road. "So?" Pete said.

"So Fiona's acting funny. I'm worried."

"Fiona's always acting funny. Big deal. I'd be more worried if she wasn't being lovably eccentric. Look, there's Jonas." Pete waved at his brother, who was coming up the drive. Sam stopped the truck and rolled down the window.

"Why are you leaving?" Jonas asked. "Didn't Pio have the horse on site?"

"We were just about to call you. Sam got cold feet." Pete shrugged.

Jonas glanced at Sam, who nodded confirmation. "Where are we headed now?" Jonas asked.

"You sure you want to do this?" Sam asked. "You don't have to go all the way with us."

"Yeah, I do." Jonas nodded. "I'll at least spend a day with you before I go back to Diablo."

"Let's head to the Cracker Barrel on the main road," Sam suggested. "I'm in the mood for fried chicken and mashed potatoes."

Pete waited until Sam started driving again. "Does Jonas know you're worried about Fiona and the ranch?"

"I've only told you. If Jonas knows I'm worried, he might not buy that ranch he wants. He'll want to come in and save the day at Rancho Diablo."

"Isn't that a decision you should let him make?"

"Maybe," Sam said, "which is why I'm talking to you."

"Oh." Pete felt warmed by his brother's trust. "I say tell him. What can it hurt? Six heads are better than none."

"Well, you're the most responsible one of us," Sam pointed out, and Pete frowned.

"Jonas takes that prize."

"Jonas is a doctor. That doesn't make him the most responsible or the smartest. That would be you."

Pete raised his brows. "I'm a simple ranch hand, doing what I've done all my life."

"Jonas knows a lot about medicine. You know a lot about life." Sam pointed at him. "Not that I'm saying you know a lot about women, because you don't."

"I think I know more about women than about most other stuff." Pete was pretty sure he should be taking offense. Any minute now he probably would, but the New Mexico night sky was so pretty, like black velvet, and the stars so numerous, that it was hard to get up the energy to be annoyed anymore. The desire to punch his slowpoke of a brother had left him as soon as they'd hit the road.

"Not really," Sam said. "Look how you've screwed up the whole thing with Jackie. Major fumble, bro."

The urge to poke Sam's nose returned full-force. Pete sat up. "I haven't fumbled anything."

"Are you engaged?"

"No." Pete sat up. "But I will be."

"Word around town is that Jackie took out an insurance policy."

Pete glowered. "So?"

"Life insurance."

Pete sat back, stunned. "Fiona told you that?"

"Not this time." Sam grinned. "Darla Cameron."

"I don't believe you."

"It was all accidental. I happened to ask how they'd managed to secure financing for The Magic Wedding Dress so fast, and Darla said Jackie had an almost instant approval because she had so much cash on hand for a down payment. She didn't even put up the house for collateral. Just cash. And I said that was damn brave of her in this economy, and Darla said that Jackie was a great businesswoman, and not to worry, that she was insured to the teeth in case anything happened to her."

Pete wondered why he should care about any of this. "Jackie's smart. She wouldn't conduct business without proper insurance."

"And I kidded around and said that they better not get into any pincushion battles or anything or Jackie wouldn't have anyone to leave her estate to." Sam paused for dramatic effect. "Darla said Jackie's estate goes to her baby. She's already had it all drawn up."

"That's nice, but really none of my business." Pete warmed up just thinking about his son. He should be the one thinking of providing for his child—a thought which instantly irritated him. His baby *was* his business. He and Jackie were raising this child together, whether she liked it or not. They should make financial decisions regarding the baby's future together—*together* being the operative word. He was supposed to be the responsible Callahan, right? "We need to hurry and get this trip over with," Pete practically snarled, and Sam laughed.

"None of your business, huh?"

Pete leaned his head back and closed his eyes. Sam had no idea how close he was coming to having that nice Callahan nose totally rearranged.

THE ROADSIDE CRACKER BARREL was hopping, which was a good thing, because Pete was in the mood for company. Color. Movement. Anything to keep his mind off his brother's remarks about Fiona. Anybody with half an eye could see that there was some truth to Sam's worry about their little aunt—she *was* acting differently. Pete had noticed it when she'd arrived at the bridal shop. She wasn't her usual giggly self. Oh, she was pleasant and social and had her pod of blue-haired friends with her, but she wasn't lighthearted Fiona.

He was going to have to have a gentle aunt-and-nephew private chat with her. Pete made up his mind to do that as soon as they got home. First Fiona, then his darling turtledove. His smart, business-minded, love apple, who was busily making plans without him about her life, about their baby. It was admirable, but she was also just a wee bit too determined to be Miss Independent for his liking. At this rate, he might not ever get back in Jackie's bed.

The thought depressed him. He lost his appetite and glared at Jonas. "So what's happening with that land you want to buy east of Rancho Diablo?"

"I'm still pondering it. I may have you come out and take a look at it." Jonas slathered a roll with butter, and munched on it happily.

Pete slid a glance at Sam, who nodded at Pete. *What was that sagacious nod for? Am I supposed to do the dirty work here?* He sighed. "Jonas, Sam's worried about Fiona. Did you ever give her a subtle check-up?"

"She slapped my hand when I tried to put my stethoscope near her." Jonas looked injured. "She's never done that before. Usually she says she likes to take advantage of what she calls my expensive over-education."

Pete nodded. "But you were persistent. Not wimpy."

"No, I was wimpy." Jonas ordered a slice of pie, apparently determined to eat the contents of the restaurant on his own, Pete thought. "I bailed. With all due respect to the little aunt, I might admit."

"I guess you can't force a patient if they don't want care," Pete said.

"Yeah, that, and the fact that she has a pretty mean

slap for a tiny woman." Jonas dug into his pie with gusto. "You'd be surprised."

"Okay." Pete was getting tired of his brothers' company. "Look, she said she hadn't been feeling well. Maybe we can convince her to see Doc Graybill in town."

"Tried that. No go." Sam looked at Jonas's pie with longing. "Are you going to be a pig or are you offering a bite to your brothers?"

"Pigging out. Get your own."

Pete looked at the checkers set up on a nearby barrel where a couple of kids were playing a game. He glanced at the fire in the fireplace, noting the happy families enjoying a meal out together. Why did their family always have to have so much drama? Nothing was ever simple. He sighed, feeling the weight of his thirty-one years. "For some reason, Sam thinks the ranch might be in trouble."

"How can it be?" Jonas asked. "Even if it had a thirty-year mortgage, it's been paid off. Mom and Dad bought it right before I was born. Surely Fiona's been making payments properly, and I doubt she's taken any liens. Any work that's ever done on the ranch, we do ourselves. And we pay cash for purchases like horses and feed and equipment. We pay the taxes out of the Callahan general fund." He speared Sam with a glance. "Why would you think that?"

Sam shook his head. "Just a strange hunch I have."

"I think she's just ready to get us married off. She's going to fix our lives." Jonas nodded. "It's preoccupying her these days."

Pete picked up his tea glass and drank. He looked at the checkers set with longing, wondering for a brief second if either of his brothers would want to play. There was no time, though. Sam was right. In some dim corner of his mind, he, too, had noticed Fiona not quite being Fiona. A little more sharp, perhaps, a bit less cheerful. "Is there a reason we don't ask Fiona to have a discussion with us on the entire business side of the ranch? Not just the buy-sell side and daily operations, which we already know about, but the financial aspect?"

Sam and Jonas looked at him.

"She's never been inclined to do so before," Jonas said.

"We've never asked. Maybe she doesn't think we're interested," Pete pointed out.

"Maybe you'd like to be the one to ask her," Sam said.

"She's going to think we think she's on her deathbed," Jonas said. "I can just hear her now."

"All the more reason to know the ranch details in-depth." Pete was warming to his topic. "Have you ever thought that she's the only person, besides Burke, I guess, who knows everything? What happened to our parents? Why did they settle here? We don't know anything. I was five when Fiona and Burke came. I don't remember much." He looked inward for a moment. Hell, his first memories were of Fiona making lunch for them, taking them to church, reading to them. Most of his memories of their parents came from the photos Fiona had put in the bunkhouse on the mantel.

Sam and Jonas stared at him, their jaws slightly agape. Pete shifted in his chair. "Well, it's true," he said, feeling defensive. "She doesn't like to discuss the past. So we've never asked. We've never even pushed her about the old Navajo who shows up on the ranch once a year. Come on. She has us totally cowed."

Fiona could cow anyone. She could cow the U.S. Marines, the Pope and the Queen of England. Pete swallowed. "In fact, I think Fiona is the one thing on Earth we're all a little bit afraid of."

"And I don't know why," Sam said. "She's been a great guardian."

"But not soft," Jonas said, "she wasn't a soft guardian. Having eleven brothers made her tough as hell."

"But maybe," Pete said, "and I'm going out on a limb here, maybe it's time to get practical. If everybody's worried, and if she's starting to do things like bring in fortune-tellers, maybe it's time to tell her we have questions. She's got answers. We want them."

Jonas and Sam sat blinking at him like owls. He wished they wouldn't do that.

"Well, you're Mr. Responsibility," Sam said.

"We elect you as spokesman. We'll back you up," Jonas said.

Pete looked at the ceiling. This was partially his fault. He'd heard Fiona hiring the fortune-teller to give his brothers some oogie-boogie story to get them to the altar. He hadn't ratted her out because he'd thought it was cute of her, in a devious-little-aunty sort of way. Frankly, he'd thought it was a great joke on his brothers. And now their suspicions were aroused. "I've got enough on my plate worrying about Jackie," he said, going weasel.

His brothers glanced at each other, then back at him. In the depths of their dark-blue eyes, he saw grave disappointment. He went to defense. "Jonas, you're the oldest, damn it. You beard the lion in its sweet little flowered kitchen."

Jonas put down his fork, pushed his plate away. "She slapped my hand just for trying to listen to her chest," he reminded them. "I don't know if I'm in particularly good graces right now. She's still miffed about that."

"Then you," Pete told Sam. "You're the baby. You can get away with anything."

"I can," Sam said, "but you're the responsible one. She'll listen to you."

"You're not responsible?" Pete demanded, knowing the answer.

"I'm twenty-six. In her eyes, that's a child. Plus, I've always followed in your footsteps. She'll know you put me up to this." Sam grinned, knowing his argument was complete baloney.

Pete stood. "I hope you're not going to make a habit of being wusses."

"We knew you'd do it," Sam said, practically crowing, "we knew we could count on you."

Jonas popped Sam on the back. Pete hesitated in the act of signing the dinner check. "We?"

"Never mind," Sam said.

Jonas nodded. "Don't mind him. Sometimes his mouth runs off without his good sense."

Pete glared at both of them, realized a family council had been held to vote him in to the position of spokesperson with Fiona. This was karma getting him. "I'll think about it," he grumbled.

"You are the most responsible," Sam said, grinning.

Pete wondered if Jackie would agree. Which made him think about how he'd rather be sleeping with her tonight than sitting here with his plotting brothers, and that made him cross all over again. "Let's get out of here," he said. "I've got much better things I could be doing."

FOUR DAYS LATER, Jackie had bad news of her own.

"Why do you want me to go into Santa Fe?" she asked Dr. Graybill. "I used to work at Diablo General. The medical care here is top-notch."

Dr. Graybill put down his chart and looked at her. "I believe you are farther along in your pregnancy than you think you are, Jackie. With your history of irregular periods, you can't be sure exactly when you conceived."

"That's true. But the doctors here can handle a routine pregnancy." She was a nurse. She had extensive training and experience. Dozens of women gave birth in Diablo every year. "I'd even considered using a midwife."

Dr. Graybill shook his head. "First, I want you to make an appointment with a specialist in Santa Fe. Or someplace else. Someone who specializes in multiple births."

Jackie stared at the doctor who'd set her broken arm when she was a child, and sutured her chin when she'd fallen on it playing street basketball with her friends. His kindly eyes looked back at her sympathetically. Jackie swallowed. "Multiple? Twins?"

"I can't tell. I hear something. It's either another fetus or some type of echo. You need to see a specialist for better information. And a sonogram." He wrote the names of a few doctors on a pad and handed it to her. "These are some specialists I know. You might plan to talk to a couple of them, get a few different opinions."

Jackie shook her head. "There are no multiple births

in my family. I never even thought I could get pregnant, Dr. Graybill. I've always had such irregular cycles, and—" She stopped, realizing she sounded incoherent. How could sex on Saturday nights result in twins? "I just don't see how," she said, dazed. "I'm an only child."

Dr. Graybill smiled at her. "Well, Rafe and Creed are twins. And you might ask about their family history. Twins may run generationally in the Callahan family."

Jackie got up from Dr. Graybill's desk, her stomach hollowed out from sudden fear. She wasn't prepared for two children. She didn't want to think that there might be a problem with her baby, either. "I'll make the appointment. Thank you, Dr. Graybill."

"You're welcome."

She gave him a feeble smile and went to check out. Her head was whirling. There was no way she could be having twins. Her stomach was only barely rounded. She had gained ten or so pounds. Dr. Graybill thought she was around fourteen weeks. Her last period had been in September, and this was the third week of January.

Chills swept her that had nothing to do with the gray skies and the cold wind whipping through Diablo. She walked to the bridal shop, opening the door, closing it without even seeing Fanny lolling at her feet.

"You look like you've seen a ghost," Darla said. "Come sit down. Is everything all right?"

Darla ushered her to a sofa. Jackie sank into it gratefully. "I think Dr. Graybill's getting old."

Darla laughed. "Jackie, there are a lot of elderly people in Diablo, most of them still running the pants off the younger generations. What did he say?"

"He wants me to see a specialist." She looked at Darla. "He thinks I might be having twins."

Darla laughed.

"What's so funny?" Jackie asked, not feeling like laughing at all.

"Two little Callahans? Pete's going to double his efforts to get you to the altar." Darla giggled at her own joke, hugging Jackie when she glared at her. "You wanted change," Darla reminded her.

"Yes, I wanted change." Jackie picked up Fanny, petting her, before shaking her head. "I bet Dr. Graybill is being overly cautious."

Darla grinned as she glanced out the shop window. "Prepare for more change," she said with a giggle. "Pete's on his way in right now. You can tell him the possible good news."

Jackie sank back into the sofa as her cowboy walked inside the store. "Pete," she said weakly.

"Jackie," he said, "Darla." He tipped his hat. Darla grinned at him.

"Congratulations, by the way."

"Why?" Pete looked at Darla.

"You made it back early," Darla said, smiling as she headed to the stockroom.

Pete's gaze went to Jackie. She swallowed. No one made her blood race like Pete. Darla was probably right. Pete was going to be a very arduous suitor when he learned he might possibly be a father to twins. He'd get it into his head that he was having twin boys, just like his father, and then there'd be some bragging.

I'm not telling him until I know for sure, Jackie decided. *There's no reason to get his hopes up, and he would. Darla's right. He'll crow, and he'll think he's*

going to win that stupid bet of Fiona's, and he'll romance me like a lovestruck cowboy.

And it would be wonderful.

Heat hit her as she thought about how Pete could
romance her. Magic hands, persuasive lips—she just
couldn't handle a super-determined Pete right now. *I'm
having a panic attack. I'd say yes, whatever you want,
Pete, and then I'd find out Dr. Graybill's made a mistake and then I'd have Pete dishonestly. Because I was
scared.*

This was not the way she wanted to get him.

It had to be about love.

"We need to talk," Pete said. "Take the rest of the
day off."

Chapter Eleven

Jackie sighed. There was kind, loving, gentle Pete, and then there was demanding Pete. Stubborn was good, Jackie told herself. A bossy, chauvinistic Pete would help her keep her eyes on her goal. "No," she said. "I can't take off. I can't leave Darla."

He sat down next to her on the sofa. "Then we'll talk here."

That might be worse. Anyone could come in at any moment, making their cozy rendezvous into some romantic foregone conclusion that wedding bells would soon be ringing. Jackie edged slightly away. "We'll close the store in a couple of hours. Surely it can wait."

He pulled her to him, kissing her thoroughly, leaving her breathless and dazed. "I've been on the road with my brothers for almost five days, if you count hours around the clock. I need time with you. And if I have to have it right here on this overstuffed floral mushroom—"

"Loveseat."

"Loveseat," Pete went on, "then I don't care who in Diablo sees us."

Jackie pulled back, blinking. This was a new Pete,

a Pete who wasn't content to wait seven days between visits. "Did something happen while you were gone?"

"You've been happening to me for five years." Pete caressed her cheek with warm fingers, and Jackie felt herself melting.

She couldn't melt.

"Pete, we can talk later." She stood up, desperate to get him out of the store and away from her before she broke down and threw herself into his big, strong arms. "I'll come by your place."

He looked at her. "My place."

"Yes." Jackie smiled at him. "Something new for us."

"I don't want new. I want old." He reached out to grab her, and she sidled away just as Fiona came in the door.

"Pete!" Fiona said. "What are you doing here? I thought you were on the road with Sam and Jonas."

"I was." Pete got up and kissed his aunt on the cheek. "I cut the trip short."

"No good horses?" Fiona asked.

"A change in plans," Pete said. "Aunt Fiona, if you have time in your busy schedule, there's something I'd like to talk to you about."

"Oh." Fiona looked from Pete to Jackie, then back to Pete. Obviously not seeing whatever she was hoping to find in their expressions, she said, "I can spare some time tonight. Will it take long? Should I have Burke make dinner for us? Jackie, will you be joining us?" Her tone turned hopeful.

"No. No Burke. No Jackie. Just you and me," Pete said.

"That sounds dull as dishwater." Fiona sniffed. Then she brightened. "Jackie, I just saw Doc Graybill, and—"

"Goodbye, Fiona," Jackie said, gently easing her out

the door. "It was so good to see you. I'm sorry you can't stay longer."

"But I can—" Fiona said.

"Goodbye!" Jackie said, closing the door. Dr. Graybill would never discuss her private health concerns. But he might have said something like *When will we be hearing wedding bells?* and that would be all the encouragement Fiona would need.

Jackie turned around, leaning against the door for support.

Pete stood in front of her, staring down at her with penetrating blue eyes. She hadn't heard him sneak up behind her. Her patience snapped. Opening the door, she said, "You don't want to be late for your meeting with Fiona."

Pete leaned down to kiss her lips, right there in the open doorway where anyone on the main drag of Diablo could see. "Don't forget to come by tonight," he reminded her, when he finally released her lips. "I'll be ready and waiting."

Her knees buckled. "About that—"

"Okay," he said, "I'll come to your place. And then you can tell me what you're hiding, Jackie Samuels."

Pete went off whistling, not that he felt all that lighthearted. It gave him something to do with his lips since he couldn't be kissing Jackie right now. All he wanted to do was kiss her. He'd nearly killed Sam and Jonas on the trip. He'd had a really short fuse with them, all from thinking constantly about Jackie. He wanted to be able to kiss her every hour on the hour. "This bachelor business is for the birds," he muttered, and Rafe appeared at his side.

"You're back," Rafe said. "Did Sam find what he was looking for?"

"I don't know if Sam knows what he's looking for. What are you doing in town?" Pete glanced around for Rafe's truck.

"Buying feed. We need some storage boxes, too."

"For?"

"Fiona's taken down all the Christmas lights. She wants to put them in color-coordinated boxes this year. Red and green, so we don't have to hunt next year. It wouldn't be so bad if she didn't have a million decorations for every holiday."

Pete nodded. Ever since they'd been boys, Fiona had insisted upon lights along the fences out front, color appropriate to every holiday, including Valentine's Day. "That means she wants the red and white ones separated for Valentine's—"

"And the green and white ones for her precious St. Patrick's. All in their own special boxes. We're going to need to build another storage shed."

Pete sighed. "Isn't there enough room in the basement?"

Rafe walked with him to the truck. "That's the thing I wanted to mention to you," he said under his breath, and Pete thought *Why am I the one elected to hear everything?*

"Fiona and Burke have been doing stuff in the basement."

"There are things I do not want to hear," Pete said, getting into his truck.

Rafe got into the truck with him. Pete was glad to have a little windbreak from the cold. He'd rather head home for a cup of hot coffee, but he couldn't exactly shove Rafe out the door.

"Not that kind of stuff, dummy," Rafe said.

"Lights," Pete said. "She's having an organizational fit, right?"

"I'm not sure. Her Navajo friend was by the other night—"

"Running Bear."

"Exactly." Rafe nodded.

"So? Chief Running Bear comes every year. Like freaking Santa Claus. Except we don't put out cookies and milk for him, and toss instant oatmeal for his reindeer."

"Yeah." Rafe looked at his brother. "After his visit, Fiona and Burke started hanging out in the basement. A lot. Every time I go to find her, she's down there. She says she's cleaning and getting ready for spring canning. But the door at the top of the stairs is always locked."

She'd locked it when they were kids, too. She was afraid one of them might fall down it in their sleep. "This is nothing new. She's just being cautious."

Rafe scrubbed at his chin. "Maybe."

"And she's probably cleaning." Fiona was a bit of a pack rat. The basement had dirt flooring and shelves where Fiona stacked her canned vegetables and dishware she used only at holidays. And of course, her decorations. There was very little lighting, just an overhead fluorescent light. "It's good that she's organizing things," Pete said, not really sure if it was or not. "I need to do some organizing myself."

"She took a long-handled shovel down there the other day," Rafe said.

Oh, hell, Pete thought. *I didn't want to hear that. Nothing good can come of Fiona and shovels.*

It means something's being dug up—or buried.

PETE WASN'T REALLY SURPRISED when Fiona wasn't at the house for their meeting that evening.

"She's gone out," Burke told him. "Emergency Books 'n' Bingo meeting."

"Right, right." Pete noted Burke was dressed in his usual natty attire, but looking even more dapper than usual. "Going out yourself?"

Burke grinned. "I've been selected as guest speaker at the Books 'n' Bingo meeting."

"Really. Where's the meeting?" Pete wondered whose house they'd snared on short notice.

"Oh, you wouldn't know them." Burke jammed a tweed driving cap on his head and headed out. "Lock up when you leave!"

Pete grimaced. He knew everybody in town, unless someone had moved in yesterday, and even if they had, Aunt Fiona would have organized a welcome committee, and he'd have heard of that. So clearly it was a secret meeting.

Fiona loved secrets.

"All right," Pete muttered to himself. "Let's just have a look-see in the basement."

He grabbed the keys from Burke's special cupboard where he kept all his butlering crap—not that Burke would appreciate his things being labeled so—and fished out the long one for the basement lock. It slipped in without hesitation. "Like taking candy from a baby," Pete said, and opened the door.

He turned on the wall sconce, heading down until

he could reach the switch for the overhead fluorescent. "And then there was light," Pete said, except there wasn't. Just a dim glow that streamed out from the ceiling. He peered into the dark basement, which looked the same as always to him. Dark and a little scary, and fit for spiders and other things that went bump in the night, as well as being a perfect spot for glass jars of preserves and vegetables. "I'm hungry," Pete said. "I could go for some pears right now."

He moved off the stairwell, debated going upstairs for a flashlight. Waste of time, he thought. Rafe was nutty. Nothing down here had been disturbed; he didn't need a camping torch to figure that out. There were boxes and boxes of Fiona's ornaments and lights, and rows of her carefully labeled foods—nothing more.

Pete didn't allow his gaze to travel over to the long rectangle in the dirt floor. As kids, he and his brothers had joshed each other about it being a buried coffin. They'd told ghost stories about it, daring each other to go digging. After so many ghost stories, none of them had ever wanted to be the brave one.

"It's silly," he muttered. "We're all grown men. We're not afraid of ghosts anymore."

Creed had told the best ghost stories. He could make the hair stand up on his brothers' arms. Once Creed finished his story, usually with some kind of banshee howl or other horrible story-ending device, the boys couldn't sleep for the rest of the night. Pete's eyes would close—then snap back open to peer restlessly around in the dark for signs of spirit life.

Creed had put Burke up to rigging a flying ghost in the trees once, right where the boys had spread out their camping gear. In the night, an ungodly howl had arisen, and suddenly, something white was flying over the boys, draping long fingers of soft spirit cloth over their faces as it whipped over their heads. The boys had fled into the house, screaming at the top of their lungs—except Creed, who they realized was outside rolling in the dirt, clutching his sides with laughter while enjoying them getting the bejesus scared out of them.

The hair stood up on Pete's arms at the memory. A nervous finger of fear tickled the back of his neck. He made himself glance at the seven-by-four-foot rectangle in the dirt, and cursed to himself.

It wasn't worth it. There was nothing here. Fiona hadn't been digging—there was no newly turned earth anywhere. She'd probably been digging in the garden and run downstairs with something she was canning.

His brothers were so busy worrying about Fiona that they were beginning to imagine she was off her rocker. But Fiona was just Fiona.

"It's nothing," he said. "My brothers just need to work a little harder to occupy their fertile imaginations."

He went back up the basement stairs. He could shower and get to Jackie's by seven if he hurried—time enough to drag her out to dinner. There was no reason for them to hide anymore—their secret was out. In fact, taking her to dinner might be the best way to help convince her that she needed to be thinking about their future. Jackie might not mind being a single mother, but he didn't want to be a single father.

If he was lucky, and played his cards right, perhaps he could convince her to let him into her bed tonight, too. She just needed to know how much she needed him. And their baby needed him, too.

He needed her. Pete grabbed the door handle, and

pulled out to make the door swing open. The handle resisted. He tried again, applying a little more force.

It was locked.

Pete banged on the door. "Burke! I'm in here! You locked me in!"

Burke had left. But maybe he'd come back and seen the open door. Pete had left the key in the lock. "Burke!" he yelled, banging on the door. "Rafe! Creed!"

Jonas and Sam were still on a wild goose chase to find themselves horses, Pete reminded himself. Sam wasn't going to buy anything because he claimed to be worried about the ranch. And Jonas was sitting on the fence about quitting his practice in Dallas and buying the land east of here to start his own ranch. That left Judah. "Judah!" Pete hollered. "Judah, open the damn door!"

There was silence on the landing above him. Pete balanced on the narrow step, and cursed to himself. His cursing was a comforting refrain of angry words.

It kept the silent darkness away.

"I can't take it," he said, pounding on the door. He couldn't get enough leverage on the narrow step to kick it. The door opened into the basement, anyway, so kicking it wouldn't help unless he was on the other side.

He was not on the other side. He was a prisoner in Fiona's basement.

"They'll be home soon," he told his jumping heart. Sinking onto the stair, he pulled out his cell phone. He'd call Judah, tell him to come let him out.

No cell service in the basement. "Of course not," he muttered, talking to himself to keep from getting weirded out. "When I get out of here, everybody's going to do exactly what I tell them. No more fibs.

No more—" He stopped as he felt a spider—or something—whisk over his arm.

Just like Creed's damn ghosts in the trees. Pete froze, his entire being tense, waiting. It was high time, he decided, to change his life. There were too many people running around like chickens with their heads cut off.

He would not join the chicken rodeo.

When I get out of here, everybody starts listening to good ol' Pete. Instead of being Mr. Responsibility they listen to and then ignore, from now on, it's all about what I want.

And what I want is Jackie.

Chapter Twelve

When Pete didn't show up that night, Jackie refused to admit that she was disappointed. She didn't want to call his phone. He'd said they had to talk—so if he was in the mood for conversation, he'd show up.

She told herself she was glad for the reprieve.

She missed the heck out of Pete, the old Pete. *I miss us the way we were,* she thought, but then she knew she didn't. That was why she'd wanted to change her life. She'd needed to move forward. Pete was not forward.

Still, she missed the easy companionship they'd shared once a week. "I'm in trouble," she muttered to Fanny. "I can't live with him, and I can't live without him."

It was too crazy to contemplate. Jackie sat on her sofa and snuggled the puppy, who was putting on weight almost as fast as she was. "You were some gift, you know?" she told Fanny. "I did not need a puppy and two babies."

The doctor had to be wrong. His hearing was probably a little compromised at his stage in life. She had a very small house. There was room for one child, but not two, not really.

She heard the doorbell, and went to find Darla on the porch. "I'm glad you're here. I needed company."

"I need a favor," Darla said. "Is Pete here?" She glanced around.

"No. He never came by." Jackie shrugged, trying to act as if it were unimportant.

"Never called?"

Jackie shook her head.

Darla sat on the sofa, putting a leg underneath her and reaching for Fanny. Jackie handed her the puppy and sat down, too. "That's not like that eager-beaver cowboy."

"Probably had to do something at the ranch. They're a little shorthanded with Sam being gone." Jackie tried to sound complacent about Pete's absence. "And since I'm avoiding telling him the truth until I get the test results, that's fine with me." It really wasn't. She missed him now. But it was for the best, until she was more settled. "I don't know where I'd put two babies."

Darla eyed her stomach. "I don't, either."

Jackie sighed. "So what did you need Pete for?"

"Oh." Darla sat up. "I want his opinion on a new car."

"What's wrong with your truck?"

"I like my truck. But I'd been thinking about getting something newer, and Sabrina wants to buy it." Darla beamed. "Pete would probably have some good ideas, or know of someone who has something they want to part with."

"When did you see Sabrina?"

"She came in after you left. She says she's enjoying working for Mr. Jenkins. And she likes living in Diablo. So she thought she might get a new truck. Hers is awfully dilapidated, you know. So then I said I might be looking to sell." Darla grinned. "Your theory of change is rubbing off on me."

"My theory hasn't been going too well, if you haven't noticed." Jackie shook her head. "I'll call Pete and see if he's still coming by." She was glad to have the excuse to call him. He was usually punctual to a fault. His cell phone kicked instantly over into voice mail. "It's not like him to be this late." Or late at all.

"Mr. Reliable," Darla said. "Let's go check on him."

"Check on him?" Jackie sat back on the sofa. "Why would we check on a grown man who lives on a ranch with a ton of other people?"

"Fiona and Burke are at Books 'n' Bingo. Jonas and Sam are out of town. Creed is in Diablo picking up supplies."

"That leaves Judah." Jackie frowned. Judah was the wild Callahan, the complete opposite of Pete. He rode bulls for a living, so that was likely the bad-boy draw for sweet, business-minded Darla. "You just want an excuse to see Judah."

Darla stood and kissed Fanny's small black nose. "Is that a bad thing?"

Jackie took Fanny and put her into the crate. "I'm not sure this is a prudent plan."

"We have no plan," Darla said.

"That's true," Jackie said, and went to get her coat.

PETE FIGURED HE'D BEEN in the basement around an hour, and he wasn't happy about it. For one thing, Jackie would probably be steamed that he hadn't shown up. For another, he hated sitting and twiddling his thumbs. He was a man of action, a man who didn't like sitting in a dark basement with no idea of when he might be sprung from exile. "This is why I never break the law," he said out loud. "I'd be no good with confinement."

Besides which, Sheriff Cartwright's tiny jail wasn't exactly home sweet home.

Then he heard it: The welcome sound of soft voices. "Hey!" he yelled, banging on the door. "Someone open the door!"

He heard footsteps, and the door sprang open. Jackie stared down at him, and a more beautiful sight he'd never seen.

"Pete? What are you doing down there?" Jackie asked, but he wasn't going to bother with explanations until he snagged a kiss from those sweet lips. He laid one on her until she was breathless, and then he was breathless, and then he realized he couldn't stand not sleeping with her another week, not even another day.

"You weren't down there a month, Pete," Darla said, and Pete broke away when he realized they had an audience.

"Sorry," he said, "it felt like a month." He grinned at Jackie, feeling better already. "To what do I owe the pleasure of your company? Which I'm very grateful for, by the way."

"What were you doing down there?" Jackie asked again.

Pete shrugged. "I went to check on something, and then someone locked the door, not realizing I was in the basement." He repressed a shudder, forced a grin and reached for Jackie again. "I made some personal decisions while I had nothing to do but think in the dark, and some of those decisions include you, my turtle-dove."

Jackie looked at him. "The door wasn't locked."

"It was." He nodded. "I couldn't budge it."

"She just opened the door when she heard you hollering like a madman," Darla said. "I watched her."

Pete stepped back, glanced at the doorjamb. "It was locked."

Jackie and Darla didn't say anything. Pete realized they didn't believe him. But it had been. He'd tugged on that doorknob with all his might, and the knob hadn't so much as offered to turn. "It must be getting old," Pete said. "I'll buy a new one and replace it."

"We came by because Darla wants to talk to you," Jackie said. Pete felt warmed and comforted just standing in her gaze. "About cars, if you're sufficiently recovered from your misadventures."

He looked at her, hearing a note of teasing in her voice. "You don't believe me. You think I'm a wuss who can't open a door in a house I've lived in all my life."

Jackie giggled. "It's a good thing Darla insisted on coming by to find you."

"Good to know someone cares," he said. "You have no idea how big the spiders are down there. I need some fresh air. Car talk over a veggie pizza, ladies?"

They headed toward the front door. Pete glanced over at the basement door, unable to get over the feeling that someone had pulled a not very funny, Callahan-style prank on him.

THEY ATE PIZZA, then Darla left, since she'd gotten "all the car advice she could stand." Pete had offered to take Jackie home, and Jackie had accepted. "This is the first time we've been out in public, thanks to Darla," Jackie said.

"I was just thinking the same thing. From now on, there's no need to hide from the lovable local busybodies." Pete grinned at her, so handsome that Jackie felt her breath catch. "I made some personal vows while I was locked in the basement that I think you should know about."

"Pete." Jackie smiled at him. "You panicked."

"I may panic at times," Pete said loftily, "but doors are not that hard for me to open. I promise I'm capable."

"I know. But everyone's known for a long time that you...you know."

"That was a rumor Jonas floated. I am not claustrophobic." Pete tried to look offended. "You know my brothers lie like rugs. Fibbing is a way of life for them."

Jackie laughed. "You are all capable of some pretty tall tales."

He put his hands over hers after the pizza had been cleared away. "Jackie, I'm not that claustrophobic."

"Just a little scared of the dark?"

"Not if you're there with me." He lifted her hand to kiss. "I can be quite brave."

She pulled her hand away, giving him a mock stern gaze. "Jonas said you were always afraid of small dark spaces, things that went bump in the night, and that at your family campouts they could always count on getting a rise out of you."

Pete shook his head. "If you'd been a favorite target of your siblings, you'd have always been looking over your shoulder, too."

"And commitment scares you. Anything that feels like it might tie you to something." Jackie tapped a finger against his hand. "Confess."

He grinned. "Try me, lady."

She sniffed. "So are you going to share some of these thoughts you had during your dark sojourn in the basement?"

"Yes." He nodded, his gaze suddenly sage. "We're getting married next week."

She blinked. "No, we're not." She had a doctor's appointment in Santa Fe next week. There were questions she wanted answered first.

"We are. Jackie, everyone always wants my advice but no one wants to take it. I'm asking you to marry me next week. We'll fly to Las Vegas. Or we'll stay here and have it done. I don't care which. But my son is going to be born with my name on his basket."

"Basket?"

"Whatever they put babies in now." Pete looked at her. "If you want me to get down on my knees right here in the—"

"No," Jackie said quickly. "Let's go discuss this rationally. This is the darkness and the small confined spaces talking, Pete. In the morning, it will wear off."

He helped her from the booth. "Nurse, your professional opinion is appreciated but not needed. I'm not having a panic attack. I was having a panic attack when I was trapped in the basement, but now I'm calm as a sleeping baby."

"A sleeping baby?"

"Well, whatever else you can think of that's calm. And I'll be calm next week when we say I do."

She sighed. It was going to be a long night. "I don't want to get married." She tried to sound bold and very determined, even if all she wanted was back in his arms.

Pete helped her into his truck. "Jackie, marrying you is my top priority."

"Priorities are great, but—"

"Glad to hear it," Pete said, "Saturday night, then."

Chapter Thirteen

"Pete, come in," Jackie said, "just for a few minutes."

They'd been silent on the ten-minute drive from the restaurant. Jackie let Fanny out of her crate, and the puppy went running to Pete with tiny yips. Pete picked her up, nestling her for a minute against his chest, before saying, "I'll take her out."

Jackie went with him. The moon was round in the January night sky, and the thousands of stars shone like diamonds. Crisp air blew gently across them as they watched Fanny explore her backyard.

Before she knew it, Pete had taken her in his arms, kissing her as though she was a delicate doll he didn't want to break. She could feel him taking his time with her, trying to show her that everything would be all right.

"Pete," she said, pulling away a little from him, however much she knew she belonged in his arms, "Dr. Graybill wants me to have some additional tests next week in Santa Fe. I really don't want to think about planning a wedding, too."

Concern flashed into Pete's eyes. "I'll take you to Santa Fe."

"No, no." Jackie shook her head. "I know you're

short-handed at the ranch. And I don't need anyone to go with me."

"I'm going," he said, and she realized tonight was Stubborn Pete night.

In a way, it felt good to know he was so concerned.

"So, what does the doctor say?" Pete asked.

They sat on the porch while Fanny explored.

"He wants me to be checked for the possibility of a multiple pregnancy." A small reassuring smile lifted her lips. "It's a wild goose chase. I think I'm having a normal, single pregnancy. But he wants me to have it checked, so I've made an appointment."

"Multiple?" Pete stared at her. "Like…twins?"

"Yes." She nodded.

"Wow," Pete said. "We have twins in our family. It's a possibility." He thought about it for a moment. "Rafe and Creed drove me nuts. They drove everyone nuts."

Jackie laughed. "I know. Pete, don't worry."

"I'm not," Pete said, "I'm trying not to yell with joy."

"Really?" Jackie looked at him shyly. "I was so scared to tell you. I thought it might be too much for you."

"You're weird," Pete said. "Every man dreams of twins."

She laughed. "Now you're overdoing it."

"Well, okay, I don't know about most men, but I wouldn't mind twins at all. Two boys," he mused. "Jackie, you're an amazing woman. All those years you thought you couldn't get pregnant, and you might just have hit the jackpot." He tickled her ribs, taking some playful nips along her neck. "I changed my mind. I don't want to get married next Saturday. I want to wait until you're big and round as a prize-winning pumpkin at the

State Fair, so everyone can see what a good shot I am. I'll grin while you waddle down the aisle."

"Pete!" Jackie pushed him away, though not very enthusiastically.

He pulled her into his lap. "My proficient little nurse," he said, "who would have ever thought your eggs would like my—"

"Pete Callahan," Jackie said, making her voice stern. "Bragging is not a good trait in a man."

"I don't care," Pete said, "my brothers are going to explode with envy. I can't wait."

"No, they're not," Jackie said, "they've set you up."

He looked at her. "What do you mean?"

She wished he hadn't brought up the bet. "Have you noticed any of them charging out to get a date?"

He frowned. "No."

"I could barely get Judah into the same room with Darla. I think they're happy to let you get tied down."

"They're slow starters," Pete said, but his frown didn't go away.

"Would you be so happy if you weren't currently beating your brothers in the race for the ranch?" Jackie asked.

"Yes, because the whole thing is dumb." Pete ran a hand over her cheek, cupping her face to his. "Fiona has a lot of harebrained ideas, and this is one of them. You have all the babies you want, my little lamb chop. We'll live right here in your house, and stack their cradles up like condominiums."

Jackie smiled. "At least I don't have a basement for you to lock yourself in," she said, and he snagged a fast kiss in retribution.

"I'm only interested in your sofa. Let's go inside so I can reacquaint myself with it."

PETE SLEPT ON THE SOFA, with Jackie's head on his shoulder. He hadn't meant to fall asleep, but she was so soft and round, and it felt like home, and the next thing he knew his watch was chiming its usual four-thirty wakeup call. He carried Jackie into her bedroom and set her on her pretty white bed, and when Fanny begged to get up, he put the puppy up beside her. Fanny snuggled into the blankets next to Jackie's stomach, and Pete wished he could do some snuggling of his own.

Instead he stole a tiny kiss from Jackie, who barely stirred. His angel needed her beauty rest, since she'd only had about four hours of sleep. His sons needed their rest, too. He grinned.

Life was just getting better all the time.

He let himself out and headed to the ranch. He'd forgotten all about the chat he was supposed to have with Fiona until he found her in the kitchen. She looked as though she'd been sitting up all night waiting for him, something she hadn't done since they were teenagers. No matter how late they'd tried to sneak in, she'd been perched at the kitchen table like an energetic owl.

"Good morning," he said, kissing her cheek. "Can't sleep or up early?"

"Early!" Fiona snorted. "You haven't gotten up earlier than me a day in your life, Pete Callahan. And Burke's out starting your chores. He didn't think you'd make it back."

Pete got himself a cup of coffee. "When have I ever slid on the chores?"

She frowned at him. "You've been off in your own world lately."

"I have? Who missed our meeting last night?"

"I forgot about the Books 'n' Bingo meeting when I said that." Fiona gave him a sour look. "Anyway, I figured whatever you wanted to talk about could wait."

"You just skipped out, Aunt," Pete said cheerfully. "I'll catch you when I get back from the morning rounds." *And then tonight, I may head over to Jackie's and let her seduce me. I'm pretty sure I won't say no.*

Fiona looked at him. "What time did you leave last night?"

"Around nine. Why?" He paused at the door, his coffee mug in his hand.

She jerked her head toward the back of the house. "Were you in the basement?"

"I got locked in down there, and Jackie and Darla let me out."

She sniffed. "And my jars?"

Pete went down the hall. The door leading to the basement was kicked off its hinges, hanging against the wall at a jagged angle. "Holy crap," Pete said as he walked down the stairs. He flipped on the overhead light, his eyes huge. Every single one of Fiona's precious jars of vegetables and preserves had been smashed. "What the hell happened?" Pete said, eyeing the pile of shattered glass on the floor.

"We thought you might know," Fiona said from behind him.

He stared, his mind refusing to accept what he saw. The mess was terrible, the smell of ruined vegetables and fruit overwhelming. "I am so sorry. All your hard work, Aunt Fiona."

"Never mind that. Who was in the house last night?"

"Just me and Jackie and Darla. Everything was just fine last night." Except it hadn't been. He wondered again about the lock. He went back up the steps, staring at the door carefully. There were no scratches on the lock. Someone had simply kicked in the door. "I locked it. I put the keys in Burke's cabinet. What time did you and Burke get back?" His blood chilled as he thought about Burke and Fiona coming in while someone was ransacking the basement.

"Around midnight." Fiona's shoulders slumped. "This isn't good."

"Have you called the sheriff?" Pete followed her into the kitchen.

"No," Fiona said on a sigh. "I can't."

He looked at her. "It's time we talked, Fiona," Pete said, and his little aunt just nodded, looking defeated.

"But I don't want your brothers to know anything," Fiona said. "It's imperative that you keep this conversation a secret, Pete."

"Secrets are bad, Aunt Fiona."

"Secrets are *necessary,*" she shot back. "Promise me."

He sighed. If Jackie was right and his brothers had set him up to be the marriage fall guy, then they were keeping secrets of their own. All his resolutions were going out the window in record time. "Fine," he said, "I think."

They sat down at the kitchen table. Pete waited for his aunt to speak. It was clear she was choosing her words carefully, not certain where to begin, so he reached over and took her hands in his.

"Bode Jenkins wants the ranch," she said, taking him by surprise.

Pete stared at her. "So? People in Hell want ice water, as you've always said."

"I can't stop him from getting it," Fiona said, and Pete realized his aunt was worried and frightened and everything a woman her age shouldn't be. He saw the suffering on her face, and knew it had been in her heart for a long time.

"I'm sorry, Aunt Fiona," Pete said. "You should have told me sooner. I had no idea you were carrying around this burden."

She shook her head. "I didn't know how. You boys… you were entrusted to me, as was this ranch. Burke and I have done our best, but—" She let out a shattering sigh. "Bode's just plain outsmarted me."

"Nah." Pete squeezed her fingers. "No one outsmarts my aunt."

She looked at him, her usually bright eyes filled with tears he knew she wouldn't shed. "Do you want me to go over there and kick his ass?" he asked, meaning it to be playful, just to put a smile on his aunt's face, but she shook her head so quickly he knew she was afraid he'd do just that.

"I couldn't tell you boys because I was afraid of what would happen. All six of you have heads like bags of microwave popcorn. I never know when the hot air might suddenly explode."

Pete shook his head. "Why don't you start at the beginning?"

Fiona nodded. "It's been happening for years, a sort of slow creep I was pretty proud I was fighting off. Cattle would disappear. I figured he was trying to run us out of business so we'd have to sell. That was easily solved, I just put up extra fence and kept the cattle elsewhere."

"Of course it's difficult to keep your eyes on five thousand acres and six nephews," Pete said, thinking about what his aunt had gone through.

"Well, we were up to the task, but Bode didn't make our lives any easier." Fiona pulled her hands back from his and put them in her lap. "As long as nothing happened to you boys, I didn't care. I wasn't worried when the acreage down near the ravine caught on fire. Didn't get overly excited when he sent a couple of brawny men over to put an offer on the ranch." She sniffed. "I sent them packing in a hurry."

Pete reminded himself that he'd just solemnly promised his aunt he wouldn't go thrash the daylights out of Bode Jenkins. He could feel the blood boiling between his ears, though, and told himself to remain calm for his aunt's sake. "I'm sure they never bargained on you," he told Fiona. "I wish you'd let us help you, though."

"You were younger then. And I was supposed to be your guardian. Frankly, I've got enough Irish in me not to be afraid of a little battle between neighbors," she said with a rueful smile. "Tell you the truth, I always thought Bode was dumber than a rock. But I didn't foresee his daughter, Julie, whom I'd held on my knees when she was a baby, growing up to be his ace in the hole." Fiona shook her head.

"How?" Pete asked, trying to imagine sweet Julie being much of a threat to anyone. She could be a rascal, and certainly raised hell on his brothers when she deemed it necessary—and he'd always admired her for it—but Julie was a lady.

"Next thing I knew, about five years ago, the discussion of eminent domain came up. That alarmed me, as you might imagine. Suddenly, the state was talking about needing our land for a highway. Burke and I fought it, of course. They weren't willing to pay a whole lot for the property, and I felt there were better avenues to consider. So we suggested alternative routes to the state, and to our surprise, they agreed with us. I thought it was over. I should have been suspicious then." Fiona took a deep breath. "We had the property paid for, the house paid off, it was all Callahan. And then Judge Julie was appointed to the state federal bench. Julie does whatever Bode wants her to do, as I suppose any good daughter would. So, we were told we had a year to relocate. It's been six months now. We've run out of appeals."

"What does this have to do with Julie?"

"Bode's buying the land. There's nothing we can do about that. He has a deal with the land commissioner— thanks to Julie—to take over the property. It's no secret that Bode may be an unpleasant person, but the old miser's a savvy investor and has been sitting on his wealth for years. And he has lots of friends in high places."

"You have lots of friends," Pete murmured, thinking of his social little aunt.

"Not political friends. My friends play bingo, read books, raise their kids. I was never politically minded. You'd be surprised what money can buy."

No, I wouldn't. Pete shook his head. "So what was the hurry for all of us to get married and have children for a ranch we were never going to get?"

"Oh," Fiona said, "I just wanted you boys to get down off your slow-poke butts and give me some babies. While we still have the ranch, while we can still have weddings here if you want to, why not? Before everyone finds out how low the Callahans are falling."

He regarded his small, determined aunt with some puzzlement. "You wanted us to find brides who would think that they were marrying into the Callahan family name, but would later find out we weren't what they thought we were?"

Fiona sniffed. "Marriage is full of surprises. Anyway, it wouldn't matter if you boys picked women who loved you."

He hesitated. Jackie wouldn't care if the Callahans still owned the biggest and best ranch around or not. *But I might.* The truth was, everything he had, everything he thought he was, was tied up in this land, a place where his sons would never run and play the way he and his brothers had. His heart felt like it was breaking. "I guess you considered selling off part of the ranch."

She nodded. "For about half a second. No longer than that. Bode would just get injunctions. I couldn't bear to part with anything my brother and his wife had built, anyway. But I do despise Bode Jenkins, who is a thief if there ever was one."

It was really hard not to get up and go kick Bode's ass. Pete couldn't stand to see the worry etched on Fiona's face. She'd carried this burden so long by herself. Pete got up. "Don't worry, Aunt Fiona," he said. "Everything is going to be fine."

"Except the basement door got kicked in," she said, and he stopped.

"Do you think Bode did that?"

She shrugged. "Nothing was taken."

"We don't keep cash in the house." That was all kept

in a locked safe, whose whereabouts only the eight of them knew. They'd been vigilant about people breaking in to their home, knowing it would be a temptation.

"I don't know for sure," Fiona said, "but I think Bode has wanted this house for so long it's just about made him crazy."

"This is simply solved. I'll just go ask Sabrina if Bode left the house last night."

"Oh, no," Fiona said faintly, "you can't ask Sabrina that."

"Why?" Pete sat back down, realizing he was about to hear more.

"Because I hired Sabrina to be a fortune-teller and tell you boys that you had to get married."

"I know." He nodded. "I heard the whole scheme."

She raised her brows. "I know that. I could see your shadow and your big ears practically pressed flat against the tent wall."

He looked at her, finally grinning. "Not much gets by you."

She nodded. "But what you didn't know is that I also hired Sabrina's sister, Seton, who is a private investigator, to dig up dirt on Bode."

Pete's jaw dropped. "Aunt Fiona!"

She jutted out her chin. "I finally decided two could play dirty, and that all was going to be fair in love and war. And I love nothing like I love my boys."

He was stunned. "We love you, too, redoubtable aunt…but is that why Sabrina McKinley is working as his caregiver? She's really a mole?"

"Sabrina is neither a fortune-teller nor your usual caregiver. She is an investigative reporter. She was doing a piece on animal cruelty, which is how she wound up at the circus. I met Sabrina and Seton through my friends. They are nieces of Corinne Abernathy."

Pete closed his eyes. "Does the sun ever rise without your cagey little brain working on a new scheme?"

"Nope," Fiona said happily. "I feel so much better now that I've told you all this, Pete. You have no idea how cleansing that was!"

His head felt as though it was about to explode. "So you want to ruin Bode?"

"I want," Fiona said with deadly purpose, "to make sure he never gets my brother's property."

"Maybe we could just talk to Julie?"

"Bah," Fiona said. "Bode's her father. Who would you believe in? Who would you want to make happy? Your father or your neighbor? The people who live on five thousand acres of prime land while you've grown up on a postage stamp of canyon in a tiny wooden foreman's house next door?" Fiona waved a hand at Pete. "He's got her convinced he's at death's door so she'll live there taking care of him, waiting on him hand and foot. She'll never marry because of that old fool. She's got her job, which makes him happy because of the political clout, and he's got her. Life is happy for Bode Jenkins, the miserable rat."

Bode wasn't the only one capable of playing the feeble card. Pete remembered Fiona working that angle a bit with Jonas. Or maybe she hadn't been. Pete scrubbed at his morning stubble. "You still don't think that telling the others would—"

"No." She shook her head. "You're the only one who's rational enough not to go do something stupid. You're the only one responsible enough to realize that there's more than one way to skin a cat without getting fur in your mouth. I can count on you, Pete."

He sighed and reached over to pet his aunt's delicate hands. "Yes, you can, Aunt Fiona. Everything will be all right."

He just wasn't sure how.

Chapter Fourteen

Pete did the lion's share of the chores he needed to do, realizing a thousand questions were still left unanswered. If anything, his aunt had given him more things to ponder. Fiona never told a whole tale—there was always one more curve just ahead of the brothers' slower brains. But one thing he did know for certain: He had to talk to Jackie.

At noon, he found her at the wedding shop. "Can I buy you lunch?"

"Oh, Pete," Jackie said, her hair delightfully mussed as she moved dresses around the shop, "today is rearranging day. Darla and I have planned to organize the merchandise by classification." She smiled at him. "But thanks for the invite."

He looked at her, wanting nothing more than to carry her off on his white steed and make love to her for about a week. He was certain he'd feel much better after he did.

Unfortunately, he had no white steed—only black-as-night Bleu—and Jackie wasn't the kind of girl who'd put up with heroic nonsense like a man just riding off with her. She'd tell him he was a chauvinistic ass and probably lame him. "Jackie, I need to talk to you."

She looked at him over the top of a wedding gown. "About?"

He brightened. "That one suits you."

"What one? Oh." Jackie hung the dress on the rack. "Don't get any ideas, Pete. I have no intention of walking down the aisle."

That was the trouble. She had no intentions. He had a short deadline. Fiona was right—he'd love to get married at the ranch, while they still had it. "Could you rethink that? I was hoping we could stick to the I-do-next-week plan."

"No. I have to get my appointment in Santa Fe taken care of. I can't think past that." She hauled another dress over to a different stand.

"Those look heavy." He frowned. "I thought wedding dresses would be airy and light. Maybe you shouldn't be carrying them."

"Pete!" Jackie laughed. "You're going to get in trouble if you try to supervise my pregnancy."

"Well." He shifted, not exactly certain how to get Jackie to succumb to his wishes. "I'm coming with you to the appointment. Wild horses couldn't keep me away."

"I might let you. Maybe." She shot him a glance. "If you don't drive me nuts between now and Monday."

"Monday?" He perked up. "So soon?"

"Dr. Graybill called their office. So they fit me in." She slid some plastic off some dresses to examine them. Pete watched her morosely. How could she stand to look at wedding gowns every day and not want one for herself?

"Is there something wrong with me?"

She glanced at him. "Other than you can't get yourself out of a basement that isn't locked, no. You seem all right to me."

He decided not to tell her that the basement had been trashed sometime in the night. Fiona hadn't really wanted their personal family business broadcast. He frowned, realizing Fiona had never mentioned who she thought might have done it. Bode wouldn't stoop that low if he thought he was already getting their ranch. Fiona had no enemies to speak of. He and his brothers might have enemies, but none of them would stoop to being so wienie as to destroy preserves. Someone had gotten into the house and locked him in—he was sure of it. Then when he'd left, they'd gone through the basement.

Someone was looking for something. And someone was watching their comings and goings. He and his brothers weren't around much. It was just Fiona and Burke, two stalwart, older folks on a big ranch where no one would hear them if they needed help.

Maybe he was overthinking it. Yet it did occur to him that the only new people in town were Sabrina and her yet-to-be-seen sister, Seton. He didn't think he completely approved of his aunt's plan to hire spies, but Fiona had never asked for his approval.

"Pete?" Jackie said, and he snapped his gaze to her face. She was lovely. Pregnancy was making her blossom. He'd always thought the myth about a pregnant woman glowing was something women said to make themselves seem desirable, but Jackie was more beautiful than ever. He wanted her, right now.

He had to put those thoughts away for the moment or he was going to ravish her in the store. "Yes?"

"Are you all right? I was teasing about the basement."

"Yeah, I know." He moved his hat back on his head. "Jackie, let me ask you a theoretical."

"Okay."

She wasn't really paying attention to him. Her gaze had gone to the window. He glanced, too, seeing nothing unusual on the Diablo town streets. "Say I had been locked into the basement."

She smiled. "All right, let's suppose you had been."

"And then you let me out, which I should reward you for later."

Jackie looked at him. "Is that part of the question?"

"No." He shook his head. "If someone went into the basement not too long after I'd been locked in, and made a big mess—although I'm not saying that happened— would you suppose the two events were related?"

Jackie shrugged. "If things had happened in that way, and no one in your house was responsible for the mess, one might think that the house was searched while you were locked in. And then when you were let out of the basement, it was searched. That's what you're trying to tell me, isn't it? Someone's been in your house?"

He held up a hand. "It was just a theoretical."

"Has someone been in your house?" Jackie's eyes were huge. "What would they be looking for?"

"No, no," Pete said, wondering why he hadn't thought about someone being in the house while he was conveniently locked away. "Don't go jumping to any ideas."

"I'm not. You are. You just wanted me to say it out loud to give your brain permission to think it. It was there all along."

"No, I wasn't."

"You set me up to give you the answer you wanted.

You know, you're more like Fiona than you think you are."

She went back to rearranging dresses, which he hated to see. He was pretty certain heavy lifting couldn't be healthy for his little wife in her condition. He wondered how Jackie would take to him mentioning that she should probably quit working until the stork arrived.

He frowned. "I'd feel better if you were staying with me."

She stared at him. "Why would I want to be in a house where there's a random thief wandering around? Isn't that what you're trying to tell me?"

He shook his head. "I said nothing of the sort, and Fiona will kill me if you share that gossip with anyone. I just want you near me. My motives are pure, I swear."

"I can't tell if you're being romantic or a pain in the ass."

"Both?"

She smiled. "Tell you what. You go away now, and I'll make you a salad for dinner."

"Salad?"

"I'm watching my weight. Too much weight gain isn't supposed to be good for the baby. And for some reason, the weight seems to be packing on pretty quickly now."

"I can handle a salad," he said, thinking she looked sexy as hell to him, "but I think my sons need more sustenance than rabbit food. How about if I bring them a steak?"

She waved him out of the store.

"Rare, medium or well done?" he called as she pushed him onto the sidewalk.

"Goodbye, Pete," Jackie said, but he swiped a fast kiss and went whistling down the sidewalk.

Jackie went back into the store, trying to remember what she'd been doing before Pete had come in, nearly undoing her resolve where he was concerned.

"I've said it before and I'll say it again. That man is crazy about you," Darla said. "How can you keep such a sweetheart at arm's length?"

Jackie shook her head. "Pete just likes the chase. He'll get tired soon enough."

Darla didn't look convinced. "Maybe you underestimate him. He seems like he's made up his mind. Once you told him he was going to be a dad, he's made a point to see you every day he can."

Jackie thought about that, the surprise of it catching her off guard. "You're right."

"Yes. And you're the happiest I've ever seen you."

Darla was right about that, too. She sighed. "Life is tricky right now. Pete and I were always about the cozy, comfortable sex. I don't know what's going on, but I know sex would not be cozy and comfortable right now. My waistline is expanding at warp speed." She shook her head. "I do not feel sexy at all."

"Give him a chance. He may like caftan-wearing, big-bellied ladies." Darla grinned. "You don't know until you strip, girlfriend."

"Eek." Jackie supposed she could keep the lights off, but she was pretty certain in the history of women trying to do the same, that plan had often backfired. "I miss the days of candlelight, don't you?"

Darla laughed. "Go for it. Buy a bunch of candles. And let that gorgeous hunk decide whether he can handle you big and babylicious or not. I'm thinking he's not going to be all that focused on anything but naked you."

Chills ran all over Jackie at the thought of Pete being

in bed with her again. She missed making love with him. She missed his deep voice whispering husky, naughty things to her. Missed his arms wrapped around her and going to sleep knowing he was beside her until the dawn. "I'm going out for a minute," Jackie said.

"Go get him, Tiger!"

Jackie hurried after Pete. "Pete!"

He was walking down the sidewalk, big-shouldered, tall and lean, and it didn't escape Jackie that about ten women were casting their eyes at him, saying hello, trying their best to get his attention. *Mine,* she thought, and then stopped, horrified. Her pregnancy wasn't easily hidden now—in fact, it was pretty obvious despite the empire-style, long-sleeved, fashionable dress she wore—and she was running after Pete.

To hell with it. "Pete!"

He turned, grinning at her, his brows raised as she made it to him slightly out of breath. "You shouldn't be running like that, angel cake. You might pull a hamstring."

She wanted to punch him. He looked so smug, so proud of himself, and he was even more handsome, if that was possible.

"Did I forget something in the store?" he asked, clearly enjoying his big moment of being the pursued.

"No," Jackie said, "and you're not making this easy on me." Out of the corner of her eyes, she could feel the faces peering out of windows watching her and Pete.

"I'm enjoying your eagerness, my pet."

"I simply wanted to tell you," Jackie said, her teeth starting to grit, "that maybe I'd feel better if you were staying with me."

"Oh, you're worried about me." He swept her into

his arms, leaving no one in any doubt about the status of their relationship. If he'd shouted *I'm the father* to the rooftops, he couldn't have been more clear. Part of Jackie rebelled at his chauvinism, but a bigger part of her snuggled against his chest. She felt the smile stretch on her face.

"Yes. I'm worried about you, you ass. You shouldn't be in a house where there are creepies hanging around."

"I can't leave Burke and Fiona."

Clearly he wanted her to beg. "Leave them a shotgun."

"Jackie!" He turned her face up so he could look down into her eyes. "Do I actually hear welcome and anticipation and—"

She pulled away. "Don't overdo it, Pete Callahan."

He laughed, sweeping a finger down her nose. "I'll be there for dinner, pumpkin pie. Don't you miss me too much between now and then. And I'll take very good care of you."

She couldn't miss his meaning. Nor could about twenty people milling around nearby, acting as though they weren't listening to every word. Jackie's face flamed. She was going to flee, until she caught sight of some of the town's more eligible females eyeing her with envy, so she rose on tiptoe and kissed him right on the mouth.

"If I'd only known how much you like an audience, my sweet, I would have insisted on our relationship being out in broad daylight a long time ago." Pete laughed, saluted her with a devilish wink in his eyes, and walked off.

Jackie stared after him, her blood pounding in her ears. Okay, she looked like she was pursuing him. She was pregnant, she was running after Pete and she didn't care who saw.

She'd caught him. And she couldn't wait until tonight.

She went to buy some candles. And then, for good measure, she bought a lacy pink and white nightie, not caring at all that the whole town would know how crazy she was about Peter Dade Callahan.

JACKIE FELT PRETTY BRAVE about her plan until Pete strolled into her house that night. He looked tall and long and lean, and raffish with his rumpled dark hair, a devil-may-care bachelor if there ever was one. And she felt frumpy.

"I brought steaks," Pete said, laying a grocery sack on the table. "But I vote we have dessert first."

"Wait, Pete." Jackie tried to avoid his hands, but he was too fast for her. She didn't have on the sexy nightie, which she was hoping would deflect the eye and make him concentrate on anything but her big tummy and boobs that would no longer fit into her bra without spilling out the top. The candles weren't even lit yet, and she needed the cover of candlelight.

"I'm done waiting." He carried her into her bedroom, kicking the door shut behind them. He laid Jackie on the bed, his mouth claiming hers, but Jackie gave him a halfhearted push. "Pete, let me get you dinner first. You must be starved."

"You guess correctly." He buried his face in her neck, nibbling kisses as he unbuttoned her dress. "There is far too much material here. You're wrapped up like a mummy. I know it's thirty-two degrees outside, but too much dress conceals the good stuff." He slipped it off her shoulders. "Jackie," he said, grinning at her, "you've been keeping things from me."

She laughed as he undid her bra. "Pete," she said, trying to hold on to her bra. He was having none of that.

"Goodness," he said, his tone admiring, "come to daddy." And then his mouth was on her breasts, and Jackie forgot to be embarrassed about the size of them. Her dress seemed to melt off her, and Jackie clutched Pete to her, pulling off his shirt, shoving his jeans down, craving his warmth.

"Hi, boys," he said to her stomach, kissing the whole rounded size of it, and the last worry Jackie had floated away. "If they're napping," he told Jackie, "I'm about to wake them up."

"Pete!" Jackie tried not to laugh, but his playful spirit washed away her insecurities. All she wanted was him. "We don't know that we're having twins."

"It's either that, sweetie, or a linebacker. Or you swallowed several pumpkins." He kissed her stomach again. "I'm going to have to turn you around so I don't hurt you."

"Why?" Jackie put her arms around his neck, pulling him down to her so she could kiss him. "You're not going to hurt me."

"I don't want to jostle them."

"Let's find out if they like being jostled."

"I don't know," Pete said, "you were hiding a lot under those baggy clothes, Jackie. I don't want to press my boys flat as pancakes."

"Either you get inside me right now," Jackie said, "or there will be hell to pay."

"Yes, ma'am," he said, sliding between her legs. And

then he was inside her, and Jackie gasped as he kissed her hard, driving her mad with feeling him again.

He only hesitated once. "Am I hurting anything?"

"For the love of Mike," Jackie said, practically growling, wanting him never to stop doing what he was doing to her.

"Pete," he said, "I prefer for the love of Pete." And then he found the sweet spot, and Jackie forgot to be mad. Closing her eyes, she let the sweet waves of pleasure claim her, going boneless and mindless and utterly content to be in Pete's strong arms. She felt him stiffen, heard him cry out, and holding him close to her, finally allowed the pleasure she'd held back to wash over her like rain.

"Pete," she murmured, "I missed you."

"Say it," he said, rising above her, still inside her, "go ahead and say you can't live without me."

She slapped his rump smartly. "I can't live without you."

"Good," he said, groaning, "because I'm pretty certain I can't live without you, either. I don't get munchies like my brothers. I get the Jackies, and I just have to have you."

She giggled as he buried his face in her neck, nibbling on her. It was so hard to be mad at Pete that it wasn't worth the effort.

I just love him too much. And I don't know how to fix that.

A HALF HOUR LATER, Pete realized he'd fallen asleep. "Oh, hell," he said, pushing himself up on an elbow so he could look down into Jackie's face, "I think I short-circuited." He kissed her to make up for the lack of pillow talk.

Jackie giggled. "You have been acting strange lately."

"It's sympathetic pregnancy pangs. They're blowing all my fuses. Are you hungry?" God, he was a louse. He shouldn't have fallen asleep like that. All his good intentions flew out of his brain when he got in Jackie's bed. He didn't think he needed food, even. He could probably just live on sex with Jackie for the rest of his life.

"Starving."

"I'll get the steaks on." He hopped up, grabbing for his jeans.

"Pete?"

He turned to look at Jackie. "Uh-huh?"

"About that other position you mentioned we might try."

Had he hurt her? He felt his heart rate jump. He'd never touch her again—at least not until his little guys were born—if he'd caused her the slightest bit of pain. "What about it?"

She crooked her finger at him.

"Oh, boy," Pete said, throwing his jeans back on the floor.

Chapter Fifteen

Forty minutes later, Pete knew he was wearing a very self-satisfied smirk. "We've got to stop meeting like this."

Jackie giggled. "Naked?"

"Once a month. Let's go back to our old routine, at least." Pete wondered how he could convince her that they needed to meet like this every night—married. "We have to buy a bigger house."

"*We* have to buy a bigger house?"

"Mmm." He kissed down her neck to her collarbone, lingering at the spectacular view. Pregnancy certainly brought out the best in his turtledove. "Now that the whole town knows we've been living in sin, we might as well go ahead and do it."

"The whole town doesn't know it."

He grinned, running a palm over her tummy. "Even if you hadn't branded me in the middle of the street today, my love, I think they suspected. It's time you make an honest man of me."

Jackie tried to roll out of her bed, but he caught her and brought her back, sneaking a hand between her thighs. He heard her breath catch, and grinned. "Say yes."

"To what?"

She sounded like she might be relaxing to the point of mindless, so he decided to press his advantage. "To the bigger house, for starters."

"Pete," she said, moving away from his hand and pushing him down on the bed so that she straddled him. He grinned at her serious expression. She was going to try to read him the riot act, and it was so cute when she tried to do it naked. It took all the seriousness right out of it. He could feel her warmth and wetness on his stomach, and if she only but knew it, his soldier was standing at attention right behind her. Waiting patiently for her to finish.

"If I'm having one baby, and that's what I think, there is no need for me to move. This house is plenty big enough. And I never said I'd share a house with you."

"This is a two-bedroom, one-bath house. We need a bigger house, Jackie, one that's far out in the country. You yell loudly when you're aroused." He kissed her fingertips, nibbling at them and then up her wrist. "You came so loudly Fanny ran under the bed. She may never come back out."

Jackie took her hand from him and crossed her arms, which did nothing but stiffen parts of him that were already at attention. He put his hands behind his head, enjoying the delicious sight of rounded, nude Jackie.

"I did no such thing. I made barely any noise."

"My sweet." He gave her a mock-ashamed look. "You're so loud that the chandelier is still swinging in the living room. I think the house moved on its foundation."

He lifted her hips and sat her on himself, grinning at her gasp. He reached up to tweak her nipples as she moved on him, enjoying watching her find the spots that pleasured her. But then she leaned over, and her breasts fell into his face so he could lick and suck on her nipples, and all Pete could think of was how much he loved Jackie Samuels, no matter how hard she tried to run away from him.

He was fast. He'd catch her yet.

"I ADVISE COMPLETE BED REST," Dr. Snead said on Monday, turning to glance at Jackie and Pete.

Pete didn't think Jackie on complete bed rest sounded all that bad. Bed was exactly where he wanted her. But Jackie looked concerned, so Pete said, "Is there a problem with the pregnancy?"

Pete had driven Jackie to Santa Fe Monday morning after the longest weekend of lovemaking he'd ever enjoyed. He thought he just about had her under his spell. Things were looking positive, anyway, since she used to shoo him off on Sundays and not open the door again until the next Saturday.

He looked at the screen the doctor had returned his attention to, and held Jackie's hand. She was squeezing him until his fingers were numb, and he squeezed back, letting her know that everything was going to be fine.

"No problem," Dr. Snead said. "It's just that the three babies are taking up a lot of space inside Jackie. And she's already mentioned having spasms. We need to keep the babies in as long as we possibly can."

The room swam around Pete. Now he was clutching Jackie's hand. The nurse pushed a stool underneath him. *"Three?"*

Dr. Snead nodded. "Three heartbeats. Three well-established babies. It's hard to make out the different bodies because they seem to be tangled up in there. But here's an arm."

Pete brightened. "Can you tell the sex?"

"Girls," Doctor Snead said. "It'll be clearer later on, but unless someone's got a thumb down there I can't see, you're having three girls, Jackie."

Jackie's face was ashen. Pete rubbed her hand in his. "I always knew you were an efficient woman, Jackie. We're going to have an entire family."

"I never even thought I could get pregnant," Jackie said, sounding close to tears. But she was smiling, and Pete realized she was pretty much in shock. "But I can't be on bed rest," she told Doctor Snead. "I have a shop to run."

"Get a recliner and a portable phone," the doctor said. "I'll send a nurse out once a week to check on you. And I suggest you, Mr. Callahan, learn how to cook and clean."

Pete grinned at Jackie, his face creased with mischievous laughter. "I can cook and clean, Doctor."

"And I'm afraid no marital relations," Dr. Snead said.

Pete patted Jackie's hand. "There goes your plan of driving me mad with sex, sweetheart. You'll have to do without the pleasure of me until after the children are born."

Jackie looked as though she had plenty to say but was refraining until the doctor and nurse had left the room. Pete was so happy he couldn't stand it.

He was having three little girls. All those squiggles and lines he couldn't make sense of on the screen were three little Callahan cowgirls.

After having nothing but brothers, he was looking forward to being the only man in the house.

"Jackie," Pete said, "it'll be hard on me to wait on you hand and foot, but it's a sacrifice I'm willing to make for the cause."

She looked as though she was about to kill him as he helped her up from the table. "What cause is that?"

"You, darling," he said. "You're my new cause in life."

"Great," Jackie said. "I'll only be half insane by this time next month. By the time the babies are born, I'll be stark raving mad."

"I've got to buy a baby name book. And a house. And baby furniture. Have you even been thinking about all this, Jackie Samuels, or has your mind only been on your new business?" Pete gave her a light pat on the rump as she bent over to slip her shoes on.

"Ugh. The next several months stretch before me endlessly." Jackie let Pete give her his arm.

"Just because you can't have sex with me," he said. "Good thing you had a lot of me this weekend."

Jackie sighed and Pete grinned. "We have to get married. We don't have a second to wait. You're not going to want to get married in a recliner, Jackie. Let's let the romance of Santa Fe lure us in to just doing it. Spontaneously."

"No." She shook her head. "Pete, I can't."

"We'll redo the vows later, if you want, after the babies are born and you've got your figure back. That's what you're worried about, isn't it? Your sexy little body fitting into a wedding gown?"

"No," she said, and he could practically hear her teeth grinding. "I just found out I'm having triplets. And I'm in love with a numbskull. That's what is worrying me."

She sailed off toward the truck, and Pete followed, happier than he'd ever been in his life.

She'd said she *loved* him. Maybe that had just slipped out from between her pretty little tightly clenched teeth, but he'd heard her. And he wasn't going to let her forget it, either.

Whistling, he followed her, feeling like a king. It was a beautiful day in Santa Fe, and he was going to be a dad—he *was* a dad—and he had a woman who loved him. All was well until he realized Jackie was raining tears like a leaky faucet.

"What is it? Are you in pain?" He leaned across the seat to look into her face.

She shook her face and blew her nose. "I wanted change. Have I ever gotten change."

"Yes, we have. Isn't change awesome?" He wanted her to cease the waterworks, though. He didn't want his little girls getting scared by all the noise their mother was making. "Change is good, right?"

"Change is great, but too much change is scaring me."

He pondered that. "Will it help if I tell you I have a surprise for you?"

She looked up at him through beautiful, watery brown eyes. His love had such limpid pools of suspicion beaming at him that all he could do was smile at her. "You look like I'm about to give you a vacuum cleaner."

"Not if you want to keep your handsome face on your block-shaped head." She sniffed.

He laughed. "Here." Reaching into the backseat of the double cab, he handed her a bag from her own wedding shop. "Be very careful how you open it, my love. My heart is in that bag."

She stared at him, more cautious than ever, and slowly pulled his gift from the bag.

"The magic wedding dress," she said, her voice awed, and Pete grinned.

"Darla said it was your dream come true. So I sneaked off with it." Pete kissed Jackie, and swept her hair back from her chin so he could see her face. He hoped to see a smile.

Instead, Jackie cried harder.

"Oh, crap," Pete said, "I knew I didn't believe in magic."

"No," Jackie said, trying not to cry, "it's sweet. You're sweet. It is my dream come true. I'm just not sure I'll ever fit into it now." Tears ran freely down her cheeks. Pete dug into the glove box for tissues. "I hate being all hormonal and emotional, especially when you're being so romantic and princely."

"You might fit into it if we hurry," Pete said, trying to tease her but really meaning it. "There's a chance you'll only grow another inch by the time we make it to a drive-through wedding chapel."

Jackie looked at him. "You're serious."

"Yes." He nodded. "Is there a better time than the present? I'm wearing my best jeans. You've got a dress. My chariot can take us there." He pounded on the dashboard. "It'll be as romantic as running off to Hawaii."

"It won't."

"I think it will be. And Callahan is a sweet last name. You might as well give in, Jackie. Remember when you told me there was no need to buy the steer if you could get the steak for free?"

"Yes," Jackie said, blowing her nose, "but now I'm not going to be getting any steak, according to the doctor."

"All the more reason to go ahead and reserve the steer for later." He kissed her cheek, and then her lips. "You can't resist me, Jackie. And those little girls are going to want to know they're fully claimed Callahan."

"I don't know, Pete. There's an awful lot to marriage besides having kids. My parents nearly got divorced when my dad went through malepause. It's bad when the parents aren't entirely suited to each other. The kids suffer." She looked at him. "Marriage is a very serious thing. You can't approach it like a rodeo, all just ride and hang on."

"Sure, that's exactly what it is. You can hang on to me for dear life." He snapped his fingers. "I knew I was forgetting something. I forgot to ask your father for permission to marry you."

He looked so upset that Jackie smiled. "You can ask him later, when we say our vows at your ranch. I always thought that if we did get married, I would love to do it at your family's ranch."

"Oh." Pete looked out the window for a second. "I don't know. Ranch weddings are kind of overdone. Eloping sounds a whole lot more spontaneous and romantic. Don't you think?" He looked at her eagerly.

She sighed. "I give in."

"Whee-hoo!" Pete yelled, punching the air with his fist. "I knew you couldn't wait to be my bride, Jackie, though you played hard to get. Awfully hard to get. *Pfew.*" He didn't want to think about that anymore. She'd agreed, and that was all that mattered. He pulled out his phone. "Now," he said, punching some buttons, "let's see how far we have to drive to get someone to marry us on the spot. I hope you have the money for this. It's bound to be expensive."

"Pete," Jackie said, laughing.

"Well, I'm not cheap. And there's still the matter of your house. If you're going to be on bed rest, I'll have to pick out the new house. Well, what do you know?" he said with satisfaction. "We can get married right here in Santa Fe. Actually, we could get married back in Diablo, but why wait? There's no blood test, you just need your license, social security number and twenty-five bucks. Do you have twenty-five bucks to buy me a marriage license?" He glanced over at her. "No? Lucky for you, I brought some spare change just in case."

"You planned this," Jackie said, and he grinned.

"Come on," Pete said. "Let's find a willing justice."

"Hang on a sec," Jackie said, "you should know I have no intention of moving."

"You just sit over there and imagine three girls fighting over one bathroom, and us waiting our turns, while I find the justice of the peace. I talked to one this morning who thought she had plenty of room in her schedule."

"Is this your version of sweeping me off my feet?"

Pete grinned. "Consider this my first act of sweeping, just like the doctor suggested."

"I don't think that's what he had in mind when he said you'd have to cook and clean."

"That's okay," Pete said, "you just visualize yourself into that so-called magic wedding gown, and let me take care of everything."

THE WEDDING DRESS fitted like, well, magic. Jackie looked at herself in the mirror, admiring the tiny crystal beads and sequins delicately placed on the white satin. It was the most lovely gown she'd ever seen. She *did* feel magical. Pete had overthought the situation as usual, slipping a pair of Cinderella-awesome shoes into the bag he'd "just happened to pick up" along with a darling bouquet of white roses he grabbed at a florist's. Jackie felt like a princess, and the glow in Pete's eyes told her she looked like one, too.

They stood in front of the justice, and Pete's voice didn't even shake when he said "I do." Jackie's knees were knocking together, but Pete was steady as a rock, his big hand holding hers. He kissed her before, during and after the ceremony, and the justice later said she'd never seen a man so eager to get his ring on.

The ring Pete surprised her with brought tears to Jackie's eyes. It was platinum, with two oval diamonds on it. "I'll get you another diamond to match, now that we know we're having three little girlies," he told her, and all Jackie could do was smile at Pete like she'd never smiled in her life.

He insisted on carrying her over the threshold of the courthouse. Jackie let him because he was so excited about it.

"Aren't you disappointed about not having a boy? You already bought boots."

"I'll take them back for some ladylike pink ropers." Pete shrugged, and she thought maybe he wasn't too terribly upset not to be getting at least one boy, since boys were all he'd talked about from the moment he'd learned he was going to be a dad. "We'll have boys next time," Pete said.

Jackie groaned. "You're still working on the bet."

"Nope," he said, "that was one of Fiona's scams." Pete looked at her strangely. "Did I forget to tell you?"

Her heart sank. "Tell me what?"

"Oh." Pete laughed, sounding a bit embarrassed.

"Keep this under your hat, but apparently we've lost the ranch."

Jackie blinked, unable to comprehend what Pete was telling her. He couldn't be so blithe about something so huge. "Pete, what are you talking about?"

He sighed. "This is probably something I should have brought up before now. I got so carried away with the babies, and planning a wedding—"

"Pete. What happened?" Nervous tremors began tickling Jackie.

"I don't know exactly. I just know that getting us all married with families was a scheme on Fiona's part because the ranch is gone. History." He looked at her. "I'm sorry, Jackie. I should have told you before—"

"How can it be gone? As in, she sold it?"

"No." He shrugged. "Some convoluted problem involving Bode Jenkins. He convinced some higher-ups to declare our land for a highway. Fiona persuaded the state that a better route could be found, and thought she'd warded off Bode's land grab. By then, the state had already determined that it should be bought by them, and the final result is that it will end up in Bode's hands. Kind of like when a certain big executive decided he wanted the city to build a big football stadium in Texas, and influenced the state that the people living nearby should have to sell and move. The state may have utilized right of eminent domain to make the people move, but everyone knows who really owns the property." Pete shrugged again. "Fiona says she feels responsible, but all I can see that she did wrong is that she should have come to us, not that I know what we could have done to change the outcome."

"That's terrible! I am so sorry, Pete." Jackie couldn't

imagine anyone taking her house and her little half acre. She'd paid for it with her own hard-earned cash and smarts, and she was pretty certain she'd have to be dragged off her property before anybody took it from her. "Where will the Callahans go now?"

"Fiona didn't say expressly, but I have a hunch that she's counting on Jonas to buy acreage east of here. He's wanting a spread, and we could move operations there. She sort of hinted around about it, although she didn't mention it to him. I'm the only Callahan she's told, and she doesn't want the others to know right now." He sighed. "But I should have told you, Jackie."

"Yes, you should have," she murmured. "I'm so sorry, Pete. I didn't know the Callahans were losing their livelihood."

"We're not," he said, then he frowned. "Well, I guess we are. I never thought of it that way." He brightened. "Let's go back to being happily married. I got a great girl, and you got a perfect guy." He carried her to his truck, and Jackie waited for the inevitable comment she knew was coming.

Pete didn't disappoint her.

"Good thing we got married today," he said, pretending to huff as he set her down. "I won't be able to carry you in a few days, my sweet."

"Not so perfect, after all," Jackie said, but Pete just smiled.

"Let's go put you in bed," he said. "I'm kind of looking forward to a captive audience."

Jackie shook her head at Pete and stared out the window as they drove away from the justice's. She couldn't help feeling some of the day's brightness steal away from her. Maybe she was still in shock over having triplets. Certainly she'd been so stunned that she'd willingly gotten married. Jackie gazed down at her lovely gown, and her beautiful ring and then glanced over at her new husband—a man who had somehow forgotten to tell her a huge new development in his life. She'd been worried that he was marrying her because of the bet between the brothers—now she wondered what else Pete was keeping from her.

He hadn't forgotten to tell her. Somehow she knew he hadn't wanted her to know.

Chapter Sixteen

Three months later, Jackie marveled at the amount of change that had taken over her life, her body and her husband.

"Pete won't leave me for more than an hour," Jackie complained to Darla, "and even then, he wants Fiona to be here to keep an eye on me." She held up a baby bootie she was knitting, a pink, not-ready-for-prime-time first attempt. "Fiona is teaching me to knit, but she says I'm pulling the yarn too tightly. She says I'm tense." Jackie put the bootie down and looked at Darla's sympathetic face. "I'm not complaining. It's just it's a beautiful day outside, and I want to be anywhere but in this recliner."

Pete had installed a leather recliner in the house, her "princess chair" he called it. She didn't feel like a princess. "I underestimated my husband's enthusiasm for keeping me in a prone position."

Darla handed her the week's sales numbers. "That will make you feel better."

Jackie cast her gaze over the numbers, glad to be talking business instead of baby for a moment. "Why are the sales up so much?"

"It's spring. When a young man's fancy turns to thoughts of love?"

Jackie wrinkled her nose. Pete hadn't mentioned anything lately about love. He had been asking her lots of questions, most of them had to do with how she felt— if she had any aches or pains, could she feel the babies kicking, did she want him to make a run for ice cream. "I want to give you the magic wedding dress to sell."

Darla handed her a glass of water and sat down cross-legged on the sofa nearest her. Fanny begged to sit in Darla's lap, and Darla scooped her up. "I know you're not allowed on the furniture," she told Fanny, "so be still for Aunt Darla and don't do anything that gets us both in trouble." She looked back at Jackie. "We can sell the magic wedding dress in a flash. But won't Pete be upset if you don't keep it? Aren't you supposed to redo vows again later?"

Jackie shook her head. "I don't need to redo anything. The first time was fine."

"You said you were in shock and can't remember much except Pete kissing you practically the entire ceremony." Darla giggled. "I would have liked to see that. Anyway, you promised I'd be your maid of honor."

"Did I?" Jackie wrinkled her brows. "I'm pretty sure once was enough for me. Why don't you wear the dress next?"

"Not me." Darla sighed. "I have no one who wants to kiss me breathless at an altar."

Jackie thought Judah was crazy if he couldn't see that Darla was the greatest girl in Diablo. Perfect for him, if he could only pull his head out—

"Anyway," Darla said, interrupting Jackie's not-so-nice thoughts, "I still think Pete would want you to be sentimental about the gown since he went out of his way to get it for you."

"He has a romantic side I never expected," Jackie admitted. "But Sabrina told me that the gown isn't to be kept. The magic has to move on."

Darla petted Fanny, her fingers kneading the border collie's back and stomach. Fanny lay stretched out across Darla, sucking up all the attention she could. "Do you think Sabrina really believes all that airy-fairy stuff she spouts?"

"Does it matter? I wouldn't want to be responsible for clogging up the magic or whatever."

"Have you told Pete?"

"Pete doesn't believe in magic," Jackie said. "He'd scoff at the idea."

"I meant, have you told Pete you're going to get rid of the dress?"

"No." Jackie shifted in the chair. "There are only so many hours in a day."

Darla laughed. "All of which you spend flat on your back, usually getting your feet rubbed or your belly oiled by your prince of a husband."

"It's not that big of a deal." Jackie didn't want to discuss the dress with Pete. "Will you take it to the dry cleaners for me?"

Darla hesitated. "I'll be happy to. Why are you in such a hurry to get rid of it?"

"I told you," Jackie said, "Sabrina told me the dress's magic is in the giving."

"I don't know," Darla said. "This feels like making stock investments based on fortune cookies or something."

"It's probably a pregnancy thing. But I want to do what Sabrina says."

"Fine by me. But what if someone had bought it that wanted to keep it?"

"I guess the magic would have just stayed wrapped up with it in the bag." Jackie couldn't explain it—she knew she'd sound too fanciful—but she *had* felt magical when she'd worn the dress. There had never been a second of doubt that when Pete gave it to her, it was a fairy-tale moment. "Why are people so silly about these things? I wouldn't expect Pete to keep the pair of jeans he was wearing when we got married."

Darla got up and rummaged around in Jackie's cabinet for a bottle of wine. "Can I get you a wineglass of organic apple juice?"

Jackie would have liked the wine. But that was several months away. "Yes, thank you. And don't change the subject."

"I'm not changing the subject." Darla handed her a glass of juice. "Maybe I will take the gown for myself, since you seem sure it really is magic. I could use a Cinderella affair in my life."

"Very selfish of you to hoard magic," Jackie said, nodding, "I approve."

Darla grinned. "It's worth a shot, isn't it?"

Jackie nodded, and sipped her juice. "We could give it a year."

"A year. I don't know, Jackie. I want Judah to fall in love with me, not some creep."

Jackie smiled, thinking about Pete and getting warm all over. "I'm sleeping every night with a big hunky cowboy now. It's worth a shot."

Darla sighed. "With my luck, all I'll catch will be geeks who live with their mothers and whose only social interaction is playing games on the internet."

"Think positive," Jackie said. "A few months ago, I was still working at the hospital and wondering if Pete and I had a future." Which seemed strange now, because she couldn't imagine not getting her hands on him every night. His protective streak got on her nerves, but that was all about the babies. Once she was out of this chair, he'd go back to being normal.

Maybe she didn't want normal with Pete.

"One year," Darla said. "That would take a lot of positive thinking. And a haircut. Maybe some clothes. A trip to Victoria's Secret." She handed Fanny to Jackie. "So, where's the dress?"

PETE WALKED IN five minutes after Darla left. He glanced around. "Where's Darla?"

"She had a few things to do." Jackie smiled up at her big cowboy. "How's the ranch?"

Pete ignored her question. "She's supposed to stay here until I get back."

Jackie frowned. "I have a phone, Pete. I don't need babysitting."

"It's not babysitting." Pete put Fanny outside. "I want someone with you at all times."

Jackie's frown deepened. "That isn't going to always be possible. Anyway, I'm fine."

"I know you are." Pete's face was slightly ashen. "I just want someone with you. Or I will be here."

There were times when he wasn't quite the prince he aspired to be. Jackie sighed. "Come over here and kiss me, you big ape, or I'll send you out for ice cream at midnight."

He kissed her, and magic that had nothing to do with a wedding dress stole over Jackie. She looked up at Pete, her gaze longing. "When I get out of this chair, you better be ready to be an eager husband."

Pete kissed her again, stealing her breath with his attention to detail. Her entire body heated up in places that remembered how good he felt.

"Oh, boy," Pete said, pulling away from her reluctantly. "I think I'll go shower."

Jackie smiled. "A shower wouldn't be too taxing on me, I'm sure. And there are things I can do for you—"

"No." Pete backed away from her chair. "The visiting nurse says you're going to have some type of IV if you keep getting those cramps. Something to help keep the babies inside."

All the warmth left Jackie. It was the first time he'd ever backed away from her in any way—ever. "I know how to take care of myself."

"I know. I know." He sat down on the sofa, a good five feet away from her. "I have baby nerves. Fiona says they'll pass. And I hope they do soon. I think I'm about to wear everyone out, including Sam. And that's not easy, let me tell you."

"Easygoing Sam?" Jackie wanted her husband in her arms right now, but it was clear that wasn't happening. So she tried to follow Pete's lead and adopt nonchalance. "Tell me ranch gossip if you're not going to let me do wifelike things to you in the shower."

Pete gulped. She smiled at him, the picture of innocence. "Wifelike things?"

She nodded. "Things that perhaps involve kissing, soap, warm water and a very skilled pair of hands. Those kind of wifelike things."

He looked at her. "I see."

"So, you were saying about the ranch?" Jackie

checked Pete's jeans, noting with pleasure that he wasn't as immune to her as he'd been acting. "Easygoing Sam doesn't appreciate you being moody?"

"I'm not moody," Pete said. "I've got a lot on my mind."

"Me, maybe?" Jackie said, unbuttoning her top.

He swallowed, watching her every move. "Maybe a little." His gaze lit on her lips, and then the expanse of skin beginning to show between the freed buttons.

He jumped to his feet. "You stay right there, Jackie. I'm going to shower. When I get out, I'll rub your feet."

He hurried off to the shower. Jackie closed her eyes, holding back a shriek of frustration. He was terrified of her doing anything that might hurt the babies.

She was going to scream if this kept up for three more months. "You're in for the surprise of your stubborn life, buddy," she said, getting up from the recliner and pulling off her clothes. She sneaked into the bathroom, where she could see Pete's strong, muscular body under the spray. His eyes were closed as he let the water beat down on his back—and an hour in the shower wasn't going to take care of the issue she could see that he had at the moment.

But she could. She slipped into the shower with him, moving her hands over his erection. Pete's eyes snapped open, and he started to pull away.

But now he was her prisoner. And she wasn't letting him go. She moved her hands along him, caressing him, until she felt his reluctance ebb away. He seemed to strengthen in her hands.

"I've missed you," she said. "You can't keep me in that recliner like a locked-away princess and not let me feel you."

His arms slowly went around her at last, and he held her against him, groaning a little as she stroked him. "I've missed you. You have no idea how much."

She pressed small kisses along his chin. "No more treating me like I'm going to break if you so much as touch me."

He leaned his chin against the top of her head, fully under her spell. "I dream of touching you." Almost reluctantly, he took her breasts in his hands, cupping them, teasing the nipples. "You're scaring me. The doctor said—"

"I'm seducing you." She gently pushed his hands away. "Kiss me. You'll like it, I promise."

So he did. Jackie pushed up against him, her hands teasing him, torturing him, but then drawing him inexorably toward pleasure. It was such a relief to touch him, feel his strong body, that Jackie wanted more, and relief from the heat of remembering what Pete could do to her body.

"After the babies are born," Pete began, and Jackie said, "The honeymoon begins ASAP," and the next thing she knew, he was shuddering against her, holding her the way she'd wanted to be held, and letting her hold him.

His arms locked around her. "You did seduce me," Pete murmured against her wet hair, and Jackie smiled.

"Yes," she said, happy to have her stubborn cowboy back in her arms. "Never think about staying away from me again."

"You win," Pete said, "I'm only a man. Not a prince."

Jackie smiled. He was her prince, but she couldn't allow him to be a tyrant in matters of marital pleasure. He was just going to have to let her please him often.

AFTER JACKIE'S RATHER SKILLED seduction of him—and Pete had to admit he'd loved every second—he made sure he put her right back in her recliner. "The home nurse says you are to stay still," he said, kissing her forehead to take the sting out of his words. "Not that I don't seriously appreciate your foxy side. But I have to think for the five of us. That means you have everything you need right here." He pointed to the TV remote, the portable phone, a glass of water and Fanny, whom he'd placed in her lap. "And I don't want you alone, either, Jackie, not even for fifteen minutes. Either me, or the home nurse, or Darla, or Fiona or even Jonas, if necessary, since he's still a doctor, must be with you."

"That's what the phone is for, Pete," Jackie said through gritted teeth. "So that people don't have to spend their days sitting here watching me like a nesting duck. I'm a nurse," she reminded him, as though Pete could ever forget it.

"But you're not a doctor," he said, dropping a kiss on her nose. "And these are my babies. I don't want to take any chances. So from now on, you don't move. I'll take care of everything."

She glared at him. "Pete, you're going to be a wonderful father. And I appreciate this newly protective side of you. Believe me when I say that in five years, I never thought you cared so much—"

"Well, you were wrong." He folded his arms across his chest. "I cared."

"But now you care a lot," she said. "Too much."

He shook his head. "Either the sofa, the bed or the recliner. But you, my love, will stay in a horizontal position until our little girls are ready to see their father's handsome face." He kissed her on the lips, ducking back when she took a gentle swipe at him. "Oh, my little hellcat. I do love you." He gently patted her tummy, then went into the kitchen. "So what can I make you for dinner, my turtledove?"

Pete smirked to himself. He was pretty certain that if he'd been anywhere near Jackie, that last statement would have gotten the remote launched at his head. His lady was impatient and on edge, and he couldn't blame her. Pete couldn't imagine being confined to a recliner. "You probably think this is all my fault," he called out to her.

"Probably," she said, and he grinned.

"Egg salad?" he asked. "Or pancakes. Fiona sent the egg salad. I can whip up mean pancakes. Your choice, my love."

"I'm not hungry."

She'd been plenty hungry for him not thirty minutes ago. Pete frowned and walked back out to the den. "I know this is hard on you. I'm trying to help."

Jackie shook her head. "I'm sorry. I know you are. And it's not bad. I have all these wonderful books to read. There are three hundred channels on the TV. I'm catching up on movie classics, and that's really fun. I've been ordering DVDs on my laptop and building a collection of family movies between researching other wedding shops across the country. But it's not the same."

"Try being the guy who can't give his wife any pleasure at the moment," he said. "It's embarrassing."

"Embarrassing?" She looked surprised.

"What do you think? While I appreciate your efforts, it's not as much fun without you screaming hallelujahs in my ear, Jackie. It's bad for my ego." He thought about it for a minute, trying to explain. "It's like yelling into a canyon and nothing comes back."

"Coming without me isn't good?"

"It's not bad," he said, "but it's not as good, either."

"Oh," Jackie said. "I thought men just—"

He held up a hand. "Common misconception. But men are not cave-dwellers in search of the one-sided orgasm. Trust me. Some of us have evolved. And we like being joined in the hallelujah chorus. In fact, several hallelujah choruses. A hat trick is best."

Jackie nodded. "Thank you for explaining that. Now I'm even more hot and bothered."

"I knew it," he said. "It's best we leave sex off the menu for now. Back to the pancakes or whatever else your heart desires."

"My heart desires you."

He sighed. "You, my sweet, must just lie there and look pretty."

She threw a pillow that caught him square in the face. "What?"

"Go," Jackie said, sounding like she meant it. "And next time you think of me, think of me in my nurse's uniform, taking your temperature in a place you won't appreciate, you male chauvinist—

"Hang on," Pete said, "I'm just saying—"

"I have knitting needles," she said. "You should go now." She brandished a needle from which hung a pink bootie that didn't look all that successful to him—not that he planned on mentioning it to his angel cake while she was in this rather surly mood.

"All right. I'm going to get pasta. With veggies, because that will be healthy. And when I get back, we'll have a picnic right here." He gave her his best how's-that-deal? smile and got a finger pointed at the door for his effort.

"I won't be gone long," Pete said. "I've got my cell phone if you need me, if you need anything at all—"

"Go!"

PETE RAN INTO CREED at the Italian family restaurant. "Why are you here?" he asked as he slid into the booth where his brother sat nursing a brewski.

"Fiona didn't cook anything tonight. She said we were on our own." Creed shrugged. "Usually she gets ruffled if some of us don't show up for dinner. But she's been acting a little moody lately."

"Must be something in the water." Pete thought about Jackie and decided she had cause to be as moody as she liked. "Is Aunt Fiona feeling all right?"

"She's fine." Creed shook his head, his black hair wild and unbrushed. He needed a shave, Pete noticed, or he was thinking about growing an unattractive mop on his face. And he looked glum. "Bode Jenkins came over, and the two of them had an unpleasant meeting of the minds, to choose polite terms."

Pete straightened. "What did Bode want?"

"I don't know. Burke told me about it. That's the only reason I can guess at what upset Fiona."

"That bastard," Pete said, "I'll kick his ass."

"No need. Judah already did. Sort of. As much as you can kick an old man's ass." Creed scratched his chin. "I think he just yelled at him and told him he'd kick him good if he didn't move his carcass off Callahan property. And Bode said it wasn't going to be Callahan property much longer, and then Fiona fainted. I think." Creed swallowed half his beer, then nodded. "Yeah. Jonas said she'd fainted."

"Damn," Pete said. "I can't tell whose butt I need to be laying out if you're going to change the facts every time you draw a breath."

"It happened so fast. Fiona's like a badger, you know, so we weren't too worried about her, but then Bode dropped his ace card and Fiona went lights out. Hell, Pete, I thought she'd kicked it."

Pete went cold. "She's tougher than that. She'll outlive us all."

"Yeah." Creed swallowed some more beer, then shook his head. "Anyway, so now we all know about the secret Fiona's been hiding. She said we're losing the ranch."

Pete shook his head. "I guess."

Creed narrowed his eyes. "Did you already know?"

"I knew a little about it," Pete said, "though I was never sure Fiona had told me everything. You know how she dribbles out bits and pieces. And it's never clear exactly what's really going on."

"But you knew. And you didn't tell any of us." Creed looked mad as hell.

Pete shrugged. "She asked me not to."

"But you knew there wasn't going to be a ranch for any of us to win. You knew that all along. You would have let us head to the altar for no reason." Creed glared at him.

Pete shrugged. "You weren't in any danger, were you?"

"I might have been! And you would have let me walk the plank!"

"Nah."

"Oh, yes, you wouldn't have stopped me." Creed jutted his scraggly chin out. "Do you have any idea how much we've been worrying about this whole marriage bet?"

"Who's we?"

"The rest of us. Those of us who weren't picking out brides."

Pete shook his head. "As I recall, you were all too happy to let me be the fall guy."

"And so we were. But we didn't know Jackie would marry you at the time. Any of us might have ordered a bride. Gotten a subscription to an online dating service. I seriously thought about it." Creed gulped. "But marriage is not for the faint of heart, and my heart is faint when it comes to commitment."

"I know," Pete said sourly. "You weren't in any danger. So cool it."

"Still. Brothers shouldn't hold back pertinent information, especially when it comes to Fiona." Creed paused. "I've been sitting here thinking, and I've worked it over pretty well in my mind, and...I'm going back on the rodeo circuit."

Pete sighed. "Don't make a hasty decision."

"There's nothing else for us to do. We're all in the process of thinking through our options. Jonas put an offer on the ranch east of here. Judah's going back to rodeo for a while. Rafe is seriously considering hiring on with the Shamrock ranch. And Sam...well, he says he'll probably be Fiona's bodyguard. Or go do some bullfighting. He'd make a damn lousy clown, in my opinion. Wasn't very good at it before. Still, a man's got to do something, and if we have no livelihood here, then what the hell can any of us do? Can't sit around on our duffs watching our family home go up in a puff of smoke."

Pete shook his head. "Nothing good can come of Sam and bullfighting."

Creed shrugged. "He says someone has to hang around to make Bode's life a misery. He says he's either going to take his aggression out on Bode or on bulls. He hasn't decided yet."

"Marvelous," Pete said, "this is all just ducky as hell."

His cell phone rang. Pete pulled it from his pocket, snapping it open when he saw the call was from Darla.

"Pete?" Darla said. "Thank God I reached you. Your phone hasn't been ringing."

He frowned. Maybe the reception in the restaurant was poor. "What's up?" he asked, his body tensing, his thoughts immediately on Jackie.

"It's nothing," Darla said, but she didn't sound like her normally bouncy self. Pete held the phone tightly against his ear so he could hear her. "At least I hope it's nothing. Jackie was having a little stomachache, a bit more cramping than usual, so she called me and I came over to sit with her. Then I decided to call the doctor and he suggested we swing her by the hospital."

Pete stood up, tossed some money on the table. He knew he shouldn't have let Jackie stand so long. Maybe hot showers weren't good for pregnant women. They'd had harsh words between them, perhaps a toxic stew for tiny angels. "I'll be right there."

He snapped the phone shut. "Jackie's gone to the

hospital," he told Creed, his body feeling queer and not part of himself anymore as he hurried to his truck.

Dear God. Please let her be fine. I only just made her mine.

Chapter Seventeen

The scary—and amazing—part was that Pete was a father faster than he'd ever dreamed he could be. One day he was thinking *marriage,* and today Pete realized they hadn't bought cribs. Diapers. Toys. Hadn't even talked about it.

Pete wasn't even sure how they were going to fit three babies into the small guest room. But he looked at Jackie's worn-out face and thought she was beautiful, tough and strong, and he knew everything was going to be fine.

He smoothed her hair away from her face. He still didn't understand exactly what had gone wrong. Or maybe nothing had gone wrong. Perhaps the babies had just decided there was too little room inside his petite wife for all of them to be comfortable. He hadn't had a chance to talk to the doctor yet.

He kissed Jackie on the forehead. "Mrs. Callahan, you have three very small, very beautiful little daughters. And do you know something? They all have your cute nose."

Jackie smiled wanly. "They have all their fingers and toes?"

"They're perfect. Little angels."

His heart hammered inside him. What was he going to do now? He had to learn how to bathe babies. He'd looked them over carefully as the nurses gently suctioned them, weighed them, measured them. It had taken every bit of self-control not to beg the nurses to be more careful with his tiny progeny—the babies looked so helpless, so fragile. More fragile than anything he'd ever seen in his life. Fanny was bigger and stronger than his daughters.

He was scared as hell.

"I love you," he said to Jackie.

"I love you, too." She closed her eyes.

"Jackie," he said, close to her ear so that she wouldn't feel like she had to open her eyes and look at him, "I'm...I'm losing it here."

She opened her eyes and reached for his hand to squeeze. "Everything is fine."

He swallowed. "You scared the hell out of me. I think I hurt you. Maybe we had too much...I mean, I can't bear that you were in pain."

She shook her head. "I've always wanted children. I didn't think I could have them. Whatever pain I had was such a small sacrifice that I've already forgotten about it."

He glanced around at the nurses, who were paying him no attention at all. Their whole focus was on his darling bundles of joy. But the emergency C-section weighed heavily on his mind. What if there'd been a problem? "Jackie," he whispered. "Is it okay with you if these are all the children we have? I don't think I can live with the fear of losing you."

But Jackie had fallen asleep so his agonized soul-searching was his alone. Pete took a deep breath and tried to get a grip on himself.

"Mr. Callahan," a nurse said, "we're going to take the babies down to neo-natal now."

The babies. He probably looked like a cold-hearted sonofagun not to be over there staring with pride at his sweet girls. But he was nervous. They'd been fixed up with tubes and warmers and things, and he didn't think he'd ever be able to change a diaper without worrying that he'd pull off a leg. Accidentally snap off a tiny toe. God, he'd seen corn kernels bigger than those toes. He gulped. "Thank you."

He looked back to Jackie, embarrassed that he didn't feel more for his daughters. Jackie was all he could think about. "Never again," he told her, though she slept like an enchanted princess. "No more pregnancies. This is it for me. I want the rest of our lives together to be one long Saturday night."

CREED FOUND PETE collapsed face-down on Jackie's shoulder, even as Pete sat bunched in a chair beside her. Creed set the flowers and the huge pink-and-white teddy bears he'd brought on a table and sighed. "Pete. You're gonna have a helluva of a backache tomorrow."

Pete didn't move. In fact, he looked as dead to the world as Jackie. And in that moment Creed realized his brother loved Jackie Samuels with all his heart and soul. It hadn't been about the bet, though maybe that had provided a push. Pete was part of Jackie, and Jackie was part of Pete, and the two of them shared something that was missing in his own life.

Creed sighed and went to find his diminutive nieces. They were wailing in the nursery, shaking tiny fists while nurses tended to them. He had to admit that his nieces didn't look much like Callahans. They weren't brawny, or beefy or beautiful. "Whew, you'd think Pete might have turned out a little better gene material than that," he muttered.

But the nurses looked a lot more appealing. Creed perked up as three nurses hovered around the bassinets. There were tubes and breathing apparatuses and things that looked painful on his nieces, so Creed focused on the shapely nurses.

He didn't want a nurse, he decided. Jackie had been a nurse. Then she'd opened a bridal salon. And then she'd done this. He rubbed his chin, wondering where he'd ever find a woman that was the other half of him, as Pete had. The trouble with women was that you couldn't buy them and sell them like cattle or horses. If you got a bad one, you were stuck.

Stuck would be bad.

Pete could handle the situation they'd all gotten him into, because Pete was responsible. Creed liked to think of himself as more footloose. Actually, he was probably more in tune with his inner being and didn't need the security of another person. Pete was needy, Creed decided. This was all Jonas's fault. If Jonas hadn't left to go to a fancy Ivy League school up north, and then stayed the hell away to get his medical degree and training, Pete wouldn't have turned out to be Mr. Responsibility.

I'm not ready for any of what Pete's bitten off.

Fiona rushed to the nursery window. "Look at them! Oh, my! Have you ever seen anything more beautiful than those little babies?"

He had, but Fiona probably wouldn't take his observation well so he kept his mouth shut. "They're no bigger than newborn piglets," he observed, and Fiona popped him a smart one on the arm.

"They'll grow." She stared happily through the window, her whole body practically vibrating with joy. Creed put his arm around his aunt, giving her a fond hug. "You've done yourself proud."

"I did?" She looked at him.

"Well, if you hadn't spurred Pete into marriage—"

He stopped when her face fell. "No, no. Focus on the babies. Look how cute they are! I think that one in the middle has your nose, Aunt Fiona."

Fiona looked distressed. "These children have no place to live. And it's all my fault."

Creed looked at her. "Why would it be your fault?"

"I lost the ranch." She gazed up at him with huge, tear-filled eyes. "And where are these babies going to grow up? Run? Play?"

"At Jackie's house?" Creed asked.

"Pooh. Jackie's house is no bigger than a dollhouse. I was there the other day. She doesn't even have a nursery set up."

He blinked. "Nothing?"

"Not even a crib. Besides which, there's probably only twelve hundred square feet in the entire cottage."

"I think that's Pete's business, Aunt Fiona," Creed said, his tone reluctant.

"These angels don't even have names! Callahan number 1, Callahan number 2 and Callahan number 3. What is that, I ask you?" Fiona peered through the glass. "Not that I care what anyone thinks, mind you, but for heaven's sakes, at least have names on the bassinets when my friends come to visit."

Creed shook his head. "That's for Pete and Jackie to decide."

"They're slow about it." Fiona looked disgusted, then brightened. "Creed, I think that little redheaded nurse is smiling at you," she said, giving him a playful dig in the side that the nurse noticed. She batted her eyes at Creed, and he stepped away from the window, his heart palpitating. In fact, he'd broken out in a nervous sweat.

His destiny was clear. He had to get out of Diablo. Fiona was done working on Pete, and if he wasn't careful, she'd turn her attention to *his* bachelor state. The sacrifice—Pete—had gone down like a newbie bull rider. And now there was no reason to worry about the ranch anymore.

She was going to work him like a bear in a circus. He did not want to be next on her to-do list.

"Don't you worry about a thing, Aunt Fiona," Creed said, giving her a kiss on the forehead even as he backed away from his plotting aunt and the attractive redhead eyeing him. "I'll see you later."

Fiona's gaze was on Pete's three daughters, and Creed made his getaway.

If he didn't watch out, he was going to end up like Pete—with a wife, babies and a gingerbread house. Creed broke into a run as he hit the exit.

"Jackie," Pete said when she opened her eyes an hour later. "Look what the teddy-bear fairy brought."

He pointed to the three enormous bears sitting up on the table. "Our daughters won't be as big as those bears when they're in fifth grade."

Jackie smiled. "They'll grow. I just need to feed them."

He jumped to his feet, realizing his beautiful wife had to be hungry. "Can I get you something? A drink? Something to eat?"

"A new body." Jackie shifted with a groan. "Pete, what do you think about the babies?"

Pete straightened. "Um, they look just like their mother. Gorgeous. They seem bossy, too. Very opinionated about what they want." He shot her a careful glance. "I like that in a woman, as you know."

Jackie looked at her husband. "Did you get within three feet of them?"

"Ah...not yet," he hedged. "But I will. When they aren't like tiny loaves of bread."

"Pete Callahan, I never thought I'd see the day when you were afraid of anything." Jackie smiled at him. "Although I don't think you were too happy when you locked yourself in the basement."

"I didn't—oh, hell." He sat down next to her. "Can you drink a beer? Wine? I feel like I need a small shot of courage."

Jackie was already tired again. "Go down and see our daughters. Then go celebrate."

"I'm not leaving you." Pete picked up her hand, caressing it with his lips. "I shouldn't have left you today."

"The babies were ready to be born, Pete. Whether or not you were there to stop it, they were coming."

He shook his head, and she knew her stubborn cowboy was having trouble dealing with everything. She loved him for it. "Don't worry. You're going to be a great father."

"How do you know? I haven't had any experience. I have no role model. I'd like to bottle them until they're eighteen, and then send them off to college."

"Pete." Jackie laughed. "You remind me of Mr. Dearborn."

"I'm nothing like Mr. Dearborn. I'm far better looking."

"Tell that to Jane. She will not agree." Jackie ran her fingers through Pete's shaggy black hair. She didn't think he'd touched a brush in twenty-four hours. Life had certainly changed a lot for her cowboy. "Do you want to go shave and change your clothes?"

"I'm not leaving. So back to Mr. Dearborn and why he gets to share my wife's mind when she thinks of me."

"He was a pain," Jackie said with a smile. "My most needy patient, by far. He wanted more attention, so he got it. And I knew he was trying to get my attention, but I couldn't help myself. He was cute when he complained. He did it so nicely, and I knew he was doing it on purpose."

Pete frowned. "But I'm not a complainer, nor am I needy."

Jackie laughed. "You're needy."

"My wife just had triplet daughters. I'm entitled to be a little off my normally rugged and independent game."

He pressed a kiss to her wrist, then put her hand down. "I have fantasies about getting in this hospital bed with you, Mrs. Callahan."

She patted the bed. "Bring it on, cowboy."

"You, me and at least a bed will be happening as soon as the doctor pronounces you healed. Until then, you're on a Pete diet." He slightly pulled away from her, leaning back in the uncomfortable chair. "So, don't you think we should discuss names?"

Jackie blinked. "Fiona, Molly and Elizabeth. Didn't you tell the nurses?"

He looked at her. "Did I miss a bulletin, wife?"

"Did we need to discuss it? I wouldn't think baby names are your thing, Pete."

"I think we should discuss everything."

"Then you choose some names."

Pete hesitated. "I haven't had time to think about names."

"Surely there are some that you like." Jackie waited, amused that her husband seemed to get more flustered by the moment.

"I don't know any girl names. And you've caught me off guard. I don't think well when I'm rattled." Pete gazed around the room as if looking for clues. "I was just thinking it was time to buy a baby book."

"I think we're past the book stage, husband. I'd go buy cribs and diapers, washcloths, towels, that sort of thing," Jackie suggested.

Pete looked horrified. "We haven't bought anything. Jackie, we have to have car seats to get the babies home from the hospital." Pete stood up so fast he nearly knocked over the chair. "I've got a lot to do."

Jackie was about to say so *go do it* when the man who walked into her room made the words go completely away.

Chapter Eighteen

Pete bristled, stepping in front of Bode Jenkins and his caregiver. "Hello, Sabrina," Pete said politely. To the man standing next to her, carrying an umbrella he used as a walking stick, Pete said, "To what do we owe the honor of this unexpected visit, Jenkins?"

Bode grinned at him. Pete told himself no new father took a swing at visitors. He held his fire.

"Your folks mentioned you'd had your babies, Jackie," Bode said, ignoring Pete. "I come bearing gifts." He handed her some flowers, beautiful pink tulips in a vase, which she had set on the nightstand.

Pete glanced at Sabrina. She shrugged at him, clearly not aware of why Bode had had her drive him to see Jackie. Every protective instinct Pete possessed roared to life. "You've given your gift, now shove off, Jenkins."

"Have a seat, Sabrina," Bode told his caregiver after Sabrina had hugged Jackie, then he sat down himself. "Pete, I'm here to make you an offer you can't refuse."

"Try me."

Bode laughed. "Don't be so hasty, son. You've got three daughters to think about. They're tiny now, but one day they'll need a place to bring their friends. And later, their dates." He smiled at Jackie. "You'd be surprised how time flies."

"It's not flying now because you're still here." Pete frowned. "What the hell do you want, Jenkins?"

Bode stretched out his legs, glancing at Sabrina as if they shared a secret. "I'm proposing to sell you five acres of your ranch, Callahan. You can build a house there that'll fit this brood you've acquired." He smiled at Jackie. "A man needs room to spread out, darlin'."

Jackie started to say something, but Pete forestalled his gentle bride's words. "*Five* acres?" It was an insult, a slap in his face to embarrass him in front of Jackie and remind him that Bode had him by the shorts. "I don't require much room, Bode. Our family will do just fine where we are."

Bode raised a brow. "Three daughters, a wife and a big man all sharing a tiny house that used to be a rental property for an elderly woman who had no means? Come on, Pete. You could use five acres. You can at least have a garden patch on five acres."

Pete's blood was on full boil. "Whatever you did to my aunt makes business between you and me impossible."

"Oh, now. Don't be sore about that. Especially when I'm offering to let you have five acres, Callahan. You've got a family to think about. It's land you could at least sell if you needed money."

So I'm supposed to beg for the crumbs of my family home. Pete squared his jaw, forcing himself not to cold-cock another man on his daughters' birthday. It would be a bad thing to do. "And if I wanted to do business with you—which would be a cold day in Hell—what would it cost me?"

"Not a dime," Bode said.

Jackie's gaze was on Pete. Her eyes were huge with some emotion he couldn't name. If Bode had meant to shame him, he was doing an excellent job. The way the man put it, Pete couldn't provide for his own family— which, though none of Bode's business, was galling if people were to think that about a man who considered himself Mr. Responsibility. "Out," he told Bode, "get out. If you have business to discuss with me, don't do it here when my wife's just given birth, you miserable sack of—" He held himself back with great effort that choked the words in his throat. "Get out before I do something to you only my brothers would do better."

"Let him say his piece, Pete," Jackie said quickly. "We agreed all decisions would be made between us."

"No, we didn't," Pete replied. "You named the babies without me."

Jackie blinked. It seemed that she shrank back a little. Her hands clutched the sheets as she stared at him. *Oh, hell. Bode wants us to doubt our marriage, wants to find our weak link.* "Out," he told the man, "before I kick your ass up between your ears and roll you down the hall."

Sabrina got to her feet and helped Bode from his chair. The tall, white-haired man allowed her to do it, but he grinned at Pete. "Let me know, son, when you want to talk business. All I want is information about the silver mine hidden on my new property, and for your trouble, five acres is all yours."

Pete jammed his hands in his jeans so he wouldn't swing. He was going to be the bigger man here. And he and Jackie were not going to have their first argument just because of a jackass.

Bode and Sabrina left, after Sabrina hugged Jackie, surreptitiously whispering something in Jackie's ear.

"What?" Pete asked after they'd left. The urge to move quickly, repair whatever damage Jenkins had done between him and Jackie, took him to his wife's side. "Why are you looking at me like that?"

"I'm not looking at you like anything," Jackie said. But her gaze fell to her hands.

"Jackie?" He felt her slipping away from him.

"I'm so tired right now," she murmured. "Good night, Pete."

She closed her eyes and he was left out, his hands in fists at his sides, even as he knew Bode Jenkins, that snake in the grass, had made a first strike.

JACKIE KNEW EXACTLY when Pete left. She feigned sleep, needing to gather her thoughts. What Bode had said about Pete needing more room scared her to death. It was true. There was no way she could insist that a big man share a bathroom and a tiny cottage with her and their daughters. It didn't make sense, and she'd been unreasonable.

Her house had been the last piece of herself she could keep, and she'd protected her turf without any thought of Pete's needs. She'd been so shocked by the pregnancy, and then finding out they were having multiple babies, that she hadn't considered living space until it was too late. She hadn't even decorated a nursery. She'd been too busy thinking about her new business.

Defense, she'd been playing defense.

A nurse came in to record her vitals. "How are you doing?"

"Fine. How are my daughters?" Jackie sat up, eager to hear.

"Doing fine and keeping everyone busy."

"When do I get to feed them?"

"In a little while, after you've rested."

Jackie looked at her. "Is my...husband at the nursery?"

The nurse shook her head. "No. His aunt and uncle are, though. They had an awful squabble a few moments ago with a visitor." She smiled at Jackie. "Your aunt won."

Bode had paid a visit to the nursery. She'd have to ask Sabrina what had happened later. Sabrina was on her side. She had whispered in her ear that Bode didn't mean any harm; he really just wanted to see the babies. And he was upset that he hadn't been invited to the wedding. But no one had been. There really hadn't been a wedding, not that she cared what Bode Jenkins thought. She wouldn't invite him, anyway, if he was always going to torture poor Fiona. "What happened?"

"I don't know exactly. She called him a thief, and he called her a mismanaging airhead. I thought she was going to lay him out. Her driver had to separate them." The nurse laughed. "We don't get many little elderly people raising a ruckus around here."

"Can you ask Fiona to come in here, please?" It was imperative that she speak to her.

"You don't need more visitors," the nurse said. "You need to rest."

Suddenly, Jackie knew exactly how Mr. Dearborn had felt—trapped and helpless. The exact way Pete was probably feeling right now, if she wasn't quick about putting things right.

But she'd learned a trick or two from Mr. Dearborn. "I was once a nurse here," she said, a little wistfully. "Sometimes I miss working with patients. And you're new at the hospital, aren't you?"

"I've been here three weeks." The nurse picked up her chart. "Is there anything I can get you?"

"Yes. You can get me Aunt Fiona," Jackie said, her voice sweetly determined. "I'll rest so much better once I see her cheery face."

The nurse walked to the door, smiling. "I heard you used to sneak some of your favorite patients chocolate. Particularly the difficult ones."

"Are you planning on bringing me some chocolate?" Jackie asked.

"Nope. But I'll get your aunt."

She left, and Jackie winced at the stitches in her stomach. "Good. I was about to get cranky with you," she muttered.

But then Fiona fluttered into the room, and Jackie launched her plan.

"The babies," Fiona said, "they are such darlings! I can't wait to hold them! How are you doing, my dear?"

She carefully leaned in to hug Jackie.

"I'm fine, Fiona," Jackie said, "but I'm afraid I need a huge favor."

"Babysitting, cooking, some new nighties from the store in town I hear you like shopping at?" Fiona said, eyeing her hospital gown.

"Darla's gone to get me some things. I didn't think I'd need a bag when she brought me to the hospital. We thought we would only be here for a quick check to soothe her nerves. I hadn't even packed a suitcase for the hospital. But I have something else that must be done. And you will have to keep it totally secret, please, Fiona. Absolutely under your hat."

"Oh, good," Fiona said, her face beaming. "Now what do you need me to do?"

"I NEED HELP," PETE TOLD JONAS. His brother sat at the rugged plank table in the bunkhouse, and the others—except Creed, who'd gone off somewhere, clearly out of cell phone reach because no one could get him to answer—lounged around the room, celebrating the birth of Pete's daughters and the successful hatching of The Plan.

But it wasn't a success yet, because his angels needed him. And their father planned to ride to their rescue.

After that, he'd rescue his wife from his total wipe-out as a husband. Bode Jenkins wasn't going to win this round. "I need help from all of you."

"If this is about my nieces, I'll do anything except change diapers," Sam said. "And clean spit-up. Hurl is hard for me to look at."

"You're a moron," Judah said. "Babies don't hurl. Not much, anyway. Not like you do after a bender, for example."

Rafe lifted a beer in Sam's direction. "You'll have to toughen up, Sam. Pete's not going to be sleeping much for the next couple of weeks, and we all need to help him out. When do the babies leave the hospital, Pete?"

"I'm not sure. They only weighed about four pounds each." That alone scared the hell out of Pete. "Does anybody remember what we weighed?"

"It would say on your birth record," Jonas said, "and Fiona's probably got that buried somewhere."

"It doesn't matter. I'm pretty sure I wasn't four

pounds." He remembered Sam when he'd arrived at the ranch. Sam had been about as big as a ten-pound sack of new potatoes. Pete's daughters were more like good-sized Idaho spuds. He glanced around at his brothers, not liking the new helpless feelings swamping him. "They're so small they could be in the hospital for a month."

"No," Jonas said. "We have to think positive. The delivering physician said that they were healthy, just underweight. That's a good sign."

Pete drew a relieved breath. "Jackie and I made no plans for anything."

"We know." Rafe grinned. "You've been very disorganized about becoming a father, which isn't like you at all. But we've been impressed that you've pulled it off, Pete. We didn't give you a snowball's chance, frankly."

"Glad you've got my back." The jackasses were ribbing him, and he appreciated the brotherly love but he still felt as if a whirlwind had blown into his life, spewing everything in forty directions. "So, are you going to help me or not?"

"What do you need?" Judah asked.

"No diapers," Sam reminded him.

"I need a nursery," Pete said. "I'd make you a list, but I have no idea what babies need."

"You want us to round up all your baby stuff?" Jonas said.

"Right." Pete nodded. "Diapers, cribs, the works."

Sam looked scared. "You want us to make a nursery?"

"It's a lot to ask. But you can do it." Pete sat straight, still boiling mad about Bode's visit. "It's got to work. My turtledove doesn't want to leave her house. Bode's offered me five acres of Rancho Diablo land in exchange for me telling him where the silver mine is."

They all stared at him.

"Silver mine?" Judah repeated. "Is that rumor making the rounds again?"

"Yes." Pete nodded. "But never mind that. It was the look on Jackie's face that warned me I have to take drastic steps. She was actually *listening* to the old coot."

"There's no silver mine," Jonas said. "So who cares what he thinks?"

"There's no nursery, either. Bode told Jackie I wouldn't be happy in her house. That it was too small. That a man needed to spread out. And she looked crushed." He took a deep breath, still angry. "Bode must be the one who locked me in the basement. And searched the house. That's why Fiona's jars and everything she'd stored were destroyed in the basement. I know he did it."

"Because he was looking for silver?" Judah asked.

"Exactly." Pete nodded. "That's why he wants the ranch."

"There's no silver," Sam said, "there's nothing but hard work here. And the Diablos."

They sat silently. Ghostly horses that ran free across the ranch, full of spirit that never could be tamed, their midnight-black manes and tails flying. They were the treasure of Rancho Diablo.

"I saw Fiona's friend the other day," Sam murmured.

Everyone stared at Sam.

"And?" Pete prompted.

"He was on a black-and-white horse, looking down the mesa at our house." Sam shrugged. "He raised a hand when he saw me, and then he left."

Pete shook his head. "Maybe Fiona gives him black-berry jelly or canned asparagus from the basement. Have any of us considered just asking her why Running Bear visits her every year?"

They all shook their heads at him. Pete sighed to himself. It didn't matter. He was moving on, if Jackie would have him forever. She just had to want him as much as he wanted her. Otherwise he'd be like one of the lobos, howling every night at her door. "What are we going to do about Fiona? And Burke?" he asked suddenly.

"I haven't entirely surrendered to the notion that Bode's getting our land," Jonas said. "In the meantime, I did make an offer on the ranch east of here. We can set up operations there. Fiona and Burke can manage the new place, if it comes to that."

Pete felt slightly better that there was a plan for their extended family members. "I haven't surrendered, either," he said, feeling a growl start in his body. "Even if Bode does get the ranch, he's not going to sabotage my marriage." Things were dicey enough. He did know one thing: It would be a cold day in Hell before he gave up one small part of his marriage to anyone, or anything.

"First things first," Rafe said. "We've got baby rig to shop for, and that alone is a tall order. Do you know if Jackie has a particular color she wants for the nursery? I think color scheme may be important to a woman."

Pete thought about Jackie's white, lacy bedroom, a place he couldn't wait to be again, with her, holding her, making her his. "White. Completely white. Maybe some pink, but white and lacy and all little girl."

"Not that I know what I'm talking about," Judah said, "but isn't white supposed to pick up dirt easily?

Is it a wise choice for three little infants who are going to do tons of…things Sam doesn't want to clean up?"

Pete smiled at his brothers, happier than he'd ever been in his life. "All white," he said, "and very, very soft. Like rose petals."

"Jeez, you've got it bad," Sam said.

"I hope I never say anything that unfortunate," Judah agreed. "Are you aware that you are starting to sound like Creed with his poetic soul? And I wouldn't be bragging about it, either."

Pete grinned. "One day," he said, "you'll find yourselves wearing wedding rings, and you won't be crying. And I'll get to enjoy every moment of your transformation."

"Great." Jonas stood. "Let's head out. We've got a lot of work to do."

Chapter Nineteen

In the end, Fiona got wind of the nursery scheme, and
that meant the Books 'n' Bingo Society got involved,
which pretty much meant the entire town pitched in on
the project. There were people coming and going for
days. There was sawing, hammering, painting and elderly people taking Fanny for walks so she wouldn't go
crazy from all the noise in the small house. Pete was
only dimly aware of what was going on. He spent almost every second at the hospital with Jackie and the
babies, only leaving to shower at Rancho Diablo. He
had a toothbrush and a few changes of clothes at Jackie's but he hadn't moved totally in yet. They'd only been
married for a few months, and he'd been traveling back
and forth between her place and his, making sure she
stayed in her recliner, and working at the ranch.

So when he finally took Jackie and the babies home,
even he was shocked at what had happened to her house.
The guest bedroom had been gutted. Two closets had
been cut out and shelved, and at least twenty baby
dresses hung in them. He couldn't tell how many nighties and other clothes were stacked neatly on the shelves,
but there were even tiny baby socks and shoes. Pete
thought it looked like an entire department store had

been bought out. The hardwood floors gleamed. The walls were repainted a soft white, and a pink-roses-and-lace curtain topper hung over the window. Three white cribs lined a wall, each with pink-and-white gingham sheets and comforters, and even mobiles from which miniature giraffes, monkeys, and elephants hung. Their names—Fiona, Molly and Elizabeth—were painted on plaques above each bed. On a white table nearby, diapers, wipes, fluffy towels and washcloths were neatly stacked. There was a rocking chair, a swing, a huge pink stroller and bouncy seats.

They wouldn't have to buy anything for years.

He turned to see the joy he knew would be on Jackie's face. She looked stunned—and not too happy.

"What did you do?" she asked him, her brown eyes huge.

"I didn't do anything. I just asked for a little help from my brothers. And everybody else pitched in. We'll be writing thank you notes for months." He couldn't believe how perfect the nursery was. It was everything little babies would dream of, if they dreamed of anything except being held and fed. "Do you like it?"

Jackie sank into the rocker, still staring at the room. She glanced at the babies in the car carriers they'd brought in. Fiona, Molly and Elizabeth were sound asleep, nestling under pink blankets and without a care in the world. "I don't know what to say," Jackie said. "It's beautiful. I've never seen anything like it."

"Good." Pete grinned at her, totally pleased with himself. "This is a comfortable room even for a man. I'm going to be in that rocker more than you are. It glides back and forth, and the baby monitor is right here. I'll be able to call you whenever I want something."

He was so proud. He was trying so hard. Jackie wanted to cry. Having to burst his happiness was going to be the hardest thing she'd ever done.

"Pete," she said, reaching out to take her husband's hand, "maybe I should have talked to you first."

"About what?"

He looked at her and Jackie sighed. "I was going to sell the house."

His handsome face stayed completely immobile. A tiny tickle of worry ran through Jackie. "I have to," she said. "You would never be happy here. You hadn't even brought most of your stuff here. It's a doll's house suitable for a single woman. But not for a man, and not for a family."

Pete's face darkened. "You shouldn't listen to Bode. He doesn't know me."

"I know." Jackie squeezed his hand. "You're the one who said that one bathroom wasn't enough for three teenage girls."

"This is true," Pete said gruffly. "A nightmare in the making. I advise against it. But we could have made the girls observe a lottery system."

She looked around the room. "This is a beautiful nursery, Pete. Thank you so much." She took a deep breath. "I'm so sorry. I should have talked to you about it. I spoke to your Aunt Fiona, but I guess she figured we had some things to work out between us before she helped me list the house. It's not that Bode was right about everything, but he did make me realize that I hadn't been thinking about my husband enough."

"It's your house. You can do whatever you want with it." But his voice was flat, dull.

She glanced around the room, her gaze taking in the nursery. "I love you, Pete Callahan."

"Where are you thinking of moving?" Pete asked her, and Jackie looked at him.

"Wherever you are," she said softly.

"Oh," he said, "why didn't you say that in the beginning?"

He was hurt, and she wouldn't have hurt him for the world. "I want to start our marriage with a clean slate. I want a place that's ours. So," she said, standing on tiptoe to lightly brush a kiss against his lips, "since I picked our daughters' names, don't you think you should have a say in our daughters' new home? Wherever that is?"

Pete grinned, realizing Saturday nights were turning into forever, after all. "I love you, Jackie Callahan," he said. "Don't ever scare me like that again. I thought you were giving up on us."

"No," Jackie said, "the only change I really wanted in my life was you."

"Change is good," Pete said, taking his wife in his arms. He glanced at his three daughters sleeping peacefully, and Fanny dozing on the fluffy pink rug, and then he kissed Jackie the way he planned on kissing her for the rest of her life, with every ounce of love he had in his heart for her.

And that was the one thing that wasn't ever going to change.

Epilogue

On the very last day in May—as soon as he could get her to the altar after the babies were born—Pete married Jackie at Rancho Diablo. He wouldn't have traded the speed wedding in Santa Fe for anything, but it was a treat to see how Fiona and her friends had outdone themselves today. Pete grinned as he watched about five hundred guests mill across the ranch where tents and awnings had been set up. They'd invited their friends out to show how much they appreciated everything that had been done for Jackie and Pete and the girls, and even Fanny. But mostly, for Pete, today was about honoring Jackie and showing her how much he loved her.

"Your parents would be so proud, nephew," Fiona said. "How I wish they could have been here."

"I love you, Aunt Fiona," Pete said, hugging his pink-dressed aunt. "None of this would ever have happened without you."

She smiled at him, and watched Jackie mingle with the guests. "Probably not." She giggled. "But you were ever willing to take direction."

"I thought you always said I was a hellion."

"Indeed." Fiona smiled. "And I wouldn't have had you any other way. Now find your bride. I have babies to hold. And should I mention to Creed it's high time to think about a bride of his own? I was just telling Burke that if anybody needs the rough edges knocked off by a woman, it's Creed."

Fiona went off, and Pete minded his aunt by taking his beautiful wife in his arms. "It's time," he told her.

"For what?" Jackie asked

"The honeymoon night."

She looked at him. "Honeymoon night?"

"Tonight," he said, giving her a husbandly kiss, "we're getting away for a couple of hours to a hidden place, just the two of us. We have a date for a romantic dinner set up by the Books 'n' Bingo ladies."

She looked at him, her gaze wide. "That sounds wonderful!"

He gave her a fast kiss on the nose. "They don't call me Mr. Romance for nothing."

"That's something I didn't know," she teased.

He pulled her close. "Mr. Romance has another surprise for his new bride. In October, just as the weather will be getting a bit nippy here, I'll be seeing you in a bikini in Hawaii. That wedding gown is beautiful, but I can't wait to see you in something skimpier."

"Oh, Pete!" Jackie pressed up against him for a kiss he thought was distinctly approving of his plans, until she had one of those little mommy worries that afflicted her occasionally, and which he found incredibly sweet. "But who will watch the babies while we're honeymooning?" Jackie asked, looking adorably concerned.

Clearly his bride hadn't figured out he was also Mr. Responsible. "Look at my three daughters," Pete said, "do they look like they're going to suffer with Dr. Jonas, assorted uncles, Aunt Fiona, Burke and a brigade of townspeople to wrap around their minuscule fingers? I had people fighting over the babysitting calendar."

Jackie smiled as he kissed her in front of the entire gathering. "The best thing I ever did was marry you, cowboy."

"I know," he said, "now let's go get you out of that magic wedding gown. It's magically making me want you."

"I thought you didn't believe in magic," Jackie said.

He carried her toward his truck as their friends and family tossed rose petals on them and called out congratulations. "I do now," he said. "Every time I touch you, I believe."

"I love you, Pete," she said, and it was the most magical thing he'd ever heard, besides sweet baby noises and his little wife saying *I do, and I always did* at the rose-festooned altar. He was a happy, happy man.

And somewhere in the distance, Pete could hear hooves, running wild and free, over Rancho Diablo land.

Magic.

* * * * *

THE COWBOY'S
BONUS BABY

Many thanks to Kathleen Scheibling
for believing in the Callahan Cowboys series
from the start. I have certainly enjoyed the past
five years under your guidance.

Also, there are so many people at Harlequin who
make my books ready for publication, most of
whom I will never have the chance to thank in
person, and they have my heartfelt gratitude.

Also many thanks to my children and my husband,
who are enthusiastic and supportive, and most of
all, much appreciation to the generous readers
who are the reason for my success.

Chapter One

"Creed is my wild child. He wants everything he can't have."

—Molly Callahan, with fondness, about her busy toddler.

Creed Callahan was running scared. Running wasn't his usual way of doing things, but Aunt Fiona's plot to get him and his five brothers married had him spooked. Marriage was a serious business, not to be undertaken lightly, especially by a commitment-phobe. Aunt Fiona had just scored a direct hit with Creed's brother Pete, who'd married Jackie Samuels and had triplets right off the baby-daddy bat. Creed was potently aware his days as a happy, freewheeling bachelor might come to an end if he didn't get the hell away from Rancho Diablo.

So he'd fled like a shy girl at her first dance. Creed didn't relish being called chicken, but Aunt Fiona was a force to be reckoned with. Creed stared into his sixth beer, which the bartender in Lance, Wyoming, a generous man who could see that Creed's soul was in torment, had courteously poured.

Anyone in Diablo, New Mexico, would attest to the powers of Aunt Fiona. Especially when she had a goal—

then no one was safe. His small, spare aunt had raised him and his five brothers upon the deaths of their parents without so much as a break in her stride. She and her butler, Burke, had flown in from Ireland one day, clucked over and coddled the five confused boys (young Sam had not yet been part of the family, an occurrence which still perplexed the brothers), and gave them an upbringing which was loving, firm and heaped with enthusiastic advice.

Creed barely remembered their parents, Jeremiah and Molly. He was the lucky one in the family, in his opinion, because he had a twin, Rafe. It had helped to have a mirror image at his back over the years. Creed was prone to mischief, Rafe was more of a thinker. Once, when the boys had wondered where babies came from—upon Sam's surprising arrival after Fiona had come to be their guardian—Creed had uprooted all of Fiona's precious garden looking for "baby" seeds. Rafe had told Aunt Fiona that he'd seen bunnies in her garden, which was true, but bunnies weren't the reason Aunt Fiona's kitchen crop had to be restarted.

Creed certainly knew where babies came from now. Watching Pete and Jackie go from a casual romance once a week to parents of triplets had underscored for him the amazing fertility of the Callahan men. They were like stallions—gifted with the goods.

With Fiona prodding about his unmarried state, Creed had hit the road. He did not want his own virility tested. He didn't want a wife or children. Pete was solidly positioned to win Rancho Diablo, for that was the deal Fiona had struck: whoever of the six brothers married and produced the most heirs inherited all five thousand acres.

But he and his brothers had worked an agreement out unbeknownst to their wily aunt: Only one of them would be the sacrifice (which had turned out to be the lucky—or unlucky, depending upon how one viewed it—brother Pete), and he would divide the ranch between the six of them. It was a fair-and-square way to keep any animosity from arising between them for the high-value prize of hearth and home. Competition wasn't a good thing among brothers, they'd agreed, though they competed against each other all the time, naturally. But this was different.

This competition wasn't rodeo, or lassoing, or tree climbing. This was a race to the altar, and they vowed that Fiona's planning wouldn't entrap them.

"And I'm safe," Creed muttered into his beer.

"Did you say something?" a chocolate-haired beauty said to him, and Creed realized that the old saying was true: Women started looking better with every beer. Creed blinked. The male bartender who'd been listening to his woes with a sympathetic ear had morphed into a sexy female, which meant Creed wasn't as safe as he thought he was. He was, in fact, six sheets to the wind and blowing south. "Six beers is not that big a deal," he told the woman who was looking at him with some approbation. "Where's Johnny?"

"Johnny?" She raised elfin brows at him and ran a hand through springy chin-length curls. "My name is Aberdeen."

He wasn't *that* drunk. In fact, he wasn't drunk at all. He knew the difference between moobs and boobs, and while Johnny had been the soul of generosity, he'd had girth appropriate for bouncing troublemakers out of his bar. This delightful lady eyeing him had a figure, pert

and enticing, and Creed's chauvinistic brain was regis-
tering very little else except she looked like something a
man who'd had six beers (okay, maybe twelve, but they
were small ones so he'd halved his count), might want
to drag into the sack. She had bow-shaped lips and dark
blue eyes, but, most of all, she smelled like something
other than beer and salami and pretzels. *Spring flowers,* he thought with a sigh. Yes, the smells of spring,
after a long cold winter in Diablo. "You're beautiful,"
he heard someone tell her, and glanced around for the
dope that would say something so unmanly.

"Thank you," she said to Creed.

"Oh, I didn't—" He stopped. *He* was the dope. *I
sound like Pete. I need to leave now.* The beer had loos-
ened his tongue and thrown his cool to the wind. "I'd
best be going, Amber Jean." He slid off the barstool,
thinking how sad it was that he'd never see Johnny/
Amber Jean again, and how wonderfully fresh and romantic springtime smelled in Wyoming.

"Oh, now, that's a shame," Johnny Donovan said,
looking down at the sleeping cowboy on his bar floor.
"Clearly this is a man who doesn't know much about
brew."

Aberdeen gave her brother a disparaging glance.
"You're the one who gave him too much."

"I swear I did not. The man wanted to talk more than
drink, truthfully." Johnny gave Aberdeen his most innocent gaze. "He went on and on and on, Aberdeen,
and so I could tell he wasn't really looking for the hops
but for a good listener. On his fifth beer, I began giving
him near-beer, as God is my witness, Aberdeen. You
know I disapprove of sloppiness. And it's against the

law to let someone drink and drive." He squinted outside, searching the darkness. It was three o'clock in the morning. "Mind you, I have no idea what he's driving, but he won't be driving a vehicle from my bar in this sloppy condition."

Her brother ran a conscientious establishment. "I'm sorry," Aberdeen said, knowing Johnny treated his patrons like family. Even strangers were given Johnny's big smile, and if anyone so much as mentioned they needed help, Johnny would give them the shirt off his back and the socks off his feet. Aberdeen looked at the cowboy sprawled on the floor, his face turned to the ceiling as he snored with luxuriant abandon. He was sinfully gorgeous: a pile, at the moment, of amazing masculinity. Lean and tall, with long dark hair, a chiseled face, a hint of being once broken about the nose. She restrained the urge to brush an errant swath of midnight hair away from his closed eyes. "What do we do with him?"

Johnny shrugged. "Leave him on the floor to sleep. The man is tired, Aberdeen. Would you have us kick a heartbroken soul out when he just needs a bit of time to gather his wits?"

"Heartbroken?" Aberdeen frowned. The cowboy was too good-looking by half. Men like him demanded caution; she knew this from her congregation. Ladies loved the cowboys; they loved the character and the drive. They loved the romance, the idea of the real working man. And heaven only knew, a lot of those men loved the ladies in return. This one, with his soft voice, good manners and flashing blue eyes… Well, Aberdeen had no doubt that this cowboy had left his fair share of broken hearts trampled in the dirt. "If you sit him outside, he'll gather his wits fast enough."

"Ah, now, Aberdeen. I can't treat paying customers that way, darling. You know that. He's causing no harm, is he?" Johnny looked at her with his widest smile and most apologetic expression, which should have looked silly on her bear of a brother, but which melted her heart every time.

"You're too soft, Johnny."

"And you're too hard, my girl. I often ask myself if all cowboy preachers are as tough on cowboys as you are. This is one of your flock, Aberdeen. He's only drunk on confusion and sadness." Johnny stared at Creed's long-forgotten beer mug. "I feel sorry for him."

Aberdeen sighed. "It's your bar. You do as you like. I'm going to my room."

Johnny went on sweeping up. "I'll keep an eye on him. You go on to bed. You have preaching to do in the morning."

"And I haven't finished writing my sermon. Good night, Johnny." She cast a last glance at the slumbering, too-sexy man on the dark hardwood floor, and headed upstairs. She was glad to leave Johnny with the stranger. No man should look that good sleeping on the floor.

A ROAR FROM DOWNSTAIRS, guffaws and loud thumping woke Aberdeen from deep sleep. Jumping to her feet, she glanced at her bedside clock. Seven o'clock—past time for her to be getting ready for church. She grabbed her robe, and more roars sent her running down the stairs.

Her brother and the stranger sat playing cards on a barrel table in the empty bar. One of them was winning—that much was clear from the grins—and the other didn't mind that he was losing. There were mugs of milk and steaming coffee on a table beside them. Both men were so engrossed in their game that neither of them looked up as she stood there with her hands on her hips. She was of half a mind to march back upstairs and forget she'd ever seen her brother being led astray by the hunky stranger.

"Johnny," Aberdeen said, "did you know it's Sunday morning?"

"I do, darlin'," Johnny said, "but I can't leave him. He's got a fever." He gestured to his playing partner.

"A fever?" Aberdeen's eyes widened. "If he's sick, why isn't he in bed?"

"He won't go. I think he's delirious."

She came closer to inspect the cowboy. "What do you mean, he won't go?"

"He thinks he's home." Johnny grinned at her. "It's the craziest thing."

"It's a lie, Johnny. He's setting us up." She slapped her hand on the table in front of the cowboy. He looked up at her with wide, too-bright eyes. "Have you considered he's on drugs? Maybe that's why he passed out last night."

"Nah," Johnny said. "He's just a little crazy."

She pulled up a chair, eyeing the cowboy cautiously, as he eyed her right back. "Johnny, we don't need 'a little crazy' right now."

"I know you're worried, Aberdeen."

"Aberdeen," the cowboy said, trying out her name. "Not Amber Jean. Aberdeen."

She looked at Johnny. "Maybe he's slow."

Johnny shrugged. "Said he got a small concussion

at his last stop. Got thrown from a bull and didn't ride again that night. He says he just had to come home."

She shook her head. "Sounds like it might be serious. He could have a fever. We can't try to nurse him, Johnny."

"We can take him to the hospital, I suppose." Johnny looked at the stranger. "Do you want to go to a hospital, friend?"

The cowboy shook his head. "I think I'll go to bed now."

Aberdeen wrinkled her nose as the cowboy went over to a long bench in the corner, laid himself out and promptly went to sleep. "You were giving milk to a man with fever?"

Johnny looked at her, his dark eyes curious. "Is that a bad thing? He asked for it."

She sighed. "We'll know soon enough." After a moment, she walked over and put her hand against his forehead. "He's burning up!"

"Well," Johnny said, "the bar's closed today. He can sleep on that bench if he likes, I guess. If he's not better tomorrow, I'll take him to a doctor, though he doesn't seem especially inclined to go."

Aberdeen stared at the sleeping cowboy's handsome face. *Trouble with a capital T.* "Did he tell you his name? Maybe he's got family around here who could come get him."

"No." Johnny put the cards away and tossed out the milk. "He babbles a lot about horses. Talks a great deal about spirit horses and other nonsense. Native American lore. Throws in an occasional Irish tale. Told a pretty funny joke, too. The man has a sense of humor, even if he is out of his mind."

"Great." Aberdeen had a funny feeling about the cowboy who had come to Johnny's Bar and Grill. "I'm going to see who he is," she said, reaching into his front pocket for his wallet.

A hand shot out, grabbing her wrist. Aberdeen gasped and tried to draw away, but the cowboy held on, staring up at her with those navy eyes. She couldn't look away.

"Stealing's wrong," he said.

She slapped his hand and he released her. "I know that, you ape. What's your name?"

He crossed his arms and gave her a roguish grin. "What's *your* name?"

"I already told you my name is Aberdeen." He'd said it not five minutes ago, so possibly he did have a concussion. With a fever, that could mean complications. "Johnny, this man is going to need a run to the—"

The cowboy watched her with unblinking eyes. Aberdeen decided to play it safe. "Johnny, could you pull the truck around? Our guest wants to go for a ride to see our good friend, Dr. Mayberry."

Johnny glanced at the man on the bench. "Does he now?"

"He does," Aberdeen said firmly.

Johnny nodded and left to get his truck. Aberdeen looked at the ill man, who watched her like a hawk. "Cowboy, I'm going to look at your license, and if you grab me again like you did a second ago, you'll wish you hadn't. I may be a minister, but when you live above a bar, you learn to take care of yourself. So either you give me your wallet, or I take it. Those are your choices."

He stared at her, unmoving.

She reached into his pocket and pulled out his wallet, keeping her gaze on him, trying to ignore the expanse of wide chest and other parts of him she definitely shouldn't notice. Flipping it open, she took out his driver's license. "Creed Callahan. New Mexico."

She put the license away, ignoring the fact that he had heaven-only-knew-how-many hundred-dollar bills stuffed into the calfskin wallet, and slid it back into his pocket.

He grabbed her, pulling her to him for a fast kiss. His lips molded to hers, and Aberdeen felt a spark— more than a spark, *real* heat—and then he released her.

She glared at him. He shrugged. "I figured you'd get around to slapping me eventually. Might as well pay hell is what I always say."

"Is that what you always say? With every woman you force to kiss you?" Aberdeen asked, rattled, and even more irritated that she hadn't been kissed like that in years. "You said stealing was wrong."

"It is. I didn't say I didn't do it." He grinned, highly pleased with himself, and if he hadn't already rung his bell, she would have slapped him into the next county.

Then again, it was hard to stay mad when he was that cheerful about being bad. Aberdeen put her hands on her hips so he couldn't grab her again. "All right, Mr. Callahan, do you remember why you're in Wyoming?"

"Rodeo. I ride rodeo, ma'am."

Johnny was back. "Truck's out front."

"Johnny," Aberdeen said, "this is Creed Callahan. Mr. Callahan is very happy you're going to take him for a ride. Aren't you, Mr. Callahan?"

"Callahan?" Johnny repeated. "One of the six Callahans from New Mexico?"

"Have you heard of him?"

"Sure." Johnny shrugged. "All of them ride rodeo, and not too shabbily. The older brother didn't ride much, but he did a lot of rodeo doctoring after he got out of medical school. Some of them have been highly ranked. You don't go to watch rodeo without knowing about the Callahans." He looked at Creed with sympathy. "What are you doing here, friend?"

Creed sighed. "I think I'm getting away from something, but I can't remember what."

"A woman?" Johnny asked, and Aberdeen waited to hear the answer with sudden curiosity.

"A woman," Creed mused. "That sounds very likely. Women are trouble, you know. They want to have—" He lowered his voice conspiratorially in an attempt to keep Aberdeen from hearing. "They want to have b-a-b-i-e-s."

Aberdeen rolled her eyes. "Definitely out of his mind. Take him away, Johnny."

Her brother laughed. "He may be right, you know."

"I don't care," Aberdeen said, gathering her self-control. He might have stolen a kiss, but the conceited louse was never getting another one from her. "He's crazy."

"That's what they say," Creed said, perking up, obviously recognizing something he'd heard about himself before.

Aberdeen washed her hands of Mr. Loco. "Goodbye, cowboy," she said, "hope you get yourself together again some day. I'll be praying for you."

"And I'll be praying for you," Creed said courteously, before rolling off the bench onto the floor.

"That's it, old man," Johnny said, lifting Creed up and over his shoulder. "Off we go, then. Aberdeen, I may not make your service today, love."

"It's okay, Johnny." Aberdeen watched her brother carry Creed to the truck and place him inside as carefully as a baby. The man said he was running, but no one ran from their family, did they? Not someone who had five brothers who'd often traveled together, rodeoed together, competed against each other? And Johnny said one of the brothers was a doctor.

People needed family when they were hurting. He'd be better off with them instead of being in Wyoming among strangers.

Aberdeen went to her room to look up Callahans in New Mexico, thinking about her own desire for a family. A real one. Her sister, Diane, had tried to make a family, but it hadn't worked. Though she had three small adorable daughters, Diane wasn't cut out to be a mother. Then Aberdeen had married Shawn "Re-ride" Parker right out of high school. That hadn't lasted long, and there had been no children. And Johnny, a confirmed bachelor, said he had enough on his hands with his two sisters. They had their own definition of family, Aberdeen supposed, which worked for them. If a woman was looking to be have a baby, though, Creed Callahan probably ranked as perfect donor material—if a woman liked crazy, which she didn't. "I don't do crazy anymore," she reminded herself, dialing the listing she got from the operator.

The sooner crazy left town, the better for all of them.

Chapter Two

Creed was astonished to see his brother Judah when he awakened. He was even more surprised to realize he was in a hospital room. He glanced around, frowning at his snoozing brother—Judah looked uncomfortable and ragged in the hospital chair—and wondered why he was here. Creed tried to remember how he'd gotten to the hospital and couldn't. Except for a ferocious headache, he felt fine.

"Judah," he said, and his brother started awake.

"Hey!" Judah grinned at him. "What the hell, man? You scared me to death."

"Why?" Creed combed his memory and found it lacking. "What's going on? Where am I?"

"We're in Lance, Wyoming. A bar owner brought you in."

"Was I in a fight?" Creed rubbed at his aching head, confused by his lost memory. He didn't remember drinking all that much, but if a bar owner had brought him in, maybe he'd gotten a little riled up. "If I was, I hope I won."

Judah smirked. "The fight you were in was apparently with a bull. And you lost. At least this round."

Creed perked up. "Which bull was it? I hope it was a bounty bull. At least a rank bull, right?"

His brother smiled. "Can I get you something? Are you hungry?"

Creed blinked. Judah didn't want to tell him which bull had thrown him, which wasn't good. Cowboys loved to brag, even on the bad rides. He told himself he was just a little out of practice, nothing more riding couldn't cure. "I feel like my head isn't part of my body."

"You've got a slight concussion. The doctor thinks you're going to be fine, but he's keeping you a few hours for observation."

"I've had concussions before and not gone to the hospital."

"This time you had a high fever. Could have been the concussion, could have been a bug. The doctors just want to keep an eye on you. They mapped your brain, by the way, and said you don't have too much rattling around inside your skull. The brain cavity is strangely lacking in material."

Creed grunted at Judah's ribbing. "Sorry you had to make the trip."

"No problem. I wasn't doing anything."

Creed grunted again at the lie. Callahans always had plenty to do around Rancho Diablo. Five thousand acres of prime land and several hundred head of livestock meant that they stayed plenty busy. They kept the ranch running through sheer hard work and commitment to the family business.

"Anyway, it's been a while since anyone's seen you. Didn't know where you were keeping yourself." Judah scrutinized him. "We really didn't understand why you left in the first place."

Now *that* Creed could dig out of his cranium. "I was next on Fiona's list, Judah. I could *feel* it." He shuddered. "You don't understand until you've had Fiona's eye trained on you. Once she's thinking about getting you to the altar, you're halfway there."

"She's thinking about all of us," Judah pointed out. "Remember, that's her plan."

"But it was supposed to be over when Pete got married. He was the sacrifice." Creed took a deep breath. "And then I realized Fiona was running through her catalog of eligible females for me. I could hear her mind whirring. I've known every woman Fiona could possibly think of all my life. And there's not a one of them I'd care to marry."

Judah nodded. "I feel the same way."

Creed brightened. "You do?"

"Sure. Occasionally I think about a certain gal, but then I think, no, she'd never have me. And then I get over it pretty fast." Judah grinned. "The sacrifice wasn't ever going to be me. I'm not good at commitment for the sake of just having a girl around. Heck, I was never even good at picking a girl to take to prom."

"That was an exercise in futility." Creed remembered his brother's agony. "I had to fix you up with some of my friends."

"And that was embarrassing because of you being a year older than me."

"I didn't exactly mind," Creed hedged. "And I didn't hear you complaining about going out with an older woman."

Judah shook his head. "My dates didn't complain

because I'm a good kisser. When you're a year younger than the girls you take out, you learn to make it up to them." He grinned. "You know, it's not that I don't like women, I just like *all* women."

"Amen, bro," Creed said happily, back on terra firma. "Women are a box of candy, you never know what you're going to get."

"All right, Forrest Gump. Go back to sleep." Judah smiled at the nurse who came in to take his brother's temperature. "I had no idea the ladies in Wyoming are so lovely," Judah said. "Why wasn't I living here all my life?"

Creed grinned at his brother's flirting. *Now* he remembered who he was. He was Creed Callahan, hotshot rider and serious serial lover of females. Wild at heart. It was good to be a Callahan. He was love-them-and-leave-them-happy, that's who he was.

And women adored him.

Creed never noticed the nurse taking his pulse and his temperature. Somewhere in his memory a vision of a brunette with expressive eyebrows nagged at him. A female who hadn't quite adored him. In fact, she might even have thought he was annoying.

It wasn't likely such a woman existed, but then again, he couldn't remember ever getting concussed by anything other than a rank bull, either. Creed closed his eyes, wishing his headache would go away, but there was greater pain inside him: His last several rides had been bombs. Not even close to eights. On par with unfortunate.

I need a break, and the only thing I manage to break is my head.

He'd just lie here and think about it a little while

longer, and maybe the fog would lift. He heard Judah and the nurse giggling quietly about something, which didn't help. Judah could score any time he liked. The ladies loved all that haunted-existentialist crap that his younger brother exuded. *But I'm not existential. Rafe, he's an existential thinker. Me, I'm just wild. And that's all I'll ever be.*

He felt really tired just connecting those pieces of information. When he got out of here, he was going to remember that a fallen rider needed to get right back up on his reindeer.

Or something like that.

But then Creed thought about dark-blue annoyed eyes staring at him, and wondered if he was running out of good luck.

ABERDEEN SAT RELUCTANTLY at the cowboy's bedside, waiting for him to waken, and not really wanting him to. There was something about him that nagged at her, and it wasn't just that he'd kissed her. Cowboys were typically a good group, but she wasn't sure about this one, though she was trying to give him the benefit of the doubt. She worked to spread faith and good cheer amongst her beat-up flock, and beat-up they were on Sunday mornings. Her congregation consisted of maybe twenty-five people on a busy Sunday, often less. Banged-up gentlemen dragged in for an hour of prayer and sympathy and the potluck spaghetti lunch she and her friends served in the bar afterward. She preached in Johnny's big barn, which had a covered pavilion for indoor riding. The cowboys and cowgirls, wearing jeans and sleepy expressions of gratitude, gratefully headed to the risers.

This man was beat-up, all right, but he didn't seem like he cared to find spiritual recovery in any form. She pondered her transient congregation. Sunday mornings were her favorite part of the week, and she rarely ever missed giving a sermon, though if she did, Johnny was an excellent stand-in, as well as some of their friends. Neither of them had grown up thinking they wanted to be preachers, but missionarying had taken hold of Aberdeen in high school, growing stronger during college. She'd majored in theology, minored in business, and Johnny had done the opposite. The two of them were a good working team. Over the years, Johnny's Bar and Grill had become known as the place to hang out six days a week, crash when necessary, and hear words of worship on Sunday. Aberdeen knew many of the cowboys that pulled through Lance. She couldn't understand why she'd never heard of the Callahans, if they were the prolific, daring riders that Johnny claimed they were.

But she'd gotten busy in the past five years, so busy she barely paid attention to anything more than what the top riders were scoring, and sometimes not even that. Her knowledge had ebbed when she started helping Johnny at the bar and writing more of her sermons. She was twenty-nine, and at some point, rodeo had left her consciousness. She'd focused more on her job and less on fun—although sometimes she missed that. A lot.

Plus she had Diane to think about. Diane was in trouble, real trouble, and nothing she or Johnny did seemed to help her. Their older sister couldn't keep a job, couldn't keep a husband—she was on her third— and had three young children, had had one a year for the past three years. Now she was going through a bitter divorce from a man who'd walked out and was never coming back. It had always been hard for Aberdeen and Johnny to understand why Diane made the choices she did.

Recently, Diane had asked Aberdeen to adopt her daughters, Ashley, Suzanne and Lincoln Rose. Diane said she could no longer handle the responsibility of being a parent. Aberdeen was seriously considering taking the girls in. If Diane didn't want to be a mother, then Aberdeen didn't want to see Child Protective Services picking up her nieces. She loved them, with all her heart.

Diane lived in Spring, Montana, and wanted to move to Paris to chase after a new boyfriend she'd met traveling through the state. Aberdeen lived in fear that their elderly parents would call and say that Diane had already skipped.

"Howdy," the cowboy said, and Aberdeen's gaze snapped up to meet his.

"Hi. Feeling better?" she asked, conscious once again of how those dark denim eyes unsettled her.

"I think so." He brightened after feeling his head. "Yes, I definitely am. Headache is gone." He gave her a confiding grin. "I dreamed about you."

Her mouth went dry. "Why?"

"I remembered your eyes. I didn't remember a lot else, but I did remember your eyes."

She'd remembered his, too, though she'd tried not to. "Good dream or a bad dream?"

He grinned. "Now, sugar, wouldn't you like to know?"

She pursed her lips, wishing she hadn't asked.

"Ah, now that's the expression I recall with clarity,"

Creed said. "Annoyance. Mainly because it's not what I usually see in a woman's eyes."

"No? What do you usually see?" Aberdeen *was* annoyed, and the second she fell into his trap, she was even more irritated. Mainly with herself.

"Lust, preacher lady. I see lust."

She leaned away from him. "Ladies do not lust."

He raised jet-black brows. "I swear they do."

"They desire," she told him. "They have longings."

He shook his head. "You've been meeting the wrong kind of fellows, sugar cake."

She got up and grabbed her purse. "It's good to see you on the mend, Mr. Callahan. Happy trails."

He laughed, a low, sensual sound that followed Aberdeen to the door. "Thank you, miss."

He hadn't placed an emphasis on *miss,* but it teed her off just the same. Made her feel naked. She wasn't an old-maid kind of miss; she was a conscientious abstainer from another marriage. *That's right, cowboy. I'm single and okay with it. Almost okay with it, anyway.*

As she rounded the corner, she plowed into a tall cowboy who looked a lot like the one she'd left in his hospital room.

"Whoa, little lady," he said, setting her back on her feet. "Where's the fire?"

She frowned. "You're not one of the Callahans, are you?"

"I am." He nodded, smiling at her. "You must be the nice lady who let us know Creed was down on his luck."

"Yes, I did. He's made a great recovery."

He tipped his hat, dark-blue eyes—just like Creed's—sparkling at her. "My name is Judah Callahan."

She reached out to shake his hand. "Aberdeen Donovan."

"We can't thank you enough, Miss Aberdeen."

He had kind eyes—unlike the flirt back in the hospital bed. "No thanks necessary. My brother, Johnny would help anyone in trouble." She smiled at him. "I've got to run, but it was nice meeting you, Judah."

"Thank you, Aberdeen. Again, thanks for rescuing Bubba."

She shook her head and walked away. Bubba. There was nothing little-brother Bubba about Creed. He was all full-grown man and devil-may-care lifestyle. She'd be a fool to fall for a man like him. Fortunately, forewarned was forearmed.

Chapter Three

Judah strolled into Creed's room. By the sneaky smile on his brother's face, Creed deduced that his visit wasn't all about rousing the patient to better health. "What?" Creed had a funny feeling he knew what was coming.

"You've got all the luck," Judah said, throwing himself into a chair. "Finding a little angel like that to rescue you."

Judah grinned, but Creed let his scowl deepen. "She's not as much of an angel as she appears. Don't let her looks fool you."

His brother laughed. "Couldn't sweet-talk her, huh?"

Creed sniffed. "Didn't try."

"Sure you did." Judah crossed a leg over a knee and lounged indolently, enjoying having Creed at his mercy. "She didn't give you the time of day." He looked up at the ceiling, putting on a serious face. "You know, some ladies take their angel status very seriously."

"Meaning?" Creed arched a brow at his brother, half-curious as to where all this ribbing was going. Judah had no room to talk about success with women, as far as Creed was concerned. Only Pete was married—and only Pete had claimed a girlfriend, sort of, before Aunt Fiona had thrown down the marriage gauntlet. Creed figured the rest of the Callahan brothers were just about nowhere with serious relationships.

Including me.

"Just that once a woman like her rescues a man, she almost feels responsible for him. Like a child." Judah sighed. "Very difficult thing to get away from, when a woman sees a man in a mothering light."

Creed stared at his brother. "That's the biggest bunch of hogwash I've ever heard."

"Have you ever wondered exactly what hogwash is?" Judah looked thoughtful. "If I had a hog, I sure wouldn't wash it."

"Hogwash just means garbage," Creed said testily. "Your literal mood is not amusing."

"I was just making conversation, since you're not in a position to do much else."

"Sorry." Creed got back to the point he was most intrigued by. "Anyway, so you met Aberdeen?"

Judah nodded. "Yes. And thanked her for taking care of my older brother. Do you remember any of what happened to you?"

"I don't know. Some bug hit me, I guess." Creed was missing a couple of days out of his life. "I didn't make the cut in Lance, so I was going to head on to the next rodeo. And I saw this out-of-the-way restaurant on the side of road, so I stopped. Next thing I knew, I was here."

Judah shook his head. "A bad hand, man."

"Yeah."

"Never want a woman you've just met to see you weak," Judah mused.

"I wasn't weak. I just got the wrong end of a ride. Or

the flu." Creed glared at Judah. "So anyway, how are the newlyweds? And Fiona? Burke? Everyone else?"

"No one else is getting married, if that's what you're asking. You still have a shot. Like Cinderella getting a glass slipper. It could happen, under the right conditions."

"I don't want a wife or children. That's why I'm here," Creed growled. "You can be the ambassador for both of us, thanks."

"I don't know. I kind of thought that little brunette who went racing out of your room might have some possibilities."

"Then ask her out." Creed felt a headache coming on that had nothing to do with his concussion. It was solely bad temper, which Judah was causing.

Just like the old days. In a way, it was comforting.

"I don't know. I could have sworn I felt that tension thing. You know, a push-pull vibe when she left your room. She was all riled like she had fire on her heels, as if you'd really twisted her up."

"That's a recipe for love if I ever heard one."

"Yeah." Judah warmed to his theory. "Fire and ice. Only she's mostly fire."

"Hellfire is my guess. You know she's a cowboy church preacher."

"Oh." Judah slumped. "That was the fire I picked up on. I knew she needed an extinguisher for some reason. I just thought maybe it had to do with you."

"Nope," Creed said, happy to throw water on his brother's silly theory. "You'll have to hogwash another Callahan into getting roped. And you are not as good as Fiona," Creed warned with satisfaction.

Judah shook his head. "No one is."

"I THINK," FIONA TOLD HER FRIENDS at the Books 'n' Bingo Society meeting, "that voting a few new members in to our club is a good idea. Sabrina McKinley can't stay shut up in the house all the time taking care of dreadful old Bode Jenkins." Fiona sniffed, despising even saying Bode's name. It was Bode who'd finally closed her up in a trap, and the fact that the man had managed to find a way to get Rancho Diablo from her rankled terribly. She was almost sick with fear over what to tell her six nephews. Pete knew. She could trust Pete. He would keep her secret until the appropriate time. And he was married now, with darling triplet daughters, a dutiful nephew if there ever was one.

But the other five—well, she'd be holding her breath for a long while if she dreamed those five rapscallions would get within ten feet of an altar. No, they'd be more likely to set an altar on fire with their anti-marriage postures. Poof! Up in smoke.

Just like her grip on Rancho Diablo. How disappointed her brother Jeremiah and his wife, Molly, would be if they knew that she'd lost the ranch they'd built. "Some guardian I am," she murmured, and Corrine Abernathy said, "What, Fiona?"

Fiona shook her head. "Anyway, we need to invite Sabrina into our group. We need fresh blood, young voices who can give us new ideas."

Her three best friends and nine other ladies smiled at her benevolently.

"It sounds like a good idea," Mavis Night said. "Who else do you want?"

Fiona thought about it. Sabrina had been an obvious choice for new-member status, because she was Corinne's niece. So was Seton McKinley, a private investigator Fiona had hired to ferret out any chinks in Bode's so-far formidable armor. "I think maybe Bode Jenkins."

An audible gasp went up in the tea room.

"You can't be serious," Nadine Waters said, her voice quavering. "He's your worst enemy."

"And we should keep our enemy close to our bosoms, shouldn't we?" Fiona looked around the room. "Anyway, I put it forth to a vote."

"Why not Sheriff Cartwright? He's a nice man," Nadine offered. "For our first male in the group, I'd rather vote for a gentleman."

Murmurs of agreement greeted that sentiment.

"I don't know," Fiona said. "Maybe I'm losing my touch. Maybe inviting Bode is the wrong idea." She thought about her words before saying slowly, "Maybe I should give up my chairwomanship of the Books 'n' Bingo Society."

Everyone stared at her, their faces puzzled, some glancing anxiously at each other.

"Fiona, is everything all right?" Corinne asked.

"I don't know," Fiona said. She didn't want to tell them that in another six months she might not be here. It was time to lay the groundwork for the next chairwoman. She would have no home which to invite them, there would be no more Rancho Diablo. Only one more Christmas at Diablo. She wanted to prepare her friends for the future. But she also didn't want the truth to come out just yet, for her nephews' sakes. She wanted eligible bachelorettes—the cream of the Diablo crop—to see them still as the powerful Callahan clan, the men who worked the hardest and shepherded the biggest ranch around.

Not as unfortunate nephews of a silly aunt who'd gambled away their birthright.

She wanted to cry, but she wouldn't. "I think I'll adjourn, girls. Why don't we sleep on everything, and next week when we meet maybe we'll have some ideas on forward-thinking goals for our club."

Confused, the ladies rose, hugging each other, glancing with concern at Fiona. Fiona knew she'd dropped a bomb on her friends. She hadn't handled the situation well.

But then, she hadn't handled anything well lately. *I'm definitely losing it,* she thought. In the old days, her most gadabout, confident days, a man like Bode Jenkins would never have gotten the best of her.

She was scared.

"I'M THINKING ABOUT IT," Aberdeen told Johnny that night. "Our nieces need a stable home. And I don't know how to help Diane more than we have. Maybe she needs time away. Maybe she's been through too much. There's no way for us to know what is going through her mind." Aberdeen sat in their cozy upstairs den with Johnny. It was Sunday night so the bar was closed. They'd thoroughly cleaned it after going by to see the recovering cowboy. He'd looked much better and seemed cheered by his brother's presence.

There wasn't much else she and Johnny could do for him, either, and she didn't really want to get any more involved. She had enough on her hands. "Mom and Dad say that they try to help Diane, but despite that, they're afraid the children are going to end up in a foster home somewhere, some day." Aberdeen felt tears press behind her eyelids. "The little girls deserve better than this, Johnny. And Diane has asked me to adopt them. She says she's under too much pressure. Too many children, not enough income, not enough… maternal desire."

That wasn't exactly how Diane had put it. Diane had said she wasn't a fit mother. Aberdeen refused to believe that. Her sister had always been a sunny person, full of optimism. These days, she was darker, moodier, and it all seemed to stem from the birth of her last child. Up until that moment, Diane had thought everything was fine in her marriage. It wasn't until after the baby was born that she'd discovered her husband had another woman. He no longer wanted to be a father, nor a husband to Diane.

"I don't know," Johnny said. "Aberdeen, we live over a bar. I don't think anyone will let us have kids here. Nor could I recommend it. We don't want the girls growing up in an environment that isn't as wholesome as we could make it. We don't even have schools nearby."

Aberdeen nodded. "I know. I've thought about this, Johnny. I think I'm going to have to move to Montana."

Her brother stared at her. "You wanted to leave Montana. So did I."

"But it's not a bad place to live, Johnny." It really wasn't. And the girls would have so much more there than they would living over a bar. "I could be happy there."

"It's not that Montana was the problem," Johnny said. "It was the family tree we wanted to escape."

This was also true. Their parents weren't the most loving, helpful people. They'd pretty much let their kids fend for themselves, believing that they themselves had gotten by with little growing up, and had done fine figuring life out themselves. So Johnny and Aberdeen had left Montana, striking out to "figure life out" on their own. Diane had opted to stay behind with their parents. Consequently, she'd married, had kids, done the wife thing—and left herself no backup when it all fell apart.

"I've been thinking, too," Johnny said. "To be honest, the red flag went up for me when the folks said they were worried. For them to actually worry and not ascribe to their typical let-them-figure-it-out-themselves theory, makes me think the situation is probably dire."

Aberdeen shook her head. "The girls need more. They're so young, Johnny. I don't know exactly what happened to Diane and why she's so determined she can't be a mother anymore, but I think I'm going to either have to get custody or fully adopt, like Diane wants me to do. They need the stability."

Johnny scratched his chin. "We just can't have them here. There are too many strangers for safety."

"That's why I think I have to go to Montana. At least there I can assess what's been happening."

Johnny waved a big hand at her. "Diane is leaving. There's nothing to assess. She's going to follow whatever wind is blowing, and our parents don't want to be bothered with toddlers."

"They don't have the health to do it, Johnny."

"True, but—"

"It doesn't matter," Aberdeen said quickly. "We just need to think of what's best for the girls."

"We can buy a house here. Maybe it's time to do that, anyway."

She looked around their home. It hadn't been in the best condition when they'd bought the building, but they'd converted the large old house into a working/

living space that suited them. Upstairs were four bedrooms, with two on either side of an open space, with
en suite bathrooms in the two largest bedrooms. They
used the wide space between the bedrooms as a family
room. For five years they'd lived here, and it was home.

"Maybe," she said, jumping a little when a knock
sounded on the front door downstairs. Aberdeen
glanced at Johnny. Their friends knew to go to the back
door after the bar was closed; they never answered the
front door in case a stranger might decide to see if they
could get someone to open up the bar. A few drunks
over the years had done that. She was surprised when
Johnny headed down the stairs. Her brother was big and
tall and strong, and he wouldn't open the door without
his gun nearby, but still, Aberdeen followed him.

"We're closed," Johnny called through the door.

"I know. I just wanted to come by and say thanks
before we left town," a man called from the other side,
and Aberdeen's stomach tightened just a fraction.

"The cowboy," she said to Johnny, and he nodded.

"He's harmless enough," Johnny said. "A little bit of
a loose cannon, but might as well let him have his say."

Aberdeen shrugged. "He can say it through the door
just the same," she said, but Johnny gave her a wry look
and opened up.

"Thanks for letting me in," Creed Callahan said to
Johnny, shaking his hand as though he was a long-lost
friend. "This is the man who probably saved my life,
Judah," he said, and Judah put out a hand for Johnny
to shake. "Hi, Aberdeen," Creed said.

"Hello, Aberdeen," Judah said, "we met in the hospital."

She smiled at Judah's polite manners, but it was his

long-haired ruffian of a brother who held her gaze. She could feel her blood run hot and her frosty facade trying to melt. It was hard not to look at Creed's engaging smile and clear blue eyes without falling just a little bit. *You've been here before,* she reminded herself. *No more bad boys for you.*

"We didn't save your life," Johnny said, "you would have been fine."

Creed shook his head. "I don't remember much about the past couple of days. I don't really recall coming here." He smiled at Aberdeen. "I do remember you telling your brother you didn't want me here."

"That's true." She stared back at him coolly. "We're not really prepared to take in boarders. It's nice to see you on the mend. Will you be heading on now to the next rodeo?"

Judah softly laughed. "We do have to be getting on, but we just wanted to stop by to thank you." He tipped his hat to Aberdeen. "Again, I appreciate you looking out for my brother. He's fortunate to have guardian angels."

Aberdeen didn't feel much like an angel at the moment. She could feel herself in the grip of an attraction unlike anything that had ever hit her before. She'd felt it when she'd first laid eyes on Creed. The feeling hadn't dissipated when she'd visited him in the hospital. She could tell he was one of those men who would make a woman insane from wanting what she couldn't have.

It was the kiss that was muddying her mind. He'd unlocked a desire she'd jealously kept under lock and key, not wanting ever to get hurt again. "Goodbye," she said, her eyes on Creed. "Better luck with your next ride."

He gave her a lingering glance, and Aberdeen could

have sworn he had something else he wanted to say but couldn't quite bring himself to say it. He didn't rush to the door, and finally Judah clapped him on the back so he'd get moving toward the exit.

"Goodbye," Creed said again, seemingly only to her, and chicken-heart that she was, Aberdeen turned around and walked upstairs, glad to see him go.

Once in Creed's truck, Judah tried to keep his face straight. Creed knew his brother was laughing at him, though, and it didn't help. "What?" he demanded, pulling out of the asphalt parking lot. "What's so funny?"

"That one is way out of your league, Creed."

Creed started to make a rebuttal of his interest, then shrugged. "I thought you said she'd probably feel responsible for me because she saved me."

Judah laughed. "Works for most guys, clearly backfired on you. Good thing you're not interested in a relationship with a woman, or keeping up with Pete, because you'd never get there if that gal was your choice. I don't believe I've ever seen a female look at a man with less enthusiasm. If you were a cockroach, she'd have squashed you."

He *felt* squashed. "She was like that from the moment I met her," Creed said. "I remember one very clear thing about the night I got here, and that was her big blue eyes staring at me like I was an ex-boyfriend. The kind of ex a woman never wants to lay eyes on again."

"Bad luck for you," Judah said, without much sympathy and with barely hidden laughter. "You're kind of on a roll, bro."

"My luck's bound to turn eventually." Creed was sure it would—he'd always led a fairly charmed existence, but when a man couldn't ride and the ladies weren't biting his well-baited hook and he was evading his wonky little aunt's plan to get him settled down, well, there was nothing else to do but wait for the next wave of good luck, which was bound to come any time.

"Take me to the airport," Judah said, "now that you're on the mend."

"You don't want to ride with me to the next stop?"

Judah shook his head. "I've got a lot to do back home."

Guilt poured over Creed. There was always so much to do at Rancho Diablo that they could have had six more brothers and they wouldn't cover all the bases. "Yeah," Creed said, thinking hard. He wasn't winning. He'd busted his grape, though not as badly as some guys he knew. Still, it probably wasn't wise to get right back in the saddle.

He was homesick. "Maybe that bump on my noggin was a good thing."

"Not unless it knocked some sense into you."

He couldn't remember ever being homesick before. It was either having had a bad ride or meeting Aberdeen that had him feeling anxious. He wasn't sure which option would be worse. With a sigh he said, "Feel like saving on an airplane ticket?"

"Coming home?" Judah asked, with a sidelong glance at him, and Creed nodded.

"I think I will."

"Suits me. I hate to fly. So many rules to follow. And I hate taking off my boots in a line of other people taking off their shoes. I guess I could wear flip-flops or slip-ons, but my boots are just part of my body." He glanced out the window, watching the beautiful land fly past, clearly happy to have the scenery to admire. "Better luck next time, bro," he said, then pulled his hat down over his eyes. "Wake me when you want me to drive."

Creed nodded. He wasn't as sanguine and relaxed as Judah. He was rattled, feeling that something was missing, something wasn't quite right. Creed kept his eyes on the road, tried to relax his clenched fingers on the steering wheel—just enough to take the white from his knuckles. It had been silly to go back to Johnny's Bar and Grill, but he'd wanted to see Aberdeen. He wanted to take one last look at her, at those springy, dark-brown curls, her saucy nose, full lips, dark-blue eyes. He'd been lying, of course. He remembered something else besides those eyes staring at him with annoyance. He would never forget the soft feel of her lips beneath his, printing her heart onto his soul. He'd felt it, despite the concussion, and he had a funny feeling he would never forget Aberdeen Donovan.

Which was a first for a man who loved to kiss all the girls with his usual happy-go-lucky amnesia. He'd wanted one more kiss from Aberdeen, but it would have taken better luck than he was currently riding and maybe a real guardian angel looking out for him to make that dream come true.

He turned toward home.

Chapter Four

When Aberdeen and Johnny got to Montana a week after the cowboy had left town, they found matters were worse than expected. Diane was already in Paris chasing after her new boy toy, and had no plans to return. Ashley, Suzanne and Lincoln Rose had been left with their grandparents—and as Aberdeen and Johnny had feared, the older folk were overwhelmed and looking to hand off the girls. Quickly.

"Why didn't you call us?" Aberdeen demanded. "How long has Diane been gone?"

"She left two weeks ago. With that man." Fritz Donovan looked at his nieces helplessly. "Seems a mother ought to stay around to raise her own kids. Like we did."

Aberdeen bit her lip. *Some raising. You left us to raise ourselves, so Diane isn't all to blame.*

"You still should have called, Dad."

May Donovan jutted out her chin. "Diane said she'd told you that she was leaving. We figured that since you didn't come, you didn't want the girls. And you know very well Diane needs a break. It's just all been too much for her since the divorce."

Aberdeen counted to ten. May's constant blind eye where her older daughter was concerned was one of the reasons Diane continued to act irresponsibly at the age of thirty-five.

Johnny got to his feet, towering in the small kitchen. "There's no need to lay blame. If Diane is gone, she's gone. Now we need to decide what to do with the little ones."

"You're taking them with you, of course," May said. "Now that you've *finally* arrived."

Fritz nodded. "We're a bit old to take care of three little kids. Not that we can't," he said, his tone belligerent, "but maybe they'll be happier with you. Since that's what Diane wanted and all. You should help your sister since she's not had the breaks in life that you two have had."

Aberdeen told herself their parents' words didn't matter right now. They had always been cold and odd, and strangely preferential toward Diane. Aberdeen loved her sister as much as they did, but she wasn't blind to her faults, either. Diane had a selfish side that one day she might, hopefully, grow out of. For the sake of her nieces, Aberdeen prayed she did. "We'll take them back with us," she said finally, glancing at Johnny for his approval, which she knew would be there. "You can come see them as often as you like to visit."

"Ah, well. That won't be necessary," May said. "We don't travel much."

Their parents had never visited their home in Lance. Aberdeen shook her head. "There's always a first time for everything. I'm heading to bed. We'll be off in the morning."

"That will be fine." The relief on May's face was plain. "You are planning to adopt them, aren't you, Aberdeen? After all, it would help Diane so much. She just can't do this, you know."

Her mother's gaze was pleading. It occurred to Aberdeen that her sister's mothering skills were basically the same as May's. It was always Johnny who kept the family together, Aberdeen realized. Johnny had been adoring of his little sister and helpful to his big sister and they'd always known they had their protective Johnny looking out for them. Not their parents. Johnny.

"I don't know, Mom," Aberdeen said. "We'd have to see if a court would allow it. We don't know what is involved with an in-family adoption when a mother is simply absent by choice. There's finances to consider, too."

"We can't give you any money," May said quickly, and Johnny said, "We're not asking you for money. We just need to proceed in a responsible fashion for the girls' sakes."

"Well, I would think—" May began, but Johnny cut her off.

"Enough, Mom. We have a lot of decisions to make in the near future. For all we know, Diane could come home next week, ready to be a mother. Maybe she just needed a vacation."

Aberdeen hoped so, but doubted it. "Good night," she said, and headed upstairs.

Part of her—the dreamy, irresponsible part she rarely acknowledged—took flight for just an instant, wondering how her life might be different if she, too, just took off, as Diane had, following a man on the whim of her heart.

Like a certain cowboy.

A big, strong, muscular, teasing hunk of six-four cowboy.

But no. She was as different from Diane as night and day. She was a dreamer, maybe, not a doer. She would never fling caution to the wind and follow a man like Creed Callahan.

Yet sweet temptation tugged at her thoughts.

"I'VE BEEN THINKING," Creed told Judah as they made their way through Colorado, "that little cowboy church preacher was a little too uptight for me, anyway."

Judah glanced at him as Creed slumped in the passenger seat, doling out some of their favorite road food. They'd made a pit stop just outside of Denver and loaded up on the junk food Fiona wouldn't allow them to have.

"What made you decide that?" Judah asked, taking a swig of the Big Red Creed had put in the cup holder for him. "Because I was pretty certain uptight might be good for you."

"Maybe in small doses," Creed said, feeling better as every mile took him farther away from temptation. "I'm pretty sure I can't handle uptight in large doses."

"I'd say narrow escape, except I don't think you were in danger of getting caught." Judah munched happily on Doritos from the open bag between the seat. "No, I'm sure you had Free Bird written all over your forehead, bro. No worries."

Creed pondered that. "I've decided to make a run for the ranch."

Judah glanced at him. "Since when?"

Since he'd met the preacher. That was weird, though, Creed thought with a frown. Women usually made him want to get naked, not own a ranch. "I don't know."

"Okay, of all of us, you are not the one to settle down and grow a large family."

"Pete's happy. I could learn by example."

"You ran away from being Pete. Remember? You ran like a hungry wolf to a picnic basket."

Creed considered that as he crunched some chips. "I think I changed when I got my bell rung."

"Creed, you get your bell rung once a year."

"This was different," Creed said. "I saw stars."

"You saw nothing. You weren't yourself for two days," Judah told him. "Anyway, it's not enough to change you. You've always been a loose goose."

"Yeah. I suppose so." Creed lost his appetite for chips and stared morosely at his soda can. "You know, I think Fiona's right. This *is* trash we're eating. I can feel my intestines turning red."

Judah sighed. "This is nectar of the gods."

"Maybe I miss home-cooking. We don't have it bad with Fiona, you know?" The past several months had outlined that to Creed. "We were lucky she raised us."

"Yeah. We could have gone into the system."

"That would have sucked." Creed turned his mind away from thoughts of being separated from his brothers. "Although I met a cowboy who'd been adopted, and he was pretty happy. Things worked out for him."

"It does. But we were in a good place with Fiona and Burke."

"And that's why I intend to fight for the ranch," Creed said with determination. "I just need a woman to help me with this project."

"It'd take you twenty years to *find* a woman," Judah said with some sarcasm, which cut Creed. "I'd say Pete is safe. Anyway, I thought we all agreed that the sacrificial lamb would do the deed, inherit the ranch and divvy it up between all of us. Thereby leaving the rest of us free to graze on the good things in life."

Creed crushed his soda can. "I'm not sure I'm grazing on the good things in life."

"Oh. You want angel food cake." Judah nodded. "Good luck with that. Let me know how it goes, will you?"

Creed rolled his eyes. Judah didn't understand. "I'm just saying, maybe we shouldn't burden Pete with all the responsibility."

"Why not? He's always been the responsible one."

"But maybe some of us should take a crack at being responsible, too. Take the pressure off him. He's got newborn triplets. It's selfish of us to stick him with all the duties."

"I think Fiona's probably realized by now that she can go ahead and award the ranch to Pete. Who could catch up with him? It would take years for one of us to find a woman and then have tons of kids. And what if the woman we found only wanted one? Or none?"

Creed gulped. He tried to envision Aberdeen with a big belly, and failed. She was such a slender woman. He liked slender, but then again, a little baby weight would look good on her. He liked full-figured gals, too.

Hell, he liked them all.

But he'd especially liked her, for some reason.

"It was the thrill of the hunt, nothing more," Judah said, his tone soothing. "Down, boy. It would have come to nothing."

Creed scowled. "I have no idea what you're babbling about."

"We are not settled men by nature. None of us sits and reads a whole lot, for example."

"Not true. Jonas read a hell of a lot to get through med school. And Sam for law school. And Rafe's been known to pick up a Greek tome or two."

"Pleasure reading. Expand-the-mind reading. That's what I'm talking about."

"Well, we're not reading romance novels, if that's what you're getting at." Creed put away the chips, beginning to feel slightly sick to his stomach. "Although maybe you should."

"What's that supposed to mean?" Judah demanded.

"Maybe if you read romance novels, you'd be able to see that which has been at the end of your nose for years, dummy." Creed jammed his hat down over his eyes, preparing to get in a few winks. "Think about it. It'll come to you." He pondered Judah's thick skull for a moment, then said, "Or maybe not."

Judah made no reply, which was fine with Creed, because all he wanted to do was sit and think about Aberdeen for a few minutes. *Judah is wrong. I owe it to myself to see if I can find a woman I could fall for. I owe it to myself to try to figure out if I'd be a good father. Maybe I would. I like kids.*

Wait. He didn't know that for sure. Truthfully, Pete's babies kind of intimidated him. Of course, they were no bigger than fleas. And fleas weren't good.

Pete's girls were cute as buttons. And they would grow. But they still made him nervous. Maybe he didn't have uncle-type feelings in him. He'd been uninterested in holding them. But they were so small and fragile. *I've eaten breadsticks bigger than their legs.*

Damn. I'm twenty-nine, and I'm scared of my nieces.
That can't be good.

"Have you held Pete's kids yet?" Creed asked Judah.

"Nah. They're kind of tiny. And they yell a lot."
Judah shook his head. "I don't want kids. I'm a quiet
kind of guy. Organized. Peaceful. Small, squalling
things are not peaceful."

Creed felt better. Maybe he wasn't totally a heel for
not bonding with his nieces. "I just think I could be
good at this, if I put my mind to it."

"At what? Being a dad?" Judah snorted. "Sure. Why
not? As long as you give up rodeo and getting dropped
on your head, you might be all right."

"Give up rodeo?" Creed echoed, the thought for-
eign and uncomfortable. He planned on rodeoing in the
Grandfather's Rodeo, if they had such a thing. They'd
drag him out of the saddle when he was cold and dead
and rigor mortis had set in. Cowboy rigor mortis. What
man didn't want to die with his boots on?

Of course, if he wasn't good at it anymore... "What
the hell am I doing?"

"Search me," Judah replied. "I can't figure you out,
bro. It'd take a licensed brain-drainer to do that."

Creed decided not to punch Judah, even though he
was pretty certain he should. All he knew was that before his concussion, before he'd met Aberdeen, he'd
been sure of who he was. He'd had a plan.

Now, he was asking himself all kinds of questions.
Judah was right: It would take a shrink to figure out
the knots in his brain.

I should have kissed her again. Then I wouldn't be
thinking about her. I'm shallow like that.

I really am.

TWO DAYS LATER, Johnny watched as a man he was particularly displeased to see walked into the bar. This reappearance couldn't have come at a worse time. Johnny shook his head, wondering why bad pennies always had to return when a man needed a lucky penny in his boot.

He wasn't surprised when Aberdeen went pale when she saw their customer. But then, to Johnny's astonishment, Aberdeen brightened, and went to hug the tall, lanky cowboy.

"Hello, Shawn," she said. "Long time, no see."

"Too long."

Blond-haired, smooth "Re-ride" Parker's glance slid over Aberdeen's curves. Johnny felt his blood begin to boil.

"Hello, Johnny," Aberdeen's ex-husband said.

"Re-ride," Johnny muttered, not pleased and not hiding it.

"Fixed this place up nicely." Re-ride looked around the bar. "I remember when it was just a hole in the wall."

"How's the rodeo treating you?" Johnny asked, figuring he could bring up unpleasantries if Shawn wanted. When Johnny had bought this place, it *had* been a hole in the wall—and Re-ride had just left Aberdeen with no means of support. Johnny had settled here to help Aberdeen mend the pieces of her shattered marriage, and seeing the cause of his sister's former distress did not leave him in a welcoming frame of mind.

"I'm not riding much these days," Shawn said, staring at Aberdeen, drinking her in, it seemed to Johnny, with an unnecessary amount of enthusiasm. "A man can't be on the circuit forever."

Johnny grunted. He followed the scores. He chatted to the cowboys who came in. Re-ride had never broken out of the bottom of the cowboy bracket. Maybe he had bad luck. Johnny didn't follow him closely enough to know. What he did know was that he seemed to get a lot of "re-rides," hence the name which had stuck all these years. In Johnny's opinion, Shawn could have quit the circuit ten years ago and no one would have missed him. "Guess not. Want to buy a bar?"

Aberdeen scowled at him. "No, he most certainly does not, I'm sure. Shawn, can we offer you a soda?"

Re-ride glanced at Johnny. "Ah, no. Thanks, though. Actually, I stopped by to talk to you, Aberdeen. If you have a moment."

Johnny felt his blood, which was already hot, heat up like he was sitting on a lit pyre of dry tinder.

"Johnny, can you listen out for the girls?" Aberdeen took off her apron, put the broom in the closet, and nodded to Shawn. "I do have a few minutes. Not long, though."

"Girls?" Shawn asked, snapping out of his lusting staring for a moment.

"Aberdeen's adopting three small children," Johnny said cheerfully, instantly realizing how to stop the man from using his soft-hearted sister for whatever reason his rodent-faced self had conjured up. What Aberdeen saw in the man, Johnny would never understand. *Sneaky like a rat.*

"Johnny," Aberdeen said, her tone warning as she opened the door. Re-ride followed her after tipping his hat to Johnny. Johnny ignored it, not feeling the need to socialize further.

This was no time for Re-Ride Parker to show up in Aberdeen's life. He resented every time the man appeared—usually about once or twice a year—but this time was different. He could tell, like a wolf scenting danger on the wind. Shawn was up to no good. He was never up to any good, as far as Johnny was concerned, but the way he'd practically licked Aberdeen with his eyeballs had Johnny's radar up. In fact, it was turned on high-anxiety.

Very bad timing, he told himself, but then again, that was Re-ride. Bad, bad timing.

"I'VE CHANGED MY MIND," Fiona told the five brothers who came by for a family council—and to eat barbecue, grilled corn and strawberry cake. Pete was at his house with his daughters and Jackie, probably juggling to keep up with bottles and diapers. Creed had promised to give him the thumbnail sketch of what happened at the meeting.

"I've had a lot on my mind. And I've been doing a lot of thinking about all of you. And your futures." She looked around at them, and Creed noticed Burke give her a worried glance as he served drinks in the large upstairs library. "I can't leave the ranch to the brother who gets married first and has the most children. That was my plan when Bode Jenkins got his cronies to try to legally seize this land for eminent domain purposes. His claim was that this particular property was too large for just one person to own—basically me—when the greater good could be affected by a new water system and schools. So I decided that if you all had children, we could make the case for the greater good, since there were plenty of Callahans. The state wouldn't have the right—nor would they dream, I would hope—of tossing a large family off the only property you've all ever known."

She nodded her head, her silvery-white hair shining under the lights, her eyes bright as she chose her words. Creed was amazed by his aunt's energy. For the hundredth time, he pondered how much she'd given up for them.

He even felt a little bad that he'd tried to thwart her plans. But fate stepped in and, just as soon as he was positive he wanted to thwart her forever, he'd met a girl who made his heart go *ding!* like a dinner bell. Maybe even a wedding bell. That was life for you.

"So," Fiona continued, "I have a confession to make. In my haste to keep the ranch out of the state's hands, and out of Bode's possession, I made a mistake. I played right in to his hands by agreeing to sell the land to a private developer. Fighting the state would have taken years in court, and money I was loath to spend out of your estate. So I chose a private buyer to sell it to, and made a deal that they would allow Rancho Diablo to be taken over by an angel investor. My offer was that we would buy the ranch back from them in five years, when Bode had turned his eyes to someone else's property or passed on, whichever came first." She took a deep breath, appearing to brace herself. "However, Bode was ahead of me, and the private investor I thought was absolutely safe and in our corner turned out to be in that nasty man's pocket. So," she said, looking around at each brother, "we're homeless in nine months. Totally. And for that, I can never say how sorry I am. I'm sorry for not being a wiser manager. I'm sorry that you men won't have the home your parents built—"

She burst into tears. The brothers sat, shocked, staring at their aunt, then at Burke, then at each other. Creed took a couple of quick breaths, wondering if he'd heard her right, if he could possibly have just heard that Rancho Diablo wasn't theirs anymore, and quickly realized this was no playacting, no manipulation, on Aunt Fiona's part.

It scared the hell out of him. His brothers looked just as stunned. But their aunt had been bearing an oh-so-heavy burden alone, so Creed got up and went to pat her back. "Aunt Fiona, don't cry. This isn't a matter for tears. We're not angry with you. We would never be angry with you. You've done the very best you could, and probably better than most people could under the circumstances."

"You *should* be angry! If you had an ounce of common sense, you would be, you scalawag." She pushed his hand away, and those of the other brothers when they came to fuss over her.

"But I probably don't have an ounce of sense," Creed said, "and we love you. Rancho Diablo is yours just as much as ours." He gulped, trying not to think about the yawning chasm that their lives had just turned into with a stroke of an errant wand. This was *home*.

Although perhaps not any more. But he only said, "Let Sam look over whatever papers you have to make certain there are no loopholes. Maybe call in some legal beagles. Right, Sam?"

His younger brother nodded. Creed got down on a knee and looked into her eyes. "You should have told us instead of trying to marry us off. Maybe we could have helped you."

"I wanted babies." She blew her nose into a delicate white handkerchief. "If I was going to lose the ranch, I wanted you to have brides who were eager to marry into the Callahan name, and live at Rancho Diablo. At least get married here, for heaven's sakes. But you're all so slow and stubborn," she said, with a glance around at each of them, "that I realized I was going to have to be honest with you instead of waiting for the spring sap to rise. Goodness knows, even the bulls are looking for mates. But not my nephews."

She sighed, put upon, and Creed glanced around at his brothers with a grin. "We tried to get hitched for you, Aunt Fiona. The ladies just won't have us."

"Well, I certainly don't blame them." She took the drink that Burke handed her, sipping it without energy. "But I'm making other plans. I'm holding a matchmaking ball, right here at Rancho Diablo. I'm inviting every single female that my friends know, and that's a ton, from as far away as the ladies care to come, all expenses paid. It's probably the last big party I'll ever have at this ranch, and I intend for it to be a blowout that will be talked about for years. Your bachelor ball, my going-away party."

"Whoa," Judah said, "there are only five of us, Aunt Fiona. We can't entertain a whole lot of women in a chivalrous manner."

"Goodness me," Fiona said, "most men would leap at the chance to have a bachelor raffle held in their honor."

"Bachelor raffle?" Jonas asked. "That sounds dangerous."

"Only if you're a wienie." Aunt Fiona gave her nephews an innocent look. "And there are no wienies in this room, I hope."

"Definitely not," Creed's twin, Rafe, said.

"No," Sam said, "but as the youngest, I'd like to put forth that I should have the lion's share of the ladies." His brothers scowled at him. "What? None of you wants to settle down. I'm not exactly opposed. At least not for the short term."

"You don't want to settle down," Jonas said, "you want to sow your wild oats. And all of us are ahead of you in the age department."

"Uh-oh," Sam said, leaping at the chance to bait his eldest brother, "do I hear the sound of a man's biological clock ticking? Bong, bong, Big Ben?"

Jonas looked as though he was about to pop an artery, Creed thought, not altogether amused. "We don't need a raffle or a bachelor bake-athon or whatever, Aunt Fiona. We're perfectly capable of finding women on our own. In relation to the ranch, if it isn't ours anymore—potentially—then there's no reason for us to hurry out and find brides. What we need to find are excellent lawyers, a whole team of them, who can unwind whatever Bode thinks he's got you strung with."

"We don't need to hire a lawyer, or a team," Aunt Fiona said, and the brothers looked at her with surprise. "We won't hire a lawyer because I hired a private investigator to keep an eye on him. I'm just positive Bode'll make a slip any day, and I'll be on him like a bird on a bug. And," she said, her doughy little face sad and tearstained with now-dried tears, "it wouldn't look good that I hired a P.I. to dig up dirt on him." She leaned close to Creed to whisper. "However, there's every chance he knows."

Creed winced. "Not unless he's bugged the house." Pete had claimed that someone had locked him in the basement last winter, searched the house and destroyed Aunt Fiona's jars of canned preserves and other stored food in an attempt to find something. What that person could have been looking for was anyone's guess.

Nothing had been stolen—no television, none of Fiona's jewelry, no tools. He supposed the house could be bugged, but the room they were currently sitting in was far away from the front doors and not easy to access. Someone would have needed several hours to search the house and plant bugs, and Pete hadn't been locked away that long. "It would be very difficult to bug this place."

"But he might know many things about us anyway," Fiona said, "because he gossips a lot."

"Bode?" Jonas said. "No one would talk about us to him."

"You think Sabrina McKinley might have told him something?" Sam asked, "since she's working as his caregiver?"

"No, Sabrina wouldn't blab," Aunt Fiona said, "because she's working for me."

Chapter Five

"Whoa," Jonas said, "Aunt Fiona, that little gypsy is a private investigator?"

Aunt Fiona nodded. "She's actually an investigative reporter, which is even better because sometimes they're nosier. It's her sister, Seton, who's the actual gumshoe. And don't sound so shocked, Jonas. You didn't think she was a real fortune-teller? She was playing a part I hired her to play."

Creed was having trouble dealing with all this new information. "But didn't she say that our ranch was in trouble, and a bunch of other nonsense?"

"Yes, but I gave her a script. I was trying to warn you, spur you along. As I mentioned, you're all quite slow. Thick, even. Why, I'd say molasses in winter moves faster than my nephews." She gave a pensive sigh. "The problem is, you don't have a home anymore. We don't have a place to run our business. And only Pete got married. At least he's happy," she said. "At least he found a wonderful woman." She cast an eye over the rest of her charges. "The rest of you will have a less favorable position to offer a wife. Your stock has dropped, as they say."

"Okay," Jonas said, "let's not think about our marital futures right now. Let's deal strictly with the business end."

"I say we go kick Bode Jenkins' skinny ass," Sam put in, and everyone shouted, *"No!"*

Sam said, "What a bunch of pansies."

"You have to be more sly than that," Fiona said sternly. "Violence is unacceptable. It's all about the mind, and I simply got out-thought."

"I'll have a friend eyeball the papers," Jonas said thoughtfully. "In the meantime, I'm closing on that land I offered on next week. We're not exactly homeless. If we have about nine months, we have enough time to move Rancho Diablo operations there. And build a house. It won't be like this one," he said, glancing around the room, "but it will be ours."

"What would you supposedly get for the house and land—if the deal is for real?" Rafe asked.

"Only ten million dollars," Fiona said. "A half of what it's worth for all the land, the house, and—"

She stopped, glanced at Burke, who shrugged.

"And?" Creed prompted.

"And mineral rights, and so on," she said, and Creed wondered if she'd just hedged some information. Fiona was known to keep her cards close to the vest. "It's a pittance, when you consider that we won't be able even to use the name *Rancho Diablo* anymore. We will truly be starting our brand from the bottom again."

Fiona's cheeks had pink spots in them and her eyes glittered. Creed could see that not only was her pride stung because Bode had outwitted her, she was crushed to have to give her nephews this hard news.

"We'll talk about it later," Creed said. "For now, this

is enough to digest. I don't think you should trouble yourself anymore tonight, Aunt Fiona."

Judah nodded. "I agree. My only question is, Bode hasn't been bothering you lately, has he?"

Fiona shook her head. "He's been pretty quiet since he thinks he got me over a barrel."

"About Sabrina," Jonas said. "What happens if Bode finds out that she's actually a reporter?"

They all took that in for a moment. Bode was known for his hot temper and grudges. He was underhanded, unforgiving. The tall, skinny man was unkind to just about everyone he knew; he kept people in his pocket by making sure he had whatever they needed. Bode was a power broker; he liked that power, and no one crossed him lightly.

Creed looked at his aunt. "Do you think involving her was a good idea, Aunt Fiona?"

"She and her sister came highly recommended. They are the nieces of—"

"Oh, no," Sam said, "not one of your Books 'n' Bingo cronies."

Fiona arched a brow at her youngest nephew. "Yes, as a matter of fact. I always hire friends, whether it's for curtain-making, preserving or tree-trimming. There's no better way to ensure loyalty and fairness in a job than to hire one's friends."

Creed's heart sank a little, too, just south of his boots. Aunt Fiona was in over her head. The expressions on his brothers' faces confirmed his own doubts. His cell phone jumped in his pocket, forestalling his worried thoughts. Glancing at the number, he frowned, wondering why he'd be getting a call from Wyoming.

Probably something to do with the rodeo he'd crashed

out of. "Excuse me for a moment, Aunt Fiona," he said, and stepped outside the library. "Hello?"

"Creed Callahan?" a man asked.

"Yes. Who's speaking?"

"This is Johnny Donovan. You were at our place—"

"I remember you, Johnny. How are you doing?" Creed's heart jumped right back up into his chest where it belonged as he wondered if Aberdeen might have put Johnny up to calling him. He could only hope.

"I'm fine. In a bit of a tight spot, actually."

"Oh?" Johnny had seemed capable of handling just about anything. "Something I can help with?"

"Actually, yes, perhaps," Johnny said. "You remember my sister, Aberdeen?"

Did he ever. "Yeah." He made his voice deliberately disinterested, not wanting to sound like an overeager stud.

"Well, I'm wondering—jeez, this is awkward," Johnny said. "I'm wondering if I paid your way back up here for a week, could you come keep an eye on my bar?"

Creed's jaw went slack. "Um—"

"I know. Like I said, it's awkward as hell. I wouldn't ask if I wasn't up against it, and if I didn't know that you were taking a bit of time off from the circuit."

"Yeah, I am." Creed sank into a hallway chair, staring out the arched, two-story windows that looked out over flat, wide, beautiful Rancho Diablo. "What's going on?"

"I need to be in Montana for a few weeks. Aberdeen needs to be there as well. We have a child custody hearing coming up."

Creed frowned. He didn't remember anything being

discussed about children. Did Aberdeen have kids? He knew nothing about her personal life—and yet, whenever he thought about her, he got an irrational shot of pleasure. *I'm doomed. I'm damned. She's not only a preacher but one with custody issues. Yee-haw.* "I see," he murmured, not seeing at all, but wanting to prod Johnny into spilling more info.

"Yeah. We can close the bar for two weeks, but I still hate to leave it unattended. This isn't the best area of town, as you know. We're kind of out of the way. I have a ton of friends here who could watch it, but frankly, I was thinking you owed me one."

Creed laughed, detecting teasing in Johnny's voice. "I probably do."

"I believe in doing business between friends," Johnny said. "The pay is generous. My bar's my livelihood. I'd like to keep it in safe hands."

Creed grinned. "And you don't want to keep it open?"

"Not necessarily, unless you want to. You don't have any experience with a bar or family-owned restaurant, do you?"

"Not so much." Creed wondered if he should back away from the offer politely or jump at the chance to see if Aberdeen still smoked his peace pipe the way he remembered she did. He was pretty certain she set him on fire all over. Sure, any woman could probably do that if a man was in the right, open mood, Creed mused— but Aberdeen seemed to do it for him even when she aggravated the hell out him.

He thought that was a pretty interesting juxtaposition. "We do have a family business, but it isn't in the same field as yours. We don't have strangers knocking on our door at all hours, not often anyway."

Johnny laughed. "So you'll do it?"

"I might. Let me run it past the family."

"Sounds mafia-like."

Creed grinned to himself. "Sometimes it can seem that way to outsiders. I'll get back in touch with you soon, Johnny. Good to hear from you."

He turned off his phone, sitting and considering this new twist for a moment. His gaze searched the wide vista outside, its dusty expanse vibrant even as night was covering the mesa. And then, he saw them, running like the wind across the faraway reaches of the ranch, black as night, fast as wind, free as spirits.

"Los Diablos," he murmured, awed by the hypnotizing beauty. "The Diablos are running!" he called to his brothers, and they came out of the library to stand at his side, watching in silence, shoulder to shoulder, knowing this might be one of the last times they ever saw the beautiful horses materializing across the evening-tinged swath of Rancho Diablo land.

"ARE YOU ALL RIGHT?" Aberdeen asked Johnny as she walked into the upstairs living room. "You look like you're thinking deep thoughts."

Johnny put his cell phone in his pocket. "No deeper than usual."

She smiled at him. "Then why are you frowning?"

"I've just been thinking about how we're going to make this all work out."

"Oh." She nodded and sat down on a worn cloth sofa. "I finally got all three girls to sleep. They are so sweet when they sleep. They look so angelic and happy."

A small smile lifted Johnny's mouth—but not for long. "Has Diane called to check on them?"

Aberdeen shook her head. "I think she probably won't for a while. I did talk to Mom and Dad today. They said Diane has decided to go around the world on a sailboat with her new boyfriend. They expect the trip to take about a year and a half."

Johnny's face turned dark. "You're kidding, right?"

"I wouldn't joke about that." Aberdeen sighed. "We need her at least to sign some forms that state we can make medical decisions for the girls while she's gone."

"I'm going over to France," Johnny said, and Aberdeen could see his jaw was tight. "I'm going to try to talk some sense into her. She just can't abandon her children. I don't know if she needs medication or what is going on—"

"Johnny." Aberdeen patted the sofa cushion beside her. "Come sit down."

He sighed. "Maybe I need a drink."

"It wouldn't help. I think you going to France is a good idea. I'll stay here with the girls and start looking for a house and school and a doctor."

"Have you ever thought how much having the girls here is going to change your life, even more than mine?"

Aberdeen blinked. "There's no point to worrying about the situation. We love the girls. Diane, as much as I hate to say it, appears to be unfit or unwilling at the moment."

Johnny sat silently for a few minutes. "I'll make a plane reservation. I may drag Diane back here kicking and screaming, though."

"Do you want me to go?" Aberdeen asked, and Johnny quickly shook his head.

"No. You've got enough to do in the next two weeks for the custody hearing." Johnny stood, going to look out a window over the parking lot. "I think I might sell the bar, Aberdeen."

She drew in a sharp breath. "Why?"

He didn't turn around. "I think it's time."

"Is this because of Shawn?" she asked, hating to ask but feeling she had to. She was aware Johnny had been biting his tongue for the past two weeks to keep from complaining about her ex-husband's frequent presence. It would be like Johnny to decide to sell the bar and move the newly enlarged family to Timbuktu if he thought he could get rid of Shawn. Johnny didn't understand her rosy daydreams of romance with Shawn were long evaporated. Shawn was comfortable, someone she'd grown up with, in a strange way.

"No," he said, but she wondered if he was being completely truthful. "But on that unpleasant topic, is there a reason he's suddenly hanging around again?"

A flush ran up Aberdeen's cheeks and neck. "I'm not exactly sure what you mean, or if he has a specific reason for his presence. He says he's changed—"

"Ugh," Johnny interrupted. "Changed what? His spots? I don't think so."

That stung. Aberdeen blinked back tears. "Johnny, he's been through a lot. It's not like I'd remarry him. You know that."

"I just think it's not a good time for someone like him to be in your life if we're serious about getting custody of the kids."

"I think he's lonely, and nothing more."

"You're not lonely right now," Johnny pointed out. "You're busy raising three little girls who really need you."

"Shawn knows me. He's a part of my past."

Johnny turned away. Aberdeen took a deep breath. "So, why are you really thinking about selling the bar? You've mentioned it a couple of times. I'm beginning to think you might really be considering it."

"Aberdeen," Johnny said suddenly, ignoring her question, "if your Prince Charming rode up tomorrow on a white horse, would you want that?"

"I think by twenty-nine a woman doesn't believe in fairy tales. The fairy godmother never showed up for me." She touched her brother on the arm, and after a moment, he gave her a hug. They stood together for a few moments, and Aberdeen closed her eyes, drinking in the closeness.

Just for a few heartbeats, she felt Johnny relax. He was sweet big brother again, not worried, not overburdened by life. She let out a breath, wishing this feeling could last forever.

The sound of a baby crying drifted across the hall. Aberdeen broke away from Johnny, smiling up at him. "Don't worry so much, big brother," she said, but he just shook his head.

"By the way," he said offhandedly as she started to leave the room to check on Lincoln Rose and her sisters. "I've got Creed Callahan coming to watch over the bar while we're away."

Aberdeen looked at Johnny. It didn't matter that her heart skipped a beat—several beats—at the mention of Creed's name, or that she'd thought she'd never see him again. "That's probably a good idea," she murmured, going to comfort the baby, wondering if her brother thought he had to play matchmaker in her life. Johnny was worried she was falling for Shawn again. So had he called in a handpicked Prince Charming?

It would be so like Johnny—but if he was meddling in her life, she'd have to slap him upside his big head.

He just didn't understand that Creed Callahan, while handsome enough to tease her every unattended thought, was no Prince Charming—at least not hers.

Chapter Six

The next day, Aberdeen wondered if her brother understood something about men that she didn't. Shawn sat at their kitchen table, watching her feed the girls and wearing a goofy grin.

"I never thought you'd be such good mother material," Shawn said, and Aberdeen looked at him.

"Why would you think I wouldn't be?"

Shawn was the opposite of Creed in appearance: blond, lanky, relaxed. Almost too relaxed, maybe bordering on lazy, she thought. Creed was super-dark, built like a bad girl's dream with big muscles and a strong chest, and not relaxed at all. She frowned as she wiped Lincoln Rose's little chin. Actually, she didn't know much about Creed. He'd been ill when she'd seen him. But she still had the impression that he wasn't exactly Mr. Happy-Go-Lucky.

Not like Shawn.

"You always seemed too career-oriented to want a family." Shawn sipped at his coffee, and smiled a charming smile at her. "I always felt like you were going to be the breadwinner in our marriage."

"Would that have been a problem?"

"For a man's ego, sure. Some men might like their

wife being the big earner, but not me. I have my pride, you know." He grabbed one of the carrots she'd put on the three-year-old's plate and munched it.

Not much pride. Aberdeen told herself to be nice and handed him Lincoln Rose. "Let's test your fathering skills, then."

"I'm a family man," he said, holding Lincoln Rose about a foot away from him. Lincoln Rose studied him and he studied her, and then the baby opened her mouth like a bird and let out a good-sized wail. "Clearly she doesn't recognize father material," Shawn said, handing Lincoln Rose back to Aberdeen.

Aberdeen rolled her eyes. "Have you ever held a baby?"

"Not that I can recall," Shawn said cheerfully. "But that doesn't mean I couldn't learn to like it. I just need practice and a good teacher." He looked at her so meaningfully that Aberdeen halted, recognizing a strange light in her husband's eyes. He looked purposeful, she thought—and Shawn and purposeful did not go together well.

"There was no double meaning in that statement, was there?" Aberdeen asked.

Shawn's expression turned serious. "Aberdeen, look, I've been doing a lot of thinking." Idly, he grabbed another carrot; thankfully, the toddlers didn't seem to mind. Aberdeen put some golden raisins on their plates to keep them happy while Shawn got over his thinking fit. "I know you're determined to adopt these little ladies."

"They will always have a home with me."

Shawn nodded. "I think that's a good idea. Diane is a great girl, but even back when you and I were married, she wasn't the most stable person, if you know what I mean."

Aberdeen bit her lip. She didn't want to discuss this with him. "Diane has a good heart," she murmured.

"I know," Shawn said, his tone soothing, "but you're doing right by these girls. I believe they need you." He gave her a winning smile. "And I know you're worried about the temporary-custody situation. I've been thinking about how I could be of assistance."

Aberdeen shook her head. "Thanks, Shawn, but I believe the good Lord will take care of us."

"I'd like to help," he said. "I really mean it."

She looked at him, her attention totally caught. It seemed the little girls in their sweet pink dresses were listening, too, because their attention seemed focused on Shawn. Handsome Shawn with the charming smile, always getting what he wanted. Aberdeen watched him carefully. "What are you getting at?"

"I just want you to know that I'm here for you." He took a deep breath, and she could see that he meant every word—at least, he did while he was speaking them. "I wasn't the world's greatest husband, Aberdeen. You deserved a hell of a lot better. And I'd like to be here for you now if you need me." He gave her the most sincere look she'd ever seen him wear on his handsome face. "All you have to do is say the word. I'd marry you again tomorrow if it would help you with custody or adoption or anything."

Aberdeen blinked, shocked. But as she looked into Shawn's eyes, she realized he was trying to atone, in his own bumbling way, for the past.

And as much as she'd like to tell him to buzz off, she wondered if she could afford to be so callous. She didn't know how the courts would regard her. She thought they would see her in a positive light, as a minister, as Diane's sister, as a caring aunt.

But what if the court preferred a married mother for these children? Aberdeen looked at her nieces. They seemed so happy, so content to be with her. Their eyes were so bright and eager, always focused on her as they banged spoons or pulled off their shoes and dropped them to the floor. Did it matter that she planned to live with them out of the state where they'd been raised? Would she look more stable with a husband? She and Johnny and Diane knew that even two-parent homes lacked stability—but would a court of law see it that way? For her nieces' sake, maybe she couldn't just write Shawn's offer off as so much talk.

"I would hope nothing like that will be necessary."

He shrugged. "I mean it, Aberdeen, I really do. If you need a husband, then, I'm your man."

"What happened to the man who didn't want to be married to the family breadwinner?" she asked, not wanting to encourage him.

He smiled. "Well, I'd feel like things were a bit more balanced since you need me, Aberdeen."

She pulled back a little and tried not to let anger swamp her. Shawn was pretty focused on his own needs; she knew that. But he was harmless, too—now that she wasn't married to him, she could see him in a more generous light. Sometimes. Creed's dark-blue eyes flashed in her memory. She could see him laughing, even as he was in pain from the concussion. The man had a sense of humor, though things hadn't been going his way. He had a roguish charm, and she'd told herself to run from it.

Because it had reminded her of Shawn. *Crazy,* she'd thought of him. *No more loco in my life.*

And yet loco was sitting here right now offering to give her the illusion of stability for the sake of her nieces. Aberdeen swallowed. Maybe she shouldn't dismiss the offer out of hand. Husband, wife, devoted uncle—not quite a nuclear family here, but close enough.

But it was Shawn. And she wanted something else. "Have some more carrots," she said absently, her eyes on her nieces. She'd been totally attracted to the cowboy from New Mexico, as much as she didn't want to admit it, and no matter how hard she'd tried to forget him, he hadn't left her memory.

But maybe it was better to deal with the devil she knew—if she needed a devil at all.

"Don't mind me," Creed said three days later, as Johnny looked around the bar one last time. "I've got everything I'll need. I'll be living like King Tut here."

"He didn't live long," Johnny pointed out, "and I think somebody might have done him in. Let's hope that your time here is spent in a more pleasant manner."

Creed grinned. "You're sure you don't want me to keep this place open for business?"

"It's too much to ask of a friend," Johnny said.

"Lot of income for you to lose," Creed pointed out. "I'm averse to losing income."

Johnny laughed. "I am, too. But this has got to be done. You just keep an eye on things, guard my castle and I'll be grateful for the imposition on your time."

Creed took a bar stool, glancing around the bar. "You did yourself a good turn buying this place, Johnny. It's nice. Did it take you long to turn a profit?"

"No. Not really. Building business was slow, but it happened over time. People like to hear Aberdeen preach, and then they remember us for snacks and beverages the rest of the week. It's a loyal crowd around here." He took a rag and wiped the mahogany bar with it. "I might sell, you know."

Creed blinked. "Do you mind me asking why?"

Johnny shook his head. "You'll see soon enough."

Creed wasn't sure what he meant by that, but if Johnny didn't want to discuss his business, that was fine by him. He wouldn't want to talk to anyone about Rancho Diablo and all that was happening back home unless he knew that person very well.

Actually, he wouldn't discuss it with anyone but family. Everything had gotten complicated real fast. He looked around the bar, trying to see himself with some kind of business set-up like this, and failed.

But he'd always think of it kindly because it had been his inn in the wilderness. If he hadn't come here—

"Here you go, sweetie," he heard Aberdeen say, and then he heard feet coming down the staircase. He watched the stairs expectantly, wondering how he'd feel about seeing her again. Certainly he hadn't stopped thinking about her. She was a pretty cute girl, any man would have to admit. In fact, probably lots of men noticed. But she was a prickly one. She would never have fitted into one of Aunt Fiona's marriage schemes. The woman was spicy and probably didn't have a maternal bone in her body.

Still, he waited, his eyes eager for that first glimpse of her.

She made it into view with a baby in her arms, holding the hand of a tiny toddler and with a somewhat larger toddler hanging on to her skirt as they slowly negotiated the staircase. Creed's face went slack, and his heart began beating hard in his chest. Three little blond girls?

"Holy smokes," he said, "you guys have been keeping secrets from me." He got up to help the small girls make it down the last few steps so they wouldn't face-plant at the bottom of the staircase. One shrank back from him, wanting to get to the landing herself, and one little girl smiled up at him angelically, and his heart fell into a hole in his chest. They were sweet, no question.

And then he looked up into Aberdeen's blue eyes, and it was all he could do not to stammer. "Hello, Aberdeen."

She smiled at him tentatively. "Hi, Creed. So nice of you to come look after Johnny's bar."

He caught his breath at the sight of those eyes. She was smiling at him, damn it, and he couldn't remember her ever being soft around him. It had his heart booming and his knees shaking just a bit. "It's nothing," he said, trying to sound gallant and not foolish, and Aberdeen smiled at him again.

"Oh, it's something to my brother. He said you're just the man he could trust to keep his bar safe."

Creed stepped back, nearly blinded by all the feminine firepower being aimed at him. "It's nothing," he repeated.

She gave him a last smile, then looked at Johnny. "We're ready for the road. Aren't we, girls?" She looked at Creed. "I'm sorry. These are my nieces. We're going to Montana for a custody hearing."

"Custody?"

She nodded. "I'm filing for temporary custody of the

girls for now. And then maybe later, something more, if necessary."

The smile left her face, and Creed just wanted it back. "They sure are cute," he said, feeling quite stupid and confused, but the last thing he'd ever imagined was that Aberdeen Donovan might one day be the mother of three little girls. He didn't know what else to say. Clearly, he didn't know as much about these folks as he'd thought he had. He'd best stick to what he'd been hired for. "Well, I'll keep the floor nailed down," he said to Johnny, his gaze on Aberdeen.

"I'll check in on you soon enough." Johnny helped Aberdeen herd the girls toward the door. "If you have any questions, give me a ring on my cell. And thanks again, Creed. I can't tell you how much I appreciate this."

"I appreciated you saving my life," Creed murmured, letting one of the tiny dolls take him by the hand. He led her to Johnny's big truck, and watched to see that she was put in her car seat securely, and then he waved as they drove away, his head whirling.

"Three," he muttered. "Three small, needy damsels in some kind of distress." He headed back inside the bar, shell-shocked. Aberdeen had never mentioned children. Of course, they'd barely spoken to each other.

At the moment, his swagger was replaced by stagger, and a rather woeful stagger at that.

"I kissed a woman who's getting custody of three children," he said to himself as he locked up the bar. "That's living dangerously, and I sure as *hell* don't want to end up like Pete."

Or do I?

Chapter Seven

A couple of hours later, Creed was lying on the sofa upstairs, nursing a brewski and pondering what all he didn't know about Aberdeen. He was certain he could still smell the sweet perfume she wore, something flowery and clean and feminine, like delicate lilies and definitely not baby powder from the three little darlings—when he heard a window sliding open downstairs. The sound might not have been obvious to most people, but since he and his brothers had done their share of escaping out of windows in the middle of the night, he knew the stealthy sound by heart.

And that meant someone was due for an ass-kicking. He searched around for appropriate armament, finding Johnny's available weaponry lacking. There was a forgotten baby bottle on the coffee table. A few books were stacked here and there, mostly addressing the topic of raising children.

This was a side of Aberdeen he had totally missed. Creed vowed that if the opportunity ever presented itself, he might ask a few questions about parenthood, a subject he found somewhat alarming. He glanced around the room again, but there wasn't a baseball bat or even a small handgun to be found. If Johnny had a gun, he probably had it locked in a drawer now that he had small angels terrorizing his abode. If Creed had children, he'd certainly have the world's most secure gun cabinet with all things that go pop safely locked away.

He was going to have to make do with his beer bottle, he decided, and crept down the stairs. There he saw his uninvited guest rooting around in the liquor bottles like a martini-seeking raccoon.

And then he spied a very useful thing: a long-handled broom. In the dim light, he could barely make out a shadow investigating the different choices the bar had to offer. The man seemed in no hurry to make his selection; apparently he was a thief of some distinction. When he finally settled on a liquor, he took his time pouring it into a glass. Creed wondered if olives speared on a plastic sword, perhaps a twist of lemon, might be next for his discerning guest.

The thief took a long, appreciative drink. Creed picked up the broom, extending the wooden handle toward the intruder, giving him a pointed jab in the side. His guest dropped his beverage and whirled around, the sound of shattering glass interrupting the stillness.

"Who's there?"

Creed grinned to himself, reaching out with the broom for a slightly more robust jab. The intruder was scared, and clearly hadn't yet located Creed in the dark room. Moonlight spilled through the windows, bouncing a reflection back from the bar mirror, so Creed had an excellent view of his shadowy target. "The devil," he said. "Boo!"

The man abandoned his pride and shot to the door. Creed stuck out the pole one last time, tripping his guest to the floor. "Not so fast, my friend," Creed said. "You haven't paid for your drink."

"Who are you?" The thief scrambled to his feet.

"Who are you?" Creed asked. "The bar's closed. Didn't you see the sign?"

"I—I wasn't doing anything wrong. I was just wetting my whistle."

"Do you do this often?" Creed asked. "Because I think the owners might object."

"They don't care. They give me free drinks all the time." He backed toward the window where he'd let himself in, realizing he wasn't going to get past Creed and his broom.

Creed put the handle out, tripping the man from behind. "Why do they give you free drinks, friend?"

"Because I was married to Aberdeen. And I'm going to marry her again. So I have a right to be here," he asserted, and Creed's heart went still in his chest.

"Are you telling the truth?"

"I never lie," the stranger said. "Anyway, I'm sorry I bothered you. I'll just be leaving the way I came in now."

Creed flipped on the lights, curious to see the man Aberdeen was going to marry. They stared at each other, sizing up the competition. "I'll be damned. I know you," Creed said, "you're that dime-store cowboy they call Re-ride."

"And you're a Callahan." Re-ride looked none too happy. "What are you doing in Aberdeen's bar?"

"Keeping it free of snakes." Creed felt the interview to be most unpleasant at this point. He almost wished he'd never heard the man break in. Marry Aberdeen? Surely she wouldn't marry this poor excuse for a cowboy.

Then again, she'd married him before, or at least that's what he claimed. It was something else Creed hadn't known about her. To be honest, Creed hadn't proven himself to be any more of a serious cowboy in Aberdeen's eyes after his rambling night on the plank bench. Aberdeen probably thought he was just as loose as Re-ride.

That didn't sit too well. "Go on," he told Re-ride. "Get out of my face. I'd beat you with this broom, but I've never roughed up a lady and I'm not going to start tonight. So *git*."

Re-ride looked like he was about to take exception to Creed's comment, then thought better of it and dove out the window. Creed locked it behind him—and this time, he turned on the security system. He couldn't risk more varmints crawling into the bar tonight—he was in too foul a mood to put up with nonsense. He put himself to bed in the guest room, feeling quite out of sorts about life in general.

Babies, beer burglars and a one-time bride—sometimes, life just handed a cowboy lemonade with no sugar in sight.

"I've looked over these papers with Sam," Jonas said to Aunt Fiona, "and I think we're selling ourselves short. Maybe."

His aunt looked at him. "How?"

"We should fight it, for one thing. Not roll over for the state or Bode Jenkins. And I'm in a fighting mood. Now that I've sold my medical practice, I have more time to help you with things," Jonas said. "I should have been more available for you all along."

Fiona looked at her oldest nephew. "It shouldn't have

necessitated your attention. Darn Bode Jenkins's hide, anyway."

Jonas leaned against the kitchen counter, eyeing his small, spare aunt. She was like a protective bear overseeing her cubs, but actually, things should be the other way around. He and his brothers needed to be protecting her and Burke, now in their golden years. Fiona had tried to convince them that she was one foot from the grave, but he'd been keeping an eye on her, and he was pretty certain Fiona was working their heartstrings. She had never seemed healthier, other than an unusually low spirit for her, which he attributed to her concern about losing the ranch.

He had decided to lift those burdens from his diminutive, sweetly busybodying aunt. "You know that land I put an offer on?"

Fiona brightened. "Yes. East of here. How's that coming?"

"I've changed my mind," Jonas said, after a thoughtful pause. It took him a minute to get his head around the words; every day since he'd made the decision, he'd pondered the situation again and again. "I've withdrawn my offer."

Fiona's eyes widened. "For heaven's sakes, why?"

"Because we're not going anywhere," Jonas said. "That's how Creed feels, and I agree with him."

"Creed! He's had a concussion recently," Fiona said with a sniff. "He's not thinking straight. Then again, when does he?"

"I think he might be thinking straighter than all of us." Jonas reached over and patted her shoulder. "I'm going to need all my resources, both time and money, to fight this theft of our land. I don't regret giving up on Dark Diablo for a minute."

Fiona looked at him. "Dark Diablo? It sounds beautiful."

He thought again about the wide expanse of open land where he could run cattle and horses and have his own place. His own sign hanging over the drive, shouting to the world that this was Dark Diablo, his own spread. But Creed had said Rancho Diablo was their home, and that they should fight for it, and fight hard. They would have to be dragged off their land—instead of rolling over because things looked dark and done. "Otherwise," Creed had said, "we're just cowards. Runners. The family stays together," he'd said. "Sic Sam on them."

Jonas's jaw had dropped. Sam didn't get "sicced" on anyone. Sam liked to ignore the fact that he'd gone to law school, barely broke a sweat passing the bar, and then gone on to prestigious internships, working his way up to cases that garnered him credit for being a steely defender who never failed to make his opponents cry. He'd become famous for his big persona. But only his family had noticed that with every big win to his credit, he became unhappier.

Sam liked winning. Yet he didn't like defending corporate cases where he knew the little guy was getting strung. And after a particularly nasty case, Sam had packed it in. Come home to Rancho Diablo to recover from big-city life. Now he mostly acted as though he hadn't a care in the world.

Except for Rancho Diablo.

Jonas winced. They couldn't sic Sam on Bode, but they could fight. "I've been thinking, Aunt Fiona, and

I'm not so certain your marriage scheme doesn't have some merit."

She radiated delight. "Do you think so?"

He shrugged. "It wouldn't be as easy for the state to take a property where there are families. I'm not saying that they care about us, but it certainly makes it easier to win public sympathy when folks realize what happens to us here could happen to them."

"Yes, but Pete doesn't even live here with his family," she said, her shoulders sagging. "And the rest of you are short-timers."

He grinned. "Are you hosting a pity party, Aunt?"

She glared at him. "What if I am? It's my party, and I can cr—"

"When Creed gets back here in a few days, we'll throw that bachelor ball you wanted."

"Really?" Fiona clapped her hands.

"Sure. He needs to settle down."

She looked at him, suspicious. "Why him?"

"He wants to settle down more than anyone. Haven't you noticed? And his days of rodeoing are over, though he'll never admit it. A woman would keep him off the road, and children would keep him busy."

"It's a great plan," Fiona said, "if you think it would work."

Better him than me. With Fiona busy with her usual plotting and planning, I'll try to figure out how to undo this problem with the ranch.

He was going to have to take a firm hand with his aunt and Burke. They weren't telling everything they knew. It was a riddle wrapped inside a mystery, but he agreed with Creed on one thing: It was better to fight than run.

AFTER A COUPLE MORE BEERS to help get him over the shock of Aberdeen's babies and the ex-husband who wanted her back, Creed decided maybe he'd be wiser to run than fight. It was three in the morning, but he couldn't sleep, and if he didn't quit thinking about her, he was going to end up having beer for breakfast. Creed sighed, not having any fun at all. Aberdeen tortured him, and she didn't even know it.

"I wouldn't be so bothered if it wasn't for Re-ride," he told a small pink stuffed bear he'd found underneath the coffee table—probably the smallest damsel's bear. He'd placed the bear on the coffee table after he'd discovered it. The bear had looked forlorn and lost without its tiny owner, so Creed had propped it on a stack of books, regarding it as he would a comforting friend. "You have to understand that the man is given to useless. Simply useless."

The bear made no reply but that was to be expected from stuffed pink bears, Creed told himself, and especially at this hour. And the bear was probably tired of hearing him debate his thoughts, because Creed was certainly tired of himself. Everything ran through his mind without resting, like a giant blender churning his conscience. "She's just so pretty," he told the bear, "I don't see what she sees in him. It's something she doesn't see in me." He considered that for a moment, and then said, "Which is really unfortunate, for me and for her. I am the better man, Bear, but then again, a woman's heart is unexplainable. I swear it is."

If his brothers were here, he could talk this over with them. They wouldn't be sympathetic, but they would clap him on the back, rib him mercilessly or perhaps offer him some advice—and at least he'd feel better. It was hard to feel bad when as an army of one trying to feel sorry for yourself, you faced an army of five refusing to let you give in to your sorrows. How many times had he and his brothers dug each other out of their foul moods, disappointments or broken hearts?

There weren't as many broken hearts among them as there might have been because they had each other to stall those emotions. When you knew everybody was working too hard to listen to you wheeze, you got over a lot of it on your own. But then, when it was important, you could count on a brother to clout you upside the head and tell you that you were being a candy-ass.

He wasn't at that point yet. "But she's working on me, Bear." He waved his beer at the toy. "I didn't come here to help Johnny. It wasn't the overwhelming reason I said yes, you know? It was her. And then, I got here, and I found out...I found out that maybe I rang my bell so hard that I didn't really pay attention to her when I met her. I think, Bear," he said, lowering his voice to a whisper, "that I have it *bad*."

Really bad, if he was sitting here talking out his woes on a baby's pink bear. Creed sighed, put the bottle on the table and shut his eyes so he wouldn't look at the bear's black button eyes anymore for sympathy he couldn't possibly find. "Grown men don't talk to bears," he said, without opening his eyes, "so if you don't mind, please cease with the chatter so I can get some shut-eye."

If he *could* sleep—without thinking about Aberdeen becoming a mother, a scenario that in no way seemed to have a role for him.

ALL ABERDEEN COULD BE when the judge had heard her case was relieved. She was sad for her sister and for her nieces, but it was good to be able to have temporary legal custody of her nieces.

"However," the judge continued, "it's in the best interests of the children that they remain here in Montana, where their maternal grandparents are, and paternal as well, who may be able to provide some assistance."

Shock hit Aberdeen. "Your Honor," she said, "my congregation is in Wyoming. My livelihood is in Wyoming."

The judge looked at her sternly. "A bar isn't much of a place for young, displaced girls to grow up. You have no house for them set apart from the establishment where there could be unsavory elements. And your congregation, as you've described it, is transient. None of this leads me to believe that the situation in Wyoming is more stable for the minors than it would be here, where at least the maternal grandparents can be trusted to oversee the wellbeing of the children."

Aberdeen glanced at Johnny. He would have to go back to Lance. She would be here alone with their parents, who would be little or no help. Tears jumped into Aberdeen's eyes when Johnny clasped her hand. She stared at the judge and nodded her acquiescence.

"Of course, should anything change in your circumstances, the court will be happy to reconsider the situation. Until then, a social worker will be assigned to you." He nodded at Johnny and Aberdeen. "Best of luck to you, Miss Donovan, Mr. Donovan."

Aberdeen turned and walked from the court, not looking at Johnny until they'd gotten outside.

"I expected that," Johnny said, and Aberdeen glanced at him as they walked toward his truck. "That's why I said I'd probably sell the bar. I was hoping it would turn out differently, but I knew Mom and Pop know the judge."

Aberdeen drew in a sharp breath. "Are you saying that they talked to him?"

Johnny climbed in behind the wheel, and Aberdeen got in the passenger side. "I don't know that they did, but I know that he would be familiar with some of our situation. To be fair, any judge hearing this type of case might have decided similarly. But I don't think him knowing Mom and Pop hurt them."

"So now what?" Aberdeen asked.

"Now we're custodians, for the time being," Johnny said. "I've got someone looking for Diane, and if they manage to make contact with her, we'll know a little more. I'll sell the bar, and we'll stay here until matters get straightened out. We're either going to be doing this for the long haul, or it could be as short a time as it takes Diane to come to her senses."

"You don't have to stay here," Aberdeen said. "I've taken this on gladly."

"We're family. We do it together." Johnny turned the truck toward their parents' house.

Aberdeen looked out the window. "I think selling the bar is too drastic, don't you?"

"I can think of more drastic things I don't want to see happen."

Aberdeen looked at him. "I think the worst has already passed."

Her brother took a deep breath, seemed to consider his words. "Look, I just don't want you even starting to think that putting a permanent relationship in your life might be the way to salvage this thing."

"You mean Shawn."

"I mean Re-ride." Johnny nodded. "Don't tell me it hasn't crossed your mind. He as much admitted to me that he wouldn't be opposed to remarrying you."

Aberdeen shook his head. "He mentioned it. I didn't take him very seriously."

"Stability might start looking good to you after a few months of Mom and Pop interfering with your life."

"So you're selling the bar to move here to protect me from myself?" Aberdeen sent her brother a sharp look. "Johnny, I'm not the same girl I was when Shawn and I got married."

"Look, I don't want to see both my sisters make mistakes is all," Johnny said. "You're not like Diane in any way, but Diane wasn't like this before her marriage fell apart, either."

Aberdeen sighed, reached over to pat Johnny's arm. "I think you worry too much, but thanks for looking out for me. I know you do it out of love and a misguided sense of protection, which I happen to greatly appreciate."

Johnny smiled. "So then. Listen to big brother."

Aberdeen checked her cell phone for messages, then went all in. "Is that why you brought the cowboy back?"

Johnny glanced at her. "I could pretend that I don't know what you're talking about, but I figured you'd suspect, so I might as well just say it doesn't hurt to have an ace in my boot."

"Johnny Donovan," Aberdeen said, "perhaps I'll start meddling in your life. Maybe I'll find a string of cute girls and send them your way to tempt you into matrimony. How would you like that?"

"I hope you do, because I'd like it very much." Johnny grinned. "Make them tall, slender and good cooks. I do love home cooking, and women who want to cook these days are rare."

Aberdeen shook her head. "Creed has no interest in me. And the feeling is mutual. Besides, he wouldn't solve my problem in any way if Diane doesn't come back. Even if he and I got some wild notion to get married, he lives in New Mexico. I don't know that the judge is going to let me take the girls anywhere if you really believe he's influenced by Mom and Pop."

"Still, he'll keep Re-ride busy," Johnny predicted, "and I won't mind that a bit."

"You have a darkly mischievous soul, Johnny," Aberdeen said, but secretly, she had liked seeing Creed Callahan again. It was too bad she and Creed were as opposite as the sun and the moon.

He could make a woman think twice about taking a walk on the *very* wild side.

Chapter Eight

Creed woke up and stretched, hearing birds singing somewhere nearby. It was different here than in Diablo. Everything was different, from the birds to the land, to the—

The pink bear stared at him, and Creed sighed. "Okay, last night won't happen again. You will not be hearing such yak from me again. I had my wheeze, and I'm over it." He carried the bear down to the room where the little girls had been sleeping, and was caught by the sight of tiny dresses, shorts and shoes spread at the foot of a big bed. There were toys scattered everywhere, and even a fragile music box on the dresser top. It was like walking into fairyland, he mused, and he wondered if Aberdeen had had a room like this when she was little.

He backed out of the room after setting the bear on the bed, decided to shower and get cheerful about the day—and there was no better way to get cheerful than to fill his stomach. That would require heading out to the nearest eating establishment, which would be a great way to see Lance. He took a fast shower, jumped into fresh jeans and a shirt, clapped his hat on his head and jerked open the bar door to take in a lungful of fresh, bracing summer air.

Re-ride stared up at him from the ground where he was sitting, leaning against the wall, clearly just awakening.

"Oh, no, this is not going to happen," Creed said, setting the security alarm, locking the door and loping toward his truck. "You and I are not going to be bosom buddies, so buzz off," he called over his shoulder.

Re-ride was in hot pursuit. "Where are you going?" he asked, jumping into the truck when Creed unlocked the door.

"I'm going someplace you're not. Get out." Creed glared at him.

"Breakfast sounds good. I'll show you the hot spots around here." Re-ride grinned. "I know where the best eggs and bacon are in this town."

Creed didn't want the company, but his stomach was growling, and if the eggs were the best… "If you give me any trouble," he said, and Re-ride said, "Nope. Not me."

Creed snorted and followed his new friend's directions to Charity's Diner two streets over. "I'm pretty certain I could have found this place myself," Creed said, and Re-ride laughed.

"But you didn't. Come on. I'll show you some waitresses who are so cute you'll want more than marshmallows in your cocoa."

That made no sense, Creed thought sourly. In fact, it was a pretty stupid remark, but he should probably expect little else from the freeloader. He followed Re-ride into the diner and seated himself in a blue vinyl booth, watching with some amazement as Re-ride waved over a tiny, gorgeous, well-shaped redhead.

"This is Cherry," Re-ride said, "Cherry, this is Creed Callahan."

Creed tipped his hat, noticing that Re-ride's hand fell perilously low on Cherry's nicely curved hip. "Pleasure," he told Cherry, and she beamed at him.

"Cocoa?" she asked Creed.

"Coffee," he said, wary of Re-ride's cocoa promise. "Black as you've got it, please."

She showed sweet dimples and practically stars in her big green eyes as she grinned back at Creed. "Re-ride, you've been hiding this handsome friend of yours. Shame on you."

Re-ride shook his head as he ran his gaze hungrily down a menu, his mind all on food now, though he still clutched Cherry's hip. Creed looked at his own menu as Cherry drifted away, surprised when Re-ride tapped the plastic sheet.

"She likes you, I can tell," Re-ride said.

"Look," Creed said, annoyed, "it's plain that you don't want competition for Aberdeen, but I don't—"

"Oh, there's no competition." Re-ride shook his head. "I told you, I'm marrying Aberdeen. I'm just trying to find you someone, so you won't be odd man out."

Creed sighed. "Odd man out of what? I'm only here for a few days."

"Really?" Re-ride brightened. "I might have misunderstood Johnny when I called him last night."

Creed perked up. "You talked to Johnny?"

"Yep." Re-ride lowered his voice. "You know Aberdeen is trying to adopt Diane's little girls, a horrible idea if there ever was one."

"Why?" Creed asked, telling himself that the Donovan family matters were none of his business, and yet he was so curious he could hardly stand it.

"Because I'm not cut out to be a father," Re-ride explained. "I don't want to be a father to Diane's children."

"Oh." Creed blinked. "Selfish, much?"

"What?" Re-ride glared at him, obviously confused.

Creed shrugged. "If you love Aberdeen, wouldn't you want what she wants?"

"No, that's not how it works. I'm the man, and I'll make the decisions about what's best for our family. There's no way a marriage can work when there's no chance for privacy right from the start. A man and his wife need *privacy,* and I'm sure you know what I mean, Callahan."

Fire flamed through Creed's gut. *Jealousy. By God, I'm jealous. I can't be jealous. That would be dumb. But how I wish I could poke this jerk in the nose. I should have beaten him a time or two with that broom handle last night, kind of paying it forward. I sure would feel better now.* "You'd be better off taking that up with Aberdeen than with me," Creed said, keeping his tone mild even as his heart had kicked into overdrive. Maybe he was getting a mild case of indigestion. His whole chest seemed to be enduring one large attack of acid.

"You paying, cowboy?" Re-ride asked. "I'm short a few at the moment."

He was short more things than dollars, but Creed just shook his head, deciding it wouldn't kill him to help out the poor excuse for a man. "I suppose," he said, and Re-ride proceeded to call Cherry back over to give her a list of items that would have fed an army.

Creed sighed to himself. If anyone had ever told him he'd be buying breakfast for the ex-husband and current suitor of a woman that Creed had a small crush on, he would have said they were crazy.

"Turns out I'm the crazy one," he muttered, and Re-ride said, "Yeah, I heard that about you."

Creed drank his coffee in silence.

WHEN CREED AND HIS unwanted companion returned to Johnny's bar, Creed said, "Sayonara, dude," and Re-ride hurried after him.

"No," Creed said, shutting the door in Re-ride's face.

"This isn't how you treat friends!" Re-ride called through the door.

"Exactly," Creed said, turning to study the bar. He decided he'd go upstairs and call his brothers, see how the old homestead was doing. He'd only been gone a day and a half—not much could have changed in his absence. He got out his laptop, too, to surf while he chatted. "This is the life," he said, making himself comfortable in the den. He ignored the banging on the door downstairs. Re-ride would go away soon, or he'd fall asleep outside the door again, and either way, it wasn't Creed's problem.

Until Aberdeen came back. Then Re-ride's constant presence would be a problem.

Yet, no. It couldn't be. Aberdeen was nothing to him, and he was nothing to her, and he was only here to pay back a favor. Not get involved in their personal family business.

Or to fall for her.

"That's right. I'm not doing that," he said, stabbing numbers into the cell phone. Re-ride had ceased banging for the moment, which was considerate of him. "Howdy, Aunt Fiona," he said, when his aunt picked up, and she said, "Well, fancy you calling right now, stranger."

"What does that mean?" Creed's antennae went straight up at his aunt's happy tone. Aunt Fiona was never happier than when she was plotting, but surely he hadn't been gone long enough for her to have sprung any plots.

"It means that you must have telekinetic abilities. We just mailed out the invitations to the First Annual Rancho Diablo Charity Matchmaking Ball!"

Creed blinked. "That's a mouthful, Aunt."

"It is indeed. And we are going to have mouthfuls of food, and drink and kissing booths—"

"I thought—" He didn't want to hurt Aunt Fiona's feelings, so he chose his words carefully. "Why are we having a…what did you call it again?"

"A First Annual Rancho Diablo Charity Match-making Ball!" Aunt Fiona giggled like a teenage girl. "Doesn't it sound like fun? And it's all Jonas's idea!"

Creed's brows shot up. He could feel a headache starting under his hatband, so he shucked his hat and leaned back in Johnny's chair. Outside the window ledge, a familiar face popped into view.

"Let me in!" Re-ride mouthed through the window, and Creed rolled his eyes.

"Get down before you kill yourself, dummy," he said loudly, and Aunt Fiona said, "Why, Creed! How could you speak to me that way?"

"No, Aunt. I'm not—" He glared at Re-ride and headed into another room. It was Aberdeen's room, he realized with a shock, and it carried her scent, soft and sweet and comforting. Sexy. And holy Christmas, she'd left a nightie on the bed. A white, lacy nightie, crisp white sheets, fluffy pillows…a man could lie down on that bed and never want to get up—especially if he was holding her.

But he wasn't. Creed gulped, taking a seat at the vanity instead so he could turn his face from the alluring nightie and the comfy bed which beckoned. It was hard to look away. He had a full stomach, and a trainload of desire, and if he weren't the chivalrous man that he was, he'd sneak into that bed and have a nap and maybe an erotic dream or two about her. "When is this dance, Aunt?"

"Be home in two weeks," she commanded, her typical General-Fiona self. "We're rushing this because Jonas says we must. I wanted to have it in a month, when I could order in something more fancy than barbecue, but Jonas says time is of the essence. We need ladies here fast. Well, he didn't say that, but that's the gist of it."

Creed sighed. "None of us dance, Aunt Fiona. You know that."

"I know. I never saw so many men with two left feet. Fortunately," Aunt Fiona went on, "you still draw the ladies in spite of your shortcomings. My friends have put out the calls, and we've already had a hundred responses in the affirmative. This should be a roaring success in the social columns, I must say!"

This didn't sound like one of Jonas's plans. "I've only been gone a few hours," Creed said, reeling, and Aunt Fiona snapped, "We didn't have time to wait on you to get back here, Creed, and heaven knows you're not one for making fast decisions. But Jonas is. And he is light on his feet when it comes to planning. I have great hopes for him."

Creed said to hell with it and moved to Aberdeen's bed, testing it out with a gentle bounce. It was just as soft and comfortable as it looked. "I'm afraid to ask, but why do we need a charity ball?"

"To get your brothers married, of course. And you, but I think you'll be the last to go." Fiona sounded depressed about that. "You're still haring around, trying to figure out what you want in life, Creed."

Right now he wanted a nap in this sweet bed. Telling himself he was a fool to do it—he was treading into dangerous territory—Creed picked up the lacy white nightie with one finger, delicately, as though the sheer lace might explode if he snagged it with his work-roughened hands. "I know what I want in life, Aunt Fiona," he said softly, realizing that maybe he did know, maybe he'd known it from the moment he'd met her, but there were too many things in the way that he couldn't solve. His aunt was right—he was still going after something he couldn't have. "What are we wearing to this shindig, anyway?"

"Whatever you want to wear," Aunt Fiona said, "but I'll warn you of this. Your brothers are going all out in matching black tuxes. Super-formal, super-James Bond. They intend to dance the night away and seduce the ladies in ways they've never been seduced."

Creed stared at the nightgown, seduced already. But what good would it do? There was an eager ex-husband jumping around outside, climbing to second-story windowsills, trying to make himself at home. And Creed was feeding him. "Sounds like fun, Aunt Fiona," he said. "Guess I'll shine up my best boots."

"I'll just be grateful if you get here and ask a lady to dance," Aunt Fiona said, "so hurry home."

"Don't worry. I'll be home very soon."

"You promise?"

"I swear I do."

"Then I hold you to that. I love you, even though you are a wily coyote. I must go now, Jonas is yelling at me to buy more stamps for the invitations. He had them made special in town, and then printed invitations in all the nearby papers. I tell you, your brother's a magician. I don't know why I didn't notice it before."

She hung up. Creed stared at his cell for a moment, finally turning it off. He was dumbfounded, in a word. Aunt Fiona must have worked a heck of a spell on Jonas to put him in such a partying mood. Jonas was not the ladies' man in the family. Nor did he have the most outgoing disposition. Creed frowned. There was something off about the whole thing, but it was Aunt Fiona and her chicanery, so "off" was to be expected.

Still, it made him tired. Or maybe Re-ride had made him tired. It didn't matter. He'd slept on the sofa last night, and he hadn't slept well, and the eggs had filled him up, and Re-ride was quiet for the moment, so Creed took one last longing look at the white lace nightie he held in his hand, and leaned back against the padded headboard just for a second.

Just for a quick moment to see what it would feel like to sleep in Aberdeen's bed. A guy could dream—couldn't he?

His eyes drifted closed.

CREED HAD NEVER SLEPT SO HARD. Never slept so well. It was as though he was enclosed in angel wings, dreaming the peaceful dreams of newborn babies. He didn't ever want to wake up. He knew he didn't want to wake up because he was finally holding Aberdeen in his arms. And she was wearing the hot nightie, which was short enough and sheer enough not to be a nightie at all. He'd died and gone to heaven. Everything he'd ever wanted was in his arms.

He heard a gasp, and that wasn't right; in his dreams, everyone was supposed to make happy, soft coos of delight and admiration. Creed's eyes jerked open to find Aberdeen staring at him—and Re-ride.

It was a horrible and rude awakening. There was no hope that he wouldn't look like some kind of pervert, so Creed slowly sat up. He removed the nightie from his grasp and shoved it under a pillow so Re-ride couldn't get more of a glimpse of it than necessary. "Hi, Aberdeen. Did everything go well?"

"Yes." She crossed her arms, glaring at him. "Shawn says you've been running all over town, not watching the bar at all. He says he had to come in and look after it last night because he thought he saw a prowler!"

Creed flicked a glance at Re-ride. The traitor stared back at him, completely unashamed of his sidewinder antics. "Did he say that?" Creed asked, his voice soft, and Aberdeen nodded vigorously.

"And may I ask why you're in my bed?"

It was a fair question, and one to which he didn't have a good answer. And he was already in the dog house. Creed sighed. "You can ask, but I don't have a good reason."

"Then will you get out of it?" Aberdeen said, and Creed got to his feet.

"I guess I'll be going." He walked to the door, glancing back only once, just in time to see Re-ride grab Aberdeen and give her the kind of kiss a man gives a woman when he's about to emblazon her hand with a diamond ring fit for a princess. Creed could hear wedding bells tolling, and it hurt.

All his dreams—stupid dreams—were shot to dust. He slunk down the hallway, telling himself he'd been an idiot ever to have trusted Re-ride. "That yellow-bellied coward. I live with Aunt Fiona and five brothers. How could I have let myself be gamed like that?" Creed grabbed up his laptop and his few belongings, and five minutes later he was heading down the stairs, his heart heavy, feeling low.

Re-ride went running past him, hauling ass for the front door. He jetted out of the bar, running toward town. Creed hesitated in the doorway, wondering if he should check on Aberdeen.

She came down the stairs, lifting her chin when she saw him. "You're still here?"

Creed blinked. "Re-ride just beat me to the door, or I'd be gone already."

She had enough ice in her eyes to freeze him, and Creed was feeling miserably cold already.

"Why were you in my bed?"

"I fell asleep. Is that a crime? It's not like I was Goldilocks and I tried out all the beds in the house and thought yours was the best. Although from my random and incomplete survey, so far it is pretty nice."

"I wasn't expecting to find you in my bed."

"I wasn't actually expecting to be in it, it just happened that way," he said with some heat, still smarting that Re-ride had painted him in a thoroughly unflattering light, and liking it even less that Aberdeen had believed the worst of him. Women! Who needed them? "I went in there, I fell asleep. End of story. And I'm not sorry," he said, "because it was damn comfortable, and I slept like a baby. Frankly, I was beat."

She looked at him for a long moment. "Would you like to sleep all night in my bed?" she asked, and Creed's pulse rocketed. Women didn't say something like that unless they meant something awesome and naked, did they?

"I should probably be hitting the road," Creed said, not sure where he stood at the moment, although the direction of the conversation was decidedly more optimistic than it had been a few moments ago.

She nodded. "Okay. I understand."

He understood nothing at all. "Understand what?"

She shrugged. "Thanks for watching the bar, Creed. And I'm sorry for what I said. I should have known better than to believe anything Shawn says."

"You mean Re-ride?" Creed glanced over his shoulder to see if the cowboy had reappeared, but there was a dust plume from the man's exit. "What changed your mind?"

"He proposed," she said simply. "And I realized he was doing it because of you."

"Yeah, well. I have that effect on men, I guess. They get jealous of me because it's obvious the ladies prefer me." Creed threw in a token boast to boost his self-esteem. Aberdeen had him tied in a cowboy's knot.

"So," Aberdeen slowly said, "the offer's still open if you're not of a mind to hit the road just yet."

Creed hung in the doorway, feeling as if something was going on he didn't quite understand, but he wasn't about to say no if she was offering what he thought she was. Still, he hesitated, because he knew too well that Aberdeen wasn't the kind of woman who shared her bed with just anyone. "Where's Johnny? And the little girls?"

"They're in Spring, Montana. I just came back to get some of our things." Aberdeen looked at him, her eyes shy, melting his heart. "And then I'll be going back."

She wasn't telling everything, but Creed got that she was saying she wouldn't be around. And she'd just told Re-ride to shove off, so that meant—

He hardly dared to hope.

Until she walked to him, leaned up on her toes, and pressed her lips against his.

And then he allowed himself to hope.

Chapter Nine

The first thing Creed noticed about Aberdeen was that she was a serious kisser. There was no shyness, no holding back. When he pulled her close and tight, she melted against him.

That was just the way he wanted her. Yet Creed told himself to go slow, be patient. She'd been married to quite the dunderhead; Creed wanted to come off suave, polished. Worthy of her. He would never get his fill of her lips, he decided, knowing at once that Cupid's arrow had shot him straight through.

She only pulled back from him once, and stared up into his eyes. "Are you sure about this?"

He gulped. That was usually the man's question, wasn't it? And here she was asking him like he was some shy lad about to lose his virginity. "I've never been more sure of anything in my life."

"Then lock the door, cowboy. Bar's closed for the rest of the day. And night."

He hurriedly complied, and then she took his hand, leading him upstairs. Creed's heart was banging against his ribs; his blood pressure was through the roof. *Let this be real, and not that horny dream I'd promised myself.* When Aberdeen locked the bedroom door behind them, he knew he was the luckiest man on earth. "Come here," he told her, "let me kiss you."

If he had the whole night, then he was going to kiss her for hours. He took her chin gently between his palms, his lips meeting hers, molding against her mouth. She moaned and he was happy to hear that feminine signal, so he turned up the heat a notch. She surprised him by eagerly undoing his shirt buttons, never taking her lips from his until she had his shirt completely undone. Then she pulled away for just a moment, her hands slipping his shirt off, her gaze roaming over his chest, her hands greedily feeling the tight muscles of his stomach and the knotted cords of his shoulders.

She looked as though she was starving for love and affection. He'd never made love to a preacher lady, but he'd figured she would have all kinds of hang-ups and maybe a go-slow button. Aberdeen acted as if he was some kind of dessert she'd promised herself after a month-long fast. And he didn't want to get drawn in to any lingering firefight between her and Re-ride, if that was what was going on here. He caught her hands between his, pressing a kiss to her palms. "Aberdeen, is everything all right?"

She nodded up at him, her eyes huge. "Yes."

"You're sure you want this?"

She nodded again. "Yes, I do, and if you don't quit being so slow, I'm going to be forced to drag you into my bed, Creed."

Well, that was it. A man could only play the firefighter so long when he really wanted to be the raging fire. So he picked her up and carried her to her white bed, laying her gently down into the softness. Slowly, he took off her sandals, massaging each delicate ankle. He unbuttoned her sundress, every white button down the front of the blue fabric, patiently, though it seemed to take a year and he wasn't certain why a woman needed so many buttons. He kissed her neck, keeping her still against the bed, his shoulders arched over her body, and still she kept pulling him toward her. In fact, she was trying to get his jeans off, and doing a better job of it than he was doing with the dress, but Creed was determined to have her out of her clothes first and lavish on her the attention he'd been so hungry to give her. Slipping the dress to the floor, he moved Aberdeen's hands to her side and murmured, "Don't worry. I'm going to take good care of you," and she sighed as though a ton of burdens had just slid off her. He slipped off her bra, delighted by the tiny freckles on her breasts, which, he noticed, happened to match the same sprinkles on her thighs. He took his time kissing each freckle, then slowly slipped a nipple into his mouth, tweaking the other with his hand. She moaned and arched against him, but he pressed her against the sheets again, keeping her right where he wanted her.

"Slow," Creed murmured against Aberdeen's mouth. "I'm going to take you very slowly."

She tried to pull him toward her, but there wasn't any way he was going to be rushed. He captured her hands in one of his, keeping them over her head so he could suck on her nipples, lick her breasts, tease her into readiness. Every inch of her was a treasure he'd been denied for so long; he just wanted to explore everything, leave nothing behind. She was twisting against him, her passion growing, and he liked knowing that she was a buttoned-up lady for everyone else but him. He let her hands go free so that he could cup a breast with one hand, shucking his boots with the other, and then started the heavenly trail down her stomach.

There were cute freckles there, too. Aberdeen gasped, her fingers tangling in his hair. He could feel her control completely slipping, which was the way he wanted her, wild with passion. Looping his fingers in the sides of her panties, he pulled them down, bit by bit revealing the hidden treasure.

And there was nothing he could do once he saw all of Aberdeen's beauty but kiss her in her most feminine place. She went still, surprised, he thought, but he had more surprises in store for her. She was too feminine to resist, and he'd waited too long. Her body seemed made for his; she felt right, she fitted him, and he couldn't stand it any longer. He slipped his tongue inside her—and Aberdeen cried out. He spread her legs apart, moving to kiss those pin-sized freckles on her thighs, but she buried her hands in his hair again, and it sure seemed like begging to him, so Creed obliged. He kissed her, and licked her, holding her back, knowing just how close he could get her before she exploded, and then, knowing she was too ladylike to beg—next time, he'd make sure he got her to totally let go—he put a finger inside her, massaging her while he teased her with his tongue.

Aberdeen practically came apart in his hands.

"Creed!" she cried, pulling at him desperately, and he fished a condom out of his wallet, putting it on in record time. Holding her tightly, he murmured, "Hang on," and kissing her, slid inside her.

She felt like heaven. This *was* heaven. "If I do this every day for the rest of my life, it won't be enough," he whispered against her neck, and when Aberdeen stiffened in his arms, he moved inside her, tantalizing her, keeping her on edge. She was holding back in spirit, in her heart, but as Creed brought her to a crying-out-loud climax, he kissed her, thinking she had no clue that she couldn't run him off as easily as she'd run off Re-ride. He just wasn't that kind of shallow.

"Aberdeen," he murmured, his mind clouding, nature taking over his body. He'd only pleasured her twice, but he couldn't stand it any longer. He rode her into the sheets, the pressure commanding him to possess her, never give her up, take her to be his. She cried out, grabbing his shoulders, locking her legs around him, crying his name, surrendering this much passion, he knew, against her will. When he came, he slumped against her, breathing great gulps of air, and murmured her name again. It was engraved in his heart.

Aberdeen just didn't know that yet. She'd be hard to convince. She'd have a thousand reasons why they couldn't be together.

But if he knew anything at all, if he understood one thing about his destiny, it was that Aberdeen Donovan was meant to be his by the glorious hand of Fate.

And he was damned grateful.

Aberdeen lay underneath Creed practically in shock. Never in her life had she experienced anything like that. She hadn't even known making love could be such… so much fun, for one thing. If you could call that fun. She felt as if she'd had her soul sucked from her and put back better.

She wiggled, trying to see if he had fallen asleep on her. Her eyes went wide. Was he getting hard again? It certainly felt like he was. He was the hardest man she'd ever felt, like steel that possessed her magically. All she had for comparison was Re-ride, and that wasn't much of a comparison. Aberdeen bit her lip as that thought flew right out of her brain. Creed *was* getting hard inside her again! She'd figured he'd want her once and go on his way, the way her ex had—and then she'd pack the things she needed and head to Montana.

He wouldn't miss her—he wasn't that kind of guy. He probably had women in every town. So she hadn't felt too guilty about seducing him. She'd just wanted a little pleasure, something for herself, an answer to the question she'd had ever since she'd seen his admiration for her burning in his navy gaze. He was too good-looking and too much of a rascal—a bad boy a woman fantasized about—for her not to want the question answered. She wasn't an angel. And right now she was glad of that, because he was hard, and he wanted her, and even if she hadn't planned on making love to Creed twice, she wasn't about to say no.

Not after the pleasure he'd just given her.

He looked deep into her eyes, not saying a word. She didn't know what to say to him. He made all the words she ever thought she might say just dry up. He made a lazy circle around one of her breasts, and she could feel him getting even harder inside her. He kissed her lips, sweetly and slowly, and Aberdeen's breath caught somewhere inside her chest.

To her surprise, he rolled her over on her stomach, and she went, trusting him. He reached for another condom, and kissed her shoulders, as if he wanted to calm her, soothe her. So she waited with held breath as he kissed down her spine, finding points which seemed to intrigue him. He kissed her bottom reverently, took a nip here and there, licked the curve of her hips.

And then the hardness filled her again as he slid inside her. She tried not to cry out, but oh, she couldn't stop herself. He held her gently, not demanding, not passionate and eager as he'd been before, and he rocked her against him, filling her with him. He tweaked a breast, rolling it between his fingers as he kissed her neck, and she couldn't stop her body from arching back against him. She didn't know exactly what she wanted, but when he put a hand between her legs, teasing her, the combination of steel and gentle teasing sent her over the edge again. "Creed," she said on a gasp, and he said, "Say it again," against her neck, and she obeyed him as he drove her to another climax. And when she said his name a third time—she heard herself scream it— he pounded inside her, taking her until his arms tightened around her and his body collapsed against hers.

But still he didn't let her go.

And now, she didn't want him to.

WHEN ABERDEEN AWAKENED, Creed wasn't in her bed. She rose, glancing around the room, listening.

There was nothing to hear.

He'd left. He'd gone back to New Mexico. Her heart racing, Aberdeen crawled from the sheets, sore in places she couldn't remember being sore before. And yet it felt good, a reminder of the passion she'd finally experienced.

No wonder the Callahans were famous. She peeked out the window, but his truck was gone. Her heart sank, though she'd expected him to head off. Men like Creed didn't hang around. Hadn't she learned that from

Shawn? Oh, he'd come back in the end, but he hadn't really wanted her. She'd figured that out quick enough when Shawn proposed to her.

She'd told him she had custody of her nieces, and he'd told her he didn't want to be a father. That had inflamed her, and she'd told Shawn that if he didn't get out of her room, out of her house, she'd set Creed on him.

Those were the magic words. Her ex had run as though devils were on his tail.

Aberdeen got into the shower, thinking she had a lot to be grateful to the Callahan cowboy for. She'd known there was no future for the two of them—there were too many differences in their lives—but still, she wished he'd said goodbye.

She took a long shower, letting the hot water calm her mind. She didn't want to think about her nieces at the moment, or custody, or cowboys she couldn't have. Raspberry body wash—her favorite—washed all the negative thoughts away, and she grabbed a white towel to wrap around her body and began to dry her hair. If she hurried, she could leave in an hour. She'd close up the bar, put on the security alarm, and drive to the next phase in her life. She doubted she'd ever see Creed again. A tiny splinter of her heart broke off, and she told herself she was being silly. Just because she'd slept with him, that didn't mean they could be anything to each other. But still, she'd started to think of him as someone in her life—

She heard the door downstairs open and close. Her pulse jumped. Creed had left, but surely he'd locked the door. She'd seen the closed sign in the window when they'd come home.

Boots sounded on the stairs. Aberdeen froze, holding her towel tightly around her. She could hardly hear for the blood pulsing in her ears.

When Creed walked into the room, her breath didn't release, as it should have, with relief. If anything, she was even more nervous. "I thought you'd gone."

He smiled at her. He'd showered, but he must have used Johnny's room, which made sense. His longish hair was slightly wet at the ends. His dark-blue eyes crinkled at the sides.

"Did you dress for me, Aberdeen?" he asked, his voice a teasing drawl.

Blush heated her face. She decided to brave this out. "As I said, I thought you'd gone."

He nodded. "I didn't want to wake you up when I went out. You were sleeping like a princess."

Of course he was well aware he'd made her feel like a princess. Her defenses went up. "Why are you here?"

His gaze swept her toes, up her calves, considered the towel she clutched before returning to her face. He gave her a smile only a rogue would wear. "Do you want me to leave?"

She wanted him, and he knew it. He was toying with her. "I don't know why I would want you here," she said, "I'm leaving today, and I'm sure you have places to go."

He took off his hat and laid it on her vanity. Her heart jumped inside her, betraying her inner feelings. "I do have places to go, things to do," he agreed.

She didn't trust the gleam in his eyes. Tugging the towel tighter against her, she lifted her chin. "Where did you go?"

"Out for a little while."

He didn't move closer, so Aberdeen felt on firm footing. "Did you come back to say goodbye? Because if you did, you can say it and go. No guilt." She took a deep breath. "I know you have a long drive."

He nodded. "I do."

She waited, her heart in a knot, too shy suddenly to tell him she wished everything could be different—

"I didn't come back to say goodbye," he said, stepping toward her now. "You need breakfast before you leave, and I need you."

She stood her ground as he came near, and when he reached out and took hold of the towel, she allowed him to take it from her body. He dropped it to the floor, his gaze roaming over her as if he'd never seen her body before. He seemed to like what he saw. He took her face in his hands, kissing her lips, her neck, and Aberdeen closed her eyes, letting her fingers wander into his hair as he moved to her stomach, kissing lower until he licked inside her, gently laving all the sore places until they felt healed and ready for him again. She moaned, her knees buckling, her legs parting for him, and when Creed took her back to her bed, laying her down, Aberdeen told herself that one more time enjoying this cowboy in her bed was something she deserved. She couldn't have said no if her life had depended on it. He made her feel things she'd never felt before, and she wanted to feel those things again, and he knew it.

He took out a new box of condoms. Aberdeen watched him, wanting to say that he wasn't going to need an entire new box since they both had places to be—but by the time he'd undressed and gotten into bed with her, murmuring sweet things against her stomach, telling her she was a goddess, Aberdeen slid her legs apart and begged him to come to her. And when Creed did, she held him as tightly as she could, rocking against him until she felt him get stronger and then come apart in her arms, which somehow felt better even than anything he'd done to her.

She was in heaven in his arms—and she didn't want to be anywhere else.

Chapter Ten

Time seemed to stand still for Creed, suspended between what he wanted and what was realistic. The sleeping woman he held in his arms was what he wanted. Realistically, winning her was going to be hard to achieve.

He had to give it everything in his power. There were a hundred reasons he could think of that Aberdeen had to be his—but convincing her would take some serious effort.

It would be worth it, if he could convince her.

He realized she was watching him. "Hello, beautiful," he said, stroking her hair away from her face.

She lowered her lashes. He liked her a little on the shy side; he enjoyed tweaking her, too. She was so cute, tried so hard to be reserved, and then she was all eager and welcoming in bed. "I want you again," he told her. "I don't know how you have this spell on me."

She stroked a hand over his chest. He kissed the tip of her nose, and then lightly bit it. She pinched his stomach, just a nip, and he grinned at her, giving her bottom a light spank. She jumped, her eyes wide, and he laughed, holding her tighter against him. "I could stay here with you for weeks, just making love to you. I don't even have to eat."

He would just consume her. He kissed her lips, taking his sweet time to enjoy that which he'd wanted for so long.

"I have to go, Creed," Aberdeen said, "as much as I would love to stay here with you."

He grunted, not about to let her go this moment. There was too much he still needed to know. "What happened to Re-ride? Why did he take off?"

She gazed at him, and Creed couldn't resist the pain in her eyes, so he kissed her lips, willing her to forget the pain and think only of the pleasure he could give her.

"He got cold feet," Aberdeen said.

"How cold?"

"Ice." She looked at him. "Arctic."

"He said he was going to marry you again." Creed palmed her buttocks, holding her close against him so he could nuzzle her neck, feel her thighs against his. She slipped a thigh between his, and he nearly sighed with pleasure. She was so sweet, so accommodating. He really liked that about her.

"He talks big." Aberdeen laid her head against his shoulder, almost a trusting, intimate gesture, and Creed liked that, too. "He didn't want me to adopt the girls, but I am going to, if I have to. If it's the right thing for them. If my sister, Diane, doesn't come back, then I'll move to the next phase. Right now, I've been awarded temporary custody. Shawn wanted to be part of my life, so he claimed, knew I was going to adopt my nieces if I had to, but when I told him I had to move to Montana, he went cold." She ran a palm lightly over his chest. "I told him if he didn't get out, you'd throw him out. Or something to that effect. I hope you don't mind."

Creed grinned, his chin resting on top of Aberdeen's head. "I never miss a chance to be a hero."

"So that's my story. What's yours?"

Creed thought his story was too long and too boring to bother anyone with. He didn't want to talk about it anyway. "I don't have a story."

Aberdeen pulled away. "That's dirty pool. You can't pull out my story, and then keep yours to yourself."

She had a point. He pushed her head back under his chin and gave her another light paddling on the backside. "Have I ever told you I don't like opinionated women?"

She made a deliberately unappreciative sound which he would call a snort. "I like my women a little more on the obedient side," he said, teasing her, enjoying trying to get her goat, only because he wanted to see what her retribution would be. He liked her spicy. Spice was good.

"I like my men a little more on the honest side," Aberdeen shot back, and Creed smiled to himself.

"That's my sweet girl," he said, and Aberdeen gave him a tiny whack on his own backside, surprising him. He hadn't expected her to turn the tables on him.

"So, your story?" Aberdeen prompted.

"I need to get married," Creed said, his gaze fixed on the vanity across the room as he thought about his life in New Mexico. "My aunt wants all of us to get married."

Aberdeen pulled away from him to look into his eyes. "And do you have a prospect back in New Mexico?"

"No," he said, pulling her back against him, "I don't.

So my aunt—who is a formidable woman—is planning a marital ball of some kind to introduce me and my four unmarried brothers to eligible ladies."

"Why does your aunt care if you're unmarried or not?"

"Because she's bossy like that." Creed loved the smell of Aberdeen's shampoo. Raspberry or strawberry—something clean and fresh and feminine. He took a deep breath, enjoying holding her. "And the women she'll have at the ball will be highly eligible. Socially acceptable. Drop-dead gorgeous."

"So what are you doing here?" Aberdeen asked, and Creed grinned, fancying he heard just a little bite in her words.

"Sleeping with you? Oh, this is just a fling." He kissed her lips, though she tried to evade him. "Didn't you say that you had to leave for Montana? So you're just having a little fun before you go back. I understand that. Men do it all the time." He sucked one of her nipples into his mouth, and Aberdeen went still, though she'd been trying to move to the edge of the bed, putting room between them.

"I don't know what this is," Aberdeen said, and he heard honesty in her voice. He released her nipple and kissed her on the mouth instead.

"You were going to say yes to Re-ride."

She looked at him, her gaze clear. "I hate to admit that I briefly considered it."

"But it didn't work out before."

She shook her head. "I suppose I was desperate enough to wonder if it might have been the best idea."

He hated the sound of that. "Because of your nieces?"

"I only have temporary custody. The judge didn't

seem to find me all that compelling as a guardian. I feel like I need more stability in my life to convince him. He pointed out that Johnny and I live over a bar, not exactly suitable for children. The clientele is transient. He doesn't know Johnny and me. He does know our parents, and made the assumption that they'll be available to help us out. What he didn't understand is that our parents didn't even raise us." Aberdeen seemed ashamed to admit this, and Creed put his chin on her shoulder again, holding her tight. "So I can't leave Montana with the kids. I think if my marital status were to change, that would be something in my favor."

"And along came Re-ride, and you saw your prince."

Aberdeen shrugged. "It made sense at the time."

Creed could see the whole picture. He understood now why Johnny had called him to come watch the bar. Johnny didn't like Re-ride. Johnny had called Creed in, hoping Creed might have an eye for his sister.

"Tell me something," Creed said, "why are you here to get your things instead of Johnny?"

"Johnny was going to come, and I was going to stay with the girls. But then Johnny said he thought it would be better if he stayed because our folks give him a little less trouble. Very few people bother Johnny. He's always been my biggest supporter."

"Protective big brother," Creed murmured, and Aberdeen said, "Yes."

And so Creed had run off the competition, just as Johnny had probably hoped. Creed could spot a plot a mile away, even if he was late to figure it out. Fiona had given him good training. He tipped her chin back with a finger. "Preacher lady, you need a husband, and it just so happens I need a wife."

She blinked. Seemed speechless. Her eyes widened, like she thought he was joking. He kissed her hand, lightly bit the tip of a finger before drawing it into his mouth. She pulled her finger away, then glared at him.

"That's not funny."

"I'm not joking." Creed shrugged.

"You're serious."

"Men don't joke about marriage." Creed shook his head. "It's a very serious matter worthy of hours of cogitation."

"Are you suggesting we have some sort of fake marriage? To fool the judge and to fool your aunt?"

"*Fooling*'s kind of a harsh word." Creed kissed her neck, ignoring her when she tried to push him away. She couldn't; he outweighed her by a hundred pounds, and he sensed she wasn't serious about moving him away from her delightful body. She just needed distance while her mind sorted the conclusion he'd already come to. "I'm just suggesting we become a stable, responsible married couple for all interested parties."

"You want to marry me just to get your aunt off your back?"

Creed laughed. "You make it sound so simple. Aunt Fiona is not that easy to fool. You'll have to be a very enthusiastic bride. Or she'll find me a better wife."

Aberdeen shook her head. "It's a silly reason to get married. I counsel people on making proper decisions regarding marriage vows. This would be a sham."

"*Sham* is also a harsh word." He kissed the tip of her nose. "I prefer *happy facade*."

Her glare returned. "*Happy facade* sounds ridiculous. Marriage should be a contract between two people who trust each other."

"Think of all the benefits. I'd sleep with you every night, Aberdeen. I promise." He tugged her up against him, so he could kiss between her breasts. "We're a good fit in bed."

"Sex isn't enough." Aberdeen tried to squirm away.

"It's not enough, but it sure is a lot." He rolled her over so he could spoon against her back and nip her shoulder lightly at the same time. "Good thing you like sex as much as you do. I wouldn't want a frigid wife."

She gasped and tried to jump out of the bed. "Aberdeen, you know you like it. Don't try to deny it." He laughed and tugged her against him. "Were you reaching for the condoms, love? If you hand me a couple, I'll give you an hour you'll never forget."

She went still in the bed. He held her against him, stroking her hips, letting her decide if she was going to be angry with him or take the bait. Either way, he had a plan for that.

"You're too crazy for me to marry," Aberdeen said, "even if you're serious, which I don't think you are."

"I'm as serious as a heart attack, love."

She flipped over to stare into his eyes. "Where would we live?"

"In my house in New Mexico. Wherever that's going to be."

"A house?" He could feel her taste the words, and realized having a house was a dream of hers.

"Mmm," he murmured, unable to resist running a palm down her breasts. "House, yard, school nearby, church, the works. Nothing fancy. But a home."

"Why would you be willing to have my three nieces live with you?" She looked as though she didn't quite believe what she was hearing.

He shrugged. "I don't mind kids. They didn't exactly run screaming from me, and I thought that was a good start. And my aunt wants us to have as many children as possible."

She crooked a brow. "Can't you have your own?"

He laughed. "Come here and let's find out."

Aberdeen squirmed away, studying his face. "Men don't get married and take on other people's children because of aunts."

"Probably not." He could feel her brain whirring a mile a minute, trying to find the trap. She didn't get it, and even if he told her, she wouldn't believe him. *I like her, I honestly like her. I like her body. I like her innocence. I think she'd like being married to me. That's as much as I know about why people get married anyway. This feels good and real, when it's always felt kind of empty before. And I think I'm falling in love with her.* "If you want to make love again, I'll try to think of some more reasons we should get married. There's probably one or two good excuses I haven't thought of yet, but—" He kissed her neck, burying deep into the curve, smelling her clean scent, wanting her already.

"Creed," she said, "I've been through one marriage. And my nieces have already been through marriages that didn't work out for their parents. Do you know what I mean?"

"I do, my doubting angel." He kissed her hand. "You want something solid for your nieces. You won't settle for anything less than a real family. And you think I'm your man. Hand me that bag on the nightstand, please."

"Not right now, Creed, this is serious." Aberdeen melted his heart with her big pleading eyes that melted his heart. She was such a delicate little thing.

He wouldn't hurt her for the world. "I feel like you're playing with me."

"Oh, no. I wouldn't. Well, sometimes I will, in fact a lot of times I will, but not about a marriage agreement. I'm very serious about agreements. Hand me my bag, sugar."

She shook her head. "Creed, I can't make love when you've got me tied in knots. I couldn't think. I couldn't focus. I just don't understand why you want to marry—"

He gave her a tiny slap on the backside. "Aberdeen, will you please hand me that sack on the nightstand? Or do I have to get it myself?"

"Here's your silly old sack," she said, snatching it up and flinging it at him. "But I'm not saying yes, so don't even ask."

He raised a brow. "No yes?"

"No. Absolutely not." She looked fit to be tied, as if she'd love to kick him out of her bed.

Creed sighed. "Is that your final answer?"

"In fact, it is. No woman can make love when the man who is in her bed is being an absolute ass."

"Whoa, them's fighting words from a preacher." Creed grinned at her. "Just so I can get this straight," he said, reaching into the bag and pulling out a jeweler's box, which he opened, "you're saying no?"

She stared at the box he opened for her to view. It contained a heart-shaped diamond, which he was pretty proud of picking out this morning on his way for the condoms and granola bars.

"Creed," she said, sounding shocked and choked-up, and he snapped the box shut and put it back in the bag.

"Too bad," he said. "The jeweler promised me no woman could say no to this ring. He said a woman would have to have a heart of stone to refuse it. He said—"

"You're crazy! I knew it when I first met you. I know you're crazy, and I know better than to throw myself to the wind like this, but I'm going to ride this ride, cowboy, and I swear, if you turn out to be a weirdo, I'll be really ticked at you."

He kissed her, and she burst into tears, and threw her arms around his neck. "There, there," he said, "having a weirdo for a husband wouldn't be that bad, would it?"

"Creed, give me my ring," Aberdeen said, trying not to giggle against his neck as he held her.

"Greedy," he murmured, "but I don't mind." He took the ring from the box and slipped it on her finger, and for a moment, they both admired it in the light that spilled into the bedroom through the lace curtains.

"You are a weirdo," Aberdeen said, "and I don't know why I'm jumping off a cliff into alligator-infested waters."

Creed just grinned at her. "I'll let you get on top, future Mrs. Callahan, if you're sweet, and this time, you can ride me bareback."

Aberdeen looked at him, not sure if she trusted him or not, not sure exactly of what she wanted to feel for him. But Creed understood she'd been let down before, so he tugged her on top of him, and then smiled to himself when after a moment she said, "This time, I'm going to please you, cowboy."

Aunt Fiona was right, as usual. This marriage stuff is going to be a piece of cake. I feel like I'm winning again—finally.

Chapter Eleven

Marriage was *not* going to be a piece of cake. It was going to be as nerve-racking as any rodeo he'd ever ridden in—only this time, he was pretty certain getting stomped by a bull was less traumatic than what he was experiencing now. Creed found himself waiting outside Aberdeen's family home, cooling his heels before the big intro. The girls were inside, getting reacquainted with their aunt and Johnny. Aberdeen wanted to introduce him to her family after she had a chance to go inside and prepare them for the big news.

He was nervous. And it was all because of the little girls. He'd thought they'd liked him for the brief moments they met him before—but what if they'd changed their minds? Kids did that. He knew from experience. He wasn't certain he would have wanted a new father when he was a kid. Maybe he wouldn't. He and his brothers probably would have given a new father a rough road—he was certain they would have. They'd given everybody a rough road on principle, except Fiona. She wouldn't have put up with that type of nonsense, and besides, she'd always been able to outthink them.

He was pretty certain the little girlies might be able

to out-think him, too. Girls had mercurial brains, and at their tender ages, they probably had mercurial set on high.

He was sweating bullets.

He should have brought some teddy bears or something. Big pieces of candy. Cowgirl hats. Anything to break the ice and get the girls to see him in a positive light.

"Creed, come in." Aberdeen smiled out the door at him, and he told his restless heart to simmer down. It was going to be okay.

He stepped inside the small Montana house—and found himself on the receiving end of frowns from everyone in the family except Johnny.

"Good man," Johnny said, clapping him on the back, and Creed felt better.

"You might have warned me you were setting me up," Creed groused under his breath, and Johnny laughed.

"You struck me as the kind of man who didn't need a warning," Johnny said. "These are our parents. Mom, Dad, this is Creed Callahan."

He was definitely not getting the red carpet treatment. Mr. and Mrs. Donovan wore scowls the size of Texas. "Hello," he said, stepping forward to shake their hands, "it's a pleasure to meet you."

He got the fastest handshakes he'd ever had. No warmth there. Creed stepped back, telling himself he'd probably feel the same way if he had little girls and some cowboy was slinking around. The girls looked up at him shyly, their eyes huge, and Creed had to smile. He did have little girls now—three of them—and he was going to scowl when boys came knocking on his door for them.

"Well," Aberdeen said, "Creed, sit down, please. Make yourself comfortable."

"You're marrying my daughter," Mr. Donovan said, and Creed nodded.

"That's the plan, sir."

"I don't think I care for that plan."

Creed glanced at Johnny, surprised. Johnny shrugged at him.

"I'm sorry to hear that," Creed finally said, trying to sound respectable. "Your daughter will be in good hands, I promise."

"We know nothing about you," Mrs. Donovan said.

"Mom," Aberdeen said, "I'm marrying him. You can be nice, or you can both be annoying, but this man is my choice. So you'll just have to accept it."

"You're not taking the girls," Mrs. Donovan said, and Creed went tense.

"Yes, I am, as soon as I clear it with the judge." Aberdeen got to her feet, abandoning the pretense of a welcome-home party. Creed felt sorry for her. Aunt Fiona had kept them in line over the years, but she'd never been rude to them. He glanced at the tiny girls, and they stared back at him, not smiling.

His heart withered to the size of a gumdrop. He wanted them to like him so badly, and at the moment they just seemed confused.

"The judge won't approve it." Mr. Donovan seemed confident about that. "He feels they are better off here, near us."

"All right. Come on, Creed." Aberdeen swept to the door. Creed recognized his cue and followed dutifully, not understanding his role in the script but sensing his bride-to-be was working on a game plan.

Mrs. Donovan shot to her feet. "Where are you going?"

"Back to Wyoming," Aberdeen said, and Johnny followed her to the door. Johnny might have set him up, Creed realized, but he definitely had his sister's back.

"You can't just leave!" Mrs. Donovan exclaimed.

"I can. I will. And I am."

"Wait!" Mrs. Donovan sounded panicked. "What are we going to do with the girls?"

"Raise them," Aberdeen said, and Creed could see her lips were tight. She was angry, loaded for bear, and he didn't ever want to see her look at him like that. "Maybe you'll do a better job with them than you did with us."

"Hang on a minute," Mr. Donovan said. "Let's just all calm down."

"I'm past calm," Aberdeen said. "Calm isn't available to me at the moment."

The little girls started to cry. Creed's heart broke. "Oh," he murmured, not sure what to do, completely undone by the waterworks. "I think I'll wait outside," he said, and headed toward Johnny's truck. This was such bad karma that he was going to kiss Aunt Fiona as soon as he got back to Rancho Diablo. He'd never realized before how much her steadfast parenting had colored his existence happy. Of course, she was going to box his ears when she found out he was getting married and she didn't get to arrange it, and that made him feel a bit more resourceful.

He sat in the truck, feeling like a teenager. After a few moments, Mrs. Donovan came to his window.

"Mr. Callahan," she said, her eyes bright. He thought she'd been crying.

"Yes, ma'am? Please call me Creed."

"Will you please come back inside and have a cup of tea before you depart?"

He looked at her, and she looked back at him with a sad expression, and he realized she was scared.

"You know," he said softly, "I'm not taking her away from you forever. And you will always be welcome at Rancho Diablo. We like having family around."

Tears jumped into her eyes. She nodded. "Tea?"

"I'd be honored," he said, and followed his future mother-in-law into the house.

"What did you say to her?" Aberdeen asked, watching her mother ply Creed with cupcakes and tea.

"I said I liked tea a whole lot."

Creed filled his plate up with sweets, and balanced Lincoln Rose on his knee as though he'd done it a thousand times before. Aberdeen was astonished. Good father material wasn't something she'd put on her checklist when she'd decided to seduce Creed. The shock of discovering that he might have potential in this area warmed her heart. The most important thing in the world to her right now was the welfare of her nieces—she'd do anything to protect their futures, make sure their lives were as comfortable and normal as possible under the circumstances.

Never had she suspected that Creed might be a truly willing participant in her goal. He sure looked like it now, with all her nieces standing close to him, eating him up with their eyes like they'd never seen a real man before. They'd had Johnny, but she and Johnny hadn't been around much, not knowing that Diane's marriage was in trouble. So Creed garnered a lot of attention from the girls. And he seemed to return that attention, with affection thrown in.

It's an agreement. We made an agreement. He's merely keeping up his part of the bargain. I wanted stability, and he wanted stability, and neither of us ever said anything about permanent. Or love.

So don't do it. Don't go falling in love when you know that's not a realistic ending to the story. Wild never settles down forever—and he never said forever anyway.

"More tea?" she said to Creed, and he smiled at her, his gaze kind and patient as he held the girls, and she felt heat run all over her. And another chip fell off her heart.

"To be honest," Johnny said to Creed when they'd gone outside to throw a ball for the little nieces, "I didn't mean for you to propose to my sister."

Creed looked at him, then back at the porch where Aberdeen was standing with her parents, watching the game. The small house framed them. If he hadn't known better, he would have thought this was a happy family. However, it wasn't anything he wasn't experienced with, so Creed felt pretty comfortable. "What did you have in mind, then?"

"I thought it would be a good idea to give Aberdeen something new to look at. Re-ride was old, you were new." Johnny grinned. "I wanted her to know that there were other fish in the sea."

"I'm sure there've been plenty of fish swimming her way," Creed said, his tone mild.

"Yeah, but she's not much for catching them." Johnny tossed the ball, and the pink toy bounced toward the girls who squealed and tried to catch it with uncoordinated hands. "Anyway, I just wanted you to know that you're taking on a pretty tall order with us."

"Tall doesn't bother me." Creed looked at the girls, then glanced back at Aberdeen. Her hair shone in the Montana sunlight and she was smiling at him. "However, you'll have to come to New Mexico to see her, my friend, so I hope you thought through your plan in its entirety."

"That's the way it is, huh?"

"That's the way it is." Creed nodded. "We've got plenty of space for you, too, if you're of a mind to see a different topography."

Johnny grinned. "I hear New Mexico is nice this time of year."

Creed nodded, but his gaze was on Aberdeen again, and all he could think about was that New Mexico was going to be really nice, better than nice, when he had his little preacher lady sleeping in his big bed. Naked. Naked, warm and willing.

She waved at him, and he smiled, feeling like the big bad wolf. The happiest wolf in the canyons.

AFTER HE'D CHARMED Aberdeen's folks—who warmed to him quickly after their initial resistance—and after he'd cleared hurdles with the judge, Creed placed one last phone call to warn his family of their impending change in lifestyle.

"Hello," Rafe said, and Creed grinned.

"Hello, yourself. If you've got the time, we need a ride."

His twin sighed. "I'm not flying up there just to pick up your lazy butt."

Creed had taken himself out to the small backyard after dinner to have this conversation. Johnny and Aberdeen were tucking the little girls into bed, so he had time to sound the alarm. "You'll be picking up my lazy butt and a few very busy little bottoms."

"Well, now, that sounds more interesting. How are these bottoms? Female, I hope?"

Creed grinned. "Very much so."

"Round and cute?"

"The cutest, roundest tushes you ever saw."

"So I should shave."

"Definitely. You'll regret it if you don't. You don't want to scare them." Creed thought about the small dolls that would be traveling with him and held back a laugh.

"You flying your own entertainment in for Fiona's charity ball?"

"You might say I am."

"Well, consider me your eager pilot. Where and what time do you need a pick-up?"

One of the benefits of having an ex-military pilot who'd spent time flying for private corporations was that the family had their own plane. Rafe was an excellent pilot, and letting him fly them home would be easier on the girls. Creed hadn't yet told Aberdeen, but he was looking forward to surprising her. "Tomorrow, in Spring, Montana. Plan on me, a friend and four damsels, you might say."

Rafe whistled. "You *have* been busy."

"Be on your best behavior. And ask Aunt Fiona to get the guest house ready for visitors, will you?"

"She's going to be thrilled that you're falling into line." Rafe laughed. "I should have known that all this talk of watching over a bar for some guy was just a ruse."

"Probably you should have."

"I don't know if Fiona's going to be cool with you sleeping in the guest house with a bunch of women. On the other hand she's not totally uptight, and she is hoping to marry you off," Rafe mused. "She did say she thought you were the least likely of all of us to ever settle down. So she'll probably be okay with it."

"My ladies are pretty fine. Aunt Fiona will be all right after the initial shock."

"Bombshells, huh? Are you sharing?"

"You can hold them any time you like. Except for my particular favorite, of course. Oh, and bring your headset. They can be loud. Girl chatter and all that. Wild times."

"You old dog," Rafe said, his tone admiring. "And everyone says you're the slow twin. Boy, did you have everybody fooled."

"See you tomorrow," Creed said, and turned off his phone. He went to find Aberdeen, who was sitting in the family room alone. She appeared slightly anxious as her gaze settled on him. "Hello."

"Hi." She smiled, but he thought she looked nervous.

"Girls asleep?"

"Johnny's reading to them. Lincoln Rose is asleep, the other two are excited about the trip tomorrow."

Creed nodded, sitting next to her on the sofa. "I hope you don't mind flying."

Aberdeen looked at him. "We're flying to New Mexico?"

"It'll be easier on the girls than a few days' drive."

"Thank you." Aberdeen smiled. "That's considerate of you, Creed."

"It is. I plan to get my reward after we're married."

Aberdeen's eyes widened. "After?"

"Well, yes. You'll have to wait to have me until you've made an honest man of me." He was pretty proud of his plan. He knew she had probably been thinking of how everything was going to work out between them. Sooner or later, she'd get worried about the silly stuff. Like, she wouldn't want to sleep with him at his ranch until they were married; it wouldn't be decent. She was, after all, a minister. She would worry about such things. She was also a new mother to children. She would be concerned about propriety. He intended to take all those worries right out of her busy little mind.

"I think you are an honest man," Aberdeen said shyly.

"Well, aren't you just a little angel cake," he said, pleased, and dropped a kiss on her nose. "But you're still not having me until you put the ring on my finger."

Aberdeen laughed. "You're horrible."

"But you like it." He put her head against his shoulder, enjoying holding her in the quiet family room.

"I'm so glad you weren't bothered by my folks," Aberdeen said softly. "They can be busybodies."

"Oh, I know all about well-meaning interference. I'm an experienced hand. I just hope you know what you're getting yourself into, little lady."

She smiled and leaned closer, and Creed closed his eyes, contented. Of course she had no idea what she was stepping into. He wasn't certain what was waiting back home for them, either. All he did know was that he'd told her she had to wait until they were married to have him again.

But they hadn't set a wedding date.

He felt like he was holding his breath—and he needed to breathe again. Soon.

Chapter Twelve

When Rafe met them at the plane, he was in full wolf mode. Dark aviator glasses, new jeans, dark Western shirt, dress boots. Even a sterling bolo with a turquoise stone. The kind of lone wolf any woman would lick her chops over.

Only Creed's ladies didn't really have chops yet, just gums. "Here you go," he told Rafe, and handed him the baby. "This is Lincoln Rose. Lincoln, don't be scared of ugly, honey. He tries hard but he's just not handsome like me."

Lincoln Rose stared at Rafe. Rafe stared back at her, just as bemused. Creed grinned and went to walk the next little girl up the stairs. "This is my brother, honey. You can call him Uncle Rafe if you want to, Ashley," Creed said, even though she didn't talk much yet. "Let's figure out how to strap your car seat in, okay? This plane has never seen a baby seat. But I'm pretty sure we can figure it out." He put her favorite stuffed animal and a small book beside her, then went back to the front of the plane. "And I see you've met my last little girl." Creed grinned at his brother, who still held Lincoln Rose as he latched eyes on Aberdeen with appreciation. "And this is the lady I mentioned was my special girl. Aberdeen, this is my brother, Rafe. Rafe, this is my fiancée, Aberdeen Donovan, and this little munchkin is Suzanne. Her sisters call her Suzu. And bringing up the rear is our nanny, Johnny Donovan."

"You look just like Creed," Aberdeen said. "Creed, you didn't tell me you had a twin."

"No reason to reveal all the sordid details." Creed waved Johnny toward the back and took Lincoln Rose from his brother.

"Details like how you travel in style?" Johnny said. "This is a sweet ride."

"Well, it helps to get around the country fast. We do a lot of deals here and there." Creed looked at Aberdeen. "Do you want to be co-pilot, honey?"

"No," Aberdeen said, "Thank you. I'll just sit back and try to decide how I got myself into this."

Creed grinned. "Make yourself comfortable. I'm going to help Rafe fly this rust bucket. Are we good to go, pilot?"

Rafe still seemed stunned as he looked over his new cargo of toys and babies. "Three little girls," he said, his tone amazed. "Are you trying to beat Pete?" he asked, and Creed glared at him.

"Do you see a fourth?" Creed asked.

"Who's Pete?" Aberdeen asked.

"Our brother who was first to the altar, and first to hit the baby lotto," Rafe said cheerfully.

"What were you supposed to beat him at, Creed?" Aberdeen asked.

Rafe glanced at Creed, who wished his brother had laryngitis. "I'm not trying to beat anybody at anything," Creed said. "Don't you worry your pretty little head about anything my numbskull of a brother says."

Rafe nodded. "That's right. Ignore me. I'm a pig at times."

"Most of the time. Let's fly." Creed dragged his brother into the cockpit.

"She doesn't know, does she?" Rafe asked as they settled in.

"I saw no reason to mention the baby-making aspects of Fiona's plan. It had no bearing on my decision."

"You sure?" Rafe asked.

"More than sure. Otherwise, there would be a fourth."

"And there's not?"

"Do you see a fourth?" Creed glared at Rafe again.

"I'm just wondering," Rafe said. "As your twin, it's my duty to wonder."

"Skip your duty, okay?"

Rafe switched on some controls. "I should have known that when you said you were keeping an eye on a bar, you meant a nursery."

"No, I meant a bar. I didn't have plans to get engaged when I left."

"So you found yourself in a bar and then a bed." Rafe sounded tickled. "And there were three bonuses, and so you realized this was a primo opportunity to get out of Fiona's line of fire. And maybe even beat Pete."

"No," Creed said, "because there's nothing to beat Pete for. We have no ranch, per se. Therefore, no need to have children by the dozen."

"Oh. You hadn't heard. You've been gone." Rafe slowly taxied on to the runway. "We're all supposed to settle down, if we want to, to try to keep Bode from getting the ranch."

"It's no guarantee."

"But you don't know that Fiona says that competition begets our more successful efforts, so he who winds up with a wife and the biggest family will get the biggest chunk of the ranch—if we keep it."

Creed frowned. "That has no bearing on my decision."

"It might when you've had a chance to think it over. You'll probably think about it next time you crawl into bed with your fiancée," Rafe said, his tone annoyingly cheerful.

Creed scowled. "Let's not talk about marriage like it's a rodeo, okay? I'm getting married because…because Aberdeen and the girls are what I need."

"To settle you down." Rafe nodded. "Believe me, I understand. I'd settle down if I could find the right woman."

That wasn't it, exactly. Creed was getting married because he and Aberdeen had struck a bargain that suited them both. He got up to glance out at his precious cargo, wanting to make certain everyone was comfortable, particularly the little ladies. Aberdeen and Johnny were staring at him. Aberdeen looked as if she might be on the verge of throwing Lincoln Rose's bear at him. Johnny looked as if he was considering getting out of his seat to squash Creed's head. "Is something wrong?" he asked, instantly concerned for the babies.

"The mike's on," Johnny said, "or whatever you call that loudspeaker thing."

Creed groaned. They'd heard everything—and probably misunderstood everything, too. "We'll talk later," he said to Aberdeen, but she looked out the window, not happy with him at all.

That made two of them.

Creed went back into the cockpit, flipping the switch off as he sat down. Rafe glanced at him.

"Uh-oh. You may be in trouble," Rafe said. He looked honestly concerned. "Was that my bad?"

"I'm not certain whose bad it was. Just think about flight patterns, bro. The sooner I get her on terra firma at Rancho Diablo, the clearer things will be."

He hoped Aberdeen was the type of woman who was willing to forgive and forget. Otherwise, he might be in for a bit of a rough ride, and, as he recalled, he'd been thrown recently. Which was how he'd ended up here in the first place.

He had no intention of being thrown again.

"THIS IS HOME," CREED TOLD Aberdeen when they arrived at the ranch a few hours later. Rafe had left a van at the small regional airport where they kept the family plane in a hangar, and very little had been said on the ride to the ranch. The girls had been sound asleep in their car seats. Though Johnny had ridden up front with Rafe, and Creed had sat next to her, neither of them had felt like talking. The bigger conversation was later. If he thought she was marrying him out of a sense of obligation, he was dead wrong. And she had no intention of "settling him down," as he'd told Rafe. He could just go settle himself down, she thought.

Now, at the family ranch, Aberdeen couldn't help but be surprised. She glanced at Johnny for his reaction to the huge house on the New Mexico plains. In the distance a couple of oil derricks worked. Cattle roamed behind barbed-wire fencing. The sky was a bruised blue, and canyons were red and purple smudges in the distance. It was in the middle of nowhere, and a sense of isolation hung over the ranch.

Until, it seemed, a hundred people flowed out of the house, coming to greet them. Creed opened his door, turning to help her out. A tiny, older woman made it to the van first.

"Aunt Fiona, this is Aberdeen Donovan," Creed said. "Aberdeen, this is the brains of the outfit, Fiona."

"Hello, Aberdeen," Fiona said. "Welcome to Rancho Diablo."

Fiona's smile enveloped her. Aberdeen thought that the same wonderful navy eyes ran in the Callahan family. She felt welcomed at once, and not nervous as she had been after listening to the men discuss their "tyrant" aunt. "Hello. Creed's told me so many wonderful things about you."

"I doubt it." Fiona smiled. "But you're sweet to fib, honey. This is Burke, the family overseer. He's the true brains of the outfit, as my rascal nephew puts it."

A kindly white-haired gentleman shook her hand. "It's a pleasure, Aberdeen. And, Fiona, I think we have some extra guests." Johnny had unstrapped Lincoln Rose and handed her out to Aberdeen. Fiona gasped.

"What a little doll! Creed, you didn't tell us you were bringing a baby!"

His brothers came forward, eager for their introduction and to catch a glimpse of the baby. Johnny handed out the last two, and Aberdeen smiled.

"This is Lincoln Rose, and Suzanne and Ashley. These are my nieces, and this is my brother, Johnny Donovan."

Johnny finally made it from the van and introduced himself to the rest of the Callahans. Fiona shook her head at Creed. "You told Rafe you were bringing bomb-shells, you ruffian."

"I couldn't resist, Aunt Fiona." Creed grinned, clearly proud of himself.

"These are the prettiest bombshells I've ever seen," Fiona said. "I'll have to send out for some cribs, though. And anything else you require, Aberdeen. We don't have enough children at Rancho Diablo, so we'll be happy to gear up for these. You'll just have to let us know what babies need. My nephews have been a wee bit on the slow side about starting families." She sent Creed a teasing smile. "Is there anything else you'd like to spring on us, Creed?"

"Introductions first, Aunt Fiona." He went through the litany of brothers, and Aberdeen felt nearly over-whelmed by all the big men around her. Johnny seemed right at home. But then, another woman came forward, pushing a big-wheeled pram over the driveway, and Suzanne and Ashley went over to see what was inside.

"Babies," Ashley said, and Creed laughed.

"This is Pete's wife, Jackie. Jackie, this is Aberdeen Donovan."

Jackie smiled at her; Aberdeen felt that she'd found a friend.

"We'll have a lot to talk about," Jackie said.

"Yes, we will," Fiona said. "Come inside and let's have tea. I'm sure you're starving, Aberdeen." She took Lincoln Rose in her arms and headed toward the house. Aberdeen and Jackie followed.

"I'm starving, too," Creed said, watching the ladies walk away.

Sam laughed. "Not for love."

Jonas shook his head. "Did you buy that big diamond she's wearing?"

Creed shrugged. "It isn't that big."

"You're getting married?" Judah asked. "You were only gone a few days!"

"It feels right," Creed said, grinning at them.

"You're trying to win," Pete said. "You're trying to beat me."

Creed clapped his brother on the back. "Nope. I'd have to go for four to win, and I'm pretty good at knowing my limits, bro. The gold medal is all yours."

Pete grinned. "I hope you warned Aberdeen."

"About what?" Creed scowled as he and his brothers and Johnny walked toward the house, each carrying a suitcase. Burke tried to help carry one, but the brothers told him diaper bags were their responsibility, and Burke gladly went to park the van instead.

"About the bet. Which is a really dumb bet, if you ask me," Pete said. "I wasn't even trying, and look what happened to me. I just wanted to get married."

"It's almost like you got hit by a magic spell," Sam mused. "Who would have ever thought you could father three adorable little girls?"

"I don't know what to say about that," Pete groused. "I think it was more like a miracle. But besides that, I'm more than capable of fathering adorable, thanks. You'll be the one who has ugly."

"There's no such thing as an ugly baby." Jonas opened the door. "Have you ever seen an ugly baby? They don't exist. I'm a doctor, I know."

"You're a heart specialist, don't overreach your specialty." Creed shook his head. "But no, we're not going to bring up the baby bet, and we're not going to talk about ranch problems or anything like that. I'm trying to get the woman to marry me, not leave in a dust cloud." It could happen. Aberdeen could get cold feet. She had that cold-feet look about her right now. Creed knew she was still annoyed about Rafe's conversation with him in the plane. He also knew she'd been a bit rattled by the size of Rancho Diablo. Or maybe by its faraway location. Whatever it was, he needed time to iron it out of her without his brothers bringing up Callahan drama. "So just pull your hats down over your mouths if you have to," he told his brothers, "and let's not talk about anything we have going on that's *unusual.*"

"Oh, he likes this one," Sam whispered to his brothers.

"You're talking about my sister like I'm not here," Johnny said.

"Sorry," Sam said. "You look like one of us. You could be a Callahan. We can be easily confused." He grinned. "We separate ourselves into the bachelors and the down-for-the-count."

"I'm not down—oh, never mind." Creed shook his head. "Johnny, don't listen to anything we say. We mean well. Some of us just blab too much."

Johnny shrugged. "I hear it all the time in the bar. Yak, yak, yak."

Jonas jerked his head toward the barn. "While the ladies chat, let us show you the set-up."

Creed hung back as his brothers headed out. He was pretty certain that if he was smart—and he thought he was where women were concerned—he'd better hang around and try to iron some of the kinks out of his little woman. She had a mulish look in her eyes whenever he caught her gaze, and he knew too well that mulish females were not receptive to men. He sat down by Aberdeen and pulled Lincoln Rose into his lap. "Take you for a buggy ride around the property when you've had a chance to rest?"

Aberdeen looked at him. "Is it story time?"

"I think so." Creed nodded. "Better late than never, huh?"

"We'll babysit," Jackie said, and Fiona nodded eagerly.

"And it's romantic on the ranch at night," Jackie said. "Trust me, Aberdeen, you want to take a spin on the ranch."

Aberdeen looked at Creed, and he smiled, and though she didn't smile back at him, he thought, she wasn't beaning him with a baby bottle, either—and that was the best sign he had at the moment.

"Romance," he said so only she could hear, "are you up for that?"

"We'll see how good your story is," she said, and Creed sank back in the sofa, looking at Lincoln Rose.

"Any tips on good stories?" he asked the baby, but she just looked at him. "I don't know any, either," he said, and Fiona said, "Then I suggest you get it in gear, nephew. Once upon a time, cowboy poets lived by their ability to tell stories. Live the legend."

Aberdeen raised a brow at him, and he decided right then and there that whatever she wanted, the lady was going to get.

Chapter Thirteen

Aberdeen could tell Creed was dying to get her alone. She wasn't entirely reluctant. Story time didn't sound horrible—and in spite of the conversation she'd over-heard between Creed and his twin, she was willing to give him a chance to explain.

And to kiss her breathless.

Burke entered the room with a tall, distinguished-looking guest, and the room went silent.

"Well, Bode Jenkins," Fiona said, rising to her feet. "To what do we owe this unpleasant occurrence?"

Bode smiled at her thinly, then glanced at Aberdeen's daughters. "A little bird told me that you were welcom-ing visitors. You know how I hate not being invited to a party, Fiona." He sent a welcoming smile to Aberdeen, but instead of feeling welcomed, her skin chilled.

Creed stood, and Jonas stood with him. Sam fol-lowed, as did Rafe, Pete and Judah. Aberdeen glanced at Creed, whose face seemed suddenly set in granite. The brothers looked ready for an old-style Western shoot-out, which bewildered her.

"Now, Bode," Fiona said, "you have no business being here."

"You should be neighborly, Fiona," Bode said, his

tone silky. "When Sabrina told me you were expecting visitors, I just had to come and see what good things were happening around my future ranch. One day," he ruminated, "I'm going to cover this place over with concrete to build the biggest tourist center you ever dreamed of."

The brothers folded their arms, standing silent. If this man's visit was about her arrival, then Aberdeen wanted no part of it. She grabbed Lincoln Rose and held her in her lap, either for comfort or to protect her from what felt like an oncoming storm, she wasn't certain. Her sisters naturally followed Lincoln Rose, hugging to Aberdeen's side for protection.

But then Ashley broke away and went to Creed, who picked her up in his big, strong arms. Bode smiled, his mouth barely more than a grimace. "Looks like you're growing quite the family, Fiona," he said, glancing at Pete's and Jackie's three daughters. "Another birdie told me that you're paying your sons to get wives and have babies so you can make the claim that Rancho Diablo has its own population and therefore shouldn't be subject to the laws of the nation. It won't work, Fiona, if that's what's on your mind."

"Never mind what's on her mind," Creed said, his voice a growl. "If you've stated your business, Jenkins, go."

Bode looked at Aberdeen. Her skin jumped into a crawling shiver. She clutched her two nieces to her. "I'm not going without giving my gift to the new bride-to-be," he murmured, his gaze alight with what looked like unholy fire to Aberdeen. "Will you walk outside with me, my dear?"

"I'm sorry that I can't," Aberdeen said. "My nieces

wouldn't like me leaving them. We've just gotten in from a long day of traveling. I'm sure you'll understand."

Creed shot her a look of approval.

"That's too bad," Bode said. "There's someone I want you to meet."

"Is Sabrina outside?" Fiona frowned. "Why don't you bring her in?"

"Sabrina says she thinks she's coming down with a cold. She didn't want to give it to anyone." Bode shrugged. "I've just learned Sabrina is a fortune-teller. I wanted her to tell your fortune as a gift, Miss—"

"Donovan," Aberdeen said. "I don't believe in fortune-telling, Mr. Jenkins. Please tell your friend I'll be happy to meet her at another time when she isn't under the weather."

But then she realized that Fiona was staring at Bode, her brows pinched and low. Aberdeen sank back into her chair, glancing at Creed, who watched Bode like a hawk.

"Sabrina is a home-care provider," Fiona said, "who happens to have a gift. Why do you sound so irregular about it, Bode?"

He smiled at Fiona, but it wasn't a friendly smile. "I think you've tried to set me up, Fiona Callahan. And I don't take kindly to trickery."

"I don't know what you're talking about," Fiona snapped. "Don't be obtuse."

"Then let me be clear. You hired Sabrina McKinley to spy on me."

"Nonsense," Fiona shot back. "Why would I do that?"

"You'll do anything you can to save your ranch."

Bode tapped his walking stick with impatience. "My daughter, Julie figured it all out," he said. "She learned from one of your sons that Sabrina had been here one night."

"So?" Fiona said, her tone rich with contempt.

"So it was an easy feat for Julie to run a background check on Sabrina. Turns out she was traveling with some kind of circus."

"Is that a crime?" Jonas asked. "Last I knew, a circus was a place for hard-working people to have a job with some travel and do what they like to do."

"I'd be careful if I was you, Jonas," Bode said, his tone measured, "your little aunt can get in a lot of trouble for helping someone forge documents of employment and employment history."

Creed snorted. "How would Aunt Fiona do that?"

"Why don't you tell them, Fiona?" Bode stepped closer to Aberdeen, gazing down at the little girls she held. "I'd be cognizant, my dear, were I you, that this family loves games. And not games of the puzzle and Scrabble variety. Games where they use you as a pawn. You'll figure out soon enough what your role is, but only you can decide if you want to be a piece that's played."

"How dare you?" Aberdeen snapped. "Sir, I'll have you know that I'm a minister. I've met people from all walks of life, heard their stories, ached with their troubles, celebrated their joy. You know nothing about me at all, so don't assume I don't know how to take care of myself and those I love."

"I only wish to give you the gift of knowledge," Bode replied.

Aberdeen shook her head. "Gift unaccepted and unneeded. Creed, I'd like to take the girls to their room now." She stood, and Burke materialized at her side.

"I'll take Miss Donovan to her room," Burke said. "The golf cart should carry everyone nicely."

"I'm going out to see Sabrina," Jonas said, and Bode said, "She's not up to seeing—"

"She'll see me," Jonas snapped.

Judah trailed after Jonas. "I'm not being a bodyguard or anything," he told Bode as he walked by him, "I'm just damn nosy."

The two men left. Creed handed Lincoln Rose to Burke. Fiona stood, looking like a queen of a castle.

"You've caused enough of an uproar for one night, Bode. Out you go."

"We're at war, Fiona," Bode said, and she said, "Damn right we are."

"That's enough," Creed said. "If you don't go, Jenkins, we'll throw your worthless hide out."

Aberdeen followed Burke outside, with a last glance back at Creed. He'd stepped close to Bode, protectively standing between his aunt and the enemy, and Aberdeen realized that Creed was a man who guarded his own. He looked fierce, dangerous, nothing at all like the man who romanced her and seduced her until she wanted to do whatever it took to make him happy.

Yet, looking back at Creed, Aberdeen also realized she had no idea what was going on in this family. It was as if she'd landed in a strange new world, and the man she'd agreed to marry had suddenly turned into a surly lion.

Johnny took one of the girls in his arms, following her out, and as their eyes met, she knew her brother was rethinking her cowboy fiancé, too.

"BUSTED," SAM SAID, and Creed nodded. Bode had left, his demeanor pleased. Whatever he'd come to do, he felt he'd succeeded.

"I think you are busted, Aunt," Creed said. "He knows all about your plan. I don't think Sabrina would have ratted you out unless he threatened her."

"Oh, pooh." Fiona waved a hand. "Bode is my puppet. He jumps when I pull his strings."

Creed crooked a brow at his aunt. "You told Sabrina to enlighten him with the fortune-teller gag?"

"Seemed simpler than having him fish around and find out she's actually an investigative reporter." Fiona shrugged, looking pleased with herself. "Now he thinks he knows something he probably won't go digging around in her background. At the moment, he thinks he stole her from me, so he's pleased. It's not that hard to do a search on the computer for people these days, you know."

Creed shook his head. "You deal with her," he told his brothers. "I have a fiancée and three little ladies to settle in to the guest house."

His brothers looked as though they wished he would keep on with the line of questioning he'd been peppering the cagey aunt with, but he had promised romance to a pretty parson, and he was going to do just that.

CREED WALKED INTO THE GUEST HOUSE right after Aberdeen had finished tidying the girls up and putting them in their jammies. The girls were tired, too exhausted for a bedtime story, so Aberdeen kissed them and put them in their little beds with rails—except for Lincoln Rose, who had her own lovely white crib. "Your aunt is amazing," she told Creed, who nodded.

"She amazes everyone."

"She's thought of everything." Aberdeen pointed around the room, showing the toys and extra diapers and even a tray of snacks and drinks on a wrought-iron tray on the dresser. "How did she do all this so quickly?"

"A lot of this is Burke's doing," Creed said, "but Fiona is the best. We were spoiled growing up."

"I could guess that." Aberdeen looked around the room. "It's clear that she spent a lot of time thinking about what children need to be comfortable."

Creed frowned. Aunt Fiona hadn't known about the girls. He hadn't told anyone, not even Rafe. He'd wanted them to get to know Aberdeen and the girls on their own, and not from anything he mentioned on a phone call.

Somehow Aunt Fiona had figured him out. He sighed. "No moss grows under her feet."

"Well, I'm very grateful. And now, if you don't mind, I'm going to bed." She turned her back on Creed, letting him know that he need not expect a good-night kiss. She wasn't ready to go into all the details of everything he was keeping from her, but at this moment she was bone-tired. And her nieces would be up early, no doubt. Tomorrow she'd make Creed tell her what was going on with the scary neighbor and Rancho Diablo.

At least those were her plans, until she felt Creed standing behind her, his body close and warm against her back. She closed her eyes, drinking in his nearness and his strength. He ran his hands down the length of her arms, winding her fingers into his, and Aberdeen's resistance slowly ebbed away.

He dropped a kiss on the back of her neck, sending a delightful shiver over her.

"I'm sorry about tonight," he murmured against her skin. "I had romantic plans for us."

"It may be hard to find time for romance with all the commotion you have going on here. I thought my family tree was thick with drama."

He turned her toward him, his dark gaze searching hers. "I know you're wondering about a lot of things. I'll tell you a few family yarns in between riding lessons with the girls."

"Not my girls," Aberdeen said, her heart jumping.

"No time like the present for them to get in the saddle." Creed winked at her. "And you, too. You'll make a wonderful cowgirl."

"Sorry, no." Aberdeen laughed. "Lincoln Rose is staying right in her comfy stroller. My other two nieces can look at the horses, but there'll be no saddle-training for them."

"We'll see," Creed said, his tone purposefully mysterious. "Learning to ride a horse is just like learning how to swim."

"Will not happen," she reiterated, and stepped away from his warmth. She already wanted to fall into his arms, and after everything she'd heard today, she'd be absolutely out of her head to do such a thing. If she'd ever thought Creed was wild, she had only to come here to find out that he probably was—at the very minimum, he lived by his own code. And the judge was looking for stability in her life before he awarded her permanent custody of her nieces. An adoption application needed to be smooth as well. She shot Creed a glance over her shoulder, checking him out, noting that his gaze never left her. He was protective, he was kind, he was strong. She was falling in love with him—had fallen in love with him—but there were little people to consider. Her own heart needed to be more cautious, not tripping into love just because the man could romance her beyond her wildest imaginings. "Good-night, Creed," she said, and after a moment, he nodded.

"Sweet dreams," he said, and then before she could steel herself against him, he kissed her, pinning his fingers into her waist, pulling her against him.

And then he left, probably fully aware that he'd just set her blood to boil. Tired as she was, she was going to be thinking about him for a long time, well past her bedtime—the rogue. And she was absolutely wild for him.

She wished Creed was sleeping in her bed tonight.

Chapter Fourteen

"You can't marry her," Aunt Fiona said when Creed went back to the main house. Fiona was sitting in the library in front of a window, staring out into the darkness. Burke had placed a coffee cup and a plate of cookies on the table. Creed recognized the signs of a family powwow, so he took the chair opposite Fiona and said, "I'm surprised you'd say that, Aunt. Doesn't Aberdeen fill the bill?"

Fiona gave him a sideways glance. "If there was a bill to be filled, I'm sure she'd do quite well. However, I don't believe in doing things in half measures, and I think that's what you're doing, Creed."

He nodded at the cup Burke placed beside him, and sipped gratefully. He didn't need caffeine to keep up with Fiona, but he did need fortification. It was going to be a stirring debate. "You're talking about the little girls."

Fiona shrugged. "They're darling. They deserve your best. We don't have a best to give them at the moment, as Bode's untimely visit indicates."

"We'll be fine. Give me the real reason you're protesting against me marrying her."

"Stability. We don't have that." Fiona sighed. "Have you told Aberdeen about this situation?"

"No. It didn't seem necessary. I'll take care of her and the children."

Fiona nodded. "I would expect that. However, we're at war here. Bode was sizing us up. I don't mind saying I'm afraid."

Creed shrugged. "I'm not afraid of that old man."

"You should be. He intends to make trouble."

"What's the worst he can do?"

Fiona looked at him. "You should know."

"I think the choice should be Aberdeen's."

Fiona nodded. "I agree. Be honest with her. Let her know that we're not the safe haven we may appear to be at first glance."

Creed didn't like that. He wanted to be able to give Aberdeen and the girls the comfort and safety he felt they needed. Protecting them was something his heart greatly desired. And yet, he knew Aunt Fiona's words of caution probably warranted consideration. "I'll think about it."

"Do you love her, Creed?" Fiona asked, her eyes searching his.

"Aberdeen is a good woman." He chose his words carefully, not really certain why he felt he had to hold back. "I think we complement each other."

After a moment, Fiona sat back in her chair. "Of course, you know that it's my fondest wish for you boys to be settled. I haven't hidden my desire to see you with families. But I wouldn't want to bring harm to anyone, Creed."

He stared at his aunt. Harm? He had no intention of causing Aberdeen any pain. Far from it. All he wanted to give her was joy. He wanted to take care of her. That's what they'd agreed upon between themselves: Each of them needed something from the other. He intended to keep his side of the bargain.

But as he looked at his little aunt fretting with her napkin and then turning to stare out the window, searching Rancho Diablo in the darkness, he realized she really was worried.

For the thousandth time in his life, he wished Bode Jenkins would somehow just fade out of their lives. But he knew that wasn't going to happen. They just couldn't be that lucky.

"If I only believed in fairy tales," Fiona murmured. "But I have to be practical."

"You pitting us against each other for the ranch is very practical." Creed smiled. "Nobody is complaining, are they?"

Fiona gave him a sharp look. "Is the ranch why you're marrying her?"

Creed drew in a deep breath. Why was he marrying Aberdeen—really? Was he using the ranch as an excuse to bolster his courage to give up rodeo, give up his unsettled ways and get connected to a future? Aberdeen, a ball and chain; the little girls, tiny shackles.

Actually, Creed thought, he was pretty sure the little girls were buoys, if anything, and Aberdeen, a life preserver. Before he'd met them, he'd been drowning in a sea of purposelessness. "I can't speak to my exact motivation for marrying Aberdeen Donovan," Creed said. "I haven't had time to pinpoint the reason. It could be gratitude, because I think she saved my life in the literal sense. It could be she appeals to the knight in me who feels a need to save a damsel in distress. It might even be that she's gotten under my skin and I just have to conquer that." Creed brightened. "Whatever it is, I like it, though."

Fiona smiled. "You do seem happy."

He grunted. "I haven't got it all figured out yet. But when I do, I'll let you know."

TWO WEEKS LATER, the magic still hadn't worn off. Mornings bloomed so pretty and sunny that Aberdeen found herself awestruck by the beauty of the New Mexico landscape. Riding in the golf cart with Burke, who'd come to get her and the girls for breakfast, Aberdeen couldn't imagine anything more beautiful than Rancho Diablo on a summer morning.

And the girls seemed tranquil, curious about their surroundings, staring with wide eyes. Horses moved in a wooden corral, eager to watch the humans coming and going. Occasionally she saw a Callahan brother walking by, heading to work—they always turned to wave at the golf cart. She couldn't tell which brother was which yet, but the fact that Creed has such a large family was certainly comforting. She liked his family; she liked the affection they seemed to have for each other.

She was a little surprised that Creed was a twin, and that his brother, Pete, had triplets. What if she had a baby with Creed? What were the odds of having a multiple birth in a family that seemed to have them in the gene pool? The thought intimidated her, and even gave her a little insight into why Diane might have become overwhelmed. *One at a time would be best for me. I'd have four children to guide and grow and teach to walk the right path. I wonder if I'll be a good mother?*

When Aberdeen realized she was actually daydreaming about having Creed's baby, she forced herself to stop. She was jumping light years ahead of what she needed to be thinking about, which was the girls and putting their needs first. They were so happy and so sweet, and she needed to do her best by them. She saw Johnny ride past in one of the trucks with a Callahan brother, and they waved at her and the girls, who got all excited when they saw their uncle. Johnny, it seemed, was fitting right in. He hadn't come in to the guest house last night, and she suspected he'd slept in the bunkhouse with the brothers. "Your uncle thinks he's going cowboy," she murmured to the girls, who ignored her in favor of staring at the horses and the occasional steer. It was good for Johnny to have this time to vacation a little. He'd had her back for so long he hadn't had much time to hang out, she realized. They'd both been tied to the bar, determined to make a success of it, buy that ticket out of Spring, Montana.

She hugged the girls to her. "Isn't this fun?"

They looked at her, their big eyes eager and excited. For the first time she felt herself relax, and when she saw Fiona come to the door, waving a dish towel at them in greeting, a smile lit her face. It was going to be all right, Aberdeen told herself. This was just a vacation for all of them, one that they needed. If it didn't work out between her and Creed, it would be fine—she and Johnny and the girls could go back home, create a life for themselves as if nothing special, nothing amazing, had happened.

As if she'd never fallen in love with Creed Callahan.

She took a deep breath as Burke stopped the golf cart in front of the mansion. Aberdeen got out, then she and

Burke each helped the girls to the ground. Aberdeen turned to greet Fiona.

"Look who's here!" Fiona exclaimed, and Aberdeen halted in her tracks.

"Mommy!" Ashley cried, as she and Suzanne toddled off to greet Diane. Aberdeen's heart went still at the sight of her older sister, who did not look quite like the Diane she remembered. Cold water seemed to hit her in the face.

"Aberdeen!" Diane came to greet Aberdeen as if no time had passed, as if she hadn't abandoned her children. She threw her arms around Aberdeen, and Aberdeen found herself melting. She loved Diane with all her heart. Had she come to get her daughters? Aberdeen hoped so. A whole family would be the best thing for everyone.

"How are you doing?" Aberdeen asked her sister, leaning back to look at her, and Diane shook her head.

"We'll talk later. Right now, your wonderful mother-in-law-to-be has welcomed me into the fold," Diane said, and Aberdeen remembered that they had an audience.

"Yes. Aunt Fiona, this is my older sister, Diane." Aberdeen followed her nieces, who were trying to get up the steps to Fiona. Aberdeen carried Lincoln Rose, who didn't reach for her mother. The minute she saw Fiona, she reached for her, though. Fiona took her gladly, and Aberdeen and Diane shared a glance.

"I'm good with children," Fiona said, blushing a little that Diane's own daughter seemed to prefer her. "It's the granny syndrome."

"It's all right," Diane said quickly. "Come on, girls. Let's not leave Mrs. Callahan waiting."

"Oh." Fiona glanced back as they walked through the entryway. "Please, just call me Fiona. I've never been Mrs. Callahan."

"This is gorgeous," Diane whispered to Aberdeen. "How did you hook such a hot, rich hunk?"

"I haven't hooked him," Aberdeen said, hoping Fiona hadn't heard Diane.

"Well, find a way to do it. Listen to big sister. These are sweet digs."

"Diane," Aberdeen said, "what are you doing here? And how did you get here?"

"Mom and Dad told me where you were, and it's not that difficult to buy a plane ticket, Aberdeen."

"What about the French guy?"

"We'll talk later," Diane said as Fiona showed them in to a huge, country-style kitchen. At the long table, the largest Aberdeen had ever seen, settings were laid, and each place had a placard with their names in gold scrolling letters. There were even two high chairs for the youngest girls, with their own cards in scrolled letters. Each of the children had a stuffed toy beside her plate, and so they were eager to sit down, their eyes fastened on the stuffed horses.

"I hope you don't mind," Fiona said. "We have a gift shop in town and the owner is a friend of mine. I couldn't resist calling her up to get a few little things for the girls."

"Thank you so much," Diane said, and Aberdeen swallowed hard.

"Yes, thank you, Fiona. Girls, can you say thank you?"

The older ones did, and Lincoln Rose saw that her sisters were holding their horses so she reached for hers, too. And then Burke brought them breakfast, and Aberdeen tried to eat, even though her appetite was shot.

They were being treated like princesses—but the thing was, she wasn't princess material. She eyed her sister surreptitiously; Diane seemed delighted by all the attention Fiona was showering on them, and Aberdeen felt like someone dropped into a storybook with a plot she hadn't yet caught up on.

"Quit looking so scared," Diane said under her breath. "Enjoy what the nice lady is trying to do for you. This is great." And she dug into the perfectly plated eggs and fruit as though she hadn't a care in the world.

"Diane," Aberdeen said quietly, so Fiona couldn't hear, even though she had her head in the fridge looking for something—a jam or jelly, she'd mentioned. "What are you doing here? Really?"

Diane smiled. "Little sister, I'm here to see my daughters. Who will soon be your daughters, by the looks of things."

"I think you should reconsider," Aberdeen said, desperation hatching inside her. "If you're not traveling with that guy, and you seem so happy now, I mean, don't you think…" She looked at her sister. "These are your children, Diane. You can't just abandon them."

"I'm not abandoning them." Diane took a bite of toast. "I simply recognize I'm not cut out to be a mother. I wish it were different, but it's not. I get depressed around them, Aberdeen. I know they're darling, and they seem so sweet and so cute, but when I'm alone with them, all I am is desperate. I'm not happy. I think I was trying to live a dream, but when my third husband left, I realized the dream had never been real." She looked at Aberdeen. "Please don't make me feel more guilty than I do already. It's not the best feeling in the world when a woman realizes she's a lousy mother. And, you know, we had a fairly dismal upbringing. I just don't want to do that to my own children."

Fiona came over to the table, setting down a bowl full of homemade strawberry jam. "I'm pretty proud of this," she said. "I had strawberries and blackberries shipped in special, and I redid my jam stock after I lost all of last year's." She beamed. "Tell me what you think of my blue-ribbon jam!"

Aberdeen tore her gaze away from her sister, numb, worried, and not in the mood for anything sweet. She glanced around at her nieces who seemed so amazed by all the treats and their stuffed horses that all they could do was sit very quietly, on their best behavior. They were obviously happy to see Diane, but not clingy, the way kids who hadn't seen their mother in a while would be. Aberdeen sighed and bit into a piece of jam-slathered toast. It was sweet and rich with berry taste. Perfect, as might be expected from Fiona, as she could tell from everything Creed had said about his aunt.

Her stomach jumped, nervous, and a slight storm of nausea rose inside her. Aberdeen put her toast down. "It's delicious, Fiona."

Fiona beamed. It *was* delicious. If Aberdeen had eaten it at any other time in her life, she'd want to hop in the kitchen and learn Fiona's secrets. There were probably secrets involved in making something this tasty, secrets that could only be passed from one cook to another. Her stomach slithered around, catching her by surprise. She felt strangely like an interloper, a case taken on by these wonderful people and Creed. That wasn't the way she wanted to feel.

And then he walked into the kitchen, big and tall and filling the doorway, her own John Wayne in the flesh, and sunshine flooded Aberdeen in a way she'd never felt before.

"It's wonderful jam," Diane said, and Aberdeen nodded, never taking her eyes off the cowboy she'd come to love. He grinned at her, oblivious to her worries, and if she didn't know better, she would have thought his eyes held a special twinkle for her. Ashley got down from her chair and tottered over to him to be swept up into his arms. Lincoln Rose and Suzanne sat in their high chairs, patiently waiting for their turns for attention from Creed. Creed walked over and blew a tiny raspberry against Lincoln Rose's cheek, making her giggle, and did the same to Suzanne. They waved their baby spoons, delighted with the attention.

Then Creed winked at Aberdeen, in lieu of a good-morning kiss, and Aberdeen forced a smile back, trying to sail along on the boat of Unexpected Good Fortune.

But life wasn't all blue-ribbon strawberry jam and gold-scrolling placards. At least not her life.

Diane poked her in the arm, and Aberdeen tried to be more perky. More happy. More perfect.

She felt like such a fraud.

Chapter Fifteen

Pete and Jackie strolled in, carrying their three babies and a flotilla of baby gear, and the mood in the kitchen lifted instantly. Creed rose to help his brother and sister-in-law settle themselves at the breakfast table.

"We figured there'd be grub," Pete said, "hope you don't mind us joining you, Aunt Fiona."

She gave him a light smack on the arm with a wooden spoon. "The more, the merrier, I always say." She beamed and went back to stirring things up on the stove. Jackie seated herself next to Aberdeen.

"So, how do you feel about the royal treatment, Aberdeen?" Jackie asked.

"It's amazing. Truly." Aberdeen caught Creed's smile at her compliment. "Jackie, Pete, I'd like you to meet my sister, Diane."

Diane smiled, shaking her head at the babies Pete and Jackie were trying to get settled in their baby carriers. "I had my babies one at a time and I still felt like it was a lot. I can't imagine it happening all at once."

Jackie smiled. "We couldn't, either. And then it did." She got a grin from her proud husband, and Aberdeen's gaze once again shifted to Creed. He seemed completely unafraid of all the babies crowding in around him—in fact, he seemed happy.

"It hasn't been bad," Pete said. "We're catching on faster than I thought we would. Jackie's a quick study."

Aberdeen didn't think she'd be a quick study. She pushed her toast around on her plate, trying to eat, wishing the nausea would pass. She caught Creed looking at her, and he winked at her again, seeming to know that she was plagued by doubts. Cold chills ran across her skin. She didn't think she'd be radiant sunshine like Jackie if she found herself with three newborn triplets. He'd probably be dismally disappointed if she didn't take to mothering like a duck to water. "Excuse me," she said, getting up from the table, feeling slightly wan, "I'm going to find a powder room."

"I'll show you," Jackie said, quickly getting up to lead her down a hall.

"Thanks," Aberdeen said, definitely not feeling like herself.

"You look a bit peaked. Are you feeling all right?" Jackie asked.

"I'm fine. Thank you." Aberdeen tried to smile. But then she wasn't, and she flew into the powder room, and when she came back out a few moments later, Jackie was waiting, seated on a chair in the wide hallway.

"Maybe not so fine?" Jackie said.

"I suppose not." Embarrassment flashed over her. "I've always been a good traveler. I can't imagine what's come over me."

"Hmm. Let's sit down and rest for a minute before we go back to the kitchen."

Aberdeen sat, gratefully.

"It can be overwhelming here, at first."

"I think you're right." Aberdeen nodded. "Johnny and I live a much simpler life. And yet, everyone here is so nice."

"Did you know your sister was coming?"

Aberdeen shook her head.

"Well, you've got a lot going on." Jackie patted her hand. "Let me know if there's anything I can do to help."

"You have three newborns." Aberdeen realized the nausea had passed for the moment. "I should be helping you."

"We all help each other." Jackie looked at her. "Your color is returning. Are you feeling better? You were so pale when you left the kitchen."

"I feel much better. I've always been very fortunate with my health. I don't think I've had more than a few colds in my life, and I'm never sick. I can't imagine what's come over me." Aberdeen wondered if she was getting cold feet. But she wouldn't get cold about Creed. He made her feel hotter than a firecracker.

"Not that's it's any of my business," Jackie said, "but the nurse in me wonders if you might be pregnant?"

Aberdeen laughed. "Oh, no. Not at all. There's no way." Then the smile slipped slowly off her face as she remembered.

There *was* a way.

Jackie grinned at her. Aberdeen shook her head. "I'm pretty certain I'm not."

"Okay." Jackie nodded. "Can you face the breakfast table?"

Aberdeen wasn't certain. Her stomach pitched slightly. "I think so."

Jackie watched her as she stood. "You don't have to

eat breakfast, you know. It's a lovely time of the day to take a walk in the fresh air. And I'd be happy to keep an eye on your little ones."

"I think…I think I might take your suggestion." Something about the smell of eggs and coffee was putting her off. She felt that she'd be better off heading outside until her stomach righted itself. "I'm sure it's nothing, but…would you mind letting Fiona know I'm going to head back to the guest house?"

"Absolutely." Jackie showed her to a side door. "Don't worry about a thing."

Aberdeen *was* worried, about a lot of things.

I can't be pregnant. I was in the safe zone of the month when we—

She walked outside, the early-morning sunshine kissing her skin, lifting the nausea. "No, I'm not," she told herself, reassuringly.

A baby would really complicate matters. As wonderful as Rancho Diablo was, Aberdeen felt as though she was on vacation—not at home. Being here was fairy-tale-ish—complete with a villain or two—and any moment she should wake up.

She didn't know how to tell Creed that as much as she wanted to keep to their bargain, she didn't know if she could.

CREED GLANCED UP when Jackie came back into the kitchen, his brows rising. "Where's Aberdeen?"

Jackie seated herself, looking at him with a gentle smile. "She's taking a little walk. Fiona, she said to tell you she'd see you in a bit." Jackie smiled at her husband, and resumed eating, as though everything was just fine and dandy.

But Creed knew it wasn't. Jackie had high marks in this family for her ability to cover things up—look at how skillfully she'd gotten Pete to the altar. So Creed's instinctive radar snapped on. "Is she all right?"

"She's fine."

Jackie didn't meet his eyes as she nibbled on some toast. "Maybe I'll go join her on that walk," he said, and Diane said, "Good idea."

Jackie waved a hand. "I think she said she was looking forward to some solitude."

That was the signal. It just didn't sound like something Aberdeen would say. Creed got to his feet. "I think I'll go check on the horses."

Diane nodded. "My girls and I are going to sit here and enjoy some more of this delicious breakfast." She whisked her sister's abandoned plate to the sink. "Fiona, if I could cook half as well as you do, I might still have a husband."

Fiona grinned. "You think?"

"No." Diane laughed. "But I would have eaten better."

Diane seemed comfortable with Fiona and company, much more so than Aberdeen did. Creed got to his feet. "I'll be back, Aunt Fiona."

"All right." His aunt beamed at him, and Creed escaped, trying not to run after Aberdeen as he caught sight of her walking toward the guest house. "Hey," he said. "A girl as pretty as you shouldn't be walking alone."

Aberdeen gave him a slight, barely-there-and-mostly-fakey smile. Creed blinked. "Are you okay, Aberdeen?"

"I'm fine. Really."

"Hey." He caught her hand, slowing her down. "You trying to run away from me, lady?"

She shook her head. "I just need a little time to myself." She took her hands from his, gazing at him with apology in her eyes.

"Oh." Creed nodded. "All right." He didn't feel good about the sound of that. "Call me if you need anything. Burke keeps the guest house stocked pretty well, but—"

"I'm fine, Creed. Thank you."

And then she turned and hurried off, smiting his ego. *Damn.* Creed watched her go, unsure of what had just happened. He wanted to head after her, pry some answers out of her, but a man couldn't do a woman that way. They needed space sometimes.

He just wished the space she seemed to need didn't have to be so far away from him.

ABERDEEN FELT GUILTY about disappearing on Fiona, and Diane—and Creed. She didn't want to be rude, but she wanted to wash up, change her clothes, shower. Think. Just a few moments to catch her breath and think about what she was doing.

She felt like she was on the Tilt-A-Whirl at the state fair, and she couldn't stop whirling.

At least I'm not pregnant, she told herself. *I'm a planner. Planning makes me feel organized, secure.*

I've got to focus.

"Hey," Johnny called, spying her. "Wait up."

He caught up to her, following her into the guest house. "It feels like I haven't seen you in days."

"That's because we're in this suspended twilight of Happyville." Aberdeen went into the bathroom to wash up. When she came out, Johnny was lounging in the common area.

"That didn't sound particularly happy, if we're hanging out in Happyville." Johnny shot her a worried look. "What's up?"

Aberdeen sat on one of the leather sofas opposite Johnny. "I don't know, exactly."

He nodded. "Feel like you're on vacation and shouldn't be?"

"Maybe." Aberdeen considered that. "I need to wake up."

"An engagement, three kids that aren't yours, a new place…" His voice drifted off as he gazed around the room. "Saying yes to a guy who lives in a mansion would freak me out, I guess, if I was a woman."

"Why?" Aberdeen asked, and Johnny grinned.

"Because your bar was set too low. Re-ride wasn't much of a comparison, you know?"

Aberdeen nodded. "I lost my breakfast, and Jackie wanted to know if I was pregnant."

"Oh, wow." Johnny laughed. "That would be crazy."

Aberdeen glared at him.

"Oh, wait," Johnny said, "is there a possibility I could be an uncle again?"

"I don't think so," Aberdeen snapped, and Johnny raised a brow.

"That's not a ringing endorsement of your birth-control method."

Aberdeen sighed. "I don't want to talk about it." The best thing to do was to concentrate, and right now, she just wanted to concentrate on what was going on with Diane. "Johnny, have you noticed that Diane seems to like her children just fine?"

"Mmm. She's just not comfortable with them. She's like Mom."

Aberdeen felt a stab of worry. "I wonder if I'd be like that."

Johnny crooked a brow. "You're not pregnant, so don't worry about it. Unless you might be pregnant, and then don't worry about it. You're nothing like Mom and Diane."

"How do you know? How does any mother know?" Aberdeen was scared silly at the very thought that she might bring a child into the world she couldn't bond with.

"Because," Johnny said, "you're different. You were always different. You cared about people. I love Diane, but she pretty much cares about herself, and whatever's going on in her world. You had a congregation that loved you, Aberdeen."

Aberdeen blinked. "I miss it. Maybe that's what's wrong with me."

"Well, I don't think that's all that's going on with you, but—" Johnny shrugged. "The pattern of your life has been completely interrupted. The bright side is that you can build a congregation here, if you want. I'm sure there's always a need for a cowboy preacher."

Aberdeen wasn't certain she wanted a new church. "What if I want my old church? My old way of life?" she asked softly.

Johnny looked at her. "I think that bridge has been crossed and burned behind us, sis."

Creed burst in the door, halting when he saw Johnny and Aberdeen chatting. He was carrying a brown paper bag, which caught Aberdeen's suspicious gaze.

"Sorry," Creed said. "Didn't realize you two were visiting."

"It's all right," Johnny said. "I'm just taking a break from ranching. I think I'm getting the hang of this cowboy gig." He waved a hand at the paper bag. "Did you bring us breakfast or liquor?"

Creed set the bag on a chair. "Neither."

Aberdeen shot her fiancé a guarded look. "Is that what I think it is, Creed Callahan?"

"I don't think so," Creed said. "It's a…lunch for me. That's what it is. I packed myself a lunch."

"You're going to go hungry, then," Johnny observed. "You can't work on a ranch and eat a lunch the size of an apple."

"It's for me," Aberdeen guessed.

"It's for us," Creed said, and Johnny got to his feet.

"I'll leave you two lovebirds alone," he said, and Aberdeen didn't tell him to stay.

"Goodbye," Johnny said, and went out the door.

"Creed, that's a drugstore bag," Aberdeen said, "and since you just bought a huge box of condoms when we were in Wyoming, I'm betting you bought a pregnancy test."

He looked sheepish. "How'd you guess?"

"Because you looked scared when you ran in here, like your world was on fire. Jackie told you, didn't she?"

"Well, everyone was worried. We thought something was really wrong with you. And Fiona started fretting, worrying that you didn't like her food, and Jackie said it was a girl thing, and she'd tell Fiona later, and then Diane blurted out that maybe you were pregnant, and I—" He looked like a nervous father-to-be. "Could you be?"

"I don't think so." Aberdeen sighed. "I mean, I guess it's possible. But not likely."

"It wasn't likely for Pete to have triplets, either," Creed said. "Maybe we'd better find out."

"I don't have to pee," Aberdeen said, feeling belligerent. She didn't want everyone at Rancho Diablo discussing her life.

"I'll get you a glass of water," Creed said, jumping to his feet, and Aberdeen said, "No!"

"Well, I might get a glass of water for me. With ice. It's hot in here."

Aberdeen closed her eyes. Just the thought of being a dad clearly was making him nervous. He'd have four children, Aberdeen realized, all at once.

"It wouldn't be what we agreed on," Aberdeen said, and Creed said, "We'll make a new agreement. After I drink a tall glass of water." He went into the kitchen and turned the faucet on full-blast. "Do you hear water running, sweetheart?"

Aberdeen shook her head. "I'm not going to take the test."

He shut off the faucet and came back in with a glass of water. "We'll drink together."

"You pee in the cup." Aberdeen ignored the glass Creed set beside her.

"I didn't get a cup," Creed said cheerfully. "I bought the stick one. It looked more efficient. And it said it could detect a pregnancy five or six days before a skipped—"

Aberdeen swiped the bag from him. "I'm not going to do it while you're here."

"Why not?" Creed was puzzled.

"Because," Aberdeen said. "I need privacy. I have a shy bladder."

He grinned at her. "No, you don't. I happen to know there's nothing shy about you, my little wildcat."

Aberdeen looked at him, her blood pressure rising. "I just want to avoid the topic a little while longer, all right?"

"Well, I feel like a kid on my birthday trying to decide which present to open first," Creed told her. "Pregnancy will probably be a very healthy thing for me."

"Is this about the ranch?" Aberdeen asked, and Creed looked wounded.

"No," he said, "that's dumb."

"Why? You said yourself—"

"I know." Creed held up a hand. "I told you getting married was about getting the ranch. I'd have three built-in daughters, and it would get Fiona off my back. I told you all that, it's true. But it's not anymore."

She looked at him, wanting to kiss him. Maybe he was falling for her as hard as she was falling for him! "What is it, then?"

"Our agreement?" Creed considered her question. "I don't know. Grab out the pee stick and we'll renegotiate based on whether you come up yes or no." He rubbed his palms together. "It's almost as much fun as a magic eight ball."

Aberdeen closed her eyes for a second, counting to ten. "Did anyone ever tell you you're a goof?"

"No. They just call me handsome. And devil-may-care." He came to sit next to her with his icy glass of water. "Drink, sweetpea?"

Chapter Sixteen

Twenty minutes later, Creed tapped on the bathroom door. It seemed like Aberdeen had been in there a long time. "Aberdeen? Are you taking a nap in there?"

"Give me a second," she said, and he wondered if her voice sounded teary. Was she crying?

His heart rate skyrocketed. "Let me in."

"No."

"Is something wrong?"

"I don't think so."

He blinked. That sounded foreboding, he decided. "Do you want your sister?"

"No, thank you."

He pondered his next attack. She couldn't be in there all day. He was about to relinquish his sentinel position outside her door when it opened.

Aberdeen walked out, and he saw at once that she *had* been crying. "Guess we're having a baby?"

She nodded.

He opened his arms, and she walked into them, her body shaking. Creed held her, and she sniffled a second against his chest, and then she pulled away.

He wanted her back. "I'm really amping up the pressure on my brothers," he said cheerfully, seeing a whole world of possibilities kaleidoscoping before him. He'd have a son to play ball with, to teach how to rope. Was there anything better than a boy to help him on the ranch?

Even if they didn't have a ranch anymore, he'd have a son.

"Aberdeen, sweetie, this is the best news I've had in my entire life. Thank you."

She looked at him. "Really?"

"Oh, hell, yeah." He sat down, checking his gut and knew every word he was speaking was true. "I feel like a superhero."

She wiped at her eyes, then looked at him with a giggle. "I feel strangely like a villainess."

"Uh-uh." He shook his head. "I mean, you're sexy and all, but there's nothing evil about you, babe, except maybe what you do to my sense of self-control. I don't suppose you'd like to have a celebratory quickie?"

She laughed but shook her head.

"It was worth a try." He liked seeing the smile on her face. "Hey, you know what this means, don't you?"

"It means a lot of things. Name the topic."

He felt about ten feet tall in his boots. "We need to plan a wedding."

She looked at him, surprised. "Isn't that rushing things a bit?"

"Not for me. I'm an eight-second guy. I'm all about speed and staying on my ride."

Aberdeen crossed her arms in a protective gesture, almost hugging herself. "When I met you, you hadn't stayed on your ride. In fact, you had a concussion. What if—"

"What if I decide to bail?" He grinned at her and

pulled her into his lap. "Lady, you're just going to have to stick around to find out."

She looked down at him from her perch. "I'm way over my head here, cowboy. Just so you know."

"Nah. This is going to be a piece of cake. Fiona can help you plan a wedding. Or we can elope. Whichever you prefer." He nibbled on her neck. "Personally, I'd pick eloping. We'll get to sleep together faster. And you'll make a cute Mrs. Callahan. I'm going to chase my Mrs. Callahan around for the rest of my life."

"I can run fast."

"I know," he said, "but I think we just learned that I run faster."

She laughed, and he kissed her, glad to see the waterworks had shut off. She'd scared him! No man wanted to think that the mother of his child didn't want him. But he was pretty certain Aberdeen did want him, just as much as he wanted her. It was just taking her a little longer to decide that she wanted him for the long haul.

He wasn't letting her get away from him. "When are you going to make an announcement?"

She sighed. "I think something was foreshadowed when you ran in here with a paper bag from the drugstore. I won't be surprised if Fiona has already ordered a nursery. And I don't even know anything about you." For a moment, she looked panicked. "You know more about me than I do about you."

He shrugged. "No mysteries here. Ask a question."

"Okay." Aberdeen pulled back slightly when he tried to nibble at her bottom lip. Maybe if he got her mind off the pregnancy, he could ease her into bed. He did his best romancing between the sheets, he was pretty certain. Right now, her brain was on overdrive, processing, and if she only but knew it, he could massage her and kiss her body into a puddle of relaxation. He felt himself getting very intrigued by the thought.

"Who's the scary guy who visited?" Aberdeen asked. "That Bode guy?"

Uh-oh. It was going to be hard to lure her into a compromising position if she was up for difficult topics. "He's just the local wacko. No one special."

"I felt like I'd been visited by the evil Rancho Diablo spirit."

He sighed, realizing he was getting nothing at the moment—even his powers of romance weren't up to combating a woman who was still trying to figure out if she wanted to be tied to his family, friends and enemies. "I'm a very eligible bachelor," he said, "you don't have to examine the skeletons in my closet. Why don't we hop down to Jackie's bridal shop and look at dresses?" he said. Surely if romance wouldn't do it, shopping might get her thinking about weddings—and a future with him.

"Bode Jenkins," she said. "Was he threatening me?"

"He was being a pest. We're used to him showing up uninvited, trying to throw a wrench into things. Don't take it personally."

"He wants your ranch."

"Yep." Creed shrugged. "I think he may be delusional. He doesn't really want the ranch. He just wants to stick it to us. That's my personal assessment." He nuzzled at her cheek. "I'll be a lot stronger in my fight against evil and doom if I'm married. Let's talk about our future, all right?"

She moved away from his mouth. "Quit trying to seduce me. You're trying to get me off topic, and it isn't going to work."

He sighed. "Most women in your shoes would be more than happy to talk about tying me down, sister."

She took a long time to answer, and when she did, it wasn't what he wanted to hear. "I can't get married at the snap of a finger, Creed. Mom and Dad would want me to get married at home—"

"We can fly them here."

"They would want me to have a church wedding—"

"But what do you want?" he asked, wondering why she was suddenly so worried about her parents. Her folks didn't seem to be all that interested in what she did. He moved his lips along her arm, pondering this new turn of events.

"I don't know. I just found out I'm having a baby. I can't really think about a wedding right now." She slid out of his lap and walked over to the window. "I'd better get back to the girls. I've left them alone too long."

"They're not alone," Creed said, surprised. "They're with their mothe—"

The glare she shot him would have knocked him back two feet if he'd been standing. She went out the door like a storm, and Creed realized he had a whole lot of convincing to do to get his bride to the altar.

In fact, it was probably going to take a miracle.

"I NEVER THOUGHT it would be so difficult to get a woman to jump into a wedding gown," Creed told his twin a few minutes later, when Rafe sat down next to him in the barn. Creed still felt stunned by the whirling turn of events in his life. "I'm going to be a father. I want to be a husband. I don't want my son coming to me one day and saying, 'Mom says you were half-baked with the marriage proposal.'" He looked at Rafe. "You know what I mean?"

Rafe shook his head. "Nope."

Creed sighed, looking at the bridle he was repairing. Trying to repair. This should have been mental cotton candy for him, and he was muffing the repair job. His concentration was shot. "Imagine finding out the best news in your life, but the person who's giving you the news acts like you're radioactive. You would feel pretty low."

"Yeah. But I'm not you. I'd just make her say yes."

Creed looked at Rafe. "Thanks for the body-blow."

Rafe grinned and took the bridle from him. "Give her some time, bro. She's just beginning to figure out that you've turned her life inside out. She needs some time to adjust."

"Yeah," Creed said, "but I want her to be Mrs. Callahan before I have to roll her down the aisle in a wheelbarrow."

Rafe looked at him. "And you wonder why Aberdeen isn't running a four-minute mile to get to the altar with you. Is that the way you romance a woman? 'Honey, let's get hitched before my brawny son expands your waistline?'"

"I never said a word about that. I just want sooner rather than later. I don't really care if she's the size of an elephant, I just want her wearing white lace pronto." Creed scratched his head, and shoved his hat back. "Truthfully, I think I wanted to marry that gal the moment I laid eyes on her. Even in my debilitated state, I knew I'd stumbled on something awesome." He looked at Rafe. "Aberdeen *is* awesome."

Rafe considered him. "You really are crazy about her, aren't you? This isn't about the ranch for you."

"Nope. I've tried every song-and-dance routine I know to get her to take me on. I've offered short-term marriage, marriage-of-convenience, and the real deal. She just doesn't set a date." He sighed, feeling worn down. "It's killing me. I really think I'm aging. And I'm pretty sure it's supposed to be the woman who plots to get the guy to wedded bliss. She sure can drag her feet."

"I don't know, man. All I know is you better shape up before the big dance tomorrow night."

Creed straightened. "That's not tomorrow night, is it?"

Rafe nodded.

"Oh, hell. I've got a bad feeling about this."

Aberdeen already seemed overwhelmed by the ranch, by Rancho Diablo, by him. How would she feel about a bachelor rodeo? He already knew. She would see his brothers hooting and hollering, trying to catch women and vice versa, and figure that he was no different from those lunkheads. That's how a woman thought. "I bet pregnant women probably jump to conclusions faster than normal, because of their hormones and stuff."

Rafe smacked him on the head. "Of the two of us, you are definitely the dumbest. Why do you talk like Aberdeen has no common sense? When beautiful, husband-hunting women are throwing themselves at you tomorrow night, she'll totally understand. It'll probably make her want you. Jealousy is catnip to a woman."

Creed groaned. If he knew Aberdeen the way he thought he did, she was going to run for the mountains of Wyoming. She was like a piece of dry tinder just waiting for a spark to set her off. He could feel her looking for reasons not to trust him. Damn Re-ride, he thought. He'd convinced her that all men were rats.

"Most men are rats," he said, pondering out loud, and Rafe nodded.

"Very likely. And women still love us."

Creed didn't think Aberdeen was going to love him if she could convince herself that he was a big stinky rodent. "I've got to get her out of here," he said, but his twin just shrugged.

"Good luck," Rafe said, and Creed figured he'd need a turnaround in his luck pattern if he wanted his bride.

He knew just who could advise him.

DIANE SAT ON A PORCH SWING, watching her daughters play in a huge sandbox the brothers had constructed for all the new babies at Rancho Diablo. Maybe it was dumb, Creed thought, to make a sandbox when the babies were all still, well, babies. Ashley and Suzu were big enough to play in the soft sand dotted with toys, but Lincoln Rose would catch up in time, and so would Pete's daughters.

Creed couldn't wait to see all the kids playing together one day. The vista of Rancho Diablo land made a beautiful backdrop for children to view, panoramic and Hollywood-like. Burke had helped, drawing off precise measurements and finding the best type of sand to make wonderful castles.

And now Diane sat on the porch swing alone, watching her two oldest, and holding her baby. He watched her for a second, and then went to join the woman he hoped would be his sister-in-law one day.

"Hi," he said, and Diane turned her head.

"Hello."

"Mind if I join you?"

"Not at all. Please do." She smiled when he sat down. "My girls really like it here. There's something about this ranch that seems to agree with them."

He nodded. "It was a pretty great place to grow up."

Diane looked back at her girls. Creed realized her gaze was following her daughters with interest, not the almost cursory, maybe even scared expression she'd worn before.

"Are you comfortable here?" Creed asked.

"I am." She nodded. "Your aunt and uncle have been very kind."

Creed started to say that Burke wasn't his uncle, then decided the tag was close enough. Burke was fatherly, more than uncle-like, and a dear friend. "How long are you staying?"

She smiled, keeping her gaze on her daughters. Creed mentally winced, his question sounding abrupt to him. He sure didn't want Diane to think he was trying to run her off.

"Your aunt has offered me a job," Diane said, surprising Creed.

"She has?"

"Mmm." She turned to look at him, and he saw that her eyes were just like Aberdeen's and Johnny's, deep and blue and beautiful. But hers were lined with years of worry. She'd had it hard, he realized—no wonder Aberdeen and Johnny were so bent on helping her. "She says she needs a housekeeper/assistant. She says all her duties are getting to be too much for her. Yet your Aunt Fiona seems quite energetic to me."

Creed shrugged. "I wouldn't blame Fiona a bit if she

felt like she needed some help. She's got an awful lot she does on the ranch."

"So it wasn't just a polite invitation?" Diane looked at him curiously.

"I doubt it. While my aunt is unfailingly polite, she's never offered such a position to anyone else that I'm aware of, and she wouldn't fancy giving up any of the reins of the place if she really didn't feel the need." He smiled. "She's pretty fierce about doing everything herself."

"So why me? Because I'm Aberdeen's sister?"

He shrugged again. "Probably because she likes you. Fiona prefers to run her own business, so if she offered, she must have felt that you'd be an asset to the ranch."

"She doesn't discuss hiring with you?"

He laughed. "She may have talked to some of my brothers. I can't say. But Fiona's business is her own. So if you're interested in a job with her, that's a discussion between the two of you. The only tip I could positively give you is that if you accept her offer, you will work harder than you ever have in your life. Ask Burke if you don't believe me."

She finally smiled. "I'll think about it, then."

"Yeah. Well, glad I could help. Not that I have any useful information to impart." He grinned at the pile of sand the two little girls were pushing around in the box with the aid of a tiny tractor and some shovels. "So now I have a question for you."

"All right," Diane said. "You want to know how I can help you to get Aberdeen to marry you."

He blinked. "Well, if you could, it would help."

She smiled. "Look, Creed. I'm going to be just as

honest with you as you were with me. Aberdeen doesn't always talk about what she's thinking. If she does, she'd go to Johnny first, and then maybe she'd come to me. I'm a lot older than Aberdeen, in many ways. But I can tell you a couple of things. First, she's afraid she's turning out like me. The fact that she's pregnant makes it feel real unplanned to her, for lack of a better word, and Aberdeen is all about planning everything very seriously. People who plan are *responsible*. Do you understand what I'm saying?" She gave him a long, sideways look.

Creed nodded. "Thank you for your honesty."

She went back to watching her daughters. "It's good to self-examine, even when it's painful. I know who I am, and I know what I'm not. I'm not a good mother, but I know I'm a good person. That probably doesn't make sense to you, but I know that in the end, the good person in me will triumph."

Creed thought she was probably right. There was a kind streak in Diane, a part of her that acknowledged strength in family, that he'd already noticed. "No one's perfect," he said. "Neither my brothers nor I would claim we've come within a spitting distance of perfect. So you're probably amongst like-minded people."

Diane placed a soft kiss atop Lincoln Rose's head. Creed wondered if she even realized she'd done it. "Back to Aberdeen. The B-part to my sister that I know and understand—though I'm not claiming to be an expert— is that there will never be another Re-ride in her life."

"I'm no Re-ride," he growled.

"I mean that, even if she married Re-ride again, it would be no retread situation. Aberdeen is not the same shy girl who got married so young. She would kick his butt from here to China if she married him and he tried to do the stupid stuff he did before."

"She's not marrying Re-ride," Creed said decisively, "and I'm no green boy for her to be worrying about marrying."

Diane sighed. "I'm sure Aberdeen is well aware that it was a real man who put a ring on her finger this time, cowboy. All I'm saying is that she's going to make her own decisions in her life now. She'll do things when she's comfortable and not before—and right now, I'd say she's not totally comfortable. Some of that is probably due to me, but—" She gave Creed a long look and stood. "I feel pretty comfortable in saying that most of her indecision is due to you," she said, kissing him on the cheek, "future brother-in-law."

He looked at her. "I don't wait well."

She smiled. "I guessed that. You may have to this time, if you really want your bride." Diane went to the sandbox and said, "Girls, we need to get washed up now," and they dutifully minded their mother. Creed watched with astonishment as they followed Diane like little ducklings. It was one of the most beautiful things he'd ever seen. He wondered if Diane had yet realized that she had no reason to be afraid of being a mother— she seemed to have all the proper components except confidence. He watched the girls go with a little bit of sentimental angst, already considering himself their father in his heart, knowing that they needed their mother, too. He'd have thought Lincoln Rose would have at least reached for him.

But no. They'd been content to spend time with their mother, an invisible natural bond growing into place.

Creed wished he could grow some kind of bond with Aberdeen. She seemed determined to dissolve what they had. "I'm not doing this right," he muttered, and jumped when Burke said, "Did you say something, Creed?"

Creed glanced behind him as Fiona's butler materialized with a tray of lemonade and cookies. "Are those for me?"

"They're for the little girls and their mother." Burke glanced around. "Are they done with play time?"

"I'm afraid so. Bring that tray over here to me. I need fortification."

Burke set the tray down on the porch swing.

"There's only one glass," Creed said.

"Yes. The lemonade is for you. It has a little kick in it, which I noticed you looked like you needed about twenty minutes ago when you ran through the house."

Creed looked at Burke. "Okay. Tell me everything you're dying to say."

"I'm not really an advice column," Burke said. "I see my role more as fortifier."

Creed waved a hand, knocking back half the lemonade. "You're right. That does have a kick. And it's just what I needed."

Burke nodded. "The cookies are for the girls. They get milk with theirs, usually."

Creed blinked. "Well, my ladies have departed me. All of them, I fear."

Burke cleared his throat. "If you don't need anything else—"

"Actually, I think I do." Creed looked at the butler, considering him. "Burke, your secret is out. We all know you and Fiona are married."

Burke remained silent, staring at him with no change in expression.

Creed let out a sigh. "I guess my question is, how did you do it?"

"How did I do what?"

"How did you convince my aunt to get to the altar?"

Burke picked up the tray. "I sense the topic you're exploring is Miss Aberdeen."

"I could use some advice. Yes." Creed nodded. "Wise men seek counsel when needed, Burke, and I know you have some experience with handling an independent-minded female. My problem is that I've got a woman who seems a little more cold-footed than the average female, when it comes to getting to the altar."

"I may have mentioned my role isn't giving advice," Burke said, "but if I had any, I would say that the lady in question seems to know her own mind. Therefore, she undoubtedly will not take well to being pushed." Burke handed him a cookie. "I must go find the young ladies. It's past time for their afternoon snack and nap."

Creed nodded. "Thanks, Burke."

The butler disappeared.

"I'm not hearing anything I want to hear," Creed muttered. "I know a woman needs her space. But I'm no Re-ride." He munched on the cookie, thinking it would taste better if Aberdeen was there to share it with him.

Between Burke's special lemonade, the cookie and the advice, he thought he was starting to feel better. Not much, just a little, but better all the same.

He was going to be a father.

He wanted to be a husband, too.

He wanted Aberdeen like nothing he'd ever wanted in his life. If his aunt had sprung the perfect woman on him, she couldn't have chosen better. He would easily trade Rancho Diablo if Aberdeen would be his wife. He wanted to spend the rest of his days lying in bed with her, holding her, touching her.

He was just going to have to hang on.

Chapter Seventeen

"I'm worried about Sabrina McKinley," Fiona said to Creed when he rolled into the kitchen. She was making a pie, blueberry, he was pretty sure.

For once, he had no appetite for Fiona's baking. "You mean because of Bode?"

"Well, I certainly didn't like his tone the other night. He made it sound like she was a prisoner or something. The man gives me the creeps." She shook her head and placed the pie on a cooling rack. "I begin to rethink my plan of planting her, I really do, Creed."

"Jonas checked on her. He'd know if something was wrong." Creed sometimes wondered if his oldest brother had developed a secret penchant for Fiona's spy. Then he dismissed that. Jonas was nothing if not boring. He'd never go for the Mata Hari type.

"I suppose." She fluffed her hands off over the sink, brightening. "On the other hand, we have news to celebrate!"

"Yeah." Creed didn't know how his aunt always managed to hear everything lightning-fast. "I'm going to be a father." He beamed, just saying the words a pleasure.

Fiona's mouth dropped open. "You're having a baby?"

He nodded. "Isn't that the news you were talking about?"

She slowly shook her head. "I was going to say that we have one hundred and fifty beautiful, eligible bachelorettes attending the ball tomorrow night." Her gaze was glued to him. "Is the mother Aberdeen?" she asked, almost whispering.

"Yes!" He stared at his aunt, startled. "Who else would it be?"

"How would I know?" Fiona demanded. "You were gone for months. I thought you had only just met Aberdeen when you got thrown at your last rodeo."

He nodded. "Absolutely all correct."

"That means you two got friendly awfully *quickly*." She peered at him, her gaze steadfast. "Goodness, you've barely given the poor girl a chance to breathe! No wonder she left."

He blinked. "Left?"

Fiona hesitated, her eyes searching his. "Didn't she tell you?"

His heart began an uncomfortable pounding in his chest. "Tell me what?"

"That she was going back home? She left an hour ago."

Creed sat down heavily in a kitchen chair. Then he sprang up, unable to sit, his muscles bunched with tension. "She didn't say a word."

"I think she said something about a letter. Burke!"

Her butler/secret husband popped into the kitchen. "Yes?"

"When Aberdeen thanked us for our hospitality and said she was leaving, did she leave a letter of some kind?"

Burke's gaze moved to Creed. "She did. I am not to give it to Creed until six o'clock this evening."

"The hell with that," Creed said, "give it to me now."

Burke shook his head. "I cannot. It was entrusted to me with certain specifications."

Creed felt his jaw tightening, his teeth grinding as he stared at the elderly man prepared to stick to his principles at all costs. "Burke, remember the chat we had a little while ago out back?"

Burke nodded.

"And you know I'm crazy about that woman?"

Burke nodded.

"Then give me the letter so that I can stop her," Creed said, "please."

Burke said. "Creed, you're like a son to me. But I can't go against a promise."

"Damn it!" Creed exclaimed.

Fiona and Burke stared at him, their eyes round with compassion and sympathy.

"I apologize," Creed said. He ran rough hands through his hair. His muscles seemed to lose form suddenly, so he collapsed in a chair. "I don't suppose she said why?" he asked Fiona.

Fiona shook her head. "She said she needed to be back home. I asked her to stay for the ball, and she said she felt she'd only be underfoot. However," she said brightly, "Diane, Johnny and the girls stayed."

"Good," Creed said, shooting to his feet, "I've got a future brother-in-law to go pound."

"He's a guest!" Fiona called after him. "He saved your life!"

Creed strode out to find Johnny—and some answers.

FIVE HOURS LATER, at exactly six o'clock—and after learning that Johnny and Diane knew nothing at all about Aberdeen's departure—Burke finally presented Aberdeen's letter to Creed, formally, on a silver platter.

The envelope was white, the cursive writing black and ladylike. Creed tore it open, aware that his family was watching his every move. News of Aberdeen's departure—and pregnancy—had spread like wildfire through Rancho Diablo. No one had had a clue that Aberdeen had wanted to leave.

Of course he'd known. In his heart, he'd known she was questioning their relationship from the minute she'd seen the ranch and the jet to the moment she'd learned she was pregnant.

> Creed,
> I want you to know how sorry I am that I will be unable to keep our bargain. As you know, at the time we made it, I was under the belief that Diane wanted me to adopt her children. I had no idea when, or if, Diane might return. But now I am hopeful that, given a little more time with her daughters and the gentle comfort of Rancho Diablo, my sister is gaining a true desire and appreciation of what it means to be a mother. This is more than I could have ever hoped for. For that reason, I'm leaving her here, in good hands, as Fiona has offered her employment. I know Diane is happy here, happier than I might ever be. It seems a fair trade-off.
> My part of the bargain to you was that marriage might cure your aunt's desire to see you married

to help keep Rancho Diablo. I don't think you'll need my help. All of you seem quite determined to keep fighting, and I pray for the best for you. Mr. Jenkins seems most disagreeable, so I hope the good guys win. After the ball tomorrow night, perhaps all of your brothers will find wonderful wives. That is something else I will be praying for.

As you know, I have a congregation and a life back in Lance that means a lot to me. When I met you, I believed you were basically an itinerant cowboy. Marrying you for your name on an adoption application didn't seem all that wrong, considering that you, too, had a need of marriage. Now that I've met your family, I know that it would be wrong for me to marry you under false pretenses. That's just not the kind of person I am. Yours is a different kind of lifestyle than I could ever live up to. In the end, though you are a wonderful, solid man, I realize that my life and your life are just too different. With Diane finding her footing with her girls, I think this is a happy ending. I have you and your family to thank for that. So I'd say that any debt that may have existed before is certainly wiped out.

I know too well that you will want visitation rights once the baby is born. You no doubt have lawyers available to you who can draw up any documents you wish to that effect.

I know we will be talking in the future about our child's welfare, so I hope we can remain friends.

All my best,

Aberdeen

P.S. I have entrusted Burke with the engagement

ring. Thank you so much for the gesture. For a while, I did feel like a real fiancée.

He looked up from the letter, his heart shattered. "She left me," he said, and his brothers seemed to sink down in their various chairs.

The silence in the room was long and hard. No one knew what to say to him. His hands shook as he stared at the letter again. She didn't feel like a real fiancée.

How could she not? Had he not loved her every chance he got? "She says she didn't feel like a real bride-to-be," he murmured. "But she's having my baby. How can she not feel like she's going to be a real wife?"

Jonas cleared his throat. "Women get strange sometimes when they're pregnant," he said, and Fiona gasped.

"That's not kind, Jonas Callahan!" She glared at him.

"It's true," Pete said. "Jackie gave me a bit of a rough road when she found out she was pregnant. There we were, this perfectly fine relationship—"

"That went on and on," Sam said. "Every woman has heard that a man who sleeps with her for a hundred years isn't serious about her, so you were only a Saturday-night fling, as far as she knew."

Pete stiffened. "But that wasn't how I felt about her. She just saw our relationship on a completely different level."

"I am never going through this," Judah said, "and if I do find a bride—and I hope I don't—but if I do, I'm going to do it right. None of this bride-on-the-run crap." He leaned back in the sofa, shaking his head.

"Maybe it's not that simple," Rafe said. "Maybe she didn't like it here."

"She didn't seem quite herself," Creed said, "but I put it down to the fact that she was worried about her nieces." Yet he'd known deep inside that hadn't been all of it. "I guess she didn't love me," he said, not realizing that he'd spoken out loud.

"Did you tell her you did?" Rafe asked.

Creed glanced up from the letter. "Not specifically those very words. I mean, she knew I cared."

"Because she was clairvoyant," Sam said, nodding.

"Hey," Jonas said, "your time is coming, young grasshopper. Go easy on Creed."

"I'm just saying," Sam said, "that it's not like she's some kind of fortune-teller like Sabrina."

Everyone sent him a glare.

"Well, I did think she was the more quiet of the two sisters," Aunt Fiona said. "I wondered about it, I must say. I put it off to her being shy, perhaps, and—"

"That's why you offered Diane a job," Creed said, realization dawning like a thunderclap. He sent his aunt a piercing look. "You knew Aberdeen wasn't happy here, and you were trying to keep her little nieces here at the ranch!"

Fiona stared at him. "Oh, poppycock. That's a lot of busybodying, even for me, Creed. For heaven's sake."

He was suspicious. "Did Aberdeen tell you she wasn't happy here? With me?"

Fiona sighed. "She merely thanked me for my hospitality and said she had parents and a congregation to get back to. It wasn't my place to ask questions."

"So she never told you we'd had an agreement based on her feeling that a husband might put her in a more favorable light to an adoption committee?" Creed asked.

"So when Fiona offered Diane a job, and Aberdeen

could see that things might be working out for her sister, the marriage contract between you two could be nullified," Judah said, nodding wisely.

"Oops," Aunt Fiona said. "I had no idea, Creed. I was just thinking to help Diane get on her feet again."

It wasn't Fiona's fault. He and Aberdeen had an agreement which, to her mind, was no longer necessary, so she'd chosen to leave him. She couldn't be blamed for that, either, since he'd never told her that he was wolf-crazy about her. Creed grunted. "What happens if Diane doesn't accept your offer of employment?"

Fiona straightened. "She will." She looked uncertain for a moment. "She'd better!"

"Because you fell for the little girls?" Creed asked, knowing he had, too. It was going to drive him mad if they left—and yet, if Diane chose to leave with her daughters, he would wish them well and hide his aching heart.

"No," Fiona said. "I would never dream of interfering in someone's life to that extent. She just happens to have recipes from around the world, thank you very much, due to all her travels. And she has experience taking care of elderly parents. And I could use a personal secretary." Fiona sniffed.

Groans went up from around the room. Fiona glared at her nephews. "Oh, all right. Is there anything wrong with giving a mother time to bond with her daughters? Perhaps all she had was a little bit of the blues. Does it matter? I like Diane. I like Johnny. And I like Aberdeen." She shook her head at Creed. "Of course I didn't mean to do anything that would give Aberdeen the license to leave you, but I didn't know the nature of your relationship. It was up to you to discuss your feelings with her, which I'm sure you did amply."

Creed grunted. "I was getting around to it."

A giant whoosh of air seemed to leave the room. His brothers stared at the ceiling, the floor, anywhere but at him. Creed's shoulders sagged for a moment. He hadn't, and now it was too late.

"Give her time," Fiona said. "If I was in her shoes, I'd want time."

He held on to this jewel of advice like a gold-miner. "You really think—"

"I don't *know*," Fiona said, "although all of you seem to think I know everything. I don't. I just think Aberdeen has a lot on her mind. I would let her figure it out on her own for a while, perhaps."

"It might be sound counsel, considering the lady in question is mature and independent-natured," Burke murmured in his soft Irish brogue. Burke didn't hand out advice willy-nilly, so he was sharing knowledge of how he'd won Fiona.

"And the baby?" Creed asked, his heart breaking.

Fiona shook her head, silent for once.

The minutes ticked by in still quiet. Creed read the letter again, feeling worse with every word. Judah got up, crossing to the window of the upstairs library. "The Diablos are running," Judah said, and though the joy of knowing the wild horses were still running wild and free on Callahan land sang in Creed's veins, he stared at out at them, not really believing their presence portended mystical blessings anymore.

Chapter Eighteen

Aunt Fiona's First Annual Rancho Diablo Charity Matchmaking Ball was a knock-out success, Creed acknowledged. Ladies of all makes and models came to the ranch by the carload. If he'd still been a single man, he might have been as holistically lighthearted as Sam, who was chasing ladies like a kid at a calf-catch. He thought Johnny Donovan garnered his fair share of attention, though the big man never seemed to do more than dance politely with any lady who lacked a partner. Jonas was his usual stuck-in-the-mud self. If anybody was ever betting on Jonas to finally have a wild night in his life, the bettor was going to lose his money to the house. Jonas was a geek, and that was all he was going to be.

The one shocker of the evening was that Judah and Darla Cameron—who'd had her eyes on Judah forever, not that his clown of a brother had the sense to realize it—actually seemed to engage in a longer-than-five-minute conversation. The chat lasted about twenty minutes, Creed estimated, even more surprised to see his brother initiate said conversation. To his great interest, he saw Darla head off, leaving Judah standing in the shadows of the house. Creed spied with enthusiasm, watching his boneheaded brother watching Darla walk away.

And then, just when he thought Judah was the dumbest man on the planet, beyond dumb and moving toward stupid-as-hell, Judah seemed to gather his wits and hurried after Darla. Creed snickered to himself and drank his beer. "Dumb, but not terminal," he muttered to himself, and thanked heaven he'd never been that slow where a good woman was concerned.

Or maybe he was. Creed thought about Aberdeen being up north, and him being here, and fought the temptation to give in and call her. Johnny said Aberdeen was stubborn. And on this Creed thought Johnny probably had a point.

He was willing to give her time, but it seemed like the cell phone in his pocket cruelly never rang with a call from her.

Creed went back to pondering Aunt Fiona's wonderful party. As bachelor busts went, it was one for the ages. Any of them should get caught. *Not me, I'm already caught, even if my woman doesn't know it. But it'll be fun for us all to get settled down, and then we'll raise a bunch of kids together, and instead of marriage feeling like a curse, we'll all look back and laugh about how determined we were to stay footloose and fancy-free.*

Except for my dumb twin. Rafe is a worm that will never turn. He watched Rafe go by, stuck in wolf mode, a bevy of absolutely gorgeous women tacked on to him like tails pinned on a donkey. Disgusting, Creed thought, that anyone considered his brother deep-thinking and existential when he was really a dope in wolf's clothing. Rafe looked like a man on his way to an orgy, dining at the table of sin with great gusto.

Disgusting.

Johnny sat down next to him on the porch swing. "You're not doing your part, dude. Aren't you supposed to be dancing?"

Creed shrugged. "I danced with a couple of wallflowers, so Aunt Fiona wouldn't be embarrassed. But I'm wallflowered out now."

"Nice of some of the local guys to show up and help out with the chores of chivalry," Johnny said.

"Everyone loves a lady in a party dress," Creed said morosely. "Heard from your sister? She's not coming back tonight to make sure I have my dance card filled? Induce me to give up my swinging-single lifestyle?"

Johnny laughed, raised a beer to Creed. "You know Aberdeen. She's the kind of woman who'll let a man hang himself with his own rope."

Creed leaned back. "It's dangerous dating a woman who's fiercely independent."

Johnny nodded. "Tell me about it."

Creed gave him a jaundiced eye. "Oh, hell, no. You're not dating anyone. Don't give me that commiseration bit."

"I'm hanging on," Johnny said. "For the right one to come along and catch me."

"Yeah, well, good luck," Creed said. "I found the right one. She threw me back."

"Patience is a virtue," Johnny said, and Creed rolled his eyes. Patience was *killing* him. He'd never been a patient man. Fiona said that he'd always wanted everything he couldn't have. He was a worker, a planner, a man of action—the crusader who rode into a forest and plucked out a maiden in the midst of battle, if need be, even before he discovered treasure and liberated it from the evil dragon.

Princess first. Ladies first. Absolutely, always.

At least that's the way he'd always seen himself. Aberdeen had him sitting on the sidelines in his own fish story. He was chomping at the bit.

"Wanna dance, handsome?" Creed heard, and glanced up, fully prepared to wave off a charming and buxom beauty, only to realize she was staring at Johnny, her eyes fast to the man whom Creed had thought might be his brother-in-law one day.

"Mind if go do my duty?" Johnny asked Creed. "I hate to leave you here alone, nursing that dry bottle, but as you can see, duty calls, and it's a beautiful thing."

Creed waved the empty bottle at Johnny. "Never let grass grow under your feet."

"Nor your ass, my friend," Johnny said with a grin, and went off with a lovely lady dragging him under the strung lights and a full moon to join the other dancers.

Creed shifted, feeling as if grass might have grown under him, he'd sat here so long. Johnny was right: He was moping after Aberdeen. If he didn't quit, he was going to end up Rip Van Winkle-ish, waking up one day to find time had passed and nothing had happened in his life. The phone wasn't going to ring; Aberdeen wasn't going to call.

He was waiting on a dream.

He had a baby on the way, a child who would bear his name. But he couldn't force Aberdeen to love him.

He would just have to be happy with knowing that at least his future had a blessing promised to him. And he was going to be a hell of a father. Because he remembered how much it had hurt when he'd lost his own father, how much it had stung not to have a dad around on the big occasions. So maybe he couldn't be a husband, and maybe his Cinderella had thrown her slipper at his heart, but this one thing he knew: He was going to wear a World's Best Father T-shirt as if it was a king-size, golden, rodeo buckle.

And his kid would know he was there for him. Always.

Eight months later

ABERDEEN HAD GROWN like a pumpkin: blue-ribbon, state-fair size. At least that's the way she felt. Johnny worried about her incessantly. "You should have stayed, accepted the Callahans' offer of employment, because you're driving me nuts," she told her brother.

"I could have," Johnny said, turning on the Open sign at the bar door, "but my livelihood is here. I'll admit I toyed briefly with the idea of staying in New Mexico and working with the Callahans. They seemed to need the help. And they sure know how to throw a heck of a dance. There were ladies from everywhere just dying to find a husband. I had a feeling if I'd hung around, Fiona might have fixed me up with a wife, too. From what I've gleaned over the past several months, no weddings went off and no one got caught, though."

Aberdeen wondered if Johnny was trying to reassure her that no one had caught Creed. She decided to stay away from that painful subject. She nodded at his pleased grin. "You could use someone looking after you."

"Women are not that simple, as I know too well."

Johnny smiled and wiped off the bar. "No, it was fun at the time, and I enjoyed the break, but I had to be near my new nephew."

She shook her head. "I don't know the sex of the baby. Quit angling for a hint."

Johnny laughed. "Okay. So what happens when the baby is born?"

"I'm going to keep doing what I'm doing. Occasionally preaching, working here, looking for a house."

Her answer was slightly evasive because she knew Johnny was asking about Creed. The truth was, she never stopped thinking about him. Yet she knew their bargain had been a fairy tale. He'd been grateful to her and Johnny; he'd wanted to help her out. She wouldn't have felt right keeping him tied to an agreement for which there was no longer a need.

"As soon as that baby is born, you know he's going to be here."

Aberdeen nodded. "That's fine." She was over her broken heart—mostly. "You know what the bonus is in all this? Diane is happy at the Callahan ranch. Her daughters are flourishing."

At that Johnny had to smile. He flew down there once a month to visit the girls and Diane, always bringing back reports of astonishing growth and learning skills. Teeth coming in. New steps taken. First pony rides. He'd even taken their parents down to visit once. They'd been impressed with the girls' new environment, and the change in Diane.

Johnny never mentioned Creed when he took his monthly sojourn to New Mexico, and Aberdeen never asked. She knew he would come to visit his baby. It would be the right thing, for the baby's sake. And he would want his baby to spend time at Rancho Diablo. *It will all work out,* Aberdeen told herself. *We're two adults, and can make this work. We are not Diane and her ex-husbands, who turned out to be sloths and degenerates of the first order. Creed will be an excellent father.*

She turned her mind away from Creed and back to the new sermon she was writing. After the baby was born, she intended to go back to school for some additional theology classes. The bar would bring in some income as she did the books for Johnny, and then she could afford a separate house.

It might not be the kind of situation she'd dreamed of with her concussed cowboy—but those had been just dreams, and she knew the difference between dreams and real life.

She went upstairs to the temporary nursery, smiling at the few things she'd put in the small room. A white crib, with white sheets and a white comforter. A lacy white valance over the small window. Diapers, a rocker, some tiny baby clothes in neutral colors: yellow, white, aqua.

It had seemed better not to know if she was having a boy or a girl. She would love either.

In fact, she couldn't wait.

Voices carried up the stairs. Johnny was welcoming some customers. She'd be glad to find her own little house, she realized. Something about having a baby made her feel protective, made her need her own space.

Her tummy jumped with a spasm, bringing another smile to Aberdeen's face. This was an active child, always on the go. The ob/gyn had said that Aberdeen needed to take it easy; the baby could come any day now.

It was too hard to sit and wait, though. The feeling of nesting and wanting everything just right had grown too great for her to ignore. She touched the baby's tiny pillow, soft satin, and told herself that in a few days, she'd be holding her own precious child.

"Aberdeen," a deep voice said, and she whirled around.

"Creed," she said, so astonished she couldn't say anything else. Her heart took off with a million tiny tremors. The baby jumped again, almost as if recognizing that its father had walked into the room.

"I bribed Johnny to let me up here without telling you I was here. Blame me for that, but I wanted to surprise you."

"I'll yell at him later," Aberdeen said.

His gaze fell to her stomach. Aberdeen put a hand over her stomach, almost embarrassed at her size.

"You look beautiful."

"Thank you." She didn't, and she knew it. Her dress was a loan from a mother in her congregation. She hadn't wanted to spend money on clothes when she was too big to fit into much other than a burlap potato sack, the kind that could hold a hundred pounds of potatoes easily. "Why are you here?" she asked, not meaning to sound rude, but so shocked by his sudden appearance that she couldn't make decent conversation.

She'd never been so happy to see anybody in her entire life. She wanted to throw herself into his arms and squeal for joy that he'd come.

But she couldn't.

"I came to see you. And my baby," he said. "I didn't want to miss you having the baby."

She swallowed. "Any day now. I guess Johnny told you."

Creed smiled. "He gives me the occasional update."

Drat her brother. "I guess I should have known he would."

"So this is the nursery?"

She ran a hand proudly along the crib rail. "For now. At least until I find a small house."

He nodded. He gazed at her for a long time. Then he said, "I've missed you."

She blinked, not expecting him to say anything like that. "I—"

He held up a hand. "It was just an observation. Not said to pen you into a corner."

She shook her head. "I know."

Another cramp hit her stomach. Her hands went reflexively to her tummy.

"Are you all right?" Creed asked, and she nodded.

"I think I'll go lie down. It's good to see you, Creed," she said. "Thanks for coming."

He nodded. "Guess I'll go bug Johnny. He's promised to teach me how to make an Expectant Father cocktail."

"Oh, boy," Aberdeen said, backing toward the door. "You two just party on."

She disappeared into the hallway, but as she left, she glanced over her shoulder at Creed. He was staring at her, his gaze never leaving her—and if she hadn't known better, she would have thought he looked worried.

If he was worried, it was because of the baby. He'd never said he loved her, never told her anything except that he'd take care of her and Diane's daughters, so she knew she'd done the right thing by letting him go.

Another cramp hit her, this one tightening her abdomen strangely, and Aberdeen went to check her overnight bag, just in case.

"So, DID THE HEART GROW FONDER in absentia?" Johnny asked.

Creed shook his head and slid onto a bar stool across from Johnny. "Can never tell with Aberdeen. She keeps so much hidden."

"Have confidence," Johnny said, putting a glass in front of him, "and a New Papa cocktail."

"I thought you were going to teach me about Expectant Father cocktails."

Johnny grinned and poured some things into the glass. Creed had no idea what the man was putting in there, but he hoped it took the edge off his nerves. He'd waited eight long months to lay eyes on Aberdeen again, and the shock, well, the shock had darn near killed him.

He'd never stopped loving her. Not one tiny inch, not one fraction of an iota. If he'd thought he had any chance with her, any at all, he'd ask her to marry him tonight.

And this time he'd spend hours telling her how much he loved her, just the same way he'd spent hours making love to her. Only now, he'd do it with a megaphone over his heart.

"Give her a moment to think," Johnny said, "and drink this. It's for patience. You're going to need it."

"I've never had to chase a woman this hard," Creed grumbled. "I'm pretty sure even a shot from Cupid's quiver wouldn't have helped. The shame of it is, I know she likes me."

Johnny laughed. "No, this is a drink for patience as

you wait to become a father. The doctor said today was her due date. Did I mention that?"

"No," Creed said, feeling his heart rate rise considerably. "All you said was today was a great day to get my ass up here. Thanks, you old dog. Now I think I'm going to have heart failure."

"You are a weak old thing, aren't you?" Johnny laughed again. "Relax, dude. I predict within the next week, you'll be holding your own bouncing bundle of joy."

Creed felt faint. He took a slug of the drink and winced. "That's horrible. What is it?"

"A little egg, a little Tabasco, a little bit of this and that. Protein, to keep your strength up."

Creed frowned. "Ugh. It's not going to keep my strength up, it's going to bring my lunch up."

"Trust me on this. It grows on you."

Creed shuddered. And then he froze as Aberdeen's voice carried down the stairs.

"Johnny?"

"Yeah?" her brother hollered up the stairs.

"I think perhaps you might bring the truck around."

Creed felt his jaw give. His gaze locked on Johnny. "What does that mean? Is that code for kick me out?"

"No." Johnny flipped the open sign to Closed and locked the door. "I think it means she wants to make a little run to the county hospital."

Creed blinked. He felt fainter. "What am I supposed to do?" He jumped up from the bar stool. "Should I carry something? Help her pack?"

Johnny said, "Hold on," and went upstairs.

A moment later, he came back down. "You might jog

up there and keep an eye on her while I bring the truck around. I'll meet you out back in a minute."

Creed's anxiety hit high gear when he realized Johnny was totally rattled. The man knocked over a liquor bottle and broke a glass—Creed had never seen him anything but sure-handed around his bar—in his haste to put things away.

But he didn't hang around to analyze his friend. He shot up the stairs to check on Aberdeen. She sat on the bed, looking puzzled.

"Do you need something?" he asked. "A glass of water? A…hell, I don't know. What can I do?"

"Nothing," Aberdeen said, panting a little. "Except I have some concerns."

"Shoot," he said, "I'm your listening ear."

She gave him a wry gaze. "Are you going to want to be in the delivery room?"

"Nothing could keep me out of there," he said, "unless you don't want me, in which case I'm not above bribing you."

Aberdeen started to laugh, then quit abruptly. "Ugh. Don't make any jokes."

"I'm not joking in the least. I have to be there every step of the way."

"Okay." She took a deep breath. "You can't look under the sheet, and if things get tricky, you have to leave. Deal?"

"I don't know," he said, "you didn't keep to our last deal. I don't guess I can trust you with another one unless it's in writing."

"Creed!" Aberdeen said, looking like she was torn between laughing and crying.

"Oh, all right," he said, "although I reserve the right to judge what is tricky."

"If I say go, then you go," Aberdeen explained, with another gasp and a pant.

He sighed. "You'll want me there. Pete's already told me that my main role is to bring you ice chips and let you squeeze the skin off my fingers. Oh, and if you cuss me out, I'm to ignore all that and tell you how beautiful you are, and how you're the most wonderful woman in the world."

Aberdeen groaned. "If you can do all that, you'll be a true prince."

A truck horn honked outside, and Creed helped Aberdeen to her feet. "Guess I got here in the nick of time," he said, to make conversation. "Isn't that what princes do? Show up to help the fair damsel?"

Aberdeen didn't say anything for a moment.

But then she looked up at him, about halfway down the stairs. "Thank you for being here," she told him, and Creed's heart soared.

Maybe, just maybe…

Chapter Nineteen

"I can't believe my mother had six of us," Creed said, after Aberdeen let out a loud groan. "Can't she have some medication to dull the pain?"

"She's too far along," the nurse said.

"Can I have some pain medication?" Creed asked.

The nurse smiled at him, at the edge of tolerance. "Perhaps you'd like to go sit outside in the waiting area. We'll take good care of Mrs. Callahan."

Aberdeen let out another gasp. Creed's gaze flew to her, his teasing spirit gone. He was panicked. There seemed to be a lot of pain involved, and he hadn't meant to do this to her. She was never going to become Mrs. Callahan.

She was going to hate him forever.

He went through his litany of jobs Pete had suggested: Ice chips, tell her she's beautiful, stay out of the way except when she wants to squeeze your fingers to the bone. Try to be helpful. Try.

Creed stayed at the bedside, scared out of his wits. Good-and-stomped cowboys suffered, but even they hadn't seemed to be in this much agony.

Creed closed his eyes and prayed.

Thirty minutes later, Aberdeen gave one final shriek

that went through Creed—he seemed to feel her every pain—and suddenly the doctor smiled with satisfaction.

"It's a girl," the doctor said, and Creed went light-headed. He sank onto a chair as nurses scurried to clean up baby and Aberdeen. He was out of breath; there was no more strength in his body.

Then it hit him. The baby that was squalling up a storm and being fussed over by the nurses was *his*. He jumped to his feet and hurried over to get a glimpse.

She was beautiful.

He went to tell Aberdeen. His heart constricted as he saw how exhausted she was.

"How are you doing?" he asked, and Aberdeen gave him a wan smile.

"How are you?" she asked. "I thought you were going to fade on me."

"No," he said. "I'm tough. Not as tough as you, though. You win." He bent down and kissed her on the lips, so she'd know she was beautiful. A kiss seemed to express his feelings better at this moment than words.

Then he remembered he was in this predicament because he'd never said the words (Sam's shot about clairvoyance came to mind), so he just threw himself out on the ledge. "You're beautiful," he told her. "I may never get you pregnant again, but I want you to know that I love you fiercely, Aberdeen Donovan. And this may not be the time to tell you, but if you don't put my ring back on your finger and marry me, I'm going to…I'm going to cry like my daughter."

Aberdeen smiled. But she didn't say anything for a long moment. She closed her eyes and he thought she looked happy. Content. He brushed her hair back from her face, thinking she really was the most beautiful woman he'd ever seen in his life. Of course he was in love with her, had been always, but now she'd given him an amazing gift, so he loved her even more.

"I saw him one day," Aberdeen murmured, and Creed said, "Who?"

"The Native American. He was on your ranch, probably a thousand feet from the house. He waved to me, so I went to talk to him. He was tall, and had long, braided hair and such kind eyes. He said he was watching over the horses."

"The Diablos?"

"He called them that, but I didn't know what he meant at the time. And he said not to be scared, that all things worked out for the Callahans. That you would know your parents through this baby."

He blinked. "He told you that?"

"I didn't understand what it meant. But now I do. He said he'd known your parents a long time ago, and this baby was a gift to them. And then he left."

Creed was shocked. He'd never spoken to Aunt Fiona's friend; neither had any of his brothers, as far as he knew. "Our parents died long ago," he said. "I'm not sure how a baby can be a gift to them. But I'm okay with the theory."

"Have you ever talked to him?"

Creed shook his head. "He comes around to talk to Fiona about once a year. I don't know why. It's one of those things Aunt Fiona is mysterious about—one of many things, I suppose."

"He was nice. I liked him. I've never seen so much peace in someone's eyes." She looked at him. "I'll marry you, Creed Callahan."

His heart soared. "You will?"

She smiled. "Yes."

A nurse came between them for a moment, handing Aberdeen her pink-blanket-wrapped baby, and a delighted smile lit Aberdeen's face. "She looks just like you."

"Don't say that," Creed said, "I want her to look just like her wonderful mother. There are no beauties in my family tree, just unfortunately unhandsome brothers."

"There's a beauty now." Aberdeen kissed the top of her baby's head. "She's so sweet."

"That she gets from your side of the family." Creed was so proud he was about to burst. "Are you really going to marry me?"

Aberdeen handed him the baby, which he took carefully, lovingly. "I am, cowboy. I've decided you're the prince I've been waiting for."

He was so happy he wanted to cry. "What took you so long?"

"I was afraid you might be the wolf in my fairy tale, not a prince. You had me fooled for a while." Aberdeen smiled. "I was determined not to make any more mistakes. But I never stopped thinking about you, and after a while, I knew you were the only man I could ever love."

"When were you going to tell me?" Creed asked. "Because I'm pretty sure the last several months have just about killed me."

"After you told me," she said simply, and he groaned.

"I'm going to tell you every day of your life how much I love you," Creed said. "I'm going to keep you convinced that you made the right decision."

"I am," Aberdeen said with conviction. "I know exactly what I'm doing. I'm marrying the most wonderful man in the world. Now name your baby."

He hesitated, glancing down at the sleeping child in his arms. "I don't know anything about naming babies. What if I pick something she hates later on?"

She smiled. "Don't you have a favorite female name?"

"Aberdeen," he said with a decisive nod.

That made her laugh as she lay back against the pillow. "I'm going to sleep now, but when I wake up, I want you to have named your little girl. Surprise me with your creativity."

"No pressure or anything," he said, and he looked down at the tiny lips, adorable closed eyes, sweet cheeks of his daughter, knowing the old Navajo was right: This baby connected him to the past he could barely remember. But he knew his parents had loved him, just as he loved this child. Joy filled him, and then it came to him. "Joy," he said, and Aberdeen opened her eyes.

"That's lovely," she said.

"It's what I feel when I look at you," he said, and she knew his heart was in his words. "And when I hold this little baby…" He leaned down to give Aberdeen a kiss. "Thank you is all I can say. And I will love you until the end of time."

"You're going to make me cry," Aberdeen said, but he sat down next to her, and touched her face, and suddenly Aberdeen didn't feel like crying, only smiling, with joy.

Creed Callahan wasn't loco, she knew. He was her prince, her man, and the hottest cowboy she'd ever laid eyes on. All hers.

All her dreams come true.

Creed leaned against her and Aberdeen drifted, loving feeling him by her side, holding their baby. It was the sweetest moment, starting their family. She murmured, "I love you," and Creed said, "Joy says you'd better," and then he kissed her again.

It was perfect.

Joy.

Epilogue

In February, the month after Joy Patrice was born, Aberdeen finally walked down the aisle into Creed's waiting arms.

Only it wasn't that simple.

First, he had to convince her that baby weight was no excuse not to marry him. Then he had to tell her that getting married at Rancho Diablo on Valentine's Day during the coldest month of the year was a swell idea—red was a great color for bridesmaid's gowns. She only had one attendant and that was Diane, but still, it took some doing. Aberdeen kept talking about waiting until springtime, when she'd lost some weight, when Joy would be a little older, when the weather would be warmer—but he wasn't about to let her weasel out of marrying him for any reason.

He'd nearly lost her before. If he'd learned anything, it was that he had to do a lot of talking with this woman. So talk he did.

And today, a day that dawned clear and sunny, he didn't relax until Aberdeen finally said, "I do." And even then, he asked her to say it again, which made her and the guests laugh.

Judah said later he'd never seen such a desperate

case. Jonas told Judah he'd better hush, because one day it might be him begging some poor woman to marry him. Sam said he thought it was romantic, if a bit weinie, of his brother to go down on bended knee and promise to love and adore Aberdeen for the rest of their lives, and Rafe said his twin had finally showed some depth of character and soul. Pete said he didn't care as long as they hurried up and cut the cake because he was starving. Keeping up with the demands of three little girls kept his appetite fired up.

Valentine's Day was a perfect day to catch his bride, in Creed's opinion. When they were finally declared husband and wife, he swept Aberdeen off her feet and carried her back down the aisle, intent on putting her right into the waiting limousine.

He intended to spend their week-long honeymoon in Bermuda making love to her constantly, and as far as he was concerned, the honeymoon began *now*.

"Wait," Aberdeen said, laughing, "Creed, put me down. We have guests. There's cake to cut."

"Oh." He put her down, reluctantly. "I'm not letting you out of my sight, though."

She took him over to the three-tiered cake. "I know. But there are some duties required—"

"Cut fast," he told her, and she made a face at him.

"We have to dance, and tell everybody thank you for coming," she said. "Creed, we just can't desert our guests. And there's Joy. I feel so guilty about leaving her. Don't you think we should wait for our honeymoon until—"

"That's it," he said, "here's the knife. Cut the cake, take a bite and let's shazaam before you get cold feet. I know you too well, parson, and I worked too hard to get you." He put cake into her mouth, waved at the applauding guests, let the photographer snap a few more photos of them, and then went over to Aunt Fiona who was holding Joy in her arms.

"This is a great party, Aunt," he said.

"But you're leaving."

He kissed her cheek. "Yes, we are. My bride wants me all to herself. Mrs. Callahan is demanding like that."

"Creed," Aberdeen said, laughing, as she bent to kiss Fiona's cheek, and then reached up to kiss Burke's.

"It's all right," Fiona said. "I've succeeded beyond my wildest dreams, so I just want to say welcome to the family, Aberdeen. And congratulations on catching Creed. I never thought I'd live to see the day, did you, Burke?"

Burke shook Creed's hand. "The limo has all your items in it, and is waiting for your call."

"Thanks for everything," Creed said, and kissed his aunt goodbye. Then he bent to kiss his baby's head. "Joy, you be sweet to your family. Aunt Diane is going to take very good care of you."

"Yes, I am." Diane closed her sister in her arms. "Congratulations, sis," she said, "I'm going to be as good an aunt to your daughter as you were to mine. I can never thank you enough for giving me time to figure out my life."

Aberdeen smiled. "I knew you would."

Johnny nodded. "I'm going to practice my uncle skills. I can't wait. Seems like I've been waiting months for this, and now I've got four babies to uncle. It's pretty cool."

"Yes," Creed said, prouder about new fatherhood

than about winning all his rodeo buckles. "All these new women in my life. Who would have ever thought it?"

"I would," Fiona murmured to Burke, who hugged her as she gazed at her growing family. "I always knew he had it in him."

"I always knew I had it in me," Creed said to Aberdeen, and she kissed him.

"Let's go, cowboy," she said, for his ears only. "I've got a special gift to give you in the limo. Because I'm pretty sure you said I wasn't having you until I made an honest man of you, and now I have."

"Hot dang," Creed said. "I'm already there, my love."

They waved goodbye to their guests under a shower of pink paper hearts, and, as Creed helped his bride run to the white limo in her long, lacy gown, he caught sight of the black mustangs running, tossing their manes and pounding their hooves, free and wild, as they chased the spirits in the wind.

Enchanted.

* * * * *

We hope you enjoyed the
COWBOYS & BABIES
COLLECTION.

If you liked reading these stories, then you
will love **Harlequin® American Romance®**.

Harlequin® American Romance® stories
are heartwarming contemporary tales of everyday
women finding love, becoming part of a family or
community—or maybe starting a family
of her own.

American Romance®

Romance the all-American way!

Enjoy for four new stories from
Harlequin American Romance every month!

Available wherever books and ebooks are sold.

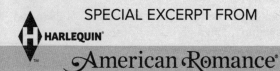
"These are your babies?"

She nodded, and he suddenly felt dizzy. The woman he loved was a mother, and somehow she'd had four children. This perfect four of a kind was hers.

It wasn't possible. He felt weak all over, weak-kneed in a way he'd never been, his heart splintering like shattered glass.

"Damn, Ash, your family… You haven't told them."

"No, I haven't."

A horrible realization sank into him, painful and searing. "Who's the father?"

She frowned. "A dumb, ornery cowboy."

"That doesn't sound like you. You wouldn't fall for a dumb, ornery cowboy."

"Yes, I would," Ash said. "I would, and I did."

He looked at the tiny bundles of sweetness in their bassinets. Two girls and two boys, he presumed, because each bassinet had colored blankets—two pink, two blue. Two of each. He felt sad, sick, really, that the woman he adored had found someone else in the nine months she'd been gone. He felt a little betrayed, sure that the two of them had shared something, although neither of them had ever tried to quantify exactly what that was. "He really is dumb, if he's not here taking care of you," Xav said, and it had to be the truth or she wouldn't be living with the woman with the wicked swing, who'd tried to crush his cranium. "Ash, I'll marry you, and take care of you and your children," he said suddenly, realizing how he could finally catch the woman of his dreams without even appearing to be the lovestruck schmuck that he was.

If anyone was father material, it was he.

Don't miss the final book in
Tina Leonard's
CALLAHAN COWBOYS *miniseries!*

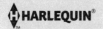
American Romance®

The Secrets Of Horseshoe, Texas

Angie Wiznowski has made mistakes—the biggest is the secret she's kept from Hardison Hollister for ten years. The man she loved has the right to know what happened following that hot Texas night long ago. And it could cost Angie the most precious thing in her life.

Hardy has no inkling he's a father…until an accident leaves a young girl injured and the Texas district attorney with an unexpected addition to his family. Blindsided by shock and hurt, Hardy can't forgive Angie for her deception. But as he gets to know his child, old and new feelings for Angie surface. While scandal could derail Hardy's political future—is that future meaningless without Angie and their daughter?

Look for
One Night In Texas
by LINDA WARREN
from Harlequin® American Romance®

**Available May 2014
wherever books and ebooks are sold.**

www.Harlequin.com

HAR75518